The Perfect Princess

Princess Charming

"True to her reputation for delivering excitement, mystery, and romance, Elizabeth Thornton crafts another breathtaking adventure set in the Regency period. *Princess Charming* is filled with delightful characterization, an intriguing plot, and sizzling sensuality. Once again Ms. Thornton gives us a delightful mixture that satisfies even the most discriminating reader and keeps us begging for more."
—*Rendezvous*

Strangers at Dawn

"An out-of-the-ordinary murder mystery set in the early 1800s with lots of suspects and a lovely romance."
—*Dallas Morning News*

"With her talent as a superb storyteller, Elizabeth Thornton skillfully blends suspense, murder and a powerful love story into a jewel of a book."
—*Romantic Times*

"Thornton has been a long-time favorite thanks to her well-told tales of intrigue peppered with sizzling romance and *Strangers at Dawn* is among the best."
—*Oakland Press*

Whisper His Name

"Thornton creates appealing characters and cleverly weaves in familiar Regency settings and customs."
—*Publishers Weekly*

"Ms. Thornton has delivered. This is a terrific book from cover to cover. The dynamic plot and characters will thrill and delight. Bravo!" —*Rendezvous*

More Praise for Elizabeth Thornton

"This book is an absolute joy to read. I loved every minute of it! We are given humor, a murderer, sensuality, scintillating dialogue, and characters to cheer for. What more could you want?"
—*Rendezvous* on *You Only Love Twice*

"If you like mystery, murder and mayhem along with your romance, then *You Only Love Twice* will be your cup of tea." —*Romantic Times*

"This witty Regency romance/mystery will keep you up all night." —*Atlanta Journal/The Atlanta Constitution* on *The Bride's Bodyguard*

"A rich, satisfying blend of suspense and passion."
—*Brazosport Facts* on *The Bride's Bodyguard*

"Cleverly plotted intrigue."
—*Publishers Weekly* on *The Bride's Bodyguard*

Nationally bestselling author Mary Balogh says, "I consider Elizabeth Thornton a major find."

Rave Reviews praises Elizabeth Thornton as "a major, major talent . . . a genre superstar."

Publishers Weekly raves: "Fast paced and full of surprises, Thornton's latest novel is an exciting story of romance, mystery, and adventure . . . a complex lot that exuberantly carries the reader. Thornton's firm control of her plot, her graceful prose, and her witty dialogue make *Dangerous to Kiss* a pleasure to read."

Also by *Elizabeth Thornton*

The Bachelor Trap
The Marriage Trap
Shady Lady
Almost a Princess
The Perfect Princess
Princess Charming
Strangers at Dawn
Whisper His Name
You Only Love Twice
The Bride's Bodyguard
Dangerous to Hold
Dangerous to Kiss
Dangerous to Love

The
Pleasure
Trap

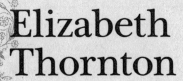

Elizabeth
Thornton

BANTAM BOOKS

THE PLEASURE TRAP
A Bantam Book / August 2007

Published by
Bantam Dell
A Division of Random House, Inc.
New York, New York

This is a work of fiction. Names, characters, places, and incidents either
are the product of the author's imagination or are used fictitiously. Any
resemblance to actual persons, living or dead, events, or locales is
entirely coincidental.

All rights reserved
Copyright © 2007 by Mary George
Cover art by Alan Ayers
Cover design by Yook Louie

Bantam Books and the rooster colophon are registered trademarks of
Random House, Inc.

ISBN 978-0-553-58957-3

Printed in the United States of America
Published simultaneously in Canada

www.bantamdell.com

OPM   10 9 8 7 6 5 4 3 2 1

For friends Alison & Elmer Preece,
for showing me the quarry garden in Hamilton.
That's what sparked the idea for this book.
Thanks muchly!

The Pleasure Trap

Prologue

Outside London, 1806

Eve moved restlessly in her small bed. Something was far wrong. Mama was leaving her. She could feel it, sense it. *Mama was leaving her.*

Eve... Her mother's voice came to her in her dream, soothing her, telling her how much she loved her, that she must not grieve too much.

"No!" She came awake on a sob. It took her a moment to get her bearings. She was in her bed, in the inn where Papa had found rooms for them while he worked at the big house, a mile or two along the road. Mama had read her a story, one of her own creations, before blowing out the candle and retiring to her chamber.

Then what was wrong? Why did she feel bereft? Where was Mama?

Eve blinked rapidly to adjust her eyes to the dim light that filtered into her chamber from the corridor. Sheba, her mother's black Labrador, had her huge paws on the bedspread and gazed intently into her eyes.

When Eve hauled herself up, the dog began to whine, a piteous sound that mirrored Eve's alarm. She stroked Sheba's great black head and felt the dampness on her hand. Sheba had been outside in the rain with Mama.

Eve didn't debate with herself how she knew this. Like her mother, she had a sixth sense that she trusted implicitly, though hers was not so well tuned as Mama's. But that was because she was still a child. Tonight, her sixth sense was vibrating like a violin string. Sheba had been out in the rain with Mama, and something was far wrong.

Heart pounding, Eve pushed back the covers and jumped out of bed. Her mother's chamber was right next door. She hared along the corridor and pushed into it. The bed was still made up and the lamp was lit, revealing her mother's notebooks and sketches spread across the small table. The coals in the grate were reduced to glowing embers.

She quelled her rising panic. "Mama?" she whispered into the silence. No words came this time, but pictures formed in her mind. The old quarry. The moon coming out from behind a cloud. Her mother falling. A lighter shadow fading into the darker shadows. Sheba, her hackles raised and her fangs bared, standing guard over the inert form on the quarry floor.

Sheba's cold nose brushed her hand. Soulful eyes looked into Eve's. Swallowing hard, Eve said, "Take me to Mama."

She delayed long enough to put on her slippers and throw a shawl around her shoulders, then, after waking the servants, she followed her dog down the stairs, out the back door, and plucked a lantern from its hook to light their steps.

She found her mother, just as she'd known she

would, on the quarry floor, still conscious but fading fast. Eve's tears mingled with the rain and coursed down her cheeks in rivulets. She knelt by her mother and took her hand.

Hush... Listen, Eve...

Eve tried to empty her mind of everything but her mother's voice, but she couldn't contain her despair. Words bubbled up and spilled over, cutting off the voice in her head. In the end, her mother's will was stronger than hers, and Eve quieted.

Listen to me, Eve. I went for a walk with Sheba and fell.

It wasn't true. Her mother wouldn't go out in the rain. Someone else had been here, someone whom Sheba had chased away. Why was her mother lying?

It was an accident, the voice inside her head insisted, then, more gently, *It was an accident.... Be careful, Eve. Don't draw attention to yourself.... Listen to what I say....*

There were no more words that Eve could distinguish, but pictures filled her mind, pictures of the various famous gardens they had visited over the years. Why was Mama thinking of gardens?

Lights appeared on the path behind Eve. Servants' voices called out to her. She thought she answered, but she wasn't sure. A cacophony of voices buzzed around her head. Sheba began to whine. Eve felt a wrenching deep inside her and quietly wept.

"The poor child! She's in shock!"

"It was an accident," she said. "Mama went out for a walk and she slipped and fell." It was what Mama wanted her to say. "Sheba found her."

As comforting hands tried to raise her, another picture flitted into Eve's mind: a ballroom with young debutantes in white dresses and their handsome partners, and beyond them, through the glass doors, the terrace and gardens, sinister beyond imagining.

Be careful, Eve...

Then all the pictures vanished and with them the sense of her mother's presence.

She had never felt so alone.

Chapter One

Henley, March 1818

Two letters that Eve was expecting arrived that morning, two letters that gave no hint of the storm they would soon let loose. Eve took them with her into the breakfast room and read them as she absently sipped her tea. The first letter she opened was from her publisher, Leigh Fleming, reminding her of the symposium and reception he hosted for all his authors and their friends every year at the Clarendon Hotel. The second was from Lady Sayers, inviting her, along with the other writers, to spend a few days at her home in London after the symposium was over. What was unusual about Lady Sayers's invitation was that her ladyship wanted Eve to extend her visit to take in the Season.

Eve didn't have to think about how she would answer Leigh's invitation. A writer's life was a lonely one, and she had come to look forward to these get-togethers with other authors, all of them females. In the last few years, their Gothic tales of romance and mystery had taken the public by storm. Women adored their stories, though gentlemen more often than not laughed themselves silly or treated their books with disdain. As a result, no writer of Gothic romances dared reveal her true identity. Instead, each used a pseudonym. They were celebrities, but invisible celebrities, except to one another and a trusted few. Eve didn't mind. The monies accumulating in her bank account were ample reward for doing what she liked to do best. She was born to be a writer. Hadn't Mama always said so?

The invitation from Lady Sayers required a little more thought. She was a fellow writer who lived in the lovely district of Kennington, and when she wasn't writing, she mixed with the cream of society. Even before Eve was published, her ladyship had been hosting these weeklong get-togethers at her house after the symposium was over. Writers looked forward to this relaxing time together, perhaps even more than they looked forward to the symposium. Lady Sayers was fun to be with. She was what was euphemistically called "an original." Though she was only fifty, she had buried four husbands. She painted her nails and face. She was outspoken. Some said she was outrageous, and in her younger days had stirred up more trouble than any Gothic heroine could hope to meet.

Eve was flattered by the invitation to prolong her visit, but she was also wary. She suspected that Lady Sayers might be playing matchmaker. All the same, Eve had an excellent reason for taking her ladyship up on her offer.

It registered that a silence had fallen on the breakfast table, and Eve looked up to find that her companion was studying her speculatively. Miss Millicent Claverley was Eve's aunt on her mother's side, and she and Eve had been close ever since Miss Claverley arrived to take over the care of her brother-in-law's household after her sister's tragic death. When Eve's father married again, Miss Claverley returned to her own house in Henley, and Eve joined her soon after. It was an arrangement that seemed to suit everyone, particularly the new step-mother.

No one knew exactly how old Miss Claverley was. Her age had hovered around her late forties for the last several years. There were no telltale threads of silver in her coiffured dark curls. Miss Claverley wouldn't have allowed it. She was an attractive woman, nicely rounded though far from plump, and liked to dress in the current mode.

Eve held up the letter from Lady Sayers. "Lady Sayers has invited us to spend a few weeks in London to take in the Season after the symposium."

Miss Claverley nodded. "Yes, I know, dear." When Eve frowned, Miss Claverley made a clicking sound. "No, I did not read your mind. That was your mother's gift, not mine. Anyhow, I received a letter from Lady Sayers, too. That's how I know. I didn't say anything until you had read your letter first."

No one, thought Eve, had ever said that the Claverleys were an ordinary family, leastways on the distaff side. Some called them fey, others called them witches. Eve called them clever. They had an uncanny aptitude for making connections, and they made the most of it. It was a game they played, just like a magician with his bag of tricks. When her Claverley cousins came for a visit, she felt that the house had been invaded by a swarm of mischievous sprites. For the most part, she regarded them with amused tolerance, but when they went too far, she was not above astounding them with a few tricks of her own.

In her own case, she put all her Claverley cleverness into her writing. As an author, she always knew what her characters were thinking and feeling. She didn't have to read their minds.

She nibbled on dry toast as her aunt spoke.

"You know, Eve, it might not be a bad thing. You need to be taken out of yourself. There's more to life than writing. And Sally Sayers will be good for you, good for both of us. She knows how to enjoy life."

Eve's response was dry. "So I've noticed. There's never a dull moment when Lady Sayers is around."

Miss Claverley smiled. "Oh, I think that's all an act. From what I've observed, it's not uncommon among writers to adopt a larger-than-life personality when they are in the public eye. You do it yourself, only with you, it's the opposite."

"I do?"

Miss Claverley nodded. "With your hair pulled back, and that lace cap on your head, you could pass for a governess or a schoolteacher."

"I do it because I want my books to be taken seriously!" protested Eve.

"Really? Good grief! If I took them seriously, I'd be frightened out of my mind. Your men are deliciously wicked, but I'm glad I can't meet them in real life. A word of advice, Eve? Pretty yourself up to look like one of your heroines. It's what your readers expect."

"But I don't want to be noticed. I don't want to be recognized when I go shopping in Bond Street. I want to protect my privacy."

"If you dress like a frump, you *will* be noticed."

Eve made a rude sound.

Undaunted, Miss Claverley topped up Eve's cup from the teapot. "Lady Sayers mentions that her niece, Liza, will join her, and now that she has turned eighteen, she'll be making her come-out."

This was what interested Eve. A young girl's come-out had given her an idea for a book.

"And," Miss Claverley went on, "it's not as though you'll be a rival for her suitors. At your age, you'll be more like a chaperon to the girl, so you need not worry that Sally will be hounding young men to pay you court. Her hopes will be pinned on her niece."

Eve almost took offense. "At *my* age? I'm only four-and-twenty! And Lady Sayers knows I would not dream of pilfering her niece's beaux. She has far more to fear from you. You see every male as a potential conquest."

"Nonsense! I'm interested in people, that's all. Men lead exciting lives. They do things women would be censored for if they tried to copy them." She thought for a moment, then said musingly, "I think that's why women are snapping up your books. They live vicariously through your heroines. They're not afraid to try anything."

Eve cupped her ear. "Was that a compliment I heard?"

Her aunt used both hands to bring her cup to her smiling lips. When she set the cup down, she said grudgingly, "I believe it was."

Eve laughed. She thoroughly enjoyed this good-natured bantering between herself and her aunt. It was like playing a game of chess.

"So, it's all settled, then," said Miss Claverley. "We're off to London to take in the Season?"

Eve's eyes narrowed on her aunt's innocent expression. "I've just realized something. It's *you* Lady Sayers wants as a companion. I can see it now. You'll be free to enjoy yourselves, and I'll be lumbered with the niece."

"Silly girl! I'll be there to chaperon *you*, you know, in case you run off with a fortune hunter."

They both chuckled at the unlikely prospect.

After a moment, Miss Claverley said, "Do you mind telling me why you want a Season in London? Dare I hope that you're seriously considering the idea of matrimony?"

"For whom?"

Miss Claverley sat back. "For you, of course."

"What would be the point? You'd only steal all my suitors. What man would look at me when my chaperon is far more dashing?"

"Someone who likes a quiet life," retorted her aunt. "Poor man, he'll wake up one morning and realize that he has been duped. You're dashing on the inside, Eve, as we both know. All right. So the subject of matrimony has been set aside for the moment. Then if you're not interested in finding a husband, why take in the Season?"

Eve's gray eyes darkened to violet, a sure sign that she was excited about something. "I'm setting my next story in London at the height of the Season. I want to be part of what's going on. I want to see how the *ton* lives. I need to know what a young girl feels at her first ball, what she hopes for, dreams about. The same goes for her parents and the young men who court her. You know me. I can't write a story until I've pinned down all the details."

Her aunt was silent for a long time. Finally, she said, "Be careful, Eve. People in high places will go to any lengths to protect their privacy. And if they find themselves in one of your books, there is no saying what they will do."

"I know better than that," protested Eve. "My characters come from my imagination. Any resemblance to a living person would be coincidental."

"All the same, be careful, Eve."

"I will. I promise."

There was an interval of silence, then Miss Claverley's expression cleared. "Now, tell me about the letter from your publisher, and before you make any arch remarks at my expense, I will own to having recognized that the address is in his handwriting. I presume he is hosting his annual reception at the Clarendon?"

Eve nodded. "For writers and their friends, so I'm counting on you to lend me your support."

Miss Claverley beamed. "I wouldn't miss it for the world."

They ate their meager breakfast of tea and toast in companionable silence. Miss Claverley was reflecting that Eve was so like her mother, Antonia, that it made her heart ache—those animated violet-gray eyes, the sooty lashes and brows, the luxuriant mane of dark hair she rarely tamed with pins or ribbons, except in company. But the resemblance went deeper than that. She'd known that one day Eve would acknowledge her mother's legacy. That day was drawing near. The signs were all there. Miss Claverley was afraid, and she didn't know why she was afraid.

Suddenly conscious that Eve's eyes were on her, she said the first thing that came into her head. "If we are going to take in the Season, we'll need suitable clothes. Is there enough time to have a few things made up before we go?"

Eve drank the last of her tea. "Lady Sayers says we should wait till we get to town before we have anything made up. Her modiste knows all the latest styles."

"But think of the cost! London prices are over the moon."

Eve rested her elbows on the table, cupped her chin in

her hands, and smiled into her aunt's eyes. "What do we care? Mrs. Barrymore is paying the shot."

"Mrs. Barrymore?"

"Aunt! That's me! Eve Dearing! You surely haven't forgotten that Mrs. Barrymore is the celebrated author who pays for all the little luxuries we enjoy?"

Miss Claverley replied with great dignity, "Of course I know who Mrs. Barrymore is. What I didn't know was that she had money to spare."

"Bags of it," said Eve, grinning.

"Mmm. Maybe I should write a book."

"Maybe you should."

When Eve left the breakfast room, her shadow, Dexter, a descendant of the beloved Sheba, left his post at the front door and trotted after her. On reaching her bedchamber, Eve went straight to her escritoire and dashed off a note to her publisher, then sat for a moment, chewing on the end of her pen as she contemplated the projected trip to town.

"You know, Dexter," she said at last, "there's something holding me back. I know I *want* to accept Lady Sayers's invitation, but I can't seem to get the words down on paper."

In her mind's eye, she saw a ballroom with glittering chandeliers. Beautiful young debutantes and their handsome partners whirled around the floor. Beyond them, through the glass doors to the terrace, lay the gardens, bathed in moonlight.

The scene was all too familiar. She'd dreamed about it for years. This was how her stories came to her, in her dreams, but only this dream had the power to make her tremble.

She corrected herself. Her other stories had taken place in settings she drew from memory, from famous gardens that she had visited as a child. The ballroom and debutantes were completely beyond her experience. Then where had this setting come from? She felt as though she recognized it.

She gave a self-conscious laugh. "Will you listen to me? I'm beginning to sound like my crazy Claverley cousins."

Dexter's soulful black eyes were trained on his mistress as she gazed into space.

Eve's thoughts had shifted to her parents, especially her mother. As a child, she'd never questioned the way things were. Her father had been busy making a name for himself as a landscape gardener. As a result, he was absent a good deal of the time, traveling all over England. Whenever it was convenient, she and her mother would pack up and join him. That carefree existence came to a devastating end when Antonia died and Eve's father remarried a scant year after her mother's death. She hadn't wanted a new mother and, with childlike doggedness, had refused to be parted from Aunt Millicent.

It was the beginning of a long estrangement between father and daughter that had lasted to the present day, not a quarrel or a falling-out but a tepid relationship that never quite warmed the heart.

It was inevitable, Eve told herself. She was passionate about her mother and could not bear to see another woman take her place. Martha, her father's wife, was the opposite of her mother, and that rankled, too. Where Antonia had been artistic in many areas—writing, sketching, playing musical instruments—Martha was happier in the stillroom, counting her jars of jam and pickles. Life with Antonia was an adventure. Martha had her feet planted firmly on the ground.

Maybe that's why her father chose someone so different from her mother to be his second wife. Maybe life with Antonia was *too* unsettling. Maybe her gift of sensing what her husband was thinking and feeling was too uncomfortable to be borne. And maybe he thought the same about his daughter.

She heaved a sigh. She should have made the effort to heal the breach long before now. Her father and his wife lived in Brighton, so there had been plenty of opportunities for her to do the right thing. She'd tried. It wasn't her father who was the problem so much as Martha. The second Mrs. Dearing made it perfectly obvious that she wasn't comfortable around her freakish stepdaughter.

And now she'd left it almost too late. Though her father wasn't an old man, his health wasn't good. He was becoming forgetful and there was something particular she wanted to ask him, something only he could tell her. She wanted to find the quarry in Kent where her mother had met with that tragic accident.

It wasn't a secret. No one had tried to keep the information from her. The simple truth was, over time, the details had become blurred. Her aunt thought Antonia had been out walking at night in the gardens of a house that was perched on a cliff. Eve remembered it as a quarry. The one thing they agreed on was that it happened in Kent, just an hour or so out of London.

Why couldn't she remember? She remembered finding her mother's body. She remembered the servants dragging her away. But most of all, she remembered the deep well of grief and guilt, all mixed up together, that had sucked her down to an unending pit of despair.

She'd learned to deal with the grief, but the guilt was something else. It felt like a chip of ice lodged in her heart, and no one and nothing had ever thawed it.

She made a clicking sound with her tongue. She wasn't usually so maudlin. What on earth had got into her? She wanted to revisit the scene of her mother's tragic accident. That was all it was.

A warm tongue licked her hand. When Eve smiled, Dexter thumped his tail and barked.

"Another mind reader in the family," Eve told her dog, "is one too many for my comfort. No, I'm not cast down. I'm happy. Look at me! I'm smiling. And why shouldn't I be? I have my writing, I have my small circle of friends in Henley and an exciting trip to London coming up. Who wouldn't be happy in my shoes?"

Dexter was an overgrown, good-hearted pup that loved everyone indiscriminately. If a burglar entered the house, he wouldn't raise the alarm. He'd want to be petted. If a rabbit bit him on the nose, he wouldn't give chase unless he thought it was a game. Maybe when he was older, his doggie instincts would come into play.

"You're going to Lady Sayers's for a little holiday," she said. "Now what do you think of that?" Eve was sure Dexter would get a warm reception, because Lady Sayers was a doggie person.

Dexter wagged his tail.

"Want to go for a walk?"

Dexter bolted to the door and looked over his shoulder to see if his mistress was following.

Laughing, Eve got up. "See, I can read minds, too. There's nothing to it."

She opened the door and followed Dexter down the stairs.

Chapter Two

Ash Denison had time to spare before keeping an appointment with his tailor, so he dropped by his favorite club, Wattiers, where he knew he could be sure of the finest French cuisine to be had in London. Not only was Ash a connoisseur of fine food, but also of fine tailoring, fine horses, fine wine, and, it went without saying, fine women.

He was a tall, athletically built young man with longish dark hair framing a face that was saved from being too handsome by a square, determined jaw. Though Ash was regarded as a dandy, his garments were conservative—dark coat impeccably tailored to his broad shoulders, and knit trousers molding his long muscular legs. What distinguished him from his conservative friends were his elaborately tied neckcloths and the quizzing glass that hung from a black ribbon around his neck. And what made him immensely popular were his easygoing manners and his unstinting generosity to anyone who needed a helping hand.

Today, he dined alone, though there were plenty of acquaintances who would have been happy to join him if given a little encouragement. Ash had positioned his chair, however, so that his back was to the other diners. He was in a reflective mood, having just encountered the former dean of his college, who had opined, in no uncertain terms, that Ash's life lacked focus and he'd expected him to have made his mark on the world by now. Ash was inclined to agree with him, but that did not mean he was unhappy or wanted to change his ways. He had no ambitions except to enjoy his life, each precious moment of it, and damned if he could see what was wrong with that.

His dinner arrived—oysters en brochette with buttered asparagus and creamed potatoes. On this occasion, the fine cuisine did not distract his thoughts for long. This was the beginning of the Season, when ambitious mamas brought their lovely daughters up to town in hopes of tempting some eligible bachelor into marriage. Until now, he had managed to disqualify himself from the hunt by claiming poverty, but he was not sure how much longer he could keep up the pretense. His grandmother had suddenly arrived in town with the express intention of taking in the Season. One word from his grandmother was all it would take to put him in the camp of eligible bachelors, and the hunt would be on.

His friends would rub their hands in glee. Most of them had fallen by the wayside, captured by lovely young women who led them straight to the altar. Ash didn't think he'd ever be ready to take that long, long walk. His own parents' marriage had not exactly been an example of domestic bliss. They were both gone now, as was his brother, Harry, and it was left to him to secure the succession.

There had to be more to life than that.

"Mind if I join you, Denison?"

The elderly gentleman who loomed over Ash didn't wait for an answer but pulled out a chair and seated himself. Ash managed a smile. Colonel Shearer commanded his respect, not only because of his advanced years but because of his record in the Spanish Campaign and, latterly, at Waterloo. Soldiering had been his life. It was also his only topic of conversation. There was nothing the colonel liked more than to corner a former comrade-in-arms and regurgitate every detail of battles gone by. As a veteran of the Spanish Campaign, Ash was an ideal audience for the colonel's reminiscences.

"You'll have a glass of wine, Colonel?" Ash asked. He raised a hand to attract the waiter's attention.

"Thank you, no. I've already dined. Too much wine in the middle of the day makes me drowsy."

Ash was startled when the colonel took the newspaper that was folded under his arm and slapped it on the table between them. "What do you make of that, Denison, eh?"

Ash noted the torn edges of the paper and wondered how long the colonel had been carrying it around. The date at the top of the back page informed him that it was a week old. Mystified, he began to scan it.

"It's a short story," Ash said. "They're a regular feature in the *Herald*. I never read such drivel myself. Too fanciful for my taste. But my grandmother dotes on these Gothic tales."

"As does my Myrtle," responded the colonel, shaking his head. "Well, it's fit only for the ladies, isn't it? But this time, the *Herald* has gone too far. I wouldn't mind if Angelo—that's the author's name, by the way—set his stories in the country homes of the high and mighty—

well, who hasn't visited Blenheim and Chatsworth?—but when one's own private domain is used as a backdrop, that is going too far. Fairfield isn't open to the public. How does this Angelo fellow know so much about my property? Not that he gives it its proper name. *Longfield* he calls it, or something similar." He thumped the paper with his index finger. "The impudence of the knave! That's my home he's writing about."

Ash wasn't sure why the colonel was so angry. "Country estates are not so very different," he ventured. "Perhaps you're mistaken. It could be another estate or something he has imagined."

The colonel brought the flat of his hand down, rattling the table. "I know my own estate." Both voice and eyes were fierce. "But that's not what gets my goat. He has resurrected an old tragedy, when one of our maids fell down the shaft of an old, disused well, and Mrs. Shearer is besieged by her friends wanting to know what really happened to Maude. And our daughters are mortified. People are snickering behind our backs. I won't have it, I tell you."

"Maude," Ash said slowly, "would be the maid?"

"Of course she's the maid! Didn't I say so?"

Ash suppressed a retort. Colonel Shearer's war record, he reminded himself, commanded respect. "When did Maude suffer the fatal fall?" he asked gently.

"Fourteen years ago. She was Mrs. Shearer's maid. And now this Angelo fellow implies that there was foul play and that her spirit will never be at peace until the mystery is solved."

Ash hardly knew what to say. The colonel was taking this preposterous story seriously. He didn't want to aggravate the old boy's distress by laughing, though that's what he felt like doing.

"It's only a story," he said. "And intelligent people don't read this kind of rubbish."

"My wife reads it."

"Ah..." Ash saw his blunder and quickly corrected it. "So does my grandmother and my cousin. I meant that gentlemen don't usually read these fanciful tales unless a wife or a grandmother points something of interest out to them."

"Reading novels! Waste of time! Never indulge in it! But I'm glad my wife showed me this piece. Who is this devil? That's what I want to know."

Ash shrugged. "Angelo is almost certainly not his real name. You probably know the fellow. He may have been a guest at Fairfield at one time and heard the story of Maude." Something else occurred to him. "He's probably a female." He flicked the newspaper with one finger. "This kind of fiction is nearly always written by females."

"My wife reads all the Gothic writers, and she doesn't recognize any of her favorites in this twaddle." Colonel Shearer sat back in his chair. "Look here, Denison. You could get me the real name of this Angelo fellow if you put your mind to it."

"I?" Ash was taken aback. "What can I do that you can't?"

"The *Herald*'s publisher is your friend, is he not? Brand Hamilton? Oh, yes, I went to see him, but he refused to divulge the blackguard's name."

Ash wasn't surprised. He could see what was on the colonel's mind. He might call Angelo out or beat him senseless. And if Angelo were a woman—

"I'm not going to call him out," the colonel stated testily, correctly reading the thoughts that were flitting through Ash's mind. "I'm going to make him tell me what he knows, and if that doesn't work, I shall sue him."

"Is that wise? I mean, suing him? Think of the trial. The gossips will have a feeding frenzy. If you ignore it, people will have forgotten the story when the next breathless installment from Angelo arrives in their morning paper."

The colonel sighed. "That's the advice I got when I asked Richard Maitland of Special Branch to track down the fellow, but—"

"You asked the chief of staff of Special Branch to intervene?"

The colonel frowned at Ash's tone. "Why are you surprised? Major Maitland served with us in the Spanish Campaign and was there at Waterloo."

"I know. But Special Branch concerns itself with conspiracies and treason and, on rare occasions, with difficult cases that have baffled the authorities."

"That's what Maitland told me, and I can't say I blame him for turning me down. His agents have their hands full." The colonel leaned forward and trapped Ash's unwary gaze in his piercing stare. In a less commanding voice, the colonel said, "I could always count on you in a tight corner, Denison. And vice versa, if I may say so. Remember Waterloo?"

Ash nodded. His horse had been shot from under him, and the colonel had ridden into the fray and carried him off under the noses of a detail of ferocious French lancers.

The colonel's gaze softened. "Will you help me, Captain Denison?"

Oh, unscrupulous! thought Ash. *To trade on our bond as war veterans.* "I'll do my best, Colonel," he replied meekly.

Shearer got to his feet. His stern expression had softened into a smile. "You deserve your good fortune, Denison."

"My ... good fortune?"

"I met your grandmother with your charming cousin at Lady Heathcote's musicale. The dowager told me that you'd come into a considerable estate."

Ash summoned a smile. That was old news that he'd suppressed in the interest of self-preservation. His grandmother had known, of course, because it was her elder brother, a crotchety old bachelor, who had left his entire fortune to Ash. That his grandmother had chosen to let the "news" out now confirmed his suspicions. Diplomacy had got her nowhere. Now she was resorting to open warfare.

He was disappointed in her, or, more accurately, he didn't understand her. She was his mother's mother, so securing the Denison dynasty could mean nothing to her. His grandfather, on the other hand, the Marquess of Forres, *was* a Denison and was threatening to disinherit him. It was an empty threat. The estate was entailed and the title would pass to Ash whether his grandfather thought he deserved it or not.

Fortunately, Grandfather Denison was happily ensconced in his estates in Scotland. He despised town life and rarely put in an appearance at Court functions unless by royal command.

A twinkle kindled in the colonel's eye. "That makes you a prize in the marriage-mart stakes, my boy. You'll have your pick of debutantes. A word of advice from an old campaigner? Take the offensive. Find the young woman who could make you happy and marry her before your escape is cut off. That's what I did with my Myrtle, and I've never regretted it."

"I'm not thinking of getting married," Ash pointed out.

"No. I daresay. My wife tells me that you're never without a pretty woman on your arm. I tell her that it's to be expected. You and all those other fine young men spent the best years of your lives fighting on foreign soil because you thought it was your duty. And you were one of the best."

He stopped abruptly and chuckled. "Will you listen to me? I do get carried away, don't I? The point I'm trying to make is that the war has been over for three years and now it's time to get on with your life. Dandy, indeed! What a whisker! You're a warrior, my boy, as no one knows better than I."

With a little salute, the colonel turned to go, then changed his mind. "You won't forget Angelo?"

"I won't forget."

"Your best lead is most likely the symposium that is coming up. There's an advertisement for it at the bottom of the page."

Ash gave the bottom of the page a cursory glance and nodded.

"My compliments to your grandmother and Lady Amanda."

"I'll pass them along."

When the colonel moved away, Ash looked down at the food congealing on his plate and decided that he had lost his appetite.

It's time to get on with your life.

What was wrong with his life? Why did everyone think he had to change?

He finished his glass of wine and called the waiter over to settle his bill. Angelo would have to wait, for he had arranged to call on his grandmother and his cousin after he visited his tailor and drive out with them in Hyde Park.

Two ladies stood at the long window in Lady Amanda's morning room and surreptitiously studied the young gentleman of fashion who seemed to be lost in contemplation at the far end of the garden. The gentleman in question was Ash; the elder lady was his grandmother, the Dowager Countess of Valmede, and the younger was his cousin, Lady Amanda Tallant.

Amanda broke the silence. "What is he doing?"

The dowager shook her head. "Enjoying the garden? Contemplating some deep, philosophical conundrum?" She looked at her granddaughter with a twinkle in her eye. "Suffering the pangs of unrequited love?"

Amanda gave a less-than-ladylike snort. "Some hope. I'll allow that Ash loves women, but he loves them in general. No woman has ever touched his heart. I don't think he'll ever marry."

"I think you're wrong," Lady Valmede observed. "He keeps up the house and estate in Richmond, doesn't he? Why would he bother if he's not thinking of getting married one of these days? After all, it's not entailed. He could sell it if he wanted to."

"I think he keeps it up to entertain his *chères amies*. I mean, it's out of the way but still close to town. Who is to know who he entertains there?"

"Amanda!" reproved the dowager helplessly. "I wish you would mind your tongue. Besides, his rooms are in Grillon's Hotel. He doesn't need a little hideaway to entertain his lady friends."

"That's true." Amanda shook her head. "Ash likes his privacy. Not for him a busybody landlady always looking over his shoulder. Or," she added emphatically, "a busybody cousin or grandmother."

The dowager crossed to a chair by the fire. After seating herself, she said diffidently, "Tell me the worst, Amanda. Have I stayed away from town too long? Have I no influence with my grandson? Am I never to see him happily settled?"

Amanda let out a soft sigh and sank into a down sofa flanking her grandmother's chair. She was a lovely young woman, a widow in her early thirties, with pale blond hair swept back from a heart-shaped face. She'd been in mourning for the last year but had been forced out of her widow's weeds by a grandmother who had come up to town determined to take her grown-up grandchildren in hand. The object, the dowager said, was to find a wife for Ash. Amanda suspected that Ash wasn't the only one her grandmother had plans for.

"You'll see Ash happily settled," she said, "when he wants to be and not before. Oh, I'm not saying he won't fall in with your wishes and escort us to any party or ball you care to name, but that's because he sees himself as the head of our family. No one can say that Ash ever shirked his duty."

"His duty? Oh, I think you're being too hard on him. He wants us to be happy because he loves us."

"Or maybe it's because he knows we love him. Maybe it's because we're all he has."

They fell into a reflective silence. Finally, Amanda stirred. "It wasn't a happy home, was it, Grandmama? I mean when Ash was a boy. His father was..." She left the thought hanging.

"A despot!" supplied the dowager. "No wonder my poor daughter went into a decline. Her father and I were never more mistaken in a man's character!" She suppressed a shudder. "I don't think Ash had a child-hood. He filled the void left by his father's neglect. Who else was there to support his mother and brother? That's why he went off to war. With both his mother and Harry gone, what was there for him here?"

Fearing the conversation had taken a turn that was too painful for her grandmother, Amanda said lightly, "Leave Ash be, Grandmama. I, for one, am happy to see him enjoying himself."

"Did someone mention my name?" demanded a voice from the threshold.

Ash crossed to his grandmother and pressed a kiss to her cheek. He caught a whiff of talcum, a scent that always reminded him of her, a comforting scent evoking happy memories.

Slightly startled at Ash's entrance when she believed him to be in the garden, the dowager said feebly, "Molly should have announced you."

"I told her not to bother."

He crossed to Amanda, ignored the hand she offered him, and planted an affectionate kiss on her brow. "What were you saying about me?" he asked.

He spied a selection of Amanda's favorite reading material stacked neatly on the sofa table, so he sat down beside her and idly fingered first one leather-bound volume, then another.

"We were wondering," said Amanda seamlessly, "what you were doing in the garden. We saw you from the window."

"Ah." Ash stretched one arm along the back of the sofa and gave his cousin a brilliant smile. "I was coaxing a stray dog to come to me. I thought the poor little fellow looked half starved. I didn't see the gentleman who was out walking him. He practically accused me of trying to steal his dog."

Amanda laughed.

Ash's mind was only half on this bantering conversation. The other half was looking for an opening to introduce the topic of Angelo without betraying Colonel Shearer's confidence. He picked up one of the volumes that lay on the table. "*The Vanishing Heiress*," he read slowly, "by Mrs. Barrymore." He looked at Amanda. "I thought you had more intelligence than to read this drivel."

Amanda snatched the book from Ash's fingers and clasped it to her bosom. She wasn't laughing now. "Don't mock what you don't understand. These are *wonderful* stories." She lifted her chin. "And Mrs. Barrymore is a wonderful writer."

There was a lilt in his voice. "Come now. I'm told these stories are all alike. The heroine is abducted by the lecherous villain and is saved by the hero from a fate worse than death in the nick of time."

"I didn't realize you read them," interjected the dowager.

"I don't," said Ash. "But they're the talk of my clubs right now."

"Men!" scorned Amanda. "What do they know? If you read Mrs. Barrymore, you'd learn something. Her heroines don't rely on any man to save them. They save themselves."

"It's a fantasy, then?" asked Ash, adding another log to the fire.

The dowager hastened to smother the flame. "They are enjoyable stories, Ash, that's all. We know that real life is quite different. Take Mrs. Barrymore's latest novel. The heroine—I forget her name."

"Brianna," supplied Amanda.

"Brianna?" Ash sounded revolted. "What kind of name is that?" He gasped when Amanda slapped her precious novel against his chest.

"Read it, Cousin, before you pass judgment."

He chuckled and gingerly replaced the volume on the sofa table. "I know all I want to know about the likes of Mrs. Barrymore and her stories."

"Pity," said his grandmother. "Amanda and I were counting on you to escort us to the Clarendon on Thursday afternoon. All our favorite writers will be there to read excerpts from their books and answer readers' questions. You did promise to escort us to any event we planned to attend."

"Escort you?" Ash was aghast. In his mind's eye, he saw a roomful of twittering, gushing females and in their midst one solitary male—himself. Not even for Colonel Shearer would he lower himself to that level.

Amanda said, "You won't be the only gentleman there. Lots of husbands, brothers, *and* cousins will be in attendance, if only to give their womenfolk moral support."

"Don't exaggerate, dear," said the dowager. "There may be a few gentlemen present, but no more than that."

"You've been before?" asked Ash.

"Not Grandmama, but I go every year without fail," replied Amanda coolly.

The dowager said confidingly, "You see, Ash, Amanda is writing a novel, too, so it's good for her to meet other writers. They spark ideas from one another."

Amanda sat up with a jerk. "Grandmama! I told you that in confidence."

"Good heavens! Ash is family! He won't tell anyone, will you, Ash?"

"Trust me, Amanda." Ash put his finger to his lips. "Your secret is safe with me."

Her good humor restored, Amanda laughed. "Of course it is. You wouldn't want it to become known in your club that your cousin writes Gothic romances. Think of the ribbing you'd get."

That reminded him of Colonel Shearer. "Now that you mention it, there was talk in my club today of one of your tribe, a fellow by the name of Angelo. He has had a few pieces published in the *Herald*."

"I've read them," said Amanda, "but I wouldn't say that he writes in my genre. They are mysteries, and the endings leave me feeling let down. Nothing is resolved."

"You don't think he could be one of your fellow writers?"

"I don't know. I think Angelo is a female, but her voice isn't one that I recognize." To Ash's blank look she added, "Her style of writing is different. I think she may be new on the scene. Perhaps we'll meet her at the symposium. Leigh Fleming will be there. He's the publisher, and if anyone knows who Angelo is, I'm sure it will be Mr. Fleming. There's a luncheon afterward, when readers and writers mix informally. Perhaps Angelo will be there."

Tempting, but not tempting enough for Ash. There must be an easier way to discover who Angelo was.

He said lamely, "I'd feel like a fish out of water at your symposium. You can't seriously expect me to accompany you?"

Amanda smiled. "Poor cornered little rabbit! Of course I don't. But I'm not letting you off easily. Read Mrs. Barrymore's latest novel and we'll call it quits. Agreed?"

He plucked the book from the table and weighed it in

his hand. Finally, he nodded. "You drive a hard bargain, Amanda."

Amanda beamed at him. "I always said you were my favorite cousin, Ash."

The dowager seized on the moment of harmony and quickly interposed, "I'll have Molly bring refreshments, shall I? Then after tea we'll go for that drive in Hyde Park."

True to his word, later that evening Ash settled himself in his favorite chair in front of a blazing fire and embarked on the trials and tribulations of *The Vanishing Heiress*. He made up his mind to give the book half an hour of his time and, if his interest wasn't caught by then, to skim to the end.

The fire died down, the candles burned low, and still Ash read on. Occasionally he chuckled. He skipped here and there, but only the sappy bits where the author described what the hero and villain were thinking and feeling. Obviously, Mrs. Barrymore didn't know the first thing about men, but she'd written a cracking good story.

When he closed the book and came to himself, he was amazed to see how late it was. He'd enjoyed the story but not enough to make him want to meet the author.

The following morning, after a hotel footman had delivered his breakfast and that morning's paper, he turned to the back page. Sure enough, there was another breathless piece by Angelo. He looked at the bottom of the page. The date, time, and place of the symposium blazed out at him.

He swallowed a mouthful of coffee and began to

read. When he came to the end of it, he sat back in his chair. His breakfast was untouched.

Now he understood Colonel Shearer's feelings of revulsion when he'd recognized his home as the backdrop to what was supposed to be a work of fiction. He was in exactly the same position. But there was more to it than that. Angelo knew things that he ought not to have known, things that Ash had never confided to anyone. If Angelo had appeared in front of him right then, he would have taken him by the throat and squeezed the life out of him.

He read the piece again and a lump formed in his throat. The story was based on the accidental death of his own brother, Harry—Harry, who'd never matured beyond a simple-minded child. He'd gone out swimming one day in the Thames, alone, and hadn't had the strength in his wasted limbs to stay afloat.

The details were sparse, but there were enough broad strokes to paint a reasonable picture of life at Denison Hall: the overpowering father; the mother who was too fragile to withstand the hardships of daily life; himself, the elder brother, who was being groomed as the heir; and Harry, the only light in that dreary pile of bricks they called home.

What stuck in Ash's craw was the faint suggestion that Harry's death might not have been an accident. After all, there were no witnesses to what had happened.

His first call that morning was to the *Herald*'s offices. Brand was not expected back for another week, he was told, and no one else could tell him what he wanted to know.

There was only one course open to him. It looked as though he would be escorting his cousin and grandmother to the symposium after all.

Chapter Three

Leigh Fleming was taken aback when he and his bevy of writers entered the Clarendon's public dining room, which served temporarily as the meeting place for the symposium. It was standing room only, and that had never happened before. Even more surprising was the presence of so many gentlemen. Men did not read romances, so why were they here? He was wishing, belatedly, that he'd hired a few strapping lackeys to evict any gentleman who thought it amusing to heckle the guests of honor.

He smiled encouragingly at his authors as he shepherded them to their places at a long table facing the audience. His fears subsided a little when he went to the lectern and the babble of voices died away. Taking a deep breath, he began his opening remarks.

Eve relaxed a little when Leigh cracked his first joke and the audience laughed along with him. All the authors were nervous, though this wasn't the first time they'd been in this position. And, really, there was nothing to fear. They would each do a short reading, answer questions from the floor, then mingle with the audience when refreshments were served.

Since staring at the audience made her nervous, Eve focused her attention on her publisher. Leigh was in his late thirties, fair of hair and complexion, with light blue eyes that seemed to take in the world and all its follies with long-suffering tolerance. To say that she was fond of him did not do her feelings justice. She admired and respected him. He had the knack of making each and every author believe in herself and her work. He and her aunt were her staunchest supporters.

Her gaze shifted to a table in the front row where Miss Claverley and a group of ladies were gazing in rapt attention at Mr. Fleming. Aunt Millicent enjoyed these writers' get-togethers more than Eve did. In fact, Eve found this part of the proceedings more of a trial. At the back of her mind, there was always the niggling fear that she would be recognized outside the hotel and hounded like a hapless fox. As a result, she dressed in her plainest garments and did nothing to draw attention to herself. What she looked forward to was when the symposium was over and they could all relax and enjoy themselves at Lady Sayers's beautifully appointed home.

A movement caught her eye. A gentleman at one of the tables in the front row was surveying the proceedings through his quizzing glass.

Ill-mannered fop, she thought, and she turned her attention back to Leigh.

Ash lowered his quizzing glass and responded to some remark his grandmother had made. He and his little party had arrived early, at Amanda's insistence, so that they could get the best seats. As Mr. Fleming introduced each writer in turn, Amanda elaborated for Ash's benefit.

"Lady Sayers you already know," said Amanda, "but in these circles she is known as Mrs. Windermere. She won't thank you if you betray her identity to her adoring readers. There was an unpleasant incident last year, when a zealous admirer besieged one of the writers in her own home. All very unpleasant! Poor Mrs. Farrar hasn't written a thing since."

Ash nodded. "Mrs. Windermere. I shall remember." The lady had buried four husbands and, in Ash's opinion, had the stamina for taking on another four. She was a straightforward, straight-spoken lady, and Ash liked her immensely. When her gaze alighted on him, he gave her a tiny salute.

The next writer was dressed from head to toe in flowing black, which accentuated her sickly, bloodless complexion.

"Mrs. Contini is mad about vampires," Amanda said.

Ash had no idea what his cousin meant, but it sounded revolting. Just looking at Mrs. Contini made his skin prickle.

The next in line, Mrs. Rivers, was not one of Amanda's favorites. "She doesn't write about love," Amanda scoffed, "but about you-know-what."

"Lust," his grandmother interjected from his other side.

That got Ash's attention, and he raised his quizzing glass to get a better look at the lady. She was a dasher, all right, and was dressed for the hunt in a form-fitting habit with a saucy hat to match. All she needed to complete the picture was a horse and hounds. Bold eyes returned his own bold stare. The symposium, Ash decided, was turning out to be quite interesting.

His grandmother elbowed him in the ribs. Correctly interpreting that silent rebuke, he swiveled his quizzing glass to take in the next lady.

"Mrs. Barrymore," said Amanda, in a voice that told Ash this writer *was* one of Amanda's favorites. "She creates the most-appealing heroines. When I come to the end of one of Mrs. Barrymore's stories, I feel that I can attempt anything."

"Incredible heroines," he agreed obliquely, earning him a sharp look from his cousin.

Mrs. Barrymore, in his view, was letting the side down. The other authors had dressed to make themselves stand out. If one was mad about vampires, whatever that meant, then Mrs. Contini with her bloodless complexion would instantly come to mind. For a lusty tale, Mrs. Rivers was her own best advertisement. There was more to it than her dramatic good looks or the clothes she wore. Every gesture, every glance from those expressive dark eyes were a challenge every red-blooded male would recognize. Mrs. Barrymore, on the other hand, looked as though she didn't want to draw attention to herself. Her plain gray walking dress hung in loose folds, concealing her figure. Her hair, likewise, was concealed by a lace cap. She was young, no more than twenty-four or twenty-five, and was pretty enough to attract any man's attention if she put her mind to it. Many ladies of rank came to him for advice when planning a new wardrobe. Now, if Mrs. Barrymore were to put herself into his hands . . .

She turned her head at that moment and their eyes collided. There was no bold stare from Ash this time. He was blinded by the temper that sizzled in her eyes before she looked away.

Uh-oh, he'd been caught staring, and the lady was

not amused. She probably thought he was lusting after her. The idea was laughable. All the same, he'd embarrassed her. The gentlemanly thing to do now was to set her mind at rest. When the symposium was over, he'd seek her out and talk to her intelligently about her book, and if that was beyond him, he'd simply tell her how much he enjoyed it.

That ought to make amends for his unthinking perusal.

Another dig in his ribs brought his attention back to Amanda.

She whispered fiercely, "Don't you know it's rude to stare?"

"What?" He dropped his quizzing glass.

"Mrs. Rivers! Don't encourage her! She's an overbearing, loud chatterbox who loves to be the center of attention. We're here to cheer on Mrs. Barrymore. Kindly remember that."

The dowager added, "Amanda dislikes Mrs. Rivers because she is always blowing her own trumpet. She never has a good thing to say about her fellow authors."

"Hush," said Amanda. "Mrs. Contini is about to read from her book."

Ash looked down at his program. *Let Sleeping Vampires Lie.* He could hardly wait.

As Mrs. Contini gave an introduction to her book, Eve edged closer to Lady Sayers. "Who is that gentleman with Lady Amanda?" she asked softly.

Lady Sayers bent her head to Eve's. "Her cousin, Ash Denison. Viscount Denison, to be precise. He is heir to his grandfather, a cantankerous old Scot who, I believe, lives in a crumbling estate near Inverness. Ash will be a marquess one of these days, and it couldn't happen to a nicer gentleman. He is immensely popular, but," she added hastily, "not for the likes of you." Her eyes twinkled. "He'll go to any lengths to avoid marriage."

Eve's tone was dry. "If he is heir to a marquess, his fate is already sealed. Some pretty little debutante will snap him up. I can't think why it hasn't already happened."

"He has no money—leastways, that's what we've all been led to believe. His grandmother—she's on his other side, by the way—says that that is an exaggeration, so no one is quite sure what to believe."

She patted Eve's arm. "Don't look so anxious. Did you think he was staring at you? You can put that idea right out of your mind. Mrs. Rivers is more Ash's style, and doesn't she know it. Look at her preen."

Eve looked. The Prima Donna, as Mrs. Rivers was referred to in private, had struck a pose: the Highwayman in woman's clothing. If she had produced a cheroot and started to smoke it, Eve would not have been surprised. Unlike the other authors, however, Eve enjoyed Mrs. Rivers's affectations. What she did not enjoy was the lady's acid tongue.

Lady Sayers was wrong about Ash Denison, though. He'd been staring at *her*, not at Mrs. Rivers. Her highly overrated sixth sense didn't come into it. Any woman worth her salt would have recognized that comprehensive, thoroughly masculine appraisal. He'd taken inventory of every small detail of her person, from her lace cap to the little half boots on her feet. Not only was she offended but she was also deeply mortified and was wishing that she'd taken Aunt Millicent's advice and worn one of the new gowns that had arrived from the modiste that morning. By dressing as a frump, she had made herself conspicuous.

Damn and blast the man! He had wounded her vanity.

She sucked in air when she was suddenly overcome by a wave of dizziness. When she could catch her breath, the dizziness gave way to a vague unease, and she looked out on the sea of faces, sensing all was not right. She sensed—she hated to use the word, but in this case, it was the right word—she sensed a malevolent presence. The air seemed to pulse with emotions: fear, hatred, rage, and she recoiled as though she'd been struck. Someone in the audience hated her.

As suddenly as they'd surged, the emotions receded. It took her a moment to come to herself. She wasn't reading someone's mind, she assured herself. She was reading their expressions. It seemed to her that there were some disgruntled gentlemen in the audience and they meant to cause trouble.

This had never happened before. They were a group of innocuous writers. What on earth had they done to stir people up?

She looked over at Ash Denison. Once again, she caught him staring at her. She dragged her eyes away and breathed deeply to calm her nerves.

The readings did not last long. Even so, by the time Mrs. Melville came to the end of her piece, some gentlemen in the audience were becoming restive.

Leigh Fleming stepped up to the lectern and said that the authors would be happy to answer questions now.

Before he could sit down again, a masculine voice

from the back shouted, "I want to know which one of these ladies is Angelo and how she comes to know so much about my business."

A murmur went through the audience and gained in volume. The authors at the long table were seen to shake their heads and whisper among themselves.

The same strident voice continued. "His short stories are on the back page of the *Herald* every Tuesday, and I've been told, Mr. Fleming, that if anyone knows who he is, it's you."

Fleming put up his hands in a placating gesture. "Well, you've been told a lie. I don't publish short stories. Angelo is not one of my authors and has nothing to do with this symposium. If you have a complaint, I suggest you take it up with his publisher at the *Herald*."

"That's not good enough!" roared the voice.

Like everyone else, Ash had turned to get a better look at the gentleman with the belligerent voice. It was not Colonel Shearer or anyone Ash recognized. The man looked out of place, like a country squire who had come up to town for the day to bid on the stock at Tattersall's.

For the first time, Ash noticed some of the other gentlemen who were flanking the country squire. They had the same air about them, belligerent and looking for trouble. Somebody had put them up to this.

Damn and blast Colonel Shearer, thought Ash. He was almost sure that Shearer was behind it. He was as eager as the colonel to discover Angelo's identity, but this wasn't the way to go about it.

When Mr. Country Squire and his cohorts began to stamp their feet, like bulls ready to charge, Ash got up and faced them. He folded his arms across his chest and went eye-to-eye with the ringleader. He didn't argue;

he didn't ask how or why the man thought Angelo was a female. In an alarmingly even tone, he said, "Mr. Fleming's answer is good enough for me." Then he went on easily, "Are there any gentlemen in the audience who agree with me?"

One by one, gentlemen at various tables got up. "I agree," said one. Others said the same. A hush descended as everyone waited to see what would happen next.

The country squire blustered, then shouted, "This is not the end of it!" and he stormed out of the room, followed closely by his cohorts.

At the lectern, a shaken Leigh Fleming said, "I think my authors need time to come to themselves after that ugly scene. Refreshments will be served directly."

Ash's claim to fame lasted all of five minutes. Everyone wanted to shake his hand and tell him what a fine fellow he was. It did not take long, however, before people wandered away to greet the real celebrities of the symposium—as was proper—Leigh Fleming's bevy of authors.

From a passing waiter's tray, Ash plucked a glass and set it to his lips. Lemonade. When the next waiter came up to him, he placed the untouched drink on his tray and asked him to fetch something stronger. Coffee, however, was the strongest brew they served at this hen party, and Ash politely declined it.

"That was well done," said a voice at his elbow.

Ash turned and acknowledged one of the gentlemen who had helped him stare down the rowdies' ringleader. "Thank you for your help."

"Don't mention it."

Jason Ford was in his late twenties, had done his bit

for king and country in the Spanish Campaign, and, after a short stint as an agent with Special Branch, had set up on his own as an investigator working on commission.

"Well, Jason," said Ash, "are you here as an investigator or are you an admirer of Gothic literature?"

Jason gave a self-conscious laugh. "I don't have much time for reading."

"Too busy tracking down criminals?"

"Hardly. The cases I take on are beneath the notice of the police or Special Branch. Sometimes I work for barristers; sometimes I'm hired by private citizens."

Ash bared his teeth in a facsimile of a smile. He was thinking of Colonel Shearer. "Let me guess. You're here to try to discover the identity of this Angelo fellow?"

Jason nodded. "He has stepped on the toes of some very important people who want me to warn him off." His gaze traveled from one group of people to another. "Why does everyone seem to think that Angelo is a female?"

"If you'd read his stuff, you'd know."

"Oh," replied Jason, who didn't seem to be any the wiser. "And why do all these authors use pseudonyms? I'm going to have the devil of a time finding out who is who."

"That's the general idea, so I'm told. Authors guard their privacy."

"Do you think Fleming knows more than he is telling?"

"You're the investigator. You tell me."

Jason sighed. "I think they all know more than they're telling, both Fleming and his bevy of authors." He looked at Ash with puppy-dog eyes. "The publisher of the *Herald*? He's a friend of yours, is he not? Brand Hamilton?"

Ash forestalled the next question. "And you want me to ask my friend if he knows who Angelo is?"

"If it's not asking too much."

Ash didn't hesitate. Not only was Jason Ford a veteran of the Spanish Campaign, but he had sustained an injury that had lamed him in one leg. Ash was always happy to give a helping hand to men who had served their country. As a result, his estate in Richmond was well stocked with former soldiers who had fallen on hard times.

"I'll see what I can do, but he won't be back in town for a few days."

Jason wasn't finished yet. His eyes scanned the crush of people. "Do you think that heckler hit the mark? Is it possible that Angelo is one of Mr. Fleming's authors?"

"Anything is possible."

Jason sighed. "I don't much relish the idea of threatening a lady." He squared his shoulders. "I say, Denison, if you find anything out, you *will* let me know?"

"If you'll return the favor." To the question in the young man's eye, Ash responded, "I have my own reasons for wanting to find out who this Angelo is."

The interest in Jason's eyes turned to speculation. "You're on the case, too?"

"Hardly! I'm curious, that's all. Well, go on. Investigate. And start with those hecklers. Maybe someone knows them."

"Right. I was just about to."

Ash smiled as young Ford began to mingle with the crush of ladies. He looked ill at ease, and Ash found that appealing. Ford, he knew, had not been born with a silver spoon in his mouth. Anything he'd got had come to him through his own hard work. Ash admired that in a man.

His gaze shifted to Mrs. Barrymore. She'd lost the little color in her cheeks and was smoothing her brow with her fingertips. He could almost hear her making her apologies as she tried to disengage from the ladies surrounding her. She looked ill.

Someone spoke to him, but Ash brushed him off. A few strides took him to Mrs. Barrymore's side. "Allow me," he said, and, ignoring her objections, he cleared a path for her from the crowded dining room through the door and into the spacious front vestibule. No stranger to the Clarendon, Ash guided her to a pretty little alcove with a sofa and two chairs. She took one of the chairs.

"I don't know what came over me," she said. "I sensed . . ." She stopped, looked up at him, and managed a weak smile. "It's Lord Denison, isn't it? You're Lady Amanda's cousin."

"And you're Mrs. Barrymore." He sat on the sofa, right by her chair. "How do you do?" He gave her one of the gracious smiles for which he was famous—not too admiring, but not shy, either. It didn't seem to work. She was gazing at him as though he threatened her in some way. Violet eyes, he noted, with pupils dilating in alarm.

His smile disappeared. "Look, are you all right? Would you like me to get you something? Lemonade? Tea? Something stronger?"

"A glass of water would do fine."

He hailed a passing waiter, asked for a glass of water, and turned to look at her again. Color was returning to her cheeks, but her beautiful violet eyes had turned to gray. A moment before she'd been off balance. Now, her eyes told him, she had herself well in hand.

He said easily, "You said you sensed something?"

"Did I?" She gestured with one hand. "The heat was too much for me. And the crowds. I became dizzy. That's all it was."

And he sensed that there was more to it than that. But he was in no position to correct her. "I wouldn't let those hecklers upset you. The ringleader was a bully, and the others were followers. We won't be seeing them again."

"Yes, it was an unpleasant business. A strange business. I don't know what to make of it. Thank you for your intervention. That was well done."

The glass of water arrived, and she drank it back as though she'd just been rescued from the Sahara Desert. It came to him that she couldn't wait to get rid of him and that as soon as she drained the glass, she would shake him off and run for cover.

He was mildly annoyed. Women didn't take to their heels when he paid them a little attention. And how this country mouse could imagine that he was anything but a gentleman was beyond belief. So he'd stared at her through his quizzing glass. Most women would have been flattered. He wanted to dress her, not undress her. The trouble with Mrs. Barrymore was that she'd been reading too many Gothic romances and was confusing them with real life.

Those lustrous gray eyes, her best feature, were staring at him as though she expected him to pounce on her. He was tempted to laugh. Since diplomacy was getting him nowhere, he came straight to the point.

"Do you know who Angelo is?"

The wariness in her eyes cleared. "Angelo?"

"The author who got on the wrong side of the hecklers."

"No." She almost smiled. "I'd never heard of him until today. I still don't understand what all the fuss is about. What did he do that was so awful?"

"I gather some of his stories are based on real events and real characters."

She set down her empty glass, but she didn't try to run away. Evidently, she was no longer wary of him. "Some of my stories are based on real events," she said. "Every writer could say the same. However, using real characters is a tricky business. If they are recognizable, an author can be sued for slander, or is it libel? I can never remember the difference."

He said carefully, "You've never read one of Angelo's stories?"

"No. I live in Henley, and the *Herald* is a London paper."

When she looked a question at him, he said, "I'm almost sure that he's a woman, one of your colleagues, perhaps."

There was a momentary silence as she digested this, then she said, "What makes you say so?"

"The style. The voice, as my cousin Amanda calls it. Angelo's work has a Gothic feel. Women don't write the same way as men, and Gothic writers in particular use flowery prose and exaggerate every emotion. I'm basing my opinion on the readings I heard today. Take your own work, for instance. I've read one of your books and—"

"Yes, Lady Amanda told me." Her voice was crisp. "What about my work? Oh, don't hold back because I'm a female. I'm a novelist, Lord Denison, not a delicate flower, and you are entitled to your opinion."

He'd been on the point of telling her how much he'd enjoyed her book, but the snap in her voice and the ice in her eyes tested his patience. He liked women, really liked them, and they liked him. Even his former lovers had nothing but good to say about him. This little harridan had gone too far.

As blunt as he could be, he said, "Your hero is too bland. Anemic, in fact. And when he takes the heroine into his arms, he shouldn't be spouting poetry or comparing her to some distant star."

By degrees they'd moved closer. They were almost nose to nose. She let out a huff of breath. "And you would know all about it?"

He almost smirked. "I'm a male. You bet I know all about it."

"So, tell me, Lord Denison, how should my hero act?"

"Like this," he said.

She gave a little start when his thumb brushed her lips and sucked in a breath when his hand cupped her neck. It took very little to bring her lips close to his. Their warm breath mingled. She didn't struggle, nor did she yield. Her eyes stared defiantly into his.

Against her lips, he whispered, "He wouldn't be talking at all. He'd be wondering how he could get her into bed."

He released her at once and steeled himself for the obligatory slap he thought he deserved. Mrs. Barrymore did the unexpected. She laughed and got to her feet.

Shaking her head, she said, "What you have to understand, Lord Denison, is that in my books, the heroes are accessories, like a fan or a handkerchief. My heroines are my heroes." She turned away, then turned back. "Thank you for the glass of water."

"My pleasure," he responded, but this time he made sure the lady understood he was not harmless.

He watched her as she made a dignified retreat. From this angle, he had a better idea of the figure she tried to hide with the shapeless gown—straight spine, small waist, and a curvaceous bottom. He really would like the dressing of her.

When she disappeared up the stairs, he got up and returned to the symposium. Jason Ford found him in quiet reflection a few minutes later.

"Why the smile?" Jason asked.

Without thinking, Ash replied, "I was laughing at myself."

"What's so funny?"

He wasn't going to tell this serious young man that he'd been *undressing* the little country mouse in his mind. Young Ford would be scandalized. "It's not important," said Ash, and it wasn't. "Did you find anything out?"

"Not about the hecklers. Mrs. Rivers is hinting that she is Angelo, but she's being coy about it. I can hardly twist her arm behind her back to get her to tell me whether she's telling the truth or not."

Mrs. Rivers. The dasher. Ash couldn't see it. He'd rather put his money on Mrs. Barrymore. He was remembering how ill she'd looked, how shaken she was after that ugly scene with the hecklers. Something had frightened her badly.

"Leave Mrs. Rivers to me," he said.

Up in her bedchamber, Eve paced back and forth. She knew that she couldn't stay here for long. She owed it to

Leigh and her readers to mingle. All she wanted was a moment or two to get a grip on herself.

Her mind was still dwelling on the inexplicable wave of hatred that seemed to assault her during the symposium. And when she'd turned around to find the source, there was Ash Denison looking straight at her.

She sat on the edge of the bed and absently hugged herself as though she were chilled through and through. According to Lady Sayers, he was immensely popular because of his gracious manners. His manners were anything but gracious when he'd talked to her about her book. The words burned inside her brain: *flowery prose, exaggerated emotions, an anemic hero.*

Her heroes were *safe*. She trusted them. She wouldn't trust Lord Denison beyond saying "How do you do?" It amused him to trifle with a country bumpkin. That's what he thought of her. That's how he'd summed her up. Well, she had more sense than to be swayed by the opinions of a man who was nothing but an affected fop.

She was tidying herself in readiness to go downstairs when her aunt entered.

"Are you all right, dear?" asked Miss Claverley. "Lady Sayers told me you were not feeling quite the thing."

"It was the heat," Eve replied. She studied her aunt for some sign that she'd sensed the presence of something malevolent, too, but Miss Claverley, who really had a sixth sense, merely looked concerned.

"It was nerves, I suppose," said Miss Claverley. "You're always so tense at these affairs. I can't think why. You do so well."

Eve shrugged. "It wasn't the best symposium I've attended."

"No, indeed. Those dreadful men trying to make

trouble! Lord Denison soon put a stop to their game. What was the fuss about? Who is this Angelo?"

"I haven't the least idea. Shall we return to the others?"

"If you're feeling up to it, dear."

"Oh, I'm up to anyone and anything," Eve stated, and she ushered her aunt through the door.

Chapter Four

On the appointed morning of Brand Hamilton's return, Ash arrived at the *Herald*'s offices in Soho. He was still determined to discover Angelo's identity. Most people would have given up at this point. It wasn't as though Angelo had committed a crime. But Ash couldn't let it go at that. He truly believed that Angelo had written about his family, and he wanted to know how Angelo had come to know so much. Who had told him? That he'd changed the names of his characters and settings didn't fool Ash for one moment. Angelo was privy to secrets that only Ash should have known, and he felt as though his innermost thoughts had been broken into and ransacked.

But that wasn't what drove him to unmask Angelo. It was the uncertainty surrounding Harry's death that constantly gnawed at him.

He found Brand at his desk with that morning's paper spread out in front of him. He and Brand had been friends since their school days. Once, they'd been alike, but now they seemed like opposites. Brand set goals for himself and strove to attain them. Ash had long since given up striving to please anyone but himself. He enjoyed the finer things in life. Brand's tastes were Spartan, though his marriage to Lady Marion had had an effect. Nothing was too good for Marion.

There was another friend, Jack, in much the same position as Brand. Ash was godfather to his friends' children. Each had an infant son who was born within a month of the other. The standing joke was that when Ash became a father, his world view would shift on its axis.

They did not know that it had shifted on its axis when Harry died.

Brand's eyebrows rose quizzically. "Now, what has put that look on your face?" he asked.

Ash's expression cleared, and he pulled up a chair. "I was thinking," he said easily, "that with the right clothes and setting, you could pass yourself off as a buccaneer."

Brand grinned. "I've been called worse."

They spent the next little while catching up on each other's news, though there wasn't much to catch up. Now that Brand had bought a house for his family in Cavendish Square, they saw each other regularly.

When the pleasantries were over, Brand said, "So, what brings you here?"

Ash had rehearsed what he was going to say. Though Brand was his friend, his knowledge of Ash's boyhood was sketchy at best, and that was how Ash wanted to keep it, especially now that Brand was a newspaper man. Brand could nose out a story a mile off. He might not publish it, for friendship's sake, but he would not let it rest until he had uncovered every dark and dangerous secret. Some family secrets were too shameful to share.

Ash said, "Your editor may have told you that I'm trying to track down one of your contributors, a fellow named Angelo?"

Brand nodded. "Yes, Adam mentioned that you'd been asking about him. What's your interest here, Ash?"

"I'm acting for a friend," said Ash, and he began to give Brand a summary of the colonel's grievance.

Brand stopped him before he got very far. "You're acting for Colonel Shearer, aren't you?"

When Ash nodded, Brand sighed. "I don't know what's got into the old boy. He seems to think that Angelo has set one of his stories in his country estate. I can't see it. These stately gardens are all the same. I've tried to tell him that these are works of fiction, but he won't listen. He seems to think I'm protecting Angelo, but I'm not." Brand spread his hands. "I don't know who Angelo is. All I know is that a batch of stories, three in all, arrived at my office with a promise of more to come if we decided to publish. We liked them and published them, and now we're waiting for the next batch to arrive."

When Brand paused, Ash said, "How did you pay for them?"

"I deposited the funds—twenty pounds it was—in Angelo's name in his bank, Ransom, Morland, and Company in Pall Mall. Those were my instructions, and I followed them to the letter."

Ash frowned and sat back in his chair. "You followed them to the letter? Isn't that a bit melodramatic? Why the secrecy? Why didn't Angelo come in person for his money?"

Brand shrugged. "Perhaps Angelo is a public figure and if his identity were to become known, it would hurt his career."

This was a new twist. "Is that what you think?" Ash asked slowly.

"Lord, no!" responded Brand at once. "I think he is a female, you know, one of those writers of Gothic romances that are all the rage right now. That's why we publish them, to appeal to our female readers. I suppose that's why Angelo chose us. Only the *Herald* publishes the kind of stories he writes."

Ash gazed down at his highly polished boots as he sifted through what Brand had told him. There were more stories to come. What was the significance of that? He discarded the idea of approaching Angelo's bank for his name and direction. Ransom, Morland, and Company guarded their clients' secrets like priests in a confessional.

Brand broke the silence. "Colonel Shearer reacted as though he'd been held up to ridicule in Angelo's story. I tried to assure him that no one would connect him to it and that the best thing to do was ignore it."

"Is that your advice to me?"

"Unless there's something you're not telling me."

That was the thing about Brand, Ash reminded himself. He was a newspaperman and could nose out a story a mile off.

"You know how it is." He spread his hands. "Shearer and I served together in the Spanish Campaign. I promised him I'd look into it and that's what I'm doing."

"You always had a soft heart!" said Brand.

"Don't I know it!"

Ash's next port of call was Leigh Fleming's house in Wimpole Street. A portly, placid-faced butler led him up a flight of stairs to a dwarfish room that had the grand title of "library."

The house was not what Ash had expected. It was too feminine, too fussy, with too many ornaments on every available flat surface. Fleming was not an effeminate man as far as appearances went, and Ash wondered whether the house was rented or was an example of artistic temperament.

Fleming seemed pleased to see him, until he realized that Amanda would not be joining them. He waved Ash to a chair, then seated himself.

"Joining us?" Ash repeated, removing an embroidered cushion from his back and depositing it on a nearby sofa.

"Well, not up here in my masculine domain. I meant in my mother's drawing room."

Enlightenment dawned. "Ah. You live with your mother."

"She's an invalid. Lady Amanda mentioned that she might drop by for a visit."

"I see," said Ash, and wasn't particularly thrilled with the thought that occurred to him. Fleming and Amanda? A man who lived in a fussy house with an invalid mother and made his living promoting romantic ideals that no one could live up to lacked something essential, in his opinion. It wasn't manly.

"So," said Fleming, "how may I help you?"

This required diplomacy and tact with a generous helping of subterfuge stirred into the mix. Ash had no desire to get Fleming all fired up before he'd got what he wanted, and what Ash wanted was information on Fleming's writers so that he could narrow the field of suspects.

Amanda had been helpful. She'd attended several

symposiums and had become friendly with some of the authors, but the information she had unwittingly passed on was superficial. Ash needed more to work with than that.

"You're aware, I suppose," he said, "that my cousin, Lady Amanda, has struck up a friendship with some of your authors?"

Fleming replied cautiously, "I'm aware of it."

"I'm not sure that I approve."

Fleming stiffened. "My writers may not be blue bloods, but I assure you they are all respectable, decent people who live quiet, uneventful lives."

"Good grief, man! That's not what bothers me! Have you forgotten what happened at the symposium? Those hecklers could have turned nasty. And now that Mrs. Rivers is practically claiming to be Angelo, I'm afraid for my cousin's safety if she is seen in her company."

Fleming's jaw worked. "Lydia? Claiming to be Angelo? She's lying! She doesn't have Angelo's vocabulary. She'd need a dictionary at her elbow before she embarked on any of his stories. That's what makes Lydia unique. Her prose is simple!"

Ash had hoped that Mrs. Rivers would turn out to be Angelo, because it would have made his task so much easier, but he wasn't surprised that Fleming ridiculed the suggestion. After his own conversation with her, he'd come to the conclusion that all she wanted was to be the center of attention, and claiming to be Angelo had certainly done that.

Fleming shook his head. "All she wants is attention. I shouldn't be angry with her. I should feel sorry for her. But really, she is her own worst enemy."

"How do you mean?"

Fleming reached across his desk for a decanter, and

when Ash nodded, he poured out two careful measures of sherry into two crystal glasses.

One sip of the sherry made Fleming's credit rise in Ash's eyes. Ash knew his sherries, and this was vintage.

In the way of a true connoisseur, Fleming rolled the sherry on his tongue before swallowing. "Lydia," he said, "keeps house for a sister who has fallen out with all her neighbors. A most unpleasant lady, I hear, but very religious. She has no idea that her younger sister has this secret life as a writer, and if she did know, she'd put a stop to it. She controls the purse strings, you see. This annual outing to London is the high point of Lydia's life. I think that she's desperate to meet someone who will offer her marriage and take her away from her dreary existence. And the more desperate she becomes, the more men keep their distance."

"Why doesn't she break away from her sister," Ash asked, "and start a new life somewhere else? She already earns her own living, doesn't she?"

Fleming shrugged. "Starting from scratch is not cheap. Where would she live? How would she find the funds to furnish a house and pay servants? And if she should stop writing or the public stopped buying her books—what then? She'd have to return to her sister's house, if she'd have her. Not a pleasant prospect, is it?"

"I had no idea."

"No. Most men don't realize how few choices women have." He sighed and sipped his sherry. "I'll have a word with Lydia," he said, "and tell her to stop claiming to be Angelo. Will that set your mind at rest?"

Ash shook his head. "There's something else. These women don't use their own names. Who are they? What are they hiding? What do they do when they leave London? Who can vouch for them?"

Fleming bristled. "I can vouch for them."

Ash spread his hands. "Please do."

He half-expected Fleming to show him the door. Instead, Fleming topped up their glasses, settled back in his chair, and finally said, "There are only four who have stayed on with Lady Sayers, so there's no point in mentioning those who went home after the symposium. You were right about the hecklers. That's what frightened them away. Where shall I begin?"

"Tell me about Mrs. Barrymore," Ash prompted. "I know she has accepted Lady Sayers's invitation."

"Her name is Eve Dearing. Like the others, she's a single woman and lives quietly with her aunt in the pretty village of Henley. She rarely comes up to town. Her father and stepmother live in Brighton. He was a landscape gardener before he retired and worked with some famous names. Lancelot Brown comes to mind."

"Capability Brown? He is a legend."

"I believe George Dearing was his apprentice at one time."

Ash thought for a moment. "What happened to Miss Dearing's mother?"

"Oh, she died in a tragic accident when Eve was very young. When Mr. Dearing remarried, Eve went to live with her mother's sister."

"I see." That suggested to Ash that Eve and her father were not very close. What interested him, however, was her father's occupation. It was true that the layout of the estates in the Angelo stories were vague, but the gardens themselves were so vividly brought to life that only someone who loved gardens could have done such a masterly job.

Was it possible that George Dearing was Angelo? Two

writers in one family? It was far more likely to be the daughter.

"Then there's Miss Claverley," said Fleming. "She is not a writer but Eve's aunt, the one in Henley I mentioned. They're very close. She is what I would call eccentric!" To the question in Ash's eyes, he elaborated, "She's 'fey,' you know, she has a sixth sense that can be quite uncanny. She is very popular with all my writers.

"As for Anna Contini, that is her real name. Anna is a wealthy widow. She has a huge spread in Cornwall that she has turned over as a refuge for broken-down donkeys and ponies. I know it's true because I've been there. She converses more easily with those animals than she does with people, but she is quite harmless."

Ash found himself warming to the vampirish lady. He had a soft spot for castoffs, whether they were people or animals.

They spoke back and forth, but there wasn't much more Fleming could tell him about this reclusive, private lady.

The silence lengthened. Fleming grew restive. Finally, he said, "I've been frank with you, Denison. Perhaps I've told you more than I ought. I can't believe, however, that a man of the world, such as yourself, would imagine that Lady Amanda would be in harm's way from these inoffensive ladies."

"I don't think it. But my original point still stands. If someone thinks that one of your writers is Angelo, then they may all be in harm's way."

"I don't understand it!" exclaimed Fleming. "There are other publishers who publish Gothic fiction. Why are my writers being singled out in this way?"

"Because," said Ash, "Angelo was good enough to

mention your symposium at the end of each story, so naturally readers thought he would be there."

"Maybe he was there, but I know the voice of each of my authors, and I can say categorically that he is not one of them."

Ash didn't know enough about writing to argue the point.

He met up with Colonel Shearer later that evening in White's club in St. James's. When he left White's and made for Grillon's Hotel, Ash had cleared up one point: Shearer had had nothing to do with the hecklers at the symposium. In fact, he'd had to placate the colonel for even suggesting such a thing.

"Conduct unbecoming in a gentleman!" had been Shearer's opinion of anyone who had tried to disrupt an orderly, lawful assembly. If he'd been there, he would have read the buggers the riot act.

Ash came away with something else. The colonel applied to one of the stewards, who obligingly found a back copy of the *Herald* with the first story that was published. Ash, however, did not recognize the landscape or the characters involved. This story was set inside a stately home where an elderly footman took a tumble down the stairs and broke his neck. There was no clue to indicate the year it had happened.

He kept thinking that he was missing something, something that was in plain view, something that ought to have occurred to him.

What was it? He dwelled on that question for a long time.

His thoughts shifted to Eve Dearing. Before long, his lips were curling in a smile. She was a refreshing change from the docile society ladies who thronged the drawing rooms and ballrooms of London now that the Season was in full swing. If any of them ever had an original thought, he had yet to hear it. His smile lingered when he recalled Miss Dearing's heated defense of her genre. The men in her stories were accessories, she said.

It made a man want to make her change her mind.

His smile vanished. Now that was a dangerous thought! Eve Dearing was, in the words of her publisher, a respectable lady who lived quietly and uneventfully with her aunt in the small village of Henley. And he never trifled with respectable ladies. That path could well end up at the altar.

Pity.

The smile tugged at the corners of his mouth again. He was safe from Miss Dearing. Everything about her proclaimed her as a confirmed spinster—the way she dressed, the way she spoke her mind, the way she looked directly into a man's eyes.

And those were lovely eyes, a cool gray when she was in command of the situation and a stormy violet when she was aroused. He'd wager that beneath that cool exterior there were other passions besides temper waiting to be tapped. It made him wonder—

He stopped right there. He was going down that dangerous path again.

Restless now, he looked at his watch. A little excitement, he decided, was all that was needed to banish the provoking image of Eve Dearing.

It was Wednesday evening and Lady Sayers and her bevy of guests were driving home to her place in Kennington after taking in the opera. There were only four of them in her ladyship's carriage, because Lydia had begged off to visit an old friend in Marylebone. The two older ladies did most of the talking; Eve and Anna listened absently to their chatter as they gazed out the coach windows at the crush of carriages, pedestrians, linkboys, and lackeys that choked the streets.

Their coach moved at a snail's pace, which suited Eve just fine. She was making mental notes on the passing scene to add color to the book she was writing.

The lamps on every front portico had been lit, as well as the streetlamps, and she had a good view of the comings and goings of late-night revelers. One couple in particular held her interest. The gentleman was leaving the house, though the lady seemed reluctant to let him go. Eve was not naive. This was not a husband taking an affectionate leave of his wife. This woman's scarlet gown, her unbound hair falling in waves around her shoulders, and her free and easy manners clearly indicated that she was a member of the *demimonde,* that hidden sphere of society that catered to gentlemen of rank and fortune, a sphere that no well-bred lady was supposed to know anything about.

Eve's eyes danced. A writer had to fall back on her imagination to fill the void. She could hardly appeal to her male relatives to divulge what went on behind closed doors. Her boldness would shock them, and they would only deny that the *demimonde* existed. Stuff and nonsense! She was no shrinking violet. She was a woman of the world, as anyone who had read her books would know.

Their carriage had stopped, and angry voices were raised as coachmen cursed other coachmen for blocking their way. Eve's gaze was still fixed on the couple standing under the lamp on the top step of the house on the corner of Haymarket and Pall Mall. It was very amusing. The lady was trying to coax the gentleman to go back inside. The gentleman stopped her words with a kiss, a thoroughly passionate kiss as far as Eve could tell, then the gentleman turned on his heel and quickly descended the stairs.

That's when Eve's smile froze. He was none other than Ash Denison, the gentleman who had made fun of her books at the symposium; Ash Denison, making a spectacle of himself on a public street! It was too funny for words.

"What's wrong, Eve? Why do you look so fierce?"

Eve's frown smoothed out and she answered her aunt's question with a smile. "I was thinking about Dexter," she said, dredging up the first thing that came to her mind. "I hope he isn't pining for me. We've been gone a long time, and he's not used to someone else looking after him."

She wasn't sure what she was saying, since she was more intent on keeping her head turned away so that Lord Denison would not see her face. She was also loath to mention his name in case Lady Sayers called him over. The only thing Eve wanted to say to that libertine wasn't fit for the ears of polite company.

The coach began to move, and the conversation shifted to the performance they had just attended. Eve suppressed every stray thought that led to Ash Denison, no easy task when the opera in question was about the most notorious libertine of his age, Don Giovanni, but she persevered and managed to laugh and make observations in all the right places.

In her dreams that night, Ash Denison would not be suppressed. He was sitting at her escritoire, reading the pages of the novel she was currently writing and making copious notes in the margins. She was there, too, dressed from head to toe in shimmering crimson satin.

"What are you doing?" she asked.

She wasn't angry. The Eve of her dreams seemed to float on air. She loved the feel of the satin against her skin and the rustle of her skirts as she moved. Her hair was unbound, and she fluffed it out with her fingers.

He continued to make notes. "I'm making suggestions. You don't have to follow them if you don't want to."

She looked over his shoulder and scanned his notes. "You want me to make the villain into the hero of my book?" Her laugh was low and rich.

"He's not a villain. He's a rogue."

"Like you?" she teased.

He looked up at her and his smile slowly died. "Eve?" he said. "You look different."

She batted her eyelashes. "Do I?"

"You're beautiful. Ravishing. That red dress suits you to perfection. You should always wear red."

She did a little pirouette. "Thank you kindly, sir."

He got up slowly and his hands cupped her shoulders. He looked like a blind man who could suddenly see. "You take my breath away," he murmured. "There's more to you than shows on the surface. Let me teach you about pleasure, Eve. That's what you want, isn't it?"

He was going to kiss her and she was going to allow it, because this was a dream. She couldn't be held responsible for what happened in her dreams.

She lifted her head and went on tiptoe. His lips

hovered over hers. Anticipation had all her senses humming. Why wouldn't he kiss her?

"You're the rogue, Eve," he said. "Oh, you're quiet on the outside, but inside you're a dasher."

Her brow puckered. "I've heard those words before. *You're dashing on the inside.* I'm dreaming, aren't I? This is nothing but a dream."

No sooner were those words out of her mouth than everything that seemed real and substantial was sucked into a swirling mist, and she was left alone.

Chapter Five

The following afternoon, a carriage pulled up outside the doors of Lady Sayers's house, and Ash helped his grandmother and Amanda to alight. The Manor, as it was called, was set in one of the prettiest districts in London, though strictly speaking it wasn't in the city. It was on the south side of the river, largely rural, with many market gardens and orchards nearby. Yet Westminster Bridge was only a short drive away.

Amanda shaded her eyes and looked into the horizon. "Is that the new Bedlam?"

Ash nodded. "St. Mary's of Bethlehem. It's quite a change from the one they demolished. It was a house of horrors. This is supposed to be a refuge for the insane."

"I thought," said Lady Valmede, "that the Manor was close to Vauxhall Gardens?"

"It is, on the other side of the house."

Amanda suppressed a shudder. "I don't think I'd like to live close to an asylum for the insane."

"Nonsense," said Lady Valmede. "It's a mile away, and no one ever escapes from Bedlam."

Ash's gaze rested reflectively on the building in question, then he turned away as the door opened.

An elderly butler ushered them into a spacious marble hall that was flooded by sunlight from a fine Venetian window on the landing at the top of the stairs. A moment later, Lady Sayers herself appeared. Her gray-brown hair was arranged in loose curls that peeked from beneath a velvet turban.

"Augusta and Lady Amanda," she said warmly. "Lord Denison. I was on the stairs when I heard your voices. The girls sent me to look for snuff, you see." She shook her head. "Well, well, what does that matter? You could not have arrived at a better time. Eve is writing about a girl's first Season, and I can hardly remember what it was like."

"Eve?" said the dowager.

"Mrs. Barrymore." Her ladyship laughed. "Eve Dearing when she's not writing. I know she won't object to my telling you her real name. We're all friends here."

"And she is writing about a girl's first Season?"

"I know it doesn't sound very Gothic, but Eve can turn the ordinary into something that is hideously exciting. I've told her as much as I can remember, but the more I try to remember, the more I seem to forget. They're all waiting for me. Shall we join them?"

Her visitors exchanged glances and gave a collective shrug. No doubt all would become clear to them in good time.

Lady Sayers kept up an animated commentary as she led them across the vast marble hall. The decorators, she said, were in the other wing of the house getting the picture gallery ready for her niece's come-out ball. The masons were outside erecting scaffolding to point the bricks, or whatever one did to bricks, in the same wing of the house, to correct and prevent water damage. They'd promised to get the work done before dear Liza arrived. But who could trust workmen to keep their promises in these free and easy times?

The house was an odd mix of old and new but charming for all that, in Ash's opinion. What had started as a stolid Tudor manor had been added to and refurbished as tastes changed in succeeding generations. There were always improvements under way at the Manor, always workmen tearing down walls and putting up new ones.

And why not, thought Ash. As one husband had succeeded the next, Lady Sayers had become immensely rich. She could afford to indulge her tastes.

She led them to the east wing of the house, the neoclassical and most recent addition. From the silk-covered walls, portraits of her four dearly departed husbands stared down on them, imposing figures all, though, according to their widow, charming, lovable rogues in their day.

The room they entered was the music room, as was evident from the grand pianoforte at one end and the golden harp in a window embrasure. Ash took in the scene at a glance. Eve was standing at a table on which was set out an array of fans. The lady sitting at the harp was Mrs. Contini. Her sepulchral appearance was made all the more ghastly, in his opinion, by the rouge Lydia Rivers was applying to her wan cheeks. Another lady, whom he took to be Miss Claverley, was embroidering by an open window.

Lady Sayers let out a warning laugh. "Look, my dears, we have company."

There was a moment of profound silence, almost a

shocked silence. In spite of Lady Sayers's assurances, their entrance had evidently come at a bad time. Mrs. Contini began to scrub at her cheeks with a handkerchief, Mrs. Rivers fluffed out her skirts and gave Ash a bold smile, and Eve Dearing dropped the fan she was holding and stared at him as though King George himself had come calling.

Ash knew a lot more about Lady Sayers's guests since his visit to Leigh Fleming, and his gaze touched briefly on each one as Fleming's words came back to him. Lydia Rivers was desperate for attention; Miss Claverley was fey; Anna Contini preferred animals to people; and Eve Dearing...His gaze lingered.

She lifted her head and their eyes met. For one charged, lightning moment, they stared at each other, then the dowager spoke and the moment passed.

"We met at the symposium," said the dowager, smiling at each young woman in turn, "and I must say that you made quite an impression on me. Isn't that so, Amanda?"

Amanda readily agreed that this was so.

Her ladyship went on. "I simply wanted to thank you in person for the many hours of pleasure your books have given me."

And that, thought Ash, was an example of why his grandmother was popular. She had the knack of putting people at their ease. He corrected himself. It wasn't a knack. She could always find something good to say about people. A few minutes in her company was as good as a tonic.

Unless you happened to be her grandson. Then she could make you squirm with shame.

Lady Sayers rang the bell for refreshments and bade

them all be seated. The conversation turned almost immediately to her niece, Liza.

"My brother's daughter, you know," said Lady Sayers.
"She should be here any day now. I haven't seen her in
years. She was always an awkward child, but her mother
tells me that she has grown into a lovely young lady."
She flashed Eve a warm smile. "Eve and her aunt, Miss
Claverley," she nodded to the middle-aged lady who was
embroidering, "have agreed to stay on and keep me
company."

The girl, thought Ash, must be a handful if she
needed three chaperons to keep her in check. He wasn't
quite sure that the three ladies who had taken on the
task had the least idea of what willful young debutantes
could get up to.

"I remember my first Season," said the dowager. She
got up, wandered over to the table where the fans were
laid out, and examined each one closely. Ash, meantime,
picked up a leather-bound volume that was lying on the
table at his elbow. It wasn't a novel, as he expected, but a
notebook. He idly riffled through it. Someone had been
making copious notes on the layout of the rooms, the
gardens, the duties of servants, and the modes of address for those with titles. He turned back to the first
page. It was inscribed *Eve Dearing*. He put the notebook
down before Eve was aware of what he was up to.

His grandmother had a fan in her hand, a painted
ivory silk that was decorated with mother-of-pearl and
white feathers. She gazed at it fondly. "I had a fan like
this once," she said. "It was a wedding present from my
husband. If you look closely, you'll see the bride and
groom and their attendants outside the church. These
days, young girls use their fans to cool their cheeks.

When I was a girl—" She gave a faint laugh. "When I was a girl, we used our fans to flirt with our beaux."

"Flirt with your beaux?" said Amanda. "With a fan?"

Lady Sayers interjected, "Go on, Augusta. Show these young things how it's done."

The dowager did not need a second bidding. She flicked the fan open with her right hand and covered her face so that only her eyes were showing. "That means 'Follow me,'" she said. In the next instant, she changed the fan to her left hand and twirled it as though she was not aware of what she was doing. "And that means, 'Careful, we are being watched.' There is no end to the messages a girl can convey to her lover when she has a fan in her hand, but the one that is indispensable is this." She snapped the fan shut and tapped it against her left cheek. "That means 'No.'"

There was a titter of laughter.

"What if the lady wants to say 'Yes'?" asked Lydia Rivers with a sideways glance at Ash.

"Oh, I think you girls can work that out for yourselves," the dowager replied.

"Shocking!" declared Amanda, and everyone laughed.

Lady Sayers let out a sigh. "I remember it all as though it were yesterday. The beauty patches we wore, the bonnets, the gentlemen so handsome in their powdered wigs and skintight breeches..."

"And those gowns with their impossible panniers to navigate through doors," reminisced the dowager in a faraway voice.

"Panniers?" Lady Sayers sat up straighter. "That was before my time, Augusta. My gowns had hoops but not those grotesque panniers my mother wore."

"Of course. Now I remember, Sally. You were just a babe in arms at my wedding."

The silence was very mellow. Ash hated to break it, but he had come with a purpose and that was to settle, once and for all, whether one of these writers could possibly be Angelo.

To Eve, he said, "Lady Sayers mentioned that you were setting your next book in town at the height of the Season."

Eve's eyes, still mellow from hearing his grandmother's musings, met his in an unguarded stare. "Yes. The idea has been floating around in my mind for some time."

The refreshments arrived at that moment, and Mrs. Rivers got up to help their hostess pass out cups of tea. She served Ash last and managed to brush her fingers against his. He gave no sign that he was aware of it.

Ash went on, "That's quite a departure for you, is it not? You usually set your stories in stately homes and landscaped gardens."

Eve stirred her tea. "I suppose I wanted to try something new. I hope I haven't taken on too much. I lead a rather quiet life in Henley." She smiled faintly. "Country ways are not the same as town ways. There is no such thing as a Season. We have assemblies from time to time and that's about all, except for meeting friends, going for long walks, and so on."

Lady Sayers looked hopefully at the dowager. "I'm not much help to Eve. As you know, I never had a Season before I married. I hardly know what gown is proper to wear for which function. I've never been a follower of rules myself."

Amanda said sweetly, "Oh, Ash can help there, can't you, Ash? Many ladies of rank come to him for advice when they are selecting a new wardrobe."

Ash sent his cousin a killing look, but he spoke gently. "I'm always happy to oblige a lady."

"There you are, Eve," said Amanda. "It's all settled then."

Eve would have liked to send Amanda a killing look, as well. She restrained herself and said as pleasantly as she could manage, "Thank you for the offer, Lord Denison, but it's not necessary. My aunt and I ordered our wardrobes when we first arrived in town, and most of our gowns are already made up."

Lydia lost no time in entering the conversation. "Is your offer open to one and all, Lord Denison? Because if it is, I would gladly accept it." She gave Eve an arch smile.

Ash's lashes lowered to half-mast. "I'd be happy to oblige."

Lady Sayers clapped her hands. "Oh, that is very generous of you, Lord Denison. Perhaps you'll do as much for my niece when she arrives in town?"

The conversation moved on, but when the topic turned to books and writers of Gothic fiction, Ash saw the opening he'd been waiting for and seized it. "What about this Angelo fellow who writes for the *Herald*? He leaves his readers hanging. Who or what are the ghosts waiting for? Why doesn't Angelo finish his stories?"

Lady Sayers shook her head. "It's no good asking us. We haven't read his stories. We've been too busy preparing for the symposium."

Ash sat back in his chair. "What, no one has read them?"

Except for Lydia, they shook their heads. She said coyly, "I have, and we'll just have to wait and see what Angelo does next."

Anna Contini said, "You're not Angelo, Lydia. You just like to tease us."

Miss Claverley was gazing into space. "I don't think he has finished yet," she said. "I think there is more to come. I wonder..." Her voice faded.

"Why do you think there is more to come?" Ash asked sharply.

Miss Claverley gazed at him for a moment with unseeing eyes, then her cheeks went pink as she came to herself. "I beg your pardon. My mind wandered. Did you say something, Lord Denison?"

"I asked why you thought that Angelo wasn't finished yet."

"I don't know how I know. It just came to me."

"Our Miss Claverley," said Lady Sayers, "is something of a seer. She can read palms, tea leaves, and tell fortunes. Oh, it's all in good fun, but she can be astonishingly accurate in what she knows about her subjects." She giggled. "That's us."

Ash turned his head and raised his brows. The silent message was meant for Amanda, a joke they could share, but it was Eve Dearing who was in his line of vision. Their eyes met briefly, then she turned her head away.

An afternoon call was supposed to last no more than thirty minutes, but this call had turned into a hen party. Lady Valmede had started something by reminiscing about the old days, and, by general consent, the ladies soon decamped for Lady Sayers's dressing room to look over the garments she had carefully packed away, cherished mementos of her youth. Ash, meanwhile, was left in the music room to twiddle his thumbs until his grandmother and cousin were ready to leave.

He spied Eve's notebook, picked it up, and began to thumb through it. Near the back, he found something he'd missed before, a map of the southeastern border of the city, stretching to Dartford in Kent. She'd marked off places of interest. It took him a moment to realize that they were all the homes and estates of people of rank and money.

He heard steps approaching the door, quickly replaced the book, and crossed to the table with its array of fans. The door opened. The faint scent of flowers was unmistakable. He recognized her perfume. "Miss Dearing," he said, as he turned to face her.

She didn't ask how he knew her real name, nor did she care. Her mind was seething with all his offenses, not least the fact that he had invaded her dreams and made her act in ways that were contrary to her nature. She'd awakened that morning in the wee hours, fretting, fractious, and vaguely afraid of the woman in her dream. Now here he was again, the man of her dream, looking as fresh and debonair as she had ever seen him, while she felt as embarrassed as a guilty schoolgirl.

"So you know my name," she said. "What of it?"

"How many names do you have, Miss Dearing? Two? Three? More?"

She took a quick step back at the sudden change in him. "I haven't the least idea of what you're talking about."

"Don't come the innocent with me! You're Angelo! Admit it!"

Her jaw sagged. "What gave you that idea?"

"Your father is a landscape gardener, isn't he?" He gestured to her notebook on the sofa table. "You've made a map of the stately homes and gardens close to town and marked some of them off. Are those your next targets? Are these where your next batch of stories will come from? Don't you care that innocent people may be hurt?"

She seemed to be rooted to the spot, then she bounded away from him, snatched her notebook from the table, and turned to face him. "You had no right—" She had to stop to suck in air. "This book is private property. If you wanted to read it, you should have asked my permission."

"You left it in plain view for anyone to read. And that's no answer. Why have you marked off those properties in Kent?"

She advanced on him on the balls of her feet, like a cat stalking its prey. Eyes flashing, she said, "Now, you listen to me, Ash Denison. I am not Angelo. My father does not give me ideas for my stories. He never did and he never will. For one thing, we're not that close. Yes, I've marked off gardens and places in Kent I want to visit, but that's because I think I may have visited those gardens with my mother. There's a quarry nearby." She faltered a little before continuing. "It's the last place we visited before she died."

She broke off and pressed her lips together. It was anger that had loosened her tongue, and now she wished she had kept her mouth shut. She didn't want to share her innermost feelings with this man. She didn't want to share anything with him.

He studied her for a moment and smiled sheepishly. "I'm truly sorry. I seem to have made a mistake. I should think before I speak."

His apology did not soften her. "Yes, you should, and also before you hold someone up to ridicule with one of your speaking looks."

The look she had intercepted between him and his

cousin had festered into a raw sore. She'd surprised those looks on other faces before now. The crazy Claverleys were a laughingstock. They belonged with the freaks at the county fair.

His voice was controlled and cool. "Explain yourself, Miss Dearing."

"I saw the look you gave Amanda when my aunt mentioned Angelo. It spoke volumes. If you knew my aunt's character, you would treat her with more respect. She is a dear, sweet lady who never thinks ill of anyone."

His voice chilled. "If you knew my character, Miss Dearing, you would know that no insult was intended."

"I know as much of your character as I want to know. You're the darling of society. You know how to dress a lady." The sleepless hours she'd spent fretting after she had awakened from her dream made her more honest than wise. "You're more at home in the *demimonde* than you are in polite society. Your only ambition is to chase women or squeeze as much pleasure from every novel experience that comes your way." She fumbled for words, unsure of how she had entangled herself in this web. "There should be more to life than that."

A deep chuckle made her tip up her chin. His head was to the side as he studied her. "So it *was* you I saw last night, spying on me out of the coach window."

She gasped. "I did no such thing! You were making a spectacle of yourself in a public place. Can I help it if I saw you?"

He scratched his chin. "And you've summed up my character because of one careless kiss? You may be a writer, but you have a lot to learn about men, and a lot to learn about pleasure, in fact."

That was a careless kiss? Her mind boggled at the thought of what a passionate kiss must be like, and she couldn't help looking at his lips. When that mouth that was made for kissing turned up at the corners, she jerked her eyes up to meet his.

"I know as much about men," she said, "as I need for my novels."

"Of course. I should have remembered. Your heroes are accessories, aren't they?"

When she didn't reply, he edged closer. "If I'd praised your books at the symposium instead of pointing out a few obvious flaws, would you, I wonder, have taken me in such dislike? Or perhaps you don't dislike me. Perhaps it's yourself you've taken in dislike." His eyes glinted with amusement. "You don't fool me. There's more to you than shows on the surface. There's no shame in that. Put yourself in my hands, Eve, and I'll teach you about pleasure. That's what you really want, isn't it?"

Her eyes went as round as saucers. "What did you say?" she asked hoarsely.

He frowned at the change in her. She seemed thoroughly confused. "It was only a game," he said. "I'm not trying to seduce you. Word of honor."

Gesturing to the table behind him, she said in a shaken voice, "Lady Sayers asked me to fetch the fans. Would you mind?"

He did not budge but stood with feet apart, studying her intently. "What is it, Eve?"

There was a step at the door. When Amanda entered, Eve took a quick step back. Ash cursed under his breath.

Amanda didn't seem to notice the strained atmosphere. As she came up to Ash, she said, "Do you have your snuffbox with you?"

He replied with less than his usual grace, "I do. Why?"

Amanda's eyes danced. "Grandmama is going to show us how to take snuff." To Eve, she said, "I had no idea that my grandmother was such a dashing lady in her younger days. I think she must have been a flirt. She's having the time of her life and she doesn't want it to end. We're all invited to join her for the opening of Vauxhall Gardens on Saturday."

As Ash handed over the snuffbox, he gave Eve a searching look. She gathered up the fans but kept her eyes averted. She was still reeling from the words he'd used, the very same words he'd used in her dream.

Amanda went on merrily, "It's a masquerade, and Grandmama and Lady Sayers between them have offered to lend every lady one of their treasured gowns. I've always fancied myself in hoops and panniers. Anyway, I've never seen such excitement. Grandmama and Lady Sayers are behaving like . . . well . . . schoolgirls." To Eve, she added meaningfully, "And we're missing all the fun."

She and Eve walked to the door. Over her shoulder, Amanda said, "I almost forgot. Grandmama says you can go, Ash. Lady Sayers has promised to send us home in her own carriage."

Eve dipped him a curtsy. "Good-bye, Lord Denison." And that was all she said.

On the other side of the door, Amanda said, "What was that all about? When I entered the music room, I thought some deity had turned you both into statues."

Eve hardly knew where to begin. Her mind was still buzzing; her feelings were still raw. She liked Amanda immensely, but they were not so close that she felt she could confide in her.

Amanda went on, "It's about Miss Claverley, isn't it? You caught the pained look on Ash's face when she mentioned Angelo. Don't be too hard on Ash. Did he mention our aunt Agatha?"

Eve shook her head.

"He's very fond of her, but he has the typical male's suspicion of what he calls 'quackery and witchcraft.' He may have a point with Aunt Agatha. She truly believes she can communicate with departed spirits and is forever holding séances at her house. Quite honestly, it's creepy. Miss Claverley, on the other hand, is entertaining." She shrugged her lovely shoulders. "I'm sure she doesn't expect us to take her seriously."

Oh, yes, she does, Eve thought darkly while managing a weak smile.

They'd arrived at the door to Lady Sayers's dressing room and could tell from the laughter and raised voices inside that the ladies were enjoying themselves immensely.

With her hand on the doorknob, Amanda said, "I hope you'll forgive my cousin. I'm sure he meant well, but he is, after all, only a male."

"Yes," said Eve, "he's only a male."

Ash barely touched the fine dinner that was sent up from Grillon's dining room. He sat at the table, drumming his fingers, contemplating the long evening that stretched ahead of him. Out of the score or so gilt-edged invitation cards that graced his mantelpiece, he'd selected five for his consideration. He'd already excused himself from the do his grandmother and Amanda were attending—another dinner party with Lady Valmede's oldest and dearest friends.

All the same, he couldn't muster a tepid interest in the invitations he'd selected, all of them from experienced women of the world. He wasn't a cad. He never trifled with gently bred girls or with women who had marriage on their minds. So what in Hades did he think he was doing with Eve Dearing?

He flicked one gilt-edged card with his thumb. Sophie Villiers was a beautiful, passionate woman who never contradicted him. She tried too hard. He flicked another card. Letitia Sutcliffe was both beautiful and intelligent. She had no sense of humor. He flicked another. Barbara Hallet had only one subject of conversation—herself. And so it went on.

What was it about Eve Dearing that made her so memorable?

She'd brought him up short and made him think about where he was going and what he was doing. Well, two could play at that game. Her life, or lack of it, didn't bear too close a scrutiny, either.

You're more at home in the demimonde than you are in polite society. She was off the mark there. He felt at home in both worlds, as did the overwhelming majority of his male acquaintances. That did not mean that they were libertines or lacked honor.

Your only ambition is to chase women. Was she blind? Hadn't she seen last night the struggle he'd put up to get away from Madame Felicité? A smile curled his lips. Of course, he hadn't struggled too hard. That would have been ungentlemanly. Perhaps he should have told Eve that the house was a gaming club, but she would probably have lectured him on the vices attached to such dens of iniquity.

He sighed and reached for his wineglass. This was the third time in the space of two weeks that he'd been taken to task for lacking a worthwhile purpose in his life. He knew what was expected of him, and that was to put his house in order, marry some eligible girl, and produce the next crop of Denisons to secure the family name and title.

And that was supposed to give his life meaning?

The faintly cynical smile on his lips became more pronounced. He'd played that game once before. He and his brother had been pawns in their father's ambitions. As a boy, he was groomed to fulfill his destiny, and he had never questioned it. Harry was the "spare," but when it became evident that Harry would always be sickly and have the mind of a child, he'd been hidden away as though he were too grotesque for Polite Company. As for their mother, she'd feared her husband more than her sons did, but she'd found solace of sorts by dulling her pain with opium.

He couldn't think of his mother or Harry without feeling that he'd let them both down. He'd been devastated when his mother died, but when Harry died, everything changed, or perhaps it was truer to say that *he* had changed. Would he ever forget his father's words to him? It was a blessing in disguise. Harry was becoming too old to keep at home. Arrangements were already under way to have him committed to a suitable asylum. Providence had blessedly intervened and provided a way out of their dilemma.

Ash had had to clench his hands into tight fists to prevent himself from strangling the life out of his father. Harry in an asylum? Harry, who'd had a deeper knowledge of life than anyone he knew? There should be more to a man's character than intelligence and ambition, and Harry's childlike innocence shamed them all. When Harry died, a great hole opened up in his heart.

Ash had never liked his father. He was a cold man whose authority was practically sacrosanct. From that moment on, however, he despised him with his whole heart. But despising his father wasn't enough for him. He'd wanted to punish him, so when the opportunity arose, he, the last Denison heir left standing, went off to war. There could be no greater tragedy for an aristocrat than to have his line die out if anything happened to his heir.

He'd been thumbing his nose at his father, but, strangely enough, the war was the making of him. His life as a soldier had been full of hardship and danger, and he had never flinched from either. In the worst of times, he'd never questioned the rightness of what he was doing. That kind of clarity came but rarely.

He took a long draft of wine as he considered how he'd spent the years after the war. He made no apology for the fact that he'd tried to make up for lost time. But pleasure was not his guiding principle, as Eve seemed to think. He rarely thought deeply about where his life was going, but now that she'd made him think, he would have to say that he'd come to a stand. What he wanted was the kind of clarity he'd found when he was a soldier.

And where was Eve Dearing's life going? She had direction in her writing, but there was a conundrum here. She was quiet on the outside, but the heroines in her stories were adventurous women who were afraid of nothing. What was he to make of that?

The door opened and Ash's personal manservant entered. Though he was young, no more than in his late twenties, his hair was silver. His expression was inscrutable, his manner was faintly respectful. He was the epitome of a gentleman's gentleman. Ash knew he was lucky to have him. Many of his peers had tried to lure

Reaper away, without success, and Ash had no idea why his manservant was so loyal.

Reaper said, "Do we go out tonight, your lordship?"

Ash looked at the invitations he'd selected and made a face. He shook his head, then thought better of it. "Wait! Send word to Hawkins that I want my coach and bays outside the front door in, say, ten minutes."

"Where shall I say you're going?"

"Richmond."

"Ah," said Reaper, and that one syllable was eloquent. He closed the door as he left.

Dusk was creeping over the city when Ash climbed up on the box seat beside his coachman. "I'll take the reins, Hawkins," he said.

Hawkins handed the reins over without a word. His master was wearing a greatcoat almost identical to his own, a coachman's coat with a cape at the back. Hawkins knew what that meant and braced himself for a wild ride.

It wasn't a long drive, no more than an hour, but as the dusk deepened, casting long shadows across the road, Hawkins reached for his musket and cradled it in one arm.

Ash shouted above the thunder of wheels and horses' hooves, "Don't worry, Hawkins. If we meet any highwaymen, I'll run them down."

Hawkins believed him. Indeed, Hawkins suspected that his lordship would welcome a confrontation with highwaymen. He had that reckless, daredevil air about him that Hawkins remembered from the war. In every charge, in every skirmish, Captain Denison was out in front, leading his men by his own example.

A mile from their destination, Ash pulled on the reins and gradually slowed his team to a trot. By the time they crossed Richmond Bridge, the horses were walking. The house was reached through an avenue of ancient limes that made a vaulted ceiling high above them. There were lanterns on poles to light their way, but the darkness was too deep, too intense, to reveal what lay beyond the watery glow of the lanterns.

When they reached the stable block, grooms came running, some pulling on their jerkins, others their boots. These surprise visits of their master were few and far between. As a result, his servants were invariably caught off guard.

Ash jumped down from the box, leaving Hawkins to see to the stabling of the horses, then he wandered off in the direction of the river. Everyone knew his lordship's custom, and one of the grooms sent a stable boy to warn the housekeeper that Lord Denison was here and would be staying the night.

At the river's edge, Ash halted. Memories of Harry filled his mind. Though Harry wasn't like other boys, he'd found joy in small things—reading, listening to music, and, above all, playing in water. When Ash came home from the university, he would take Harry boating in the river or allow him to float, as long as someone was there to keep him safe from the current. More than anything, Harry had wanted to learn to swim. Ash had tried to teach him, but it was no use. Harry's wasted muscles couldn't protect him from the river's ebb and flow.

In his whole life, Ash had never loved anyone as much as he loved this young brother who looked up to him as if he were a demigod. He wondered what Harry would think of him now.

His gloomy thoughts dissipated when he entered the

house. His servants always gave him a warm welcome, fussing over him, anticipating his every need. That he spent so little time here made him feel guilty. He was torn two ways. On the one hand, he could never part with the house that held so many memories of his mother and brother. On the other hand, not all those memories were happy. His father had lived here, too.

He always made up for his neglect by spending the day with his steward, visiting his tenants, and ensuring that his estate was kept up to the mark. He had good people running things, though allowances had to be made for veterans who had a hard time adjusting to their new estate.

He did not consider himself a hard master, but if any of his servants tried to take advantage, they were shown the door. The army had taught him that discipline was essential or chaos would result.

When he climbed the stairs to his bed, his thoughts had taken a different turn. He was thinking of Eve Dearing, wondering what she would look like in crimson satin—and where in blazes had that thought come from?

Chapter Six

Eve knew that she was dreaming, but she could not force herself to waken. She was that twelve-year-old girl again, listening to the sound of her mother's voice. Sheba was there, her great black head damp with rain.

Even in sleep, she could feel her heart pounding, taste the panic rising in her throat. She saw herself sprinting along the corridor to her mother's room. She saw that the bed had not been disturbed, that the fire had died down. She saw her mother's notebooks and sketches strewn across the table. She roused the servants, followed Sheba out the back door, and snatched a lantern from its hook to light their steps.

Everything rushed together in her mind, like flotsam in a tumultuous storm—her mother on the quarry floor, the servants dragging her away, her mother's voice trying to impress on her to be careful. At the end, she saw the ballroom with the glass doors leading onto the terrace. Someone was waiting for her beyond those doors, someone...

She came awake on a panicked cry.

Eve gulped in several quick breaths, as though she'd been drowning and had just come up for air. When she had control of her breathing, she got out of bed and lit a candle from the embers in the grate.

Hugging herself, she sat close to the fire and thought about her dream. She'd always wondered where the picture of the ballroom and debutantes had originated, and now she knew. Now she remembered. It was the picture her mother had put into her mind in her last moments, a warning of things to come.

Why now? Why had the memory of that night come back to haunt her now?

It was her conversation with Ash Denison that had resurrected that memory. She'd told him about the quarry and she'd been thinking about it all night. It wasn't a dream, it was a memory. Everything that had been vague before was now sharply etched in her mind. Antonia had given her a glimpse into the future, a warning of things still to come.

Gardens. Antonia loved gardens and would frequently make notes or sketch something that had caught her fancy. She was also interested in the fine homes the gardens set off. When it was permitted, Papa would take them on a tour.

This is a happy house, Mama would sometimes say. Occasionally, she would grow quiet, shake her head, and say the opposite. Papa always became angry when Mama spoke like this. He called her superstitious, but the child, Eve, knew better. Mama had a sixth sense about such things.

Thoughtful now, Eve sat back in her chair. She'd asked her father about her mother's notebooks, but he said he didn't know what had happened to them. The night Mama died, everything had been in such confusion that the notebooks had been the least of their worries. They were supposed to have been sent on with her boxes, but Eve suspected that either her father or the fiercely efficient second Mrs. Dearing had destroyed them. Martha wouldn't want any reminders of a former wife, especially one she regarded as a freak.

Suddenly conscious that her hands were clenched into fists, she deliberately relaxed them. *A freak.* Isn't that what Ash Denison thought her aunt was? He hadn't said the words, but she'd caught the look on his face when he'd turned away. Heaven only knew what he'd make of her crazy Claverley cousins if he should ever meet them. She wasn't a true believer, but there were some things that defied explanation.

"Eve?"

She gave a start when someone rapped on the door. Quickly rising, she went to open it. Lady Sayers bustled in.

"A dreadful business," exclaimed Lady Sayers. "Some poor wretch has escaped from the asylum, and one of the keepers is at the door demanding to search the house."

"What?" Eve's mind was still trapped in her memories.

Lady Sayers heaved a sigh and started over. "A woman has escaped from Bedlam, and the keepers and dogs are trying to track her. They think she may be in the house. I've given them permission to look everywhere except the bedchambers that are occupied. Well, I didn't have a choice, really. There's no need to upset yourself. This will only take a few minutes, but you're to stay upstairs. I must tell the others."

She was almost at the door when she turned back. "Eve, where is Dexter?"

Eve's mind was fully awake now. "Perhaps he's with Andy." Dexter had the run of the house and Andy, the bootboy, looked after him when Eve was too busy. But Dexter always spent the night in her room.

Lady Sayers nodded and went out.

Eve's brow knit in a frown. When had she last seen Dexter? She'd let him out before going to bed and told Andy to let him in. Then where was he? Had Andy forgotten?

She went to the window and looked out. Men with lanterns were brandishing sticks and beating at the shrubbery like gamekeepers rousing pheasants for the shooters. There were dogs sniffing at bushes, but it seemed to her that they had lost the scent.

"Poor wretch," she said under her breath. Who wouldn't want to escape from Bedlam?

There was a knock at the door, and when Eve answered it, a footman told her that she was wanted downstairs. Heart beating a little faster, she followed him out. Just inside the front door, one of the keepers had Dexter on a leash, and in his free hand he clutched what looked like a filthy stocking.

His face was red with anger, though he spoke civilly enough. "Is this your dog, ma'am?"

Eve looked at Dexter. Oblivious to the trouble he'd caused, he gazed happily back at her.

"Yes," she said. "He's my dog. Thank you for bringing him home. I hope he hasn't been a trouble to anyone."

"Trouble!" The keeper breathed in and moderated his tone. "I'll tell you what your dog has done. He has taken this stocking," he waved the article in question, "and laid a false trail for my dogs to follow. I've had to call them off."

As contritely as she could manage, Eve said, "Did the stocking belong to the woman who ran away from the hospital?" When the keeper nodded, she went on, "I'm truly sorry. I'll see that it doesn't happen again."

The keeper muttered something under his breath, unhooked Dexter, and abruptly left the house.

Eve lost no time in returning to her room with Dexter at her heels, then she sat on the bed and scratched his ears. His head was damp. "At least tonight we can be happy for that poor woman. If it's raining, the dogs won't pick up her scent."

Her hand stopped scratching Dexter as she became lost in thought. A runaway from Bedlam was no laughing matter. The woman could be dangerous. But there must be a better way to treat these poor wretches than to lock them up in an insane asylum, then forget all about them.

She heard the tramp of feet as men left the house, then the sound of feminine voices outside her door. Lady Sayers's voice rose above the others, telling everyone to get back to bed and that they'd talk about it in the morning.

When Eve slipped between the sheets, she left the candle burning. Dexter's weight at her back was a great comfort. She listened as she heard the sound of the rain, no more than a whisper at first, then louder as the heavens opened. That would wipe out the woman's scent so the dogs could not pick it up again.

She closed her eyes, but sleep would not come, and after tossing and turning for half an hour, she threw back the bedclothes and got up.

The unpleasant encounter with the keeper kept running through her mind. She wondered where the runaway was and whether she'd found a dry shelter and had enough to eat. She was torn two ways. Maybe Bedlam was better than letting her die of exposure or starvation. Who was she to say?

St. Mary's of Bethlehem Royal Hospital. It was a grand-sounding name, but the name didn't change what went on inside the building. Everyone knew that shackles and physical punishments were still the most common method of controlling the deranged. There were other more humane places of confinement, but they cost the earth. Only rich people could afford them. There were no influential patrons at Bedlam to protect the interests of the patients.

Eve knew one thing. She wouldn't wish her worst enemy in Bedlam.

Her restlessness made Dexter restless, too. He was scratching at the door to get out. For once, she didn't mind. The keepers and their dogs were long gone, and a short walk might clear her mind and calm her fidgets.

After lighting a fresh candle, she put on her warmest coat, pulled on stout walking boots, and draped a shawl over her head. Even in April, the nights could be chilly. Commanding Dexter to heel and cupping the flame of the candle with one hand, she left her chamber and traversed the long corridor to the door to the servants' staircase.

Halfway down the stairs, Dexter sniffed the air, then scampered past her before she could stop him. What was worse, her candle went out. Feeling her way with one hand on the rail, she descended the stairs one careful step at a time. On the landing, she halted. It was highly irrational, but she couldn't persuade her feet to move. Ears straining, she listened. At the very least she should hear Dexter whining to get out. There was nothing, not even the sound of his breathing.

The minutes dragged by. She had to talk herself into moving. In all likelihood, Dexter was devouring something one of the kitchen maids had inadvertently left out or something he'd pilfered from the slop pail, or perhaps one of the servants was still up, or ... or ...

The woman who had run away from Bedlam.

She went down the stairs as silently as she could manage and entered the kitchen. There was some light to guide her, a soft glow from the embers in the grate, but there was no sign of Dexter or anyone else. She lost no time in lighting her candle from the embers, then she turned and surveyed the room. Everything was just as it should be.

She wasn't afraid. She didn't want to call Dexter to her. The image of the runaway from Bedlam had become so fixed in her mind that her one aim was to do nothing that would frighten her off.

With the stealth of a cat, she flitted from room to room and found them in the laundry room. Dexter saw Eve first and gave a little whine, but he didn't leave the woman's side. She was huddled against the big copper boiler that heated water from morning till night for the exhaustive demands of Lady Sayers's household.

When the woman saw Eve, she jumped up. Her eyes were wide with alarm; her breathing was shallow and strained. In one hand, she held a hunk of bread.

"Don't be afraid." Eve's voice was as gentle and as unthreatening as she could make it. "I won't hurt you or tell anyone you're here."

Her words seemed to make no impression. The eyes were still wide with fear. *She's only a girl,* Eve thought, and she took in the threadbare gown mired in mud and the hair tangled with leaves and burrs. Her feet were bare and scratched.

She looked into those fear-bright eyes. "You've made friends with my dog. I want to be your friend, too."

She didn't know where the soothing words were coming from, but they weren't having an effect. "My name is Eve," she went on. "What's yours?"

No response, but the girl's eyes darted to the door behind Eve, and Eve wondered whether she was barring the girl's only way out or whether the girl was afraid there was someone with her.

"I'm all alone," she said. "Just Dexter and me."

The girl was racked with shivers. Eve put down her candle, stripped off her coat, and draped it over the back of a chair. "Take my coat," she said. "It will keep you warm. I promise, I won't keep you here or tell anyone where you are. If you want to leave, you can go, but at least take my coat." She removed her shawl, then her boots, and set them on the chair. "These are for you," she said.

The girl's panic seemed to have died down, but she was still poised for flight. "You must be hungry," said Eve. "I'll go to the pantry and get you something to eat. Do you like cheese? Then we'll talk about what we're going to do. I'd like to send you to my home in Henley—" She broke off and shook her head. She was rattling on before she'd taken stock of the situation. This girl had escaped from Bedlam. She could be dangerous. For all Eve knew, she might well be violent. Eve didn't relish the thought of grappling with a madwoman.

But something else was at work in her. She was roused by her mother's memory tonight and could hear Antonia's voice telling her to trust her instincts.

When in doubt, trust your instincts, Eve.

That was how she'd chosen her first pony, though he'd looked like the runt of the stock. But Ginger had proved his mettle by winning ribbon after ribbon at every fair they'd visited.

Trust your instincts, Eve. She did, but Dexter's presence was an added bonus. Dexter would protect her to the death if need be.

The girl's mouth worked. "Nell."

Oh, ye of little faith, thought Eve, and smiled. "Is that your name?"

The girl gave a tiny nod.

"I'll get you something to eat, Nell."

Eve left the candle on a table and slowly backed out of the laundry room. It took her several minutes to feel her way into the kitchen. Once there, she lit the candle on the mantel and got what she wanted from the pantry. When she returned to the laundry, the girl had gone, and so had the clothes she'd set out for her. The door to the side of the wooden tubs was ajar. Eve pushed it open a fraction and saw that it was the door to the coal cellar.

So that's how the girl had got in. She'd taken refuge in the cellar and had been drawn to the laundry by the heat from the boiler.

Eve closed the door and was on the point of locking it when she paused. If the girl screwed up her courage to enter the house so that she could warm herself at the boiler, what harm was in that? She wasn't dangerous. Nothing could convince Eve that the girl was dangerous. She was like a stray dog that had been abused by its master. The keepers at Bedlam had done this to her.

Dexter poked his nose into her palm. "I'm not angry at your friend," she told him. "I'm angry at the world in general." She let out a long breath. "Let's give her time to get away. We can always go out later."

They padded back upstairs. Eve went straight to the window and looked out. Nothing moved except the branches of the trees as the wind rustled through their leaves.

Chapter Seven

The gown Eve wore for the outing to Vauxhall Gardens was on loan from Lady Valmede, who had bought it for her trousseau to wear to the opera. It was an appliqued red satin with a small padded bustle and was so low across the bosom that Eve had unfurled her fan and positioned it to preserve her modesty. Her hair was piled high and powdered; a beauty patch was glued to her cheek. She knew she had never looked lovelier, but she had never felt so uncomfortable, either. Her stays were killing her! A laugh, a cough would burst her strings, and she couldn't sit down without squirming. She didn't understand why women had ever put up with it.

Oh yes, she did. She wondered what Ash Denison would think when he saw her decked out in crimson satin.

She wasn't playing fair. Lydia had wanted this particular gown, too, but Eve had talked her out of it. Crimson satin, she'd said, made Lydia look older, so Lydia had reluctantly given up her claims in favor of a gold brocade. And very nice she looked in it, too.

But gold brocade could not compare to crimson satin. The dress made Eve feel liberated, bold, desirable, just like the heroines in her books.

Just like the Eve in her dreams.

A reluctant smile tugged at the corners of her mouth. Maybe her dream man knew a thing or two. Just to test her theory, she'd rewritten the first two chapters of her story, making the villain, with a few adjustments, the hero of the piece. The result was electrifying. Her poor, capable heroine had her work cut out for her just to tame the beast. She didn't know what would happen next, because her characters seemed to have developed a will of their own. If the dialogue got any hotter, the pages would catch fire.

"Isn't it beautiful?" said Anna Contini, gesturing with one hand.

Eve dragged her thoughts from Ash and looked out on the scene. "Beautiful," she agreed.

It was dark now, and the gardens looked as though they'd been plucked from a fairy tale. The lights from thousands of lamps shimmered as far as the eye could see—in the supper boxes, in the rotunda where the dancing took place, and along the tree-lined avenues and walks. To complete the fantasy, the strains of a stately minuet floated on the air.

Lady Valmede's party was scattered among several supper boxes. It was a large party, and Eve had a hard time remembering so many faces and names. Some had wandered off to take in the sights. Those in the boxes watched the continuous flow of people or helped themselves to the wine and refreshments offered by an army of footmen who flitted from box to box.

In Eve's box were Lady Sayers, Leigh Fleming, Anna Contini, and Mr. Henderson. He was a barrister and one of the gentlemen who had stood up with Ash to confront the hecklers. He wasn't Eve's idea of a barrister. He was too handsome, too suave, and too debonair. If she set him in one of her books, she'd make him a highwayman—

Books again! Think pleasure, she told herself. Naturally, that made her think of Ash Denison.

He was in the box next to hers, and with a will of their own, her eyes kept straying to him. He was, she thought, magnificent in his blue velvet coat with its huge turnback cuffs that showed a profusion of white lace at the throat and wrists. She'd wager there wasn't a wrinkle on his skintight white satin breeches or on his white silk stockings. His powdered wig was tied back with a black ribbon, but it was the mask that made her catch her breath. He looked as though he had stepped out of the pages of her own novel.

Eve looked away, and when she looked again, Ash was leading a striking brunette toward the rotunda where the dancing was in progress.

"That's Lady Sophie Villiers," whispered Lady Sayers in Eve's ear. "I thought their affair was over. Seems I was mistaken."

Lady Sophie looked ravishing in a silver tissue gown with a scrap of silver lace that served as a mask. Even her laugh was silvery. That was one lady, Eve decided, who needed no lectures from Ash Denison on how to enjoy herself.

Philip Henderson got up, excused himself, and wandered over to Lady Valmede's box.

"I don't know if that's wise," said Lady Sayers in the same hushed tone.

Eve followed the path of Lady Sayers's gaze. Mr. Henderson was bending over Amanda's hand, obviously requesting her to partner him in the dance. Amanda's profile might have been chiseled in ice. It looked as if she would refuse, but her grandmother said something to her, and she rose gracefully to her feet and allowed him to lead her from the box.

Eve looked at Lady Sayers, waiting for her to elaborate, and when she didn't, Eve carefully prompted, "Why isn't it wise?"

Lady Sayers hesitated, as though reluctant to pass on gossip, but her reluctance lasted no more than a moment. "Oh, when Amanda was engaged to Mark, she suddenly broke it off and became engaged to Mr. Henderson. I don't know all the ins and outs of it, but I do know that Mark was heartbroken. There was a duel, and the next thing we knew, Amanda had given up Henderson and was engaged to Mark again. That happened ten years ago and, as far as I know, they haven't spoken to each other since."

"I suppose," said Eve dryly, "that Mark was wounded in the duel?"

Lady Sayers's brows rose. "Oh, you've heard the story?"

"No. But I've used the same plot in one of my novels."

Anna leaned toward Eve and whispered, "Don't look now, but a ragamuffin just lifted an end of ham from a table over there and stuffed it under his coat, then ran off."

"I didn't know beggars were allowed in Vauxhall."

"They're not, poor devils, but hunger drives them in. And who can blame them? They must eat."

Under Eve's mystified gaze, Anna took one of the linen napkins lying on the table and wrapped it around

two breasts of chicken. "Just wait and see," said Anna.
"When we leave our table, the ragamuffins will come out
and play."

Eve looked at Anna curiously. She was an odd sort of
person who didn't have much to say for herself. It wasn't
that she was shy. She lived a hermit's existence in the
wilds of Cornwall, but she wasn't lonely, or she never
complained of loneliness. Tonight, in her flaring black
domino with its cowl, she could have passed for a monk.

"St. Francis," Lydia called her, because she cared for
stray and abused animals. It seemed that Anna's vocation extended to people, as well.

Thinking of Nell, Eve sighed.

"Why the long face?" Anna asked.

"I was thinking of the runaway from Bedlam." Eve's
eyes searched the crowds. "I hope she's found a safe
haven far, far away from here."

"I doubt it."

Eve shifted to get a better look at Anna's face. "You
doubt it?"

Anna's shoulders lifted in a tiny shrug. "Where
would she go? Who would look after her? Someone
must have committed her to Bedlam. What's to stop
them doing it again? Oh, no, our runaway has nowhere
to go. She'd be much better off here with the beggars, if
she could ever bring herself to trust anyone, and that's
doubtful. I don't think we'll find her at Vauxhall. Too
many people."

"You sound," said Eve slowly, "as though you are on
her side."

Anna replied quietly, "And you sound as though you
know more than you've told me."

Anna's hard stare did not intimidate Eve. It was
something in the older woman's voice that thawed Eve's

misgivings. "Oh, Anna," she said impulsively, "she isn't mad or deranged. She's only a frightened girl. She can hardly speak. If you'd only heard her try to say her name. I'd like to help her, but she's as nervous as a creature of the wild."

Anna nodded sympathetically. "It's the same with my donkeys. Some of them have been so abused that they never learn to trust people. But we do what we can."

Eve expected more questions, but none came. Anna suddenly got up. To the others at the table, she said in a loud, bright voice, "Why don't we take a turn around the rotunda?"

When they returned to their table, Anna's napkin was gone.

Eve was listening idly to her aunt's glowing account of the many amiable people she had met at Vauxhall when a shadow fell across her and a masculine voice said, "Miss Dearing, would you do me the honor of taking a turn around the gardens with me?"

The voice belonged to Ash Denison.

Their progress was slow because the walks were choked with strollers and Eve hadn't quite mastered the art of managing her hoops. Not everyone was in costume. In fact, the majority of people were in evening clothes and had chosen to wear only masks and those voluminous cloaks called dominoes to comply with the rules of admission.

The silence between them was beginning to annoy Eve. Here she was, decked out in crimson satin, looking perfectly ravishing, or as ravishing as she'd ever hoped to look, and not one little compliment passed his lips. This was not the man of her dreams. She wished she knew what he was thinking, but over the course of the evening she'd discovered that his mind was impervious to her little probes. It was no less than she expected. Claverleys couldn't pick and choose whose thoughts they could read, and when it came to reading thoughts or receiving messages, she was practically a novice.

Ahead of them on the path were Lady Amanda and Jason Ford, one of Lady Valmede's "spare" gentlemen who, like Mr. Henderson, had attended the symposium. They were laughing and talking, their two heads close together. As pleasantly as she could manage, Eve observed, "Lady Amanda seems to be enjoying herself. I don't think I've seen her so animated."

"You might want to copy her example."

She searched his face for signs of humor, but he wasn't joking. Stung, she replied, "What have I done now?"

He shrugged. "In spite of your fine feathers, you look as though you could be a mourner at a funeral. Do you know what I think, Eve? I think you miss your notebook, the one where you jot down your impressions of people and things to use later in your stories."

He wasn't even close to the truth. If she looked disgruntled, it was because her stays were killing her. She couldn't tell him that because the subject of stays was too delicate to mention in mixed company.

She navigated her hooped skirts around several stragglers before she spoke. "We can't all be grinning monkeys, making a spectacle of ourselves over every little joke," she gave him a spare smile, "or ogling every pretty woman who catches your eye."

He was amused and didn't mind showing it. "So you've been spying on me again? I'm flattered, Eve."

Her voice chilled. "Don't be. I was merely observing the scene before me. That's what writers do."

He steered her into a side path where there were fewer people to obstruct their progress. She went ahead of him, but as soon as he came abreast of her, he took up where they'd left off. "There's a time and place for everything, I suppose, but these are pleasure gardens. People come to Vauxhall to enjoy themselves. *Pleasure,* Eve. It's not a bad word."

She shot him a look from below her fiercely drawn brows. "We've had this conversation before. Your only ambition is to enjoy yourself, and I say there should be more to life than that."

He was so quiet that she chanced a quick look at him. For one heart-stopping moment, she felt as though she'd said something to hurt him. He was very pale, and that mockery of a smile was on his lips. It was a look that spoke volumes, and for all her Claverley charisma, she didn't know what to make of it.

A stately lady resembling a galleon in full sail was bearing down on them. There was no room to pass. They had to turn back or step off the path.

Ash guided Eve to one of the small ivy-covered arbors that were set out at intervals along the walk. The galleon in full sail passed them, but Ash made no move to rejoin the strollers on the path. Light from the lanterns outside filtered through the foliage and slats of the arbor, making patterns wherever it touched.

She looked at him, really looked at him, and her heart sank. The moment of serious introspection had passed, and he looked his usual, mocking self. But nothing could wipe the impression from her mind that her careless words had touched a nerve.

"Ash? Lord Denison?" she said softly.

He gave his rogue's grin. "Eve," he said, "this is a masquerade, not a church picnic. Every self-respecting lady expects some gentleman to steal a kiss from her in the course of the evening. Where is your sense of adventure? Where is your curiosity as a writer?"

So he wasn't going to confide in her. She had no choice but to follow his lead. "I don't have to experience everything firsthand to write about it," she said lightly.

"So, I was right. You've never been kissed before."

She knew where this was leading. He was going to kiss her, but only if she allowed it. A sensible woman would take to her heels. She didn't want to be sensible. She wanted, hoped, to find the man in her dream. He had vanished before their lips met, and she'd been left hanging ever since.

This kiss, she told herself, was inevitable, and that settled any inner debate that might have pulled her two ways.

The kiss was inevitable.

She watched him remove his own mask, breathed slowly when he removed hers, then sucked in a breath when he traced the outline of her mouth with the tip of one finger.

"You're wearing the kissing patch, Eve," he said. "That tells me far more than your empty words."

Flirting wasn't her forte, but she gave it a try. "You're making that up. It was given to me by your grandmother."

He captured her hand and dispensed with the fan, then her reticule. Something about her open palm seemed to fascinate him. The muscles in her abdomen tightened.

"My grandmother," he said, "is a devious old woman.

Who do you think pointed out to me that you were wearing the kissing patch?"

Did everyone know she'd never been kissed? Why couldn't people mind their own business? She frowned.

He smiled. "And you sent me a message with your fan."

"What message?"

"Damsel in distress."

"I was cooling my cheeks, that's all."

"After taking lessons from my grandmother? You'll have to do better than that."

He wasn't in a hurry. He pressed a kiss to her hand, then brushed kisses to the inner curve of her arm and lingered over the sensitive shell of her ear. Much to her dismay, she was finding it hard to keep her spine straight. Her knees were beginning to buckle and her breathing was becoming audible.

The brush of his hand against her cheek startled her into opening her eyes wide. His face filled her vision. "Eve?" he murmured.

Her voice was breathless. "Yes?"

"Are you making mental notes for your next novel?"

"My next . . . novel?" she repeated blankly.

A smile barely touched his lips. "I thought not."

His head descended. Hers lifted. Their lips met and clung. She didn't pull away, not even when he put his hands on her waist and drew her closer. It was like sipping fine champagne. One sip made her happy, two sips went to her head. After that, she stopped counting. She wanted to drink and drink till she was drunk on him. He didn't threaten her. He was a rogue on the outside, but inside he was chivalrous and thoughtful and kind.

She made a small, choked protest when he brought the kiss to an end. Unsmiling, he studied her face for a moment. It was an intense look that bordered on disbelief.

"I must be crazy," he muttered.

She gave a muffled yelp when his arms suddenly wrapped around her and she was dragged against the full length of his body. "Crazy," he muttered, and he took her lips again.

That kind, chivalrous gentleman was nowhere in evidence. She was in the arms of some primitive being who wanted her with a passion she hadn't known existed. She wasn't afraid. She was enthralled. Men always treated her with deference. In Ash's arms, she felt more alive, more female, more liberated than she'd felt in her life.

Drinking champagne was nothing like this. She reveled in her new-found feminine power. If she was moved, so was he. Beneath the pads of her fingers, she could feel his muscles bunch and strain. There was a catch in his breath. She could hear it as his lips brushed over her cheeks, her throat, her brows before he took her lips again, desperate lips that found an answer in her own desperate response.

She came out of the clouds when his hands began to wander. He was kneading her hips, her spine, pulling her hard against the lower half of his body. She was stunned by the proof of his desire, then shocked when his hands dipped lower and squeezed her bottom.

His head lifted. "What the devil is that?" he demanded, and he squeezed her again.

Warm color surged into her face. "My bustle." Her voice was clipped.

He began to laugh. "Saved by the bustle," he choked out, "or should we try again?"

She wriggled out of his arms and tried to adjust the bustle.

"Allow me." One yank set it to rights. "I won't say I'm sorry," he went on, "because I'm not. You've exceeded my wildest dreams, Eve Dearing."

His allusion to dreams made her feel guilty and just the tiniest bit ashamed. But, as she kept telling herself, she had no control over her dreams. They didn't mean anything.

"Don't make too much of it," she said. "I was curious, that's all."

He laughed softly. "In the interests of your next torrid romance?"

His jibe hardly registered. She was still shaken. No wonder he'd thought her heroes were anemic. She hadn't known the first thing about men, but she was learning.

She cleared her throat. "Naturally. What else could it be?"

He cupped her chin in one hand and held her face up to the light. His eyes were searching. His expression was serious.

"What?" she asked tremulously.

"There's more to you, Eve Dearing, than shows on the surface."

When it looked as though he would kiss her again, she said in a shaken voice, "We should get back to the others."

He found her fan, her mask, and her reticule, then ushered her out of the arbor. The steady stream of people was all going in one direction, to the fireworks display on the far side of the booths. Ash kept up a flow of small talk, to which Eve said not one word. She was still in a sensual daze.

Someone called her name, and she gave a guilty start

when she saw Leigh Fleming bearing down on them. He gave Ash a look of mingled annoyance and suspicion before he spoke to Eve.

"I've been looking for you everywhere. The fireworks display is about to begin. I thought we agreed to stay close to the Grove?"

She relinquished Ash's arm and tucked her hand in the crook of Leigh's elbow. "We went for a walk," she said. "That's all."

Ash was quite happy to fall into step behind them, since there wasn't room on the path for three people to walk abreast, but when Eve and Fleming excluded him from their conversation, he began to feel mildly irritated.

He left the path, found a cheroot in his pocket, and lit it from one of the low-hanging lamps. He didn't want company, so he ducked into the entrance of a nearby arbor, where he could watch the passing scene undisturbed.

He inhaled and blew out a stream of smoke. Tonight, she'd been ravishing in the gown she had borrowed from his grandmother. Men couldn't keep their eyes off her. Perversely, all he'd wanted was to wrap her in his cloak and stare down any man who got too close.

His brow wrinkled. Crimson satin. There was something familiar about that gown, some forgotten memory that skirted the edge of his mind—Eve and crimson satin. It would come to him eventually.

Tonight, he hadn't been able to resist her.

He blew out another stream of smoke. A persistent inner voice was telling him to try harder, because if he wasn't careful, he'd be harnessed to the kind of life he despised—marriage to some eligible girl, and begetting heirs to secure the succession.

So he was taken with her. In time, that would pass. They were incompatible. She was an incurable romantic, and he was a disillusioned idealist.

The kiss was a mistake.

Why had she permitted it?

They'd both got more than they'd bargained for.

So much soul-searching was making him restless. To blazes with Eve Dearing. He didn't want to change any more than she did.

Cursing softly, he threw the stub of his cheroot into the shrubbery and went to join the others.

Chapter Eight

Eve noted the dreamy smiles on her companions' faces and grudgingly admitted that Ash Denison was probably right. The party at Vauxhall was over. They were back at the Manor, trudging upstairs to their beds, and every lady looked as if she were floating on air.

Whether or not they'd been kissed, they had evidently had the time of their lives.

No need to look at Lydia. She hadn't stopped talking since they'd arrived home. So many beaux vying for her favors! So many invitations to places where no lady should go! So many gentlemen of rank begging her not to leave London. "And as for Lord Dension," she gushed with a sideways glance at Eve, "I'm sure I'm quite dizzy from all the outrageous compliments he paid me."

Lydia had always liked to hold center stage, but tonight she was different. She seemed as wound up as a little girl on Christmas Day. What present was she going to open first? More to the point, who had put that sparkle in her eyes? It had to be a man.

Could it be Ash Denison? And why was everyone looking at her? Did they think she was jealous?

It was a great relief to slip into her own chamber and shut the door on the world. The maid helped her undress, then left her to her ablutions. After completing her nightly toilette, she sank into her soft feather mattress and drew the covers up to her chin.

Thoughts turned in her mind in a never-ending circle. Nell. Anna. Ash Denison. Her first kiss. Ash Denison. Her first kiss. Ash Denison...

She was twenty-four years old and she'd received her first kiss tonight. Why wasn't she smiling? Why wasn't she floating on air? As kisses went, she thought it must be superlative. After all, Ash Denison had had a great deal of practice. How many women had he kissed, anyway? A hundred? A thousand? More? Kissing her would hardly rate a yawn. She, on the other hand, had no one to compare him to.

How far would he have taken her if she hadn't stopped him?

Her mind flirted with the thought. Suddenly aware that she was smiling, she gave herself a mental shake. She wished she would stop thinking about Ash Denison and go to sleep.

Concentrate! Think of something else!

Her lashes fluttered and her breathing slowed as she began to drift. Pictures of gardens filled her mind, the gardens she had visited with her mother. She felt free and happy just being with her mother, and the sweet scent of orange blossoms filled the air. Orange blossoms...

She drifted further into the stream of sleep and let the current take her.

Strange. She was lying on a grassy bank with the sun

beating down on her face. A shadow blocked out the rays of the sun. She opened her eyes to see Ash's face hovering above her. He was stretched out beside her, propped on one elbow, and his crooked smile was so devastatingly sweet that her heart turned over.

"You're the only man who has ever kissed me," she told him.

He laughed, but it was a pleasant laugh with no sting behind it. "As I am well aware." He plucked a blade of grass and chewed on it as he looked out over the horizon. "Now tell me something I don't know, Eve." This time his voice was serious. "Tell me why you throw up a wall whenever I get too close to you."

"Because," she said, "you're always finding fault with me."

"I could say the same about you."

"You make me feel inadequate—as a female, I mean."

"Ditto—as a male, I mean."

Since he was smiling, she knew he wasn't annoyed. "That," she said, "is sheer bravado on my part, with a dash of self-preservation thrown in for good measure. I've never met anyone like you, you see."

"What am I like?" He sounded like a sleepy lion.

She held her face up to the sun's rays as she considered his question. "You're every woman's idea of a dream lover."

And that's what he was, a dream. That's why she could say and do anything she wanted. You couldn't be held responsible for what you said or did in dreams.

"I'm flattered."

He didn't sound flattered, so she opened her eyes and looked appealingly into his. "But that's only a part of it. You make me want things I know are out of my reach.

When I'm with you, I want to be beautiful and desirable."

"And that frightens you?"

"Because I feel so inept. I could meet you on the dueling field with pistols at twenty paces, but in the boudoir, I'm a complete novice. I'd be hiding in the closet or under the bed."

He blocked out the sun's rays again as he bent over to study her face. Shaking his head, he said slowly, "*I* think you're beautiful. *I* desire you. But what I admire most is that your life has direction. You're a wildly successful writer. You can't know how much I envy that."

His words made her heart sing. She looped an arm around his neck. "Your life has direction. You make people feel good about themselves. You don't have to work at it. It's a gift."

He said seriously, "Tell me what you want from me, Eve."

She answered him seriously. "Teach me how to be a woman, Ash. Teach me about pleasure. You promised you would."

She sensed his smile as their lips met, then the smile dissolved as he pressed the softest kiss to her lips, her brows, her throat. He gave a low throaty chuckle and threw a handful of confetti in the air, only it wasn't confetti.

"Kissing patches," he told her, and they both laughed as the patches floated down and came to rest on every part of her person.

That was when the kissing began in earnest.

There was no hesitation on her part. All her scruples were blissfully asleep. His every kiss and caress drowned her with wonder.

She abandoned herself to the wonder. Who would

have believed that passion could be so pleasant? She felt as though she were languidly drifting in a tropical stream. The sun warmed her skin; the breeze was as soft as swansdown. Her limbs were fluid and weightless. She smiled dreamily.

Everything changed when his kisses became hotter. Her eyes opened wide and a sudden tightness gripped her throat. She could hardly breathe. The tightness spread to her breasts and the lower part of her body. This wasn't pleasure. This was torment. Heat followed every brush of his lips till she was sure that she would burst into flames. She moved restlessly, trying to get her breath. How many kissing patches were there?

"What's this?"

He had found the birthmark on the back of her left shoulder. She hadn't realized that she'd disrobed. That was the thing about dreams. Things happened and you had no memory of them.

"I was born with it," she said, her breath catching. "It's the Claverley ruby and is passed on from mother to daughter, like a family heirloom."

The tickle of his hair on her back as he kissed the Claverley ruby was suddenly too much to bear. She turned, wrapped her arms around him, and kissed him as he'd kissed her, and she gloried in his response. Sensation was building inside her. She knew she was going to shatter.

Sudden tears welled in her eyes. What she felt was more than pleasure. She didn't want a chivalrous English gentleman—and where had that thought come from? She wanted this difficult, confusing man who was so much more than he allowed the world to see. She'd been blind, but now she could see clearly. Sadness. Guilt. Something...

There was something important she had to ask him, something about his brother.

He raised a little as he felt her hands pushing at his shoulders.

"Ash," she began, and got no further.

A terrible scream rent her mind, and a whirlwind of disjointed thoughts overwhelmed her. Ash dissolved before her eyes, sucked into the swirling gale. As swiftly as the whirlwind had surged to life, it subsided, and a different picture formed in her mind. A woman in white was fighting for her life outside her window. A man was there. He had a knife in his hand and murder in his heart. He raised his knife to finish her off and someone else screamed, distracting him from the woman who had collapsed on the ground.

Gasping, Eve pushed herself out of bed. Her limbs felt leaden; she could hardly breathe. She was inside the mind of a murderer. Rage. Hatred. Fear. She was crippled with the fury of a murderer's emotions. Words were forming in her mind.

Kill her! Kill them both! Stupid bitches! They know too much!

What's that? Who's there?

Nell.

He'd seen Nell. She could sense the surge of fear sweep through him.

Eve stumbled to the window and flung it wide. "You down there," she yelled. "I see you. Dexter, get him. Attack!"

It was a ruse, but it was the best she could come up with on the spur of the moment. Dexter was at her side, his hackles raised and fangs bared in a snarl that would have shocked those who thought of him as an overgrown puppy.

She turned from the window and ran. Others had heard the scream and had come out of their chambers to find out what was going on. Footmen in their nightshirts were donning coats and shouting for lanterns. Eve waited for no one. She let Dexter lead the way. He made straight for the shrubbery below Eve's window. When he began to whine and bark, the footmen converged on him.

Eve knelt beside the inert form of a woman. Lydia. She had changed into one of her own gowns, a floating white gauze. The scarlet poppy that bloomed on the bodice came from her own blood. She was very still but breathing softly.

Eve ordered one of the footmen to fetch the doctor and the constable. Pointing to another, she told him in a hard voice that she needed his nightshirt. The man's jaw dropped, but he did her bidding when he saw the feral gleam in her eyes.

To the others who were standing gaping, she yelled, "What are you waiting for? There's a murderer out there! Search the grounds. Find him." Nell was safe. She didn't know how she knew it, but Nell was safe.

As they moved off, she tore the shirt in two and set to work to stanch the bleeding. She knew what to do because she'd learned the technique of dressing wounds to add credibility to one of her heroines, who'd had to doctor her brother.

There was another technique she'd learned that she'd repudiated a long time ago, the gift that came to her from her mother. It was the Claverley charisma that had saved Lydia tonight, not Eve Dearing.

She got up when she'd finished her task, then ordered one of the footmen to tear down one of the shutters to use as a stretcher to carry Lydia to her bed. There was no end, she thought bitterly, to what she'd learned in order to make her stories come alive. If only she had cultivated her charisma instead of pretending that it did not exist, she may well have prevented what happened tonight.

As they trudged back to the house, she opened her mind to the man who had attacked Lydia. The sense of his presence was swiftly fading. She suppressed a shudder as the next thought gripped her mind. He would be back, driven by rage, hatred, and ... fear, fear of Lydia, fear of the girl, and fear of ... ? Her mind went blank.

It would come to her eventually, but now there was nothing to be done but take care of Lydia.

On the top step she halted and looked over her shoulder. All was calm. No shiver of apprehension disturbed her mind. Nell was safe. Emptiness. Silence. She turned and entered the house.

Across the river, in his rooms at Grillon's, Ash flung himself out of bed. He hadn't wanted the dream to end. He was still hard with wanting her, so close to taking her. Air was rushing in and out of his lungs. God in heaven, it seemed too real to have been a dream. If it hadn't been for the woman's scream ...

Where in Hades had that scream come from?

Ignoring his nudity, he stormed into his manservant's room and halted just inside the door. He didn't have to see Reaper to know he was there. He could hear his snores. If a woman had screamed, Reaper would have heard it. Neither sleep nor the effects of a night of heavy drinking had ever dulled Reaper's uncanny ability to waken at the sound of danger.

He shut the door and returned to his own room, then

went straight to the window and looked out. Carriages were coming and going. He saw a watchman strolling on the pavement, waving a lantern in one hand, clutching a truncheon in the other. Nothing seemed amiss.

After closing the window, he sat on the edge of his bed and combed his fingers through his hair. If nothing was wrong, why was he shaking like a greenhorn before his first battle?

He couldn't sleep now. He debated one moment more, then made his decision. A fast gallop to Kennington and back would help him unwind. And if there were lights in the house, he might call in to make sure that everyone had got home safe and sound.

Having settled on a logical response to his illogical alarm, he wakened his manservant, told him to tell Hawkins to have two horses saddled and waiting, then he began to dress.

Like a wild thing fleeing the hunters, the girl dashed into a clump of bushes and shrank into the darkest shadow. Crouched over, hand cupping her mouth to stifle the sound of her breathing, she waited in dread of discovery. She couldn't make sense of what she'd seen. The big house wasn't Bedlam, yet people still did terrible things.

She froze when she heard the crunch of boots on gravel. She knew that sound! He was taking his time, knowing that she was nearby.

Men came round the corner, and the man she now thought of as "the bad man" moved off quickly toward the river. She waited a moment, then she, too, took off, going round the back of the house and coming out on the other side.

Her heart was bursting, her lungs were close to collapse when she reached her destination, a dense thicket of briars that covered all that was left of a broken-down cottage. The cellar was almost intact. Groping her way forward, she tumbled onto a bed of dried grasses.

It was a long time before sleep claimed her.

Chapter Nine

Ash knew something was wrong the moment the Manor came into view. Men with lanterns were combing the grounds, and the house was ablaze with lights.

He and Hawkins were stopped at the gatehouse, and though the men on guard recognized them, they refused to let them pass until the constable had given his permission. As a result, they were left dawdling for ten minutes while one of the porters went in search of the constable. The porter finally returned with the message that her ladyship was expecting them and they were free to enter.

They rode in not much the wiser. All anyone would tell them was that there had been a vicious attack on one of Lady Sayers's guests.

When he reached the front portico, Ash slid from the saddle with only a passing glance to make sure that Hawkins caught the reins. He was wound up like a child's top and took several deep breaths to calm himself as he mounted the front steps.

In the entrance hall, Lady Sayers and her guests were talking in whispers, looking up the stairs as though waiting for someone to appear. There was no sign of Eve.

Before he could demand to know what was going on, Miss Claverley came to meet him. "A terrible business," she said. "Lydia was attacked—stabbed, in fact. The doctor is with her now."

"Where is Eve?"

"She's with the doctor. You can't go up there!"

"Oh, can't I?"

With a rudeness that shocked the ladies, he brushed off Miss Claverley's restraining hand and took the stairs two at a time.

"So that's the way of it," murmured Miss Claverley under her breath.

A footman was standing guard outside the door in the corridor and stepped in front of Ash as he reached for the doorknob. "You can't go in there, my lord, not without the doctor's permission."

"Then get it for me!" said Ash, flinging the words at the hapless man.

The footman rapped on the door and, when a masculine voice bade him enter, Ash pushed by the footman into the room.

His eyes were immediately drawn to the bed. Lydia was ashen-faced but seemed to be in a deep sleep. Eve was on a chair close by, her hand clasping Lydia's. A maid was gathering up bloody towels and bandages, and the gentleman whom Ash presumed was the doctor was drying his hands on a towel.

"It's Lord Denison, is it not?" said the doctor. "Lady Sayers said that she would send for you. I'm Braine, by the way, Archie Braine."

He was young to be a doctor, in Ash's opinion. He had a countryman's complexion weathered by wind and sun, and Ash could quite easily picture him as a shepherd, tramping across the hills with his dogs and flocks.

Ash did not correct the doctor's assumption that he'd been sent for by Lady Sayers. He hadn't decided yet how to explain his presence, but he knew he wasn't going to allude to his illogical alarm for Eve. He waited until the maid quit the room before he spoke. "Mrs. Rivers looks as though she's sleeping peacefully," he said.

"She's a very lucky woman," the doctor replied, "very lucky indeed. The knife did not penetrate any vital organs, though she lost a lot of blood. But she did suffer a concussion, and I'm more concerned about that." He nodded toward Eve. "It's my view that Miss Dearing saved her life. She knew not to move her until she had stopped the bleeding, and a very good job she made of it, too. I was amazed that a woman would know so much."

Though he spoke to the doctor, Ash's eyes never left Eve's face. "The thing you have to understand about Miss Dearing, Doctor, is that she researches all the subjects that crop up in her novels. I'd wager that one of her heroines had to stop some poor devil from bleeding to death. Am I right, Eve?"

She gave a watery smile. "Marianne in *The Hounds of Crathes.*"

"What did I tell you?"

The doctor smiled. "All the same," he said, "women on their own are easy prey. That villain might have attacked you, too, Miss Dearing. Have you thought of that?"

"I had my dog with me, and the servants were close

behind. Dexter would attack anyone who tried to harm me."

She looked so pale and fragile that Ash hated to press her about the attack. It was the thought of the villain hanging around to finish what he'd started that made the decision for him.

"Eve, what happened tonight? How did Lydia come to be attacked? I gather they haven't found her assailant, because I passed servants searching the grounds when I rode in."

She cleared her throat. "A woman's scream awakened me. She was right below my window. I threw the window wide and yelled that my dog was on the grounds and would kill anyone who was out there." She shook her head. "I can't remember my exact words. It wasn't true. Dexter was with me in my chamber."

Ash said slowly, "You were wakened by a woman's scream?"

"Yes, I heard a woman's scream. Then I ran outside with Dexter and found Lydia."

They all turned when the door opened and Lady Sayers entered the room. "Eve," she said, "the constable wants to question us. Why don't you tidy yourself before you come downstairs? Ah, Dr. Braine. The constable would like a word with you first. I'll stay with Mrs. Rivers."

Eve got up, and for the first time since he entered the room, Ash became aware that she was in her night-clothes. She'd draped a long shawl over her shoulders, not, he guessed, for warmth or for modesty's sake but to hide the blood that spattered her nightgown.

With her dark hair hanging in a thick plait down her back, and violet smudges under her eyes, she looked like a child who had seen too much and knew too much.

He'd seen that look on the faces of young recruits who had survived the horror of their first battle.

She'd acted quickly to prevent a murder. She'd taken charge, sending for both the doctor and the constable. She'd stanched the bleeding. She was competent with pistols on the dueling field at twenty paces. In the boudoir, however, she was a complete novice.

He gave his head a shake as if to clear his brain. Where were these wild thoughts coming from?

By the time Eve joined them, Ash had a fair idea of how events had unfolded. Nothing was certain, however, because Lydia had yet to come round. She'd been unconscious when Eve found her, so no one knew whether she'd recognized her assailant or what she was doing outside the house when everyone was asleep.

They were waiting for Lady Sayers in a small upstairs parlor, sitting around a fire that was hot enough to scorch his boots. Apart from the constable, Ash was the only gentleman present. He got up when Lady Sayers arrived and he offered her his chair, then he took up a position at the sideboard, where he had a good view of everyone. They were all looking expectantly at the constable, who was seated in the big wing armchair that flanked the fireplace.

Ash smiled when Constable Keble made a notation in a small notebook he held in one hand. It made him think of Eve. Keble was fiftyish, of medium height, with dark hair that was grizzled with silver, and he had the same ruddy complexion as the doctor. Ash knew all about these country constables and had little hope that Keble had much idea of how to proceed, in spite of the official-looking notebook. Constables were local men of some standing, but they were rank amateurs and worked at other jobs to make ends meet. If Lydia had not survived the attack on her, he had no doubt that someone from London would have taken over the investigation.

Keble looked up and treated his audience to a spare smile. "I hope you'll bear with me," he said. "I know you have already made statements, but there are some points I want to clarify. In cases such as these, the victim usually helps us in our inquiries. The doctor advises me, however, that Mrs. Rivers suffered a concussion when she fell, trying to escape her attacker. Nothing serious, you understand, but it may be a few days before I can question her, and in my business, time is of the essence."

His remarks were met with a general murmur of sympathy, then the questioning began, with the constable noting every small detail in his little book: the masquerade at Vauxhall; the time they arrived home; who heard the scream; who was first on the scene; who saw Mrs. Rivers last; and so on.

"Can't these questions wait?" asked Lady Sayers at one point. "Whoever attacked Lydia is long gone. We can answer them just as well after we've had a good night's rest."

Anna Contini shook her head. "I doubt if I will sleep a wink."

The constable tapped his pencil on his notebook. "There's a reason for asking these questions now. Everything is fresh in your minds. By tomorrow, you may have forgotten some small detail that could lead to the arrest of the person who stabbed Mrs. Rivers."

He gave them a moment to consider his words, then went on brusquely, "Did Mrs. Rivers have any enemies? Think, ladies, you must know something."

Lady Sayers shook her head. "We wouldn't know, not really. We're colleagues, not friends." She sighed. "Lydia isn't what you'd call popular, but that's not the same as having enemies."

Anna Contini leaned forward in her chair. "There hasn't been time for Lydia or any of us to make enemies. We've only been here for little more than a week." She threw Lady Sayers a reproachful look. "I consider Lydia my friend, but that's because I've tried to get to know her."

"Oh?" The constable smiled. "And what did you discover?"

Anna bit down on her lip.

"Mrs. Contini," the constable said, giving her a hard look from beneath his bushy brows, "I insist that you tell me."

Anna visibly stiffened under that frown. As though the words were dragged from her, she said, "She keeps house for her sister in a small village near Warwick. It's not much of a life. What I mean is, it's very dull, and her sister is very demanding. When Lydia comes up to town, she likes to spread her wings and enjoy herself."

"Now that," said Keble, "is very helpful." He made another notation, then his gaze fastened on Eve. "I've been told," he said pleasantly, "that you and Mrs. Rivers did not always see eye to eye, that there was, in fact, a running battle between you on your books and," he flicked an eye in Ash's direction, "other matters. Jealousy, was it?"

There was an audible gasp. Ash, who had propped one elbow on the sideboard, immediately straightened. This was news to him.

Miss Claverley was bristling. "That's a lie! And what,

pray tell, has it to do with anything? Eve saved Lydia's life tonight. The doctor told us."

Eve's frigid voice cut across the babble of voices raised in her defense. "I'm not aware of any quarrel between myself and Mrs. Rivers. But even if there was, that's not a strong enough motive to do her physical harm. Why would I stanch the bleeding if I wanted to kill her? Everyone saw me. I'm not hiding anything."

The constable spoke to his little book. "It's possible that you stabbed her, then returned to the house and went through the motions of opening your window to warn the attacker off."

Ash was about ready to grab the constable by the throat.

Lady Sayers's voice arrested him. "Oh, no, Constable Keble," she said. "We all heard the scream and came out of our rooms at the same time. Eve was in her nightgown, and there wasn't a spot of blood on it when she left the house. By the time we caught up to her, she was drenched in blood, so I draped my shawl over her to hide it." She shivered. "It was awful."

After a prolonged silence, Keble nodded sympathetically. "So," he said, "no one has any idea who might have attacked Mrs. Rivers."

When no one answered, he looked a question at Lady Sayers. She sighed and said, "I'm of the opinion that Lydia had a tryst with some unknown gentleman who became violent when she resisted his advances."

Miss Claverley said slowly, "At Vauxhall tonight, Mr. Fleming said that Lydia was playing a dangerous game by pretending to be Angelo. Perhaps one of the hecklers came after her."

"Who the devil is Angelo?" demanded the constable. "It's the first time his name has cropped up."

"A writer of short stories," Ash replied. No one seemed to know what to say beyond that, so he gave the constable a summary of what had taken place at the symposium but left off his own vested interest in discovering Angelo's identity.

After hearing him out, the constable said, "Sounds to me like a storm in a teacup. Maybe Angelo doesn't enter into it. In my experience, the attack on Mrs. Rivers looks more like the action of a jealous lover."

Miss Claverley looked thoughtful, but she didn't say anything.

Some other suggestions were thrown out: It was a gypsy; it was the woman who had run away from Bedlam; it was a housebreaker whom Lydia had caught in the act.

Suddenly, Constable Keble snapped his notebook shut and everyone fell silent. "Ladies," he said, "you have been most helpful." He nodded to each of them in turn. "Only one more thing. I must ask you to remain in town for a day or two until I've had a chance to look over my notes. I may have other questions for you."

Keble turned to Ash. "Lord Denison, would you mind seeing me out?"

Ash had known his turn would come but was surprised that the constable had decided to speak to him in private. In the front vestibule, Keble picked up his hat and cane, then dismissed the footman on duty. There was no one to overhear them now.

Keble came straight to the point. "Lady Sayers thinks you're here because she sent for you, but that's not the case, is it? Her servant told me that you were not at your hotel when he tried to give you her message."

"I went out riding with my groom," Ash replied easily. "I do that sometimes when I can't sleep. The porter at my hotel will tell you when I left and so will the man at the livery where I stable my horses." He paused, then said quizzically, "Do you suspect *me*, Constable?"

"It's Captain Denison, isn't it, of the Guards? My son served with you in Spain. Gerry Keble? If you had wanted to murder Mrs. Rivers, you wouldn't have botched it, and there would have been no scream."

Ash had a fleeting impression of a daredevil, fair-haired young man who served in a special unit he had commanded for a time. "Lieutenant Gerry Keble," he said, nodding. "He was a good soldier." As he remembered, Keble had lost his life at Waterloo.

"Thank you," said Keble. "He thought very highly of you." He gave a low chuckle. "It was Captain Denison this and Captain Denison that, till his mother and I were ready to tear our hair out."

Ash didn't know how to reply to this, so he said nothing.

Keble went on. "I want the names of all your guests at Vauxhall Gardens tonight. Of course, I may not need them if Mrs. Rivers comes round and can tell us who attacked her."

Ash nodded. "There's quite a list. As I remember, there were about thirty people in all, but I'll get the names to you as soon as I check with my grandmother."

"Thirty? Good God, I hope I don't have to interview them all." After a moment's thought, Keble said, "These ladies are like sitting ducks. It doesn't matter which way you look at it—if someone is stalking them, they are easy targets."

"You think someone is stalking them?"

Shrewd blue eyes gazed into his. "There are some bad people in this world, Lord Denison. Maybe this scoundrel has a grudge against Angelo or maybe against females who have become more successful than he, or maybe he has a grudge against Mrs. Rivers. It's early days yet to draw conclusions."

"Then you'll be happy to hear," said Ash, "that I'm moving in here until you've caught this scoundrel or our writers-in-residence have departed for their own homes."

Keble's brows rose. "That's a very handsome gesture, sir."

"Not as handsome as it sounds. I'm getting tired of hotel life."

That was the easy answer, but there was more to Ash's decision than that. Lydia had hinted that she was Angelo, and tonight Lydia had a close call with death. If ever he was to discover Angelo's identity, this was the place to be.

Preoccupied, Keble shoved his hat on his head. "The night is just beginning for me. I'm wanted at Vauxhall. Seems some poor blighter was set on by footpads and they bashed in his head."

"Wait," called Ash as the constable opened the door. "Mind if I come with you? I'd like to make sure that he's not one of my grandmother's guests."

"I'd be glad of the company."

The murdered man was in an arbor similar to the one Ash and Eve had taken shelter in when the gardens were bustling with visitors. Now the place was deserted, except for officers of the law and groundsmen who were left to tidy up.

An officer held his lantern up while Keble turned the man over. "Is he one of your grandmother's guests?" the constable asked.

Ash had seen enough bodies with terrible wounds in the war not to flinch as he gazed into those sightless eyes. "No," he said, "he's not one of my grandmother's guests."

"Know him, do you, sir?" asked the officer.

"Yes," said Ash. "Leastways, I recognize the face, or what's left of it." He looked at Keble. "This man was the leader of the hecklers at the symposium."

Chapter Ten

On the second day after the attack on her, Lydia came out of her deep sleep and seemed to be well on the way to a full recovery. Everyone, of course, wanted to rush to her bedside to see her and speak to her, but Dr. Braine wouldn't allow it. Lydia was still very weak, he said, and what she needed was a restful atmosphere until she had regained her strength. The ladies continued to sit with her in shifts to ensure that someone was always there if Lydia needed anything. Ash's presence was accepted without comment. Lady Sayers had asked him to stay on until things were more settled, and she had no idea that she was falling in with his wishes.

Ash was beginning to have a healthy respect for this awkward young doctor with the gruff manner, who put the interests of his patient first. Even the constable was kept waiting and allowed only five minutes to ask his questions.

When he came downstairs, Constable Keble looked thoughtful. "At this point," he said, "all she remembers is that when she returned to her box after watching the dancing in the rotunda, she found a note tucked into her glove. She'd taken them off, you see, during supper. The note was signed *Angelo* and invited her to meet him for a little tête-à-tête after everyone had gone to bed."

"God in heaven!" Ash rubbed the back of his neck. "Has the woman no sense? What was she thinking?"

"I gather she thought it was romantic."

There was a long, disbelieving silence, at least on Ash's part.

Keble nodded. "Appearances to the contrary, our Mrs. Rivers has led a sheltered life. Leastways, that's my opinion. She cannot conceive that any fine gentleman she met at Vauxhall could turn out to be a villain. Well, now she knows, and all she wants is to go home to her sister in Warwick."

"Did she recognize her attacker?"

"No. It was too dark."

"So what happened to the note?"

"She can't remember what she did with it. I'm betting that it will turn up. She'd want to keep it as a memento. Let's go outside, where we can speak more freely."

On the front steps, Keble said, "You told no one about the murdered man we found in Vauxhall?"

"No. I did exactly what you asked me to do. There are groundsmen patrolling the gardens day and night. Why? What have you found out?"

"Nothing much. The victim's name was Robert Thompson, and he leaves behind a wife and two small children. His wife had no idea that he was going to Vauxhall." The constable shook his head. "It happens all the time. A respectable man likes to slip his leash and mix with low company once in a while."

"Was he respectable?"

"He owned and managed the Three Crowns on Gloucester Road. It's a respectable inn."

Ash thought for a moment. "Do you think Thompson's death is connected to the attack on Mrs. Rivers?"

"At this point, I'd say he was robbed and murdered by footpads. Vauxhall is a favorite haunt, you know, for thieves and beggars. Never a week goes by but someone is attacked. Thompson was unlucky. Someone hit him too hard."

"From his injuries, I'd say they panicked."

"Or he fought back."

Ash wasn't ready to accept the obvious answer. The fact that Thompson had been present at the symposium and was murdered the same night that Lydia Rivers was attacked raised more questions than answers in his mind.

He looked at Keble and wondered whether the constable knew more than he was telling. "So where do we go from here?" he asked.

The constable smiled at Ash's words. "You take care of the ladies and I'll take care of the investigation, and if something turns up, I'll let you know about it." He descended the stairs, turned, and said as an afterthought, "I wouldn't mention this conversation to Lady Sayers or any of her guests. When or if Thompson's name comes up, I'd like to be the one to question them."

He left Ash to think over his words, and what Ash was thinking was that he'd like to dig a little deeper into Thompson's background before he dismissed him from the investigation. He didn't want to step on Keble's toes, but Jason Ford could act for him. Jason was discreet, well-liked, and ambitious. And Jason did not have money to spare. The commission would not go amiss.

Ash had seen very little of Eve since he'd come to stay at the Manor, but he didn't think she was avoiding him. Lydia's care had taken up all her time, and not only hers but that of all the ladies. When they weren't taking turns in the sickroom, they were snatching a few hours' sleep for themselves. After his chat with Keble, however, he was impatient to talk to her. Lydia might have told Eve more than she was willing to tell the constable, and Eve had been first on the scene when Lydia was attacked. It was possible that Eve had seen or heard something that she hadn't passed on, not realizing its significance.

His chance came when he was in the breakfast room, looking out the window as he ate a solitary luncheon. Eve came into his line of vision and he threw down his napkin and got up. A closer view revealed that she was taking Dexter for a walk. Drinking back his coffee in two gulps, he set the cup down and went after her.

Eve did the walking. Dexter, as usual, took off like a rocket, chasing flocks of crows or running in circles. But he always came to heel on command, and, as he went after her, Ash idly indulged in a pleasant reverie of Eve tamed to his hand as Dexter was tamed to hers.

A curious sensation came over him. He'd had this dream before, only it was far more lurid. He probed his mind, trying to recall the dream. The details were sketchy, but he remembered that Eve was everything he'd sensed she kept tightly submerged below the surface and that he was the one who had forced her to let go and come up for air. The Eve of his dreams was playful, sensuous, and sweetly giving. And like any red-blooded male, he'd wanted to take things to their logical conclusion.

Had he frightened her? Was it she who had screamed in his dream? Had his conscience, even in his dreams, permitted him to go so far and no further?

At least he did not have to apologize for his impetuous ardor. More to the point, he was not obliged to offer her marriage. No harm done. It was only a dream.

A self-mocking smile briefly twisted his lips. Eve Dearing was a capable, courageous, determined young woman who would no more think of marrying him than she would a wandering vagrant. The few minutes they'd spent in the arbor at Vauxhall convinced him that he could bring her to passion, but that wouldn't influence Eve when she came to choose a husband. She'd want a man with character and ambitions.

That is, if she ever came to choose a husband. She'd set the bar very high, too high for him to vault over, and he wasn't in the mood to try. She might make some man sublimely happy, but he doubted it. If they should quarrel, her poor husband might find himself facing her at twenty paces on the dueling field with a pistol in his hand.

A duel at twenty paces? Why had that thought cropped up again? And why was he smiling?

Dexter suddenly charged out of a clump of bushes toward him, came to an abrupt halt, and sat at attention, looking expectantly up at Ash.

"Good boy," said Ash, and fished in his coat pocket for the crust of bread he'd put there especially for Dexter. He was in the habit of taking Dexter with him when he made his rounds, and Dexter had come to expect his reward for fetching sticks and scaring off crows.

Eve had turned back and was coming toward him. "Ash Denison!" she called out between laughter and exasperation. "Don't you know when you're being exploited? That dog gets more treats than is good for him. Everybody is doing it. And Dexter knows just how to look to keep up the supply."

Dexter, by this time, had bolted, ostensibly to chase a butterfly, leaving Ash to face the music alone.

She was out of breath when she reached him, but that was not what killed his smile. Her skin was like parchment and there were dark smudges under her eyes. He'd seen her tired, but now she looked ill.

"What the devil does Dr. Braine think you are?" he demanded. "A workhorse? You look all in. There are others who could nurse Lydia as well as you."

She was surprised at his harsh tone, then peeved because he'd caught her when she was looking her worst. She'd hardly slept a wink in the last two nights for reliving that moment when her mind locked on the thoughts of Lydia's attacker, and when she did fall asleep, her dreams were all of that heartrending moment when she'd found her mother on the quarry floor. To add to her misery, she was worried about Nell. She hadn't seen or sensed Nell's presence since the night Lydia was attacked.

Little wonder that she looked like a tired old workhorse. It was exactly how she felt.

"Don't blame Dr. Braine," she said quietly. "He's doing more than any of us. He's so patient, so gentle, and never thinks of himself. He's an inspiration to us all, so naturally we want to do our part."

Ash was thinking that if she went on in this vein much longer, he could take a thorough dislike to the inestimable doctor. He lifted a hand to her face. "So pale, Eve." He took his hand away before she pushed it away. "How is Lydia?"

"She's slipping in and out of sleep, but the doctor

says that's only to be expected. She wants to go home to Warwick, but that's out of the question at the moment."

"Home to the sister?"

"I know. She's a bully, but after what happened, maybe a bully is what she needs."

She had turned her face up to the sun to catch its rays, and Ash had another flash of recall. Eve on a grassy bank without a stitch on, holding her face up to the sun's rays. It seemed more like a memory than a dream, and he had to clench his hands to keep from reaching for her.

"Eve," he said, "I want to talk to you about Angelo. Do you think you're up to it, or would you prefer to enjoy your walk by yourself? We can always talk later."

"Shall we walk while we talk?" she said. "I've been cooped up in the house too long, and I need the exercise."

Lady Sayers's acres were not laid out in any particular style. She knew what she liked and her own gardeners followed her directions. On the whole, she'd kept the Manor's setting rural. There was no man-made lake, but there were vast orchards of apple and plum trees, and pastures that were let to local farmers for their horses and cattle, and once in a while something that seemed out of place—a Greek folly in a thicket of trees, a bandstand in the middle of a pasture.

"I've been told," said Ash, "that the bandstand is used by musicians at the May Fair. That's when all the locals from miles around come out to party and dance till their feet give out."

Eve laughed. "What about the Greek folly?"

"She had that built after she visited Greece, but now that the trees have swallowed it up, I think she has forgotten its existence."

They stopped at a fence that enclosed a small pasture where three donkeys were quietly grazing. When the donkeys became aware of their visitors, they brayed and glared with baleful eyes.

"Donkeys?" said Ash. "Where did they come from?"

"They're Anna's donkeys. They were due to go to market…well…I'll spare you the gory details, but when she heard about it, she raised a fuss, bought the beasts, and persuaded Lady Sayers to take them in until she can transport them to Cornwall."

Dexter whined and gazed longingly at the donkeys, as though he wanted to make friends with them. "He thinks they are big dogs," Eve explained, "but Anna would have a fit if I let him get too close to them. She doesn't like dogs."

"I'm surprised she isn't bedding down with the donkeys."

"Oh, she may, if she can't find someone to look after them." She squinted up at him. "Do you think she's peculiar?"

Sensing a trap, he replied easily, "Anyone who doesn't like dogs must be peculiar."

She gazed at him straight-faced, then her lips wobbled into a reluctant smile.

"About Angelo," Ash finally said. "What do you think is going on?"

Her eyes were trained on the donkeys when she answered him. "Well, we know now that Lydia isn't Angelo. She thought she was going out to meet him." She shook her head. "Why did he attack her?"

"Because she repelled his advances? Because he wanted to punish her for stealing his thunder? That seems a bit extreme. No sane man would behave like that."

She waited for him to go on, and when he remained silent, she finally prompted, "What do you make of it all?"

He replied slowly, thoughtfully, "I don't think it was Angelo who attacked Lydia. Either she has lied about the note in her glove or she doesn't want us to know who she was going out to meet that night." He turned his head and looked directly into her eyes. "I think Lydia was attacked because someone thinks *she* is Angelo. Didn't Fleming say that she was playing a dangerous game when she claimed to write those stories? I know a number of people who would gladly wring Angelo's neck. Poor Lydia just got in the way."

Eve was shaking her head. "That seems a bit extreme, too, doesn't it? Stories don't provoke readers to do murder. They're only stories."

He gave her a small, dry smile. "I take it you haven't read the stories."

"No. Only Lydia has."

He plucked a blade of grass and began to chew it. "You were first on the scene," he said. "Did you see something, hear something that you haven't told us about?"

When his eyes trapped hers, her pulse jumped and began to race. What could she tell him? That she'd felt the killer's rage as though she were inside his mind? That she knew Lydia was the victim before she'd knelt down beside her and looked into her face? He wouldn't believe her, or he'd put her down as a charlatan.

She put as much indignation into her voice as she could manage. "What could I possibly have heard or seen that I wouldn't pass on?"

He held up his hand. Smiling awkwardly, he said, "I

believe you. But sometimes we see something that we're not aware of until we have time to think about it."

"Not in my case. I told the constable everything I know."

She knew that her answer had come too readily and braced for the next question, but he merely propped himself against the fence and gazed at the donkeys.

At last he said, "I don't think I told you that Angelo set one of his stories in my home in Richmond. It was a personal tragedy for my family, a tragedy involving my brother."

She'd got most of the story from Amanda, but it was very vague. Ash's younger brother had some devastating wasting disease and had drowned while swimming in the Thames. Ash was away at the time and had taken the boy's death very hard.

"When I read that story," he said, "I felt violated." He turned his head and spoke with a kind of suppressed savagery. "I was told it was an accident, but Angelo is insinuating that murder was done. One way or another, I'm going to find Angelo. I'd like you to help me. You're a writer. I want you to read Angelo's stories and see if they strike a chord. If you don't recognize the writer's voice, maybe you'll recognize the house and gardens where each story takes place. After all, your father is a landscape gardener, and you told me that your mother used to take you to stately homes and gardens around London. So far, I know of only two that Angelo has used. That means there is another estate. I'd like to know where it is and who owns it. Will you help me, Eve?"

In one of her dreams, she'd sensed the same pain at his center that she sensed now. There was something important she had wanted to ask him. *Tell me about your brother.* The words were never said. Even now, she feared to say them. He might take offense, snub her, tell her to mind her own business. Though she knew it was useless, she opened her mind to him, but his mind was too impervious to allow easy access to his thoughts. Besides, that's not how her gift worked. Claverleys didn't choose their subjects. Their subjects, all unknowingly, chose them.

What difference did it make if he snubbed her? Nothing ventured, nothing gained. As she stood there, undecided, it came to her that she wanted with her whole heart to understand this complex man.

She laid her hand on his arm. "Of course I'll read the stories," she said, "but tell me about your brother. What happened to him? Amanda told me that he died tragically while swimming in the Thames."

There was a long pause while Ash looked at her with eyes wide and clear, then his lashes veiled that unguarded look and he shrugged carelessly, as though the question was unimportant.

"Was it a tragedy?" he wondered aloud. "My father didn't think so. He said it was a blessing in disguise. You have to understand, Harry would never get well. His condition would only deteriorate. There were already plans under way to place him in an asylum—where he could be properly cared for, my father said." The level tone of his voice took on a razor edge. "Months later, I learned from the doctor who was treating Harry that, though his illness was incurable, there could be long stretches where it might become arrested. Harry might have lived for years, but in an asylum if my father had had his way."

He squeezed one hand into a fist. "Out of sight, out of mind—that's how my father's mind worked. He had his heir in me. Harry was expendable. Ye gods, he was only a child, a boy of ten, who found pleasure in little things. How could anyone have wished him ill?"

There was a brief silence when neither of them moved. "You loved your brother," she said then, "and hated your father."

"Yes, I loved my brother." His smile was sparse but gentle. "It would be truer to say that Harry first loved me. When I was sad, he was sad. When I was happy, he was happy. He was so easy to love. As for my father..." Those broad shoulders moved again in a shrug that bordered on indifference. "Hate is too passionate a word for what I felt. I despised him. He was, I suppose, no better or worse than other men of his time, with ambitions fitting his rank. I was groomed and educated as his heir, impressed with my duty to marry well so that our line could continue, I presume, into infinity. You'll pardon me if I say that my father's ambitions left me quite unmoved."

She stood there in miserable silence, sunk in remorse. She couldn't separate herself from the father he despised. His only aim in life, she'd told Ash, was to enjoy himself. Who was she to set herself up as judge and jury? She'd known nothing of his circumstances.

His hands captured hers in a firm clasp. "I've told you all this," he said, "so that you'll understand my resolve to discover Angelo's identity. I wasn't there when Harry died. Whatever my father told me, I had to take on faith, but it never seemed right to me. Harry would not have gone into the water with no one to help him. Angelo says much the same thing in his story. How does he know so much? If my brother was murdered, I want to know who was responsible."

"If it's in my power," she replied, thinking of her Claverley charisma, "I'll help you discover the truth."

His smile was slow and infinitely sweet. "Thank you. That's all I ask of you."

On the way back to the house, the conversation returned to the attack on Lydia and whether she had added anything to what she'd told the constable since she'd regained her senses.

"Nothing," said Eve. "All I can tell you is that she is afraid to be left alone, and who can blame her?"

After that exchange, they walked in silence, but Eve's mind buzzed with questions she would have liked to put to Ash, questions that were too personal for her even to consider. She valued her privacy, so why should she impose on his?

She was, however, free to speculate, and she couldn't help wondering about Ash's years as a soldier. The sole heir did not usually go off to war when his untimely death would also be the death of his dynasty. Was that Ash's way of punishing his father, by courting death? And when his father died, how could he punish him then?

He'd bring his line to an end.

Now she was being fanciful. No one carried revenge to that extreme, least of all someone like Ash.

She darted a sideways glance at him, then quickly averted her eyes. The more she got to know him, the more of a mystery he became. The man in her dreams was a figment of her imagination. The words he spoke were words she'd put into his mouth. The real Ash Denison was still hidden from her.

And she wanted, desperately, to get to know him better.

When they rounded the corner of the house, Ash said, "Seems we have visitors."

A groom stood at the heads of two fine bays harnessed to a very ordinary carriage. Eve's gaze, however, was riveted on the gilt-edged carriage that two liveried coachmen were driving to the stable block. "I think that Lady Sayers's niece has finally arrived," she said.

Chapter Eleven

Ash and Eve found the visitors in the music room taking tea and cake, talking about Lydia and the lucky escape she'd had, but at their entrance, the conversation faded away. The gentlemen got up when they saw Eve—the doctor, who seemed more than usually awkward, and Philip Henderson, who seemed his usual, urbane self. Eve was surprised to see Amanda in the same room with Henderson and looking quite composed. At Vauxhall, she had stiffened up like a wooden doll whenever he came near her.

Eve turned her gaze to a young woman whose bright eyes were fixed on her. This must be the niece, she thought, a beautiful, dark-eyed creature dressed to the nines in a ravishing gown the likes of which Eve had seen only in the pages of *La Belle Assemblée*.

Lady Sayers jumped up and came toward Eve with a smile that was oddly anxious. "Liza has arrived at last," she said, and after making the introductions, she embarked on a disjointed explanation of what had delayed the arrival of dearest Liza. Eve gathered that Liza's father, General Hollander, was responsible for the delay. Though too old to fight in the Spanish Campaign, much to his sorrow, he'd been fired up by some old cronies to accompany them on a tour of the most noteworthy battlefields in Spain, leaving his wife and daughter to entertain themselves in Paris while they waited for his return.

"It was no hardship," Liza said. "There is always plenty to do in Paris." She turned her lustrous eyes upon the doctor. "Have you ever been to Paris, Dr. Braine?"

"No, I have not," was the gruff reply.

Liza sighed. "They call it the City of Love, but that's where my heart was broken." Her wan smile suddenly turned brilliant. "So here I am, hoping to mend my broken heart."

Those lustrous eyes now turned upon Ash. "I never expected to meet up with you, Lord Denison, not so soon, at any rate. I must tell you that your presence is still greatly missed in Paris."

"Oh?" said Amanda, eyes dancing. "By whom, pray tell?"

Liza returned merrily, "By any lady who has not reached her dotage."

"You do me too much honor, Miss Hollander," remarked Ash, his expression as wooden as the doctor's.

The merriment ceased when the doctor spoke. "It was kind of you to invite me to take tea," he said, addressing Lady Sayers, "but I have other patients I must attend to. Mrs. Rivers is in good hands. I think I can safely leave her to your care until tomorrow. Might we have a word in private?"

His leave-taking was punctilious but not particularly cordial.

When the door closed, Liza said doubtfully, "I don't think he likes me."

Miss Claverley delicately wiped her fingers on her napkin. "Don't be too hasty to make judgments, my dear," she said. "Dr. Braine doesn't show to his best in company. When you get to know him better, I think he may surprise you."

The mischievous look that her aunt slanted in her direction had Eve shifting in her chair. That look told her that Miss Claverley's sixth sense was humming, and Eve made a determined effort to head her off. "Would anyone like more tea?" she asked brightly.

"Heavens, no," said Amanda. "Miss Claverley has promised to read our tea leaves. Shall we turn our cups over now?"

"That would be best," replied Miss Claverley.

Eve tried to catch her aunt's eye, to no avail. She was excruciatingly aware that neither Ash nor Mr. Hamilton had turned their cups over, and she fetched the teapot and refilled their cups as well as her own.

Philip Henderson said, "I have an aunt who reads tea leaves."

Eve glared at him. She was ready to glare at Ash, too, but he said nothing, merely looked at her with wide, innocent eyes.

Eve felt her nerves stretch taut. This wasn't a party game. This was serious. Her aunt knew what she was doing, but she was doing it in the wrong setting with the wrong people.

She drew in a quiet breath. She had no intention of allowing anyone to embarrass her aunt. One wrong word out of Messrs. Denison or Henderson and they would have *her* to deal with.

Miss Claverley flashed Eve a reassuring smile, then

went on to respond to Henderson's comment. "I don't really need the tea leaves. That is just a prop. The cup is all I need. Nothing earth-shattering is going to happen. You can believe what you want to believe. Now, who wants to go first?"

"Oh, take my cup," cried Liza.

Holding the cup in both hands, Miss Claverley stared into its depths. After a moment, she said, "I see your heart's desire, and you've been looking for it in the wrong places. When you stop looking, your heart's desire will find you."

Liza stared as though mesmerized. Philip Henderson spoke in an inaudible whisper in Ash's ear. Ash shrugged. Eve's hands fisted in the folds of her gown.

A slow smile—a genuine smile—curved Liza's lips. "I don't know, Miss Claverley," she said, "whether or not you are a seer, but I do believe that you are very wise."

"Do Lady Amanda's cup, Miss Claverley," interjected Mr. Henderson. "Tell us what's in her future."

"Oh, I can't tell the future," she replied. "No one can. People are free to choose their own path."

"Well, that's a relief!" replied Henderson.

"But there are a few gifted people who can look into the future and see what might be possible. The future can be changed, if we know what lies ahead."

There was a collective silence as everyone mulled over these obscure words. Eve's eyes darted to Ash. He was completely focused on stirring his tea.

"May I, Lady Amanda?" said Miss Claverley gently.

Amanda wasn't smiling now. Eve detected a certain reluctance as she handed over her cup.

Miss Claverley studied it for a moment, then smiled into Amanda's eyes. "My advice to you is the opposite of what I said to Miss Hollander. Your heart's desire is within your reach. Grasp it, Lady Amanda, before it moves beyond you."

Amanda looked puzzled. Eve, on the other hand, had a fair idea of her aunt's train of thought and interceded to avoid what could easily turn out to be an embarrassing situation.

"There you are, Lady Amanda," she said. "One of these days, you *will* be a published author!"

Amanda's expression cleared and she laughed. "I have to finish the book first! Thank you, Miss Claverley. You've given me new hope."

Liza looked at Eve. "Aren't you going to have your tea leaves read, Miss Dearing?"

Miss Claverley answered the question while Eve was groping for words that would offend no one. With a sideways glance at Eve, she said, "My niece doesn't hold with anything that cannot be explained by her intellect or her five senses."

"A wise philosophy," remarked Henderson.

Lady Sayers entered the room and the conversation turned to Dr. Braine's instructions for Lydia's care. The one thing he insisted on, said Lady Sayers, was that she not be agitated by questions about the night she was attacked. There would be time enough for that when her strength had returned, and so he would tell the constable.

Lady Sayers shook her head. "This is a sad business to drag you into, Liza. Had there been time, I would have written to your mother to cancel the visit, but, you see, I expected you at any moment. If you wish to return to Paris, and I'm sure you must, I shall arrange it as soon as may be."

"Return to Paris!" Liza sounded shocked. "I wouldn't dream of it! Here I was, thinking that London would be boring, and it isn't boring at all. What could be more exciting than living with such talented, celebrated ladies, with a mystery to solve and danger lurking just around the corner?" Her eyes sparkled with pleasure at the prospect. Gradually, her enthusiasm ebbed and she said more moderately, "Besides, I can't return to Paris. Mama and Papa are touring Provence, and I don't know how to reach them."

That, of course, settled the matter.

Philip Henderson managed to have a quiet word with Ash before he left. As he accepted his hat and gloves from the footman, he said, "I believe you're acting for Colonel Shearer in this business of Angelo?"

Ash was instantly on the alert. "Who told you that?"

Philip shrugged. "Word gets around, and the colonel isn't exactly closemouthed. The thing is, I'm in much the same position as you. I have a client who would dearly love to sue this Angelo fellow. I've told her, it would never come to court. No crime has been committed. She won't listen. The thing is, I can't turn her off because she's my mother's dearest friend. Her name is Lady Trigg, and she has a lovely country home in Crawley."

"She must be the lady whose footman fell down a flight of stairs and broke his neck."

"That's the one, and now she thinks everyone is pointing fingers at her behind her back."

"Tell her that she's not alone. Anyone who has the misfortune to play a part in one of Angelo's stories feels the same. The colonel would like to wring his neck."

"And I'd like to sue him."

They both laughed.

Ash walked down the front steps with Philip. "Maybe we can work together to discover Angelo's identity."

"Not my strong suit, old friend. I'm not a policeman. Bring me the evidence and I'll do the rest. I thought, however, that you should know about Lady Trigg. This happened a long time ago, fourteen years to be exact. It seems strange to me that someone would resurrect this old tragedy."

Ash nodded as he made a mental note. All three accidents had taken place within a year of each other.

As Philip entered the carriage, Ash thought that it was good to be on friendly terms with him again. The estrangement with Amanda had made things awkward between the men, though the upset had taken place when Ash was soldiering in Spain. He'd never understood the ins and outs of Amanda's curious behavior. He'd liked both Philip and Mark and would have been happy to see her married to either.

Now she was a widow, and Philip had invited himself into her carriage for the drive home. Ash wasn't sure how Amanda would feel about that. As far as he could tell, she was still in love with Mark.

He hadn't always admired Philip as much as he did now. Philip was a younger son and would inherit very little when his father died. So Philip had taken up a profession, but it was more than a profession. The law was his vocation.

As for himself, Ash was the only heir, and nothing much had ever been expected of him except that he marry and beget heirs. The prospect had never appealed to him, and after Harry's tragic death, he had completely repudiated the course his father had laid out for him.

He'd told Eve more than he meant to but not nearly

as much as he might have. Harry's sudden death had opened his eyes to many things he'd never questioned before. He saw his father's ambitions in a new light. They had no relevance and no substance, and he wanted no part of them. His father had tried to make him in his own image and, thank God, he had failed.

She was lucky to have Miss Claverley. She was a lady with a big heart. He hoped Eve had taken note of how respectfully, how utterly gentlemanly he'd behaved when Miss Claverley performed her parlor tricks. In his opinion, Philip was lucky to have escaped with his whole skin. Eve had the instincts of a guard dog where her aunt was concerned. A wrong look or a wrong word could have her baring her fangs, and those were ferocious fangs.

He'd seen another side of her at Vauxhall. As for the Eve in his dreams...

He shook his head, silently chiding himself. Every stray thought seemed to lead back to Eve Dearing. It was unmanly. He had more important things to think about. He was bound and determined to find Angelo and find out the truth about Harry's death.

He was getting restless again. He looked out over the grounds. A brisk walk might settle his fidgets, he decided, and he struck out on the path to Kennington Common.

As the coach bowled along Kennington Road, Philip said, "I don't often see you without your grandmother. Is her ladyship indisposed?"

"No, she's quite well, thank you. Her goddaughter, Henrietta, has a new baby, and my grandmother has gone for a little visit. They live near Barstow."

He seemed surprised. "You're not alone in that big house of yours?"

"Of course not. My old nurse is staying with me until my grandmother comes home."

This stilted conversation was beginning to fray her nerves, and she was quite happy when a silence fell between them.

"What did you think of her?" he suddenly asked.

Since this seemed like a safe topic, she expressed an opinion. "Liza? She is a curious mixture of innocence and worldliness. I took to her at once."

He nodded. "I think she's charming."

"But a bit startling for a debutante. I'm sure Eve and Lady Sayers between them will keep her right."

"Oh, I hope not. I like her just the way she is." He gave her a fleeting glance. "She reminds me of you at that age."

Her control wasn't nearly as good as she thought it was. She fought back the rush of temper, but some of it spilled out. "And look where it got me! People laughing at me behind my back or pitying me! I don't know which is worse."

His face had gone white. "Amanda—"

"No. You listen to me, Philip Henderson. I don't want you in my life at any price. You deliberately lured me away from Mark, then you challenged him to a duel. You might have killed him!"

"I did what I thought was best for all of us. No, don't interrupt. I have something I want to say to you. Oh, not about the past. That is ancient history and best forgotten. It's the present that concerns me. It's quite likely that we shall meet at various functions now that you're to take in the Season."

"And?" she prompted when he paused.

His fierce look cooled. "I'm going to be married, Amanda. The engagement hasn't been announced yet. I thought you should be the first to know."

Something inside her seemed to shrivel. When she could find her voice, she said faintly, "Who is the lucky girl?"

"Ardith Rose. I met her last year when I was prosecuting a case in Bristol."

The silence that fell between them was arctic cold and stayed with Amanda until she arrived home. She mounted the stairs to her chamber, unaware that Miss Penny, her nurse, had called out a greeting.

As in a dream, she removed her outer things and sat down at her escritoire. Miss Claverley had told her that her heart's desire was within reach. It was only a parlor game. All the same, Miss Claverley's words had touched a chord deep inside her, only she wasn't sure what she wanted.

She missed her husband. He was a good man and had always been kind to her. But no amount of wishing would bring Mark back.

Heaving a sigh, she opened the top drawer of her escritoire and extracted a sheaf of closely written pages, the first chapter of her novel. She'd rewritten it several times. If Miss Claverley's oracle was to come true, she'd better get started on the next chapter.

After finding a fresh page, she dipped her pen in the inkpot. That was as far as she got. Not a single word came to her.

Miss Claverley greeted Eve warmly when she opened her chamber door to Eve's knock. "Come in, Eve. I've been expecting you. Why don't you sit down and get every-thing off your chest."

Eve ignored the allusion to her aunt's uncanny sixth sense and came straight to the point. "Do you think it wise to play with other people's lives by advising them on what they should do?"

"You mean by reading tea leaves?"

"Of course I mean by reading tea leaves. It could do so much damage."

Miss Claverley's brow wrinkled, but her expression remained friendly, almost maternal. "What kind of damage, Eve?"

"What if they believe you and act on what you've told them?"

"Then they'd be a lot happier. No. Listen to me, Eve. I know that you're trying to protect me from ridicule, and I appreciate your concern, but it won't do. I don't push myself forward. I don't misuse my powers, but when I see someone struggling and I have it in me to help them, I feel I must."

Eve's eyes narrowed as her aunt's words turned in her mind. At length, she said, "Lady Amanda is struggling? And Liza, too?"

"They're at a turning point in their lives and looking for direction. I can't be more specific because I don't always understand the messages that come to me. The message is for them. If they have eyes to see it, well and good. If not, no harm done. I don't prophesy doom and gloom."

After a long silence, Miss Claverley said, "But this conversation isn't really about me, Eve, is it? It's about you. You're thinking about your mother and father, aren't you?"

Eve would have argued the point, but her aunt was,

after all, a Claverley, so there could be no room to wriggle here. Her answer was a shrug.

Miss Claverley's voice gentled. "Your father was—is—a good man. He loved your mother. I never doubted that, and neither did Antonia. Don't judge him too harshly."

"I don't," said Eve sadly. "He thought that love would carry the day and discovered that he was wrong." She rallied with a smile. "What normal man wants to wake up one morning and find that he has shackled himself to a witch?"

She was trying to make light of it, but she was remembering the quarrels, the heartache, and, most of all, the regret. Her parents never should have married, and they'd both come to see it when it was too late.

Miss Claverley looked troubled and took Eve's hands into her own. "Don't confuse Lord Denison with your father. The viscount is not narrow-minded. The scope of his—"

"Ash Denison!" Eve pulled her hands from Miss Claverley's clasp. "How did he come into the conversation?" Now she was wriggling for all she was worth, trying to get free of her aunt's hook. "I was talking about Papa and Mama. Lord Denison is a viscount, for heaven's sake. I'm a gardener's daughter. There can never be anything between us."

"Oh, I don't know." Miss Claverley touched a finger to her lips to quell an incipient smile. "He's unconventional. I don't think he'd let a little thing like that stand in his way."

Eve got up with as much dignity as she could summon. "That's not the point. I don't think I shall ever marry. I won't be locked into the kind of marriage my parents had."

Miss Claverley's brows snapped together as she studied Eve. "If you don't possess the charisma," she said slowly, "and you've always denied that you have it, how could your marriage possibly turn out to be like your mother's?"

Eve hesitated too long.

Her aunt rose and gave her a searching look. "Your powers are coming back to you," she said. "That's it, isn't it?"

Eve's laugh was short and mirthless. "Yes and no. In fits and starts. I feel like an infant learning to read. Every letter, every symbol is a puzzle I have to laboriously decipher."

"Give it time. You'll improve with practice."

Eve nodded, but she was thinking that time was something that was fast running out.

"Do you want to talk about it?"

Eve's eyes jerked up to meet her aunt's anxious gaze. For a moment she hesitated, then checked the impulse. Her gift was leading her into danger, and she did not want her aunt to worry. And if her aunt started worrying about her, Eve would start worrying about her aunt, then they'd both be miserable.

She smiled into her aunt's anxious eyes. "Don't worry, Aunt Millicent. Antonia is guiding me."

It was said unthinkingly, but as soon as the words were out, Eve realized that she truly believed it. *Antonia is guiding me.*

Eve wakened with a start. Someone was knocking softly on her door, repeating her name over and over in a pleading undertone. Dexter was on the other side of the door, too, whining as though he were hurt. It took her only a moment to shrug into her dressing robe and open the door.

Andy, the bootboy, a tall, dark-haired lad of about twelve or thirteen summers, was shifting uneasily from foot to foot. He was devoted to Dexter, and that was enough to make Eve like and trust him.

Andy often took Dexter out for a late-night walk, but not this late. "What happened, Andy? Did Dexter wander off on his own? You should have left him to it. One of the porters would have let him in when he decided to come home."

"It's a tinker girl, miss," he croaked out. "Dexter found her in the boiler room and, well, she needs help. She asked for you. I think she has broken her ankle."

Tinker girl. Eve knew at once that he must mean Nell. Only something like a broken ankle would induce her to seek help. And who else would she come to?

"Lead the way."

Nell's fear-bright eyes fixed on Eve when she entered the boiler room, then the fear faded and she gave Eve a shy smile. "Eve," she said.

As Eve knelt beside her, she said to Andy, "Does Cook keep a stockpot on the boil?"

"Always."

"Then fetch me a cup—a big cup, mind you." In a gentler voice, she said to Nell, "What happened?"

"Fell."

And that, thought Eve, was all she was going to get out of her. "Show me your ankle."

Nell's shoes, the shoes that Eve had given her, were warming beside the boiler, but the clothes she was wearing were nothing but rags, fit only for burning.

Shaking her head, Eve examined the painfully thin

leg Nell stretched out and gently probed the ankle. It was swollen, but not broken.

Andy arrived with the cup of stock, and after testing how hot it was, Eve gave the cup to Nell. As Nell sipped slowly and carefully, Eve said, "I'll need something to bind Nell's ankle, Andy. A tea towel would do. And wring it out in hot water."

When Andy came back with the tea towel, Eve set to work. Dexter whined, but not a whimper passed Nell's lips. Though she knew that she was wasting her breath, Eve told Nell she would have to rest her foot and bind it every few hours as she was doing. Finally, losing patience, she said, "If only you would let me send you to my home in Henley—"

She didn't complete the sentence before Nell shook her head violently.

"It won't do, miss," said Andy. "Tinkers and gypsies is wild. You can't tame them to live in houses like ordinary folk. They're like deer or foxes. They have to be free."

"And what would you know about tinkers and gypsies?" Eve demanded. Her voice was rough, not because she was angry but because she knew Andy was right.

"My pa was a gypsy. He stayed with my mam for a little while, but when I was three or four, he went off wandering and we never saw him again."

Eve wanted to kick herself. She shouldn't be taking her frustration out on Andy. "I'm sorry, Andy. That was mean-spirited. You've been so helpful. Do you think you can do one more thing for me? See if you can find something in the laundry room for Nell to wear. Oh, and get her something to eat, as well."

When she was alone with Nell, she said, "You were under my window when Mrs. Rivers was attacked, weren't you?"

Nell's only response was in her eyes. They returned Eve's steady stare.

"You screamed when you saw the man attack Mrs. Rivers—I mean, the lady in the white dress?"

Nell answered with the faintest motion of her head.

"Did you see his face?"

"Too...dark."

Eve let out a long breath. "He doesn't know that, though. I don't think it's safe for you here anymore. Is there someone I can take you to? Somewhere else you'd like to go? Someone in town, perhaps?"

Nell's dark eyes flared with fear. "Stay here! Safe here!"

Eve spread her hands. "It's all right. I won't force you to do anything you don't want to do."

Andy returned with a bundle of clothes. "This was all I could find." After handing them over, he fished a hunk of bread and a bigger hunk of cheese from his pockets.

Eve took the clothes. Nell took the bread and cheese and had a healthy bite of each.

"Boy's clothes," said Eve. She slowly shook them out. "You've done well, Andy. Now leave us alone for a minute."

Eve thought she might have a tussle on her hands, but Nell reached for the clothes and stroked them reverently. "For me?"

"For you."

Nell buried her nose in the bundle of clothes. Her eyes were sparkling when she looked at Eve. "Smell nice."

"That's because they're newly laundered."

Nell smiled at Eve, and Eve's heart turned over. She looked so young, so pretty, and so innocent. How could anyone have had this child committed to Bedlam?

Eve blinked to rid herself of the hateful burning in her eyes. That burning itch only got worse when she helped Nell disrobe and get dressed—the thin shoulders, the flat chest, the protruding ribs. "We need to put some flesh on your bones." She gave a little cough to clear the gruffness from her throat. "I'll think of something, but just remember, if you're ever in trouble, you can come to me."

Fatuous words! How much worse trouble could Nell be in?

When Nell was dressed, Eve was amazed at the change in her. She really did look like a boy. "This will do very well," she said. "No one will recognize you as Nell. Maybe we should change your name, you know, give you a boy's name."

Nell's beaming smile was thank you enough for Eve.

Andy poked his head around the door. "Someone's coming. We can't stay here."

Eve waved him away. "You go first. Take the back stairs and try not to be seen."

She reached for Nell's discarded clothes, but Nell snatched up her coat—Eve's coat—and put it on. "Warm," she said, then she reached for her shoes and, last of all, the bread and cheese.

Eve nodded. Snow wasn't unheard of in April. She bundled up the rest of the clothes and made one last plea. "Won't you let me send you to Henley?"

Nell shook her head and with a half smile pushed past Eve, then turned and limped through the door to the coal cellar.

It was all such a muddle, thought Eve. She should talk to Anna. Maybe Anna could think of a way to help Nell.

In the long corridor that ran past the servants' hall

and the kitchens, Eve came face to face with the man with the silver hair. It took a moment for her to place him: He was Ash's valet. Under one arm he carried a bundle of white linen shirts. He didn't explain why he was up so late, and neither did she.

"Good evening, Mr. Reaper," she said.

"Ah...oh, good evening, Miss Dearing."

To Dexter, Reaper was almost a stranger and the dog gave a low-throated growl as they passed.

Chapter Twelve

It was supposed to be a small, informal reception to introduce Liza to society, but as Eve looked over the crush of people, she was sure there must be close to a hundred guests.

There were a number of young people of Liza's age in attendance, and they seemed to be as pleased to make her acquaintance as she was to make theirs. They were in the drawing room, but the adjoining doors to the music room had been opened to accommodate the crush. Someone was playing the piano, and the boisterous rhythm of a country dance had them all tapping their toes.

Eve's eyes traveled the room and came to rest on Lydia. She was huddled in a chair by the empty grate, with Anna on one side to keep her company and Dr. Braine on the other. He was here as a guest, but the ever-dutiful doctor could not help keeping an eye on his patient. More than a week had passed since the attack, and though Lydia was making a remarkable recovery, she was a changed woman. She was fearful and could not be left alone for long. As a result, whenever the ladies went out, one of them always remained behind at the Manor to keep Lydia company.

Eve's train of thought was interrupted by Lady Sayers. "I think," said her ladyship, "that Lydia is a lot better than she makes out. She has her eye on the doctor and, if I'm not mistaken, he has his eye on her." She nodded sagely. "If she were to make a complete recovery, there would be no need for Braine to visit the house."

The thought startled Eve. The doctor did not seem to her to be glamorous enough for Lydia's taste. A thought occurred to her. "Is that why you invited Dr. Braine to the reception? Because you think he is sweet on Lydia?"

Her ladyship's eyes gleamed. "No. I would have invited him anyway. His late father owned quite a spread out here, so we've always been on the friendliest terms. However, this is the first time young Braine has accepted an invitation to one of my receptions, and I'm beginning to see why."

Eve gazed at the doctor, then at Lydia. She'd been doing it all evening, fixing her gaze on one person then another as though she could read their minds. It wasn't idle curiosity on her part. She was trying to get inside Angelo's head. She was coming to the conclusion, however, that he wasn't here or her charisma was too feeble to be of any use to her in a crowd.

"Any word of Lydia's sister?" she asked Lady Sayers.

Her ladyship shrugged. "I know that Lydia has written to her but she hasn't responded."

"That doesn't sound as though she has told her sister how seriously she was injured."

"No," her ladyship said serenely. "And I can see why she wouldn't. If Bertha—that's her sister's name, by the way—were to arrive now and carry Lydia off to Warwick, that could well put an end to the doctor's interest; you know, out of sight out of mind."

Latecomers arrived at that moment. On Mr. Philip Henderson's arm was a lovely young woman whom Eve had met at the opera—Miss Rose, as she remembered. It was the other guest, however, who captured her interest: Lady Sophie Villiers.

Eve remembered Lady Sophie very well. At Vauxhall, she'd watched Ash lead the stunning brunette into the rotunda where the dancing was in progress. Eve knew that she had never looked better, in her new pastel blue muslin and her hair pinned up with silver combs, but in the presence of such a dasher, she felt oddly inadequate, like warm milk compared to vintage champagne.

Well, the stunning dasher would have her work cut out for her here. The darling of society was much in demand by equally stunning ladies, and to escape their clutches, he had attached himself to the guest of honor, much like an elder brother with a sister half his age.

Ash came into view, but not with Liza as she expected. He was alone, and Lady Sophie lost no time in crossing to him and taking his arm. He threw Eve a look she could not interpret and allowed the beauty to lead him away.

A voice at her ear dragged her from her gloomy thoughts. Amanda's voice. "Come along, Eve. I think you and I could do with a breath of fresh air."

They walked slowly along the corridor, stopping from time to time at various paintings of pastoral scenes, but Eve hardly heard a word Amanda said until she mentioned Lady Sophie's name. Then her ears pricked up.

Amanda thought she was jealous and had rushed to her rescue! Was she so obvious?

She laid a hand on Amanda's arm. "I'm not jealous. I'm surprised." She repeated the words she'd once heard from Lady Sayers. "I thought their affair was over. Seems I was wrong."

Her little prod worked. "It *is* over," said Amanda, "on Ash's part at least. She, however, has always wanted Ash and has never tried to conceal it. What would you have him do—turn tail and run?"

That seemed like a reasonable course of action to Eve. "I don't expect anything," she protested. "Ash means nothing to me."

Amanda responded as though Eve had not spoken. "I don't believe that she is interested in marriage. It's the chase she likes. She's a widow and can do pretty well what she pleases, and it pleases her to hunt any man who takes her fancy. Ash knows all this. Most men are putty in her hands, but..."

Her voice trailed to a halt. Eve turned to see what had arrested Amanda's interest. Philip Henderson had just walked by with Miss Rose on his arm. There was no need to draw on her powers of intuition to deduce how that made Amanda feel. Having just been attacked by the same green monster, she truly sympathized.

She linked arms with Amanda. "She's charming, isn't she? Liza, I mean. I think all the young men are half in love with her already."

Amanda blinked and came to herself. "Except for Dr. Braine," she responded.

"She's easy to please, too, and that is an attractive quality in a young debutante, don't you think?"

They continued in this vein until Leigh Fleming came to claim Amanda for supper.

"Did you have a chance to look over Angelo's stories?"

Eve plucked a grape from her plate and nibbled on it as she put her thoughts in order. Ash and she had found a quiet nook with sofa and chairs in an embrasure in the hall outside the music room, where they could talk with some degree of privacy. Supper was being served in the dining room, but guests were free to pick up their plates and wander at will. They were, however, not allowed to wander in the gardens, except for the gentlemen who wished to smoke. This was at Ash's insistence. He feared that Angelo might still try to harm Lydia.

"Yes," she said in reply to his question, "I've read the stories and, quite honestly, I'm at a loss. I don't recognize the style or the writer's voice. It could be anyone, perhaps someone who has not been published previously."

"There must be something that can point us in his direction!" Ash's voice was rough with frustration.

Eve said, "Well, one thing is certain. He *knows* these homes and gardens."

"And you don't?"

"I might recognize them if I visited them, but I can't place them. As for Angelo," she shrugged, "I haven't a clue, only theories."

He smiled at her choice of words.

"Why the smile?"

"I was remembering," he said, "that when I was a boy, I wanted to be a Bow Street Runner when I grew up and was forever running around the estate looking for clues to crimes that had never been committed. All that my noble ambition achieved was to stir everyone up and get a thrashing for my trouble."

"That sounds a bit harsh. What did you do?"

"I caught one of the stable hands in flagrante delicto with one of the dairymaids. I was in the hayloft and was so shocked that I lost my footing and fell on top of them."

"And the stable hand thrashed you?"

"No. The dairymaid did."

She began to laugh. "So what did you take up next?"

"Girls," he replied with a straight face.

The glib reply made her shake her head.

"What?" he asked.

"That doesn't sound like the character of the elder brother in Angelo's story, the story you claim is yours. In fact, I don't recognize him as you. I find him…" She groped for words.

"Pathetic?" he threw out carelessly.

"No! *Sympathetic* is what I was going to say. A lonely boy, shy, friendless, who never put a foot wrong, bullied by his father—"

"Stop!" He was grinning when he held up his hand. "You're reading too much into one small paragraph in that story. Don't let your writer's imagination run away with you. I didn't make friends easily, but I did have a few friends."

"What happened, Ash? What changed that book-worm of a boy into the celebrated man-about-town?" Fearing that the question was too personal and she shouldn't have asked it, she tried to retreat a little. Smiling, shaking her head, she said lightly, "I'll say this for Angelo, he knows how to hook his readers. Look at me, I can't wait to know all the whys and wherefores." Then very softly, because she really wanted to know: "Something must have happened to change you so radically. Was it Harry's death?"

She half-expected him to refuse to answer, but after regarding her thoughtfully over the rim of his glass, he shook his head. "It happened before Harry died. And I didn't change, not then. It was how people viewed me that changed."

He took a mouthful of punch. "It was Morag's doing," he said, "and before you chew me to pieces, let me tell you that Morag MacRae is my cousin. She was Morag Denison back then and came down to London to have her trousseau made up for her marriage to Lord Roderick MacRae. I was eighteen and in my first year at Oxford. I didn't deliberately set out to mislead the other boys in my dormitory, but I didn't correct them when they began to assume that Morag and I . . . well, that we were lovers. Morag thought it was a great hoot, and she played her part to the hilt."

He stroked his chin with his index finger, a half smile hovering on his lips. "Needless to say, some of my classmates tried to cut me out and take Morag under their protection, but she soon cut them down to size."

"I can't imagine how they could have been so misled!"

"Oh, it started innocently enough. I was always on hand to take Morag shopping. Nothing but the best for Morag, so we went to London's most prestigious modistes. I signed the bills, but it was Grandfather Denison who banked me. My friends assumed the worst and, I'm afraid, I let them."

"Is that how you got your reputation as an expert on ladies' fashions?"

"That's how it started. I've learned a lot since then."

Though she couldn't help laughing, she was shocked. "Didn't your cousin care about her reputation? What would her betrothed have said if he'd found out?"

"Morag said that Roderick would call me out and that would only add to my credit among my peers."

"It might also have caused your death," she retorted indignantly. "Have you thought of that?"

"Ah . . . no. I don't think so. One thing I could do well was fence. Besides, Morag said that she would break the engagement and that would break Roderick's heart. He was head over heels in love with her."

She sat back and studied his dancing eyes. "You're making this up!"

"Not completely. I'm embroidering the facts a little to make me out to be a more interesting fellow than I really am."

She was ready to take umbrage, but he stopped her scalding words by popping a grape into her open mouth.

"I lied about Roderick," he said. "He would have laughed himself silly if anyone had tried to tell him that Morag was taking up with me. 'A timorous beastie,' he called me. He knew better than to think I was man enough for Morag."

He leaned toward her and stared deeply into her eyes. "I've told you all this in the strictest confidence. I wouldn't want it to get about that I was a fraud. I have my reputation to think about."

He was making fun of her! She gave him back his soulful stare, only she was in earnest. "I can see into your soul, Ash Denison," she breathed out softly, "and though I believe every word you've told me, you haven't told me every word."

"I'm an open book," he protested.

She sat back and stared at him thoughtfully. "Then tell me what happened to your mother. Angelo calls her 'a fragile flower.' What does he mean?"

His brows rose, then he reached for his wineglass and took a long swallow. "Well," he said finally, "no one would ever call you a 'timorous beastie,' Miss Dearing, but that is one of your qualities that I have always admired."

He didn't sound as though he admired her, and by referring to her as "Miss Dearing," he had put some distance between them.

She was saved the trouble of apologizing when Anna Contini stopped by their alcove. She had a small wicker basket over one arm. Indicating the two plates on the sofa table, Anna said, "Have you finished eating, because if you have, I'll just choose a few treats for my dear little donkeys."

"Oyster tarts?" Ash queried when Anna swept the contents of his plate into her basket. "Your donkeys eat oyster tarts?"

"It's amazing what donkeys will eat," she replied serenely, now eyeing Eve's plate. "Do you want that pork pie, Eve?"

"No, I was saving it for your donkeys."

"So kind."

As Anna moved away, Ash said, "That woman really is peculiar. Now, if I had the dressing of her . . ."

He looked at Eve, she looked at him, and they both smiled.

But Eve knew something that Ash did not. The treats were not for Anna's donkeys but for their little runaway from Bedlam. She and Anna had put their heads together and come up with a plan to make sure that Nell was well supplied with food.

The ice was broken. Ash said, "Eve, can we get back to what we started out to do? You said you didn't recognize the gardens. Can we go on from there?"

She was glad to follow his lead. "I made a few notes on my impressions," she said, and she proceeded to withdraw a folded piece of vellum from her reticule. "And no snide remarks will be tolerated."

"I thought you might have brought your little notebook."

"That comes very close to a snide remark."

"I'm all ears."

She unfolded her page of notes, then sighed. "All I have are questions."

"Fine. Let's see if your questions are the same as mine."

She heaved another sigh. "What happened when Angelo published his stories?"

"I can only speak for myself. I was incensed. He resurrected an old tragedy and implied that murder had been done. I wanted to wring his neck."

"Maybe that's why Angelo published those stories—oh, not to get his neck wrung, but to draw attention to accidents that were, in fact, murders."

"*What?*" He was scowling.

"It's only an opinion I'm offering you," she said quickly. "You asked me to read the stories and give you my impressions. Well, I don't see those stories in the same light as you. They're sad, yes, but I don't think they are malicious."

"They're malicious if they're not true."

"I suppose so," she said, and fell silent.

He thought for a moment as he stared at her bent head. At last, he said, "I don't know why I'm taking my frustration out on you. You're not telling me anything that hasn't occurred to me, as well. I didn't want to believe it, that's all."

His black brows were knotted tightly above his

brooding eyes. Eve was wishing she'd kept her mouth shut. She was giving him her impressions, not her convictions. It seemed to her that all she'd achieved was to open an old wound. It must be devastating to think that his brother had been murdered.

His brows relaxed and he exhaled a long breath. "If your hypothesis is correct," he said, "Angelo, for whatever reason, published his stories to draw attention to the murder of three innocent people. If I were the murderer, I'd be afraid of what Angelo would do next. I'd want to silence him before he exposed me."

"Which would explain the attack on Lydia," she added tentatively.

His unsmiling lips gradually turned up. "That's a very neat theory," he said, "but raises almost more questions than it answers."

"I know," she replied glumly.

"Such as, if Angelo believed murder was done, why didn't he write separately to me, Colonel Shearer, and Lady Trigg to tell us? Why wait for us to read his stories in the *Herald*? And what if the *Herald* had not accepted his stories? What then? And why wait so long before he raised all these doubts in our minds?"

Her shoulders slumped. "I have no idea."

"But the thing that troubles me most is why anyone would murder three innocent people all those years ago. I can't speak for Colonel Shearer's maid or Lady Trigg's footman, but I know my brother. Harry was an invalid. What offense could he possibly have committed to rouse the wrath of a killer? Until that question is answered, the villain in my mind is still Angelo."

She spread her hands. "I have no quarrel with that. His name is so firmly fixed in my brain as the villain that I'd find it almost impossible to change it. But that doesn't mean to say that my mind is closed to other possibilities."

"Point taken." He got up and held out his hand. "We've been cloistered here too long. Let's see what the youngsters are up to."

The youngsters were dancing their feet off, and not only the youngsters but those who were young at heart. As she and Ash stood watching at the edge of the dance floor, Eve let her gaze wander. She was doing it again, trying to focus her charisma as though it were a compass and could direct her to the villain. Angelo.

Her mind was suddenly engulfed in a whirlwind of seething emotions—excitement, the thrill of the chase, and anticipation of the final victory. For a moment, she thought she was in Angelo's mind, but the vision of Sophie Villiers took possession of all her senses. There was fury there, too, the fury of a scorned woman seeking revenge.

"Ash," said the Fury, as she deliberately stepped in front of him, "I've been looking all over for you." Her voice was light and teasing. "Rumor has it that you're in rake's heaven with your own private harem of lovely ladies."

Eve looked at Ash. She couldn't tell what he was thinking. His mind was closed to her. As for his expression, he looked vaguely bored and not the least put out by Lady Sophie's remarks.

"And you are?" said Lady Sophie, addressing Eve.

"I'm one of the harem," Eve quipped, and felt a blast of temper pass right through her.

"I beg your pardon," Ash said easily. "I thought you

knew each other. Lady Sophie, may I introduce Miss Dearing? Eve, this is Lady Sophie Villiers."

Eve smiled, Lady Sophie smiled, but her hungry eyes were fixed on Ash as she speculated on who had replaced her as his mistress and was now sharing his bed.

The thing to do now, thought Eve, was block the lady from her mind. It was unscrupulous to eavesdrop on the thoughts of innocent, unsuspecting people. She was discovering that it was easy to be virtuous when there was no temptation, and the temptation here was irresistible. If Ash had a mistress, she wanted to know who she was.

Lady Sophie's gaze never wavered from Ash's face, and Eve saw him through the other woman's eyes.

That crooked smile, which added to his charm in Eve's opinion, had taken on a wickedly sensual slant. His eyelids seemed heavier, and his eyes were veiled by the sweep of his thick lashes. Eve's heart began to beat a little faster. Lady Sophie did not see Ash Denison as a well-bred man of the world. She saw him as a seducer, a dangerous predator like herself.

Lady Sophie's lips were moving, but Eve wasn't listening to the banal words. She had a vision of the lady—for want of a better word—in nothing but a flimsy nightgown that plunged to her navel and clung sinuously to every voluptuous curve. The image changed when she reached for Ash and collapsed with him on the bed! And what a bed it was, a great vulgar affair with crimson velvet drapes adorned with gold frogging and tassels. They were in Lady Sophie's bedchamber, and Eve was reliving the memory as though she were right there.

This had gone too far. She had to break away. Her one thought was to escape and fill her lungs with pure fresh air.

She said the first thing that came into her head—something about having to find Miss Claverley—and hurried away. She didn't know where she was going and she didn't care. Her vulgar curiosity had opened a Pandora's box. She felt as though she was going to be sick. She was hurt, angry, and completely humiliated. She might as well have been a fly on the wall for all the notice those two paid to her. They had eyes only for each other.

Eve wasn't up to talking to anyone, and she crossed the hall to a small antechamber that served no useful purpose as far as she could tell. She had hardly stepped inside the room when she felt a hand on her shoulder. Sucking in a startled breath, she whirled to find Ash facing her.

"Eve," he said, "what the devil got into you? Why did you run off like that?"

She flung the words at him before she considered the wisdom of what she was saying. "I make it a rule never to get between lovers. Not that my presence was noticed. What was it your mistress said? I'm only one of your harem."

His anger was equal to hers. "No, Eve. You said that. And Sophie isn't my mistress. We parted company a long time ago."

So it was true. All that she'd seen was true. Her palm itched to slap him. Since no ready response came to her, she glared at him in silence.

His eyes narrowed on her face. "I'm asking myself why you should care. You've never made any secret of the fact that you want me to keep my distance. I might have believed you, except that your performance with Sophie just now . . . well, it leaves me to wonder."

"What?" she asked, bringing her chin up.

"Are you jealous, Eve?"

She wasn't jealous. She was furious. This unconscionable rake had worked his way into her good graces, and she'd foolishly allowed herself to forget what he was. Just a short time ago, her heart had gone out to him when he'd related the touching story of his loveless childhood. She doubted that he had a cousin called Morag. What a fool she was to be taken in like that. He loved women. He knew how to please them, how to woo them, how to seduce them.

"What I was," she said coolly, "was offended. Lady Sophie was obviously repeating gossip. If that's what everyone thinks, that you're hiding out here with your own private harem, then maybe it's time you went back to your rooms at Grillon's."

"It's a joke, Eve. Nobody takes it seriously."

"I'm sure I'm speaking for my friends when I say that we prefer not to be the butt of such ill-bred humor." She stopped when she realized she was beginning to sound self-righteous.

He touched a hand fleetingly to her cheek. "What a pretty speech. Oh, I'm sure you meant every word, but your hasty flight from Sophie will provoke more ill-bred humor than Sophie's remark that no one overheard but we two."

She didn't want to argue with him; she didn't want to talk to him. All she wanted was a little time to herself so that she could nurse her wounds in private.

"No one will think any such thing," she declared.

She meant to quit the room with all the dignity of a duchess, but his hand snaked around her wrist and dragged her back. In as curt a tone as she had ever heard from him, he said, "You had better unfreeze your expression if you want to avoid malicious tongues. Put a smile

on your face and allow me to escort you to your aunt."
When she stood there fuming, he went on, "I shall mention an outing to the theater and you will endeavor to
sound pleased at the prospect. Understood?"

"Understood." She spoke through her teeth, but she
dipped him an elegant curtsy and smiled into his eyes to
show him that she could playact as well as he.

He offered her his arm. When she placed her fingers
upon it, he dipped his head and whispered in her ear, "I
would have been disappointed if you had not been jealous, Eve. No, no. You promised to smile. Shall we go?"

Color high, she allowed him to lead her from the
room.

Chapter Thirteen

The reception was over. All the guests had gone home. Even the effervescent Liza had lost some of her fizz and had happily trooped off to bed, leaving her aunt and friends to enjoy a few minutes' relaxation over a glass of sherry amid the debris in the dining room. Everyone agreed that Liza had acquitted herself well at her first major hurdle of the Season. She was vivacious, she made friends easily, but she also made time for the older generation.

"That's what she calls us," said Anna. "I overheard her telling that young man she had taken under her wing that some of the older generation were planning a trip to Hatchard's Bookshop and she felt obligated to go, too."

They had a good laugh about that, especially as Eve had yet to reach her twenty-fifth birthday.

Anna said, "They seem to think that anyone past one-and-twenty must be in her dotage."

"I didn't know," said Lydia, "whether to laugh or take

offense. She sat out several dances just to keep me company."

Anna added, "She did the same with that nice young man who has a slight limp and doesn't dance. Jason Ford, that's his name."

Miss Claverley put in, "Young girls always take a fancy to soldiers, and a limp, however slight, is seen as a badge of courage."

Lady Sayers beamed. "I must say that my niece is greatly improved since I last saw her. She was a precocious child, you know. I suppose that comes from being spoiled by parents who are so much older than she. 'Hot at hand' was what my late husband called her. But now, well, she is a darling."

"I wonder," said Miss Claverley, and all ears pricked as though the Delphic oracle had spoken.

"Well, don't stop there, Millicent," said Lady Sayers. "Have you had a premonition?"

"Of course not," responded Miss Claverley tartly. "I don't have premonitions. It's just an observation. Precocious children don't usually turn out to be darlings. That's all I meant."

Eve added diplomatically, "Liza is high-spirited and that is part of her charm, but my aunt and I like her immensely, don't we, Aunt Millicent?"

"Of course. I like a girl with spunk."

"And Liza has plenty of that," Lady Sayers declared, and everyone laughed.

When they had finished their sherries and were wending their way upstairs, Eve kept up her smiles and her end of the conversation, but as soon as she entered her room, she collapsed against the door and let out a weary sigh. Keeping up appearances could be horribly draining, but she thought she had carried off her part rather well. She'd been on tenterhooks, fearing someone else might invade her mind uninvited. She need not have worried—nobody did, not even Ash, and he was the one person whose mind she would not have minded dipping into.

Where were her scruples now?

She was sorry she had ever left Henley and sorrier still that she'd decided to set a book during a girl's first Season. Her so-called "gift" was turning out to be more of a liability than a help. She didn't know how to control it. It was all very well for her aunt to say that that would come in time, but time was running out. That's what she felt whenever she read Angelo's stories, and she'd read them many times. Time was running out. How could she explain what she sensed to Ash? He wanted her to come up with clues, not some vague feeling that was not based on logic.

Her eye was caught by the nightgown her maid had laid out for her, a voluminous cotton monstrosity with a frilled yoke that buttoned to the throat and long, equally voluminous sleeves that buttoned at the wrist. In short, it was the kind of nightgown her grandmother might have worn.

Eve crossed to the bed, swiped the cotton shift from the covers, and shook it out for a better look. A family of tinkers, she thought disgustedly, could easily use it as a tent if they propped it up with a pole and pegged down the hem. There were two more just like it in her dresser.

She crushed the nightgown into a ball and tossed it onto the nearest chair. If the fire had been lit, she would have tossed it on the coals. When she'd come up to town to have a few gowns made up, she hadn't given a thought to nightclothes. But that was before she'd seen the vision of Lady Sophie and Ash in that moment of passion. Sophie Villiers's nightgown was so skimpy, Eve wondered why she had bothered to wear it.

And why had she been given a peek into Sophie Villiers's mind? What was the point of that? She wanted to do great things with her gift, important things, such as save lives and unmask murderers. Lady Sophie was hardly in that class.

Peeved, out of sorts, she wandered over to the bed, hoisted herself up, and flopped back against the pillows. She shouldn't blame Ash for something he couldn't control. It was Sophie Villiers's memory she'd been sucked into. But even knowing that, she couldn't help what she was feeling.

Out of her depth.

She wasn't up to exploring why she felt so let down, so she forced her thoughts to something else—the conversation she'd had with Ash about Angelo.

There was something about those stories that reached deep inside her and touched a chord, but the harder she tried to reach it, the further it moved away. She hadn't lied to Ash. She didn't recognize either the stories or the gardens. Then what was she reaching for? Or was it reaching out to her?

Ash...

Maybe it was Ash who was reaching out to her, not the man she knew now but the elder brother she'd taken such a liking to in Angelo's story. Her next thought made her chuckle. Maybe she was supposed to save Ash from Lady Sophie. Now wouldn't that be something?

She cast her mind back to the conversation they'd had about his early years. He'd told her that he hadn't lied, only embroidered the facts a little. When she compared his version of events to Angelo's story, she would have to say that the embroidery was in how the story was told. Ash could never be serious. He always made light of everything. It was his way, she supposed, of protecting his privacy. She had her own ways of keeping people at arm's length. In spite of what he said, no one wanted to be an open book that anyone could read at will.

All the same, it would be comforting to have one special person to whom she could unburden her heart and tell all her secrets. She wasn't that brave, so she could hardly expect Ash to be different. For a time there, she'd felt close to him—until she'd mentioned his mother.

Thoughts like these always brought her own mother to mind. Antonia believed she'd found her soul mate in her husband, and look what a disaster that had turned out to be.

Eve sighed and turned on her side. Her eyelids grew heavy.

Outside the Manor, concealed in a stand of leafy laburnums, Nell bided her time. The last carriage had left a long time ago, and most of the groundsmen had gone off duty. Only the night porters were still up, and they were inside the house. She knew their routine now, knew when it was safe to leave her cover and find the basket that would be waiting for her in the old rabbit hutch.

It was hunger that made her leave the safety of her burrow and look for food. The big house frightened her. Something bad had happened here, but that was a long time ago. Maybe the bad man had been caught and taken away. Each time she came to the house and no bad man appeared, she felt a little safer.

She buttoned Eve's coat up to her throat and pulled

up the collar. Half crouched over, she left the trees and wended her way toward the house, taking extra care not to be seen when she passed the side door with its shining lantern.

Her ankle had healed, but she still limped when she tried to run. She felt a kinship with the animals of the wild who were too old or frail to outrun the hunters. The thought made her heart begin to race. Fear was never far from her mind.

Her hearing was acute, and though the night was far from silent, she could distinguish that one odd sound that she hadn't expected to hear—the stealthy tread of a boot on gravel. Sucking in air, she sank down, her eyes desperately searching for the source of the sound. Long minutes passed, then a shadow moved in the herb garden, close by the rabbit hutch. He was lying in wait for her! The bad man was lying in wait for her!

Numb with fear, she inched away. Her hand closed around a rock and she grasped it automatically. All her senses were alive to her danger. Eve was still up. There was a light in her window. Eve...

When the shadow burst from cover, she straightened and leaped away. He didn't expect her to run to the house. As she passed Eve's window, she threw the rock as hard as she could manage.

She was in the ballroom, and girls in white dresses were twirling around the floor with their handsome partners. At one end of the ballroom were French doors giving onto the terrace. It would all end on the terrace. Someone threw a stone and cracked the window.

Eve came awake on a cry.

Dexter was sitting at the side of her bed, whining and

pawing her hand. Disoriented, she looked around her chamber. The nightgown she'd tossed away was still lying on the chair. She was on top of her bed, still fully dressed. The candle on the mantel was still burning.

Her sense of relief was palpable. It was only a dream, only a dream.

When Dexter whined again, she swung her legs over the edge of the bed and scratched his ears. "It was only a bad dream," she said. "And why are you here? Shouldn't you be with the groundsmen patrolling the grounds?"

She looked at the clock. Two hours had passed since she'd come upstairs. *Two hours.* How could that be? She must have been flitting in and out of sleep. Of course, Dexter wasn't needed to patrol the grounds at this time of night. Only the night porters would be on duty patrolling the corridors.

Something wasn't right, something about her dream. The window had cracked. That had never happened before.

She flew to the window and examined each small pane. Then she found it, a small crack beside the sneck.

Dear God, what was going on?

A sudden shaft of fear almost brought her to her knees. She was inside his mind. Shadows. Swirling gusts of white-hot rage. A labyrinth waiting to swallow her up. She had to fight it! She was in control. If she wanted to break free, she had the power to do it.

He was outside the house, searching for the girl.

What girl? What girl? her mind screamed.

The girl in the blue coat. She could ruin everything. She knew too much. She was a witness. He had to find her and silence her. Silence them all. No one ever crossed him and lived to tell the tale.

Eve's mind flinched as shadows formed behind her

eyes, then faces emerged, the faces of his victims—not three victims as she might have expected, but more than she could count. When his voice came to her, loud and clear, she surged to her feet.

Now I see you, little bitch!

He was hunting Nell! He'd recognized the coat. *In the dark?* her mind screamed. Nell must have come too close to one of the porch lanterns when she came for Anna's basket of provisions. Oh, what fools they'd been to put that poor child at risk.

She had to stop him.

Moving quickly now, she went to the clothes press and found a dark coat to conceal her pale gown and stout shoes in case she had to make a run for it. A few steps took her to the escritoire, where, since the attack on Lydia, she kept her pistol, primed and ready. She knew how to handle a pistol. And if worse came to worst, a shot from her pistol would rouse the house or the porters on duty. But she could only bring the porters to her side as a last resort. The last thing she wanted was to save Nell, only to have her sent back to Bedlam.

"Dexter, heel!"

When Dexter obeyed, she opened her door a crack and peered out. There were no servants about. Good.

"Softly now, Dexter," she said, and they flitted from the room.

"Eve?"

The voice that came to her in the darkened corridor belonged to her aunt. Now what should she do?

"Eve?"

Aunt Millicent's voice had risen a notch. Eve managed to say calmly, "Dexter is scratching to get out. Go back to bed. I'll have one of the night porters take care of him."

"I'll come with you."

"No. This is something I have to do by myself." She brushed by her aunt, hesitated, then turned back. "Look," she said, "there's a girl in trouble out there. Nell. She's the runaway from Bedlam. I'm going to help her. I know what I'm doing. Trust me. I haven't time to explain."

Leaving the house was ridiculously easy. She simply waited for her moment and, when the night porter had made his rounds, she slipped past him and left by one of the French doors in the library.

The moon provided some light but not enough to see the way ahead clearly. Small sounds made her heart jump—shrubbery rustling in the breeze; the creak of a loose shutter; a cat hissing somewhere close by. What she could not detect was Angelo's presence, and that alarmed her. Where was Nell? What had he done to her?

Her fingers tightened around her pistol and she brought it up.

Dexter whined.

"What is it?" she whispered.

He started forward and waited till she had caught up to him, then he took the lead at a faster pace, but not too fast. She lengthened her stride to keep up with him. There was no time for doubt or hesitation or questioning Dexter's instincts. He was far more sure of himself than she was of her own powers. For years, she had suppressed them. The result was that her instincts had atrophied from lack of use. Weak as they were, however, her instincts were telling her to trust Dexter. What else could she do?

When they came to the end of the turf, they entered a

dense wilderness of trees and shrubbery, and their pace slowed. Eve knew that if they kept going in this direction, they would eventually come to Vauxhall Gardens. Is that where Nell would hide? Maybe she'd found a way into the gardens at night, though there was a high wall to scale and the great iron gates would be locked. The deserted gypsy camp was nearby. Is that where Nell was making for? Was Angelo hot on her trail? And what about Nell's ankle? She wouldn't get far before it gave out.

When she stopped to get her breath, Dexter stopped a few yards ahead of her, then trotted back and nuzzled her hand. Eve shivered. Her mind was a blank. She'd lost Angelo. All the discomforts of her position began to make themselves felt. Cold was seeping through the folds of her robe. The soles of her shoes weren't as stout as she thought they were and offered little protection against the pebbles she'd stepped on. They were getting too far from the house for the groundsmen to hear a shot from her pistol.

She turned back to look the way they had come. "Dexter, heel!" she said. For the first time in her memory, Dexter disobeyed her command. He tossed his head and moved off in the direction of Vauxhall. With a small exclamation of surprise, Eve went after him.

Chapter Fourteen

His action was automatic. One moment he felt the hand grasp his shoulder, the next, wide awake, Ash lashed out and sent the intruder reeling back on his heels.

"Bloody hell!" exclaimed Reaper, picking himself off the floor. "What's got into you?" He rubbed his elbow. "That hurt."

Ash got up and rolled his shoulders to ease his aching muscles. "You should know better." He yawned. "You have a wrestler's grip, as I've told you before."

"How do you come to know about wrestlers?"

"Wrestling and fencing were the only things I excelled at when I was at Oxford." He looked at the clock. "Good Lord! Is that the time? You'd better have a good reason for wakening me in the middle of the night."

"There's a lady to see you," said Reaper.

"Eve? Miss Dearing?"

Reaper smirked. "No. Her aunt. She won't tell me what she wants. She'll speak to no one but you."

"Show her in."

He'd fallen asleep, fully clothed, on top of the bed and had left a candle burning on the mantelpiece. In fact, he wasn't sorry that Reaper had wakened him. He'd been lost in a nightmare, desperately trying to find Eve. And before that he'd been dreaming of a ballroom... Everything was mixed up in his mind. What he remembered most was how afraid he'd been.

He did no more than adjust the cuffs of his shirt before Miss Claverley entered. His smile died when he saw the worry lines etched into her face. "What is it, Miss Claverley?" he asked. "How may I help you?"

Miss Claverley sighed. "She's going to be very cross with me for carrying tales out of school, but I can't let that stop me. She shouldn't have gone off like that."

"Eve?" He felt as if he'd been kicked in the stomach. "Eve has gone off on her own?"

"Well, no, it's not as bad as that. Dexter is with her. And she has her pistol. She's gone to look for Nell."

"How long ago was this?"

The sharp tone made Miss Claverley's lower lip tremble. "Half an hour, maybe less."

"And who is Nell?"

"You'll have to ask Eve. I can't betray her confidence."

With a muffled oath, Ash reached for his pistol and yelled for Reaper to find Hawkins and tell him to meet him outside.

Dexter set a fair pace, and Eve had to run to keep up with him. A time or two she tripped over a tree root or some obstacle on the path, but she managed to right herself before she took a tumble. For the most part, it was an easy run. They were on a well-worn path.

Suddenly the trees thinned out and she burst into a clearing at the edge of uncultivated pastureland. One arm was clamped under her breasts to ease the stitch in her side. Her other arm ached from the weight of her pistol. It took her a moment or two to catch her breath and straighten her spine.

There were no clouds now to shroud the light of the moon, and she knew at once where Dexter had led her. This was where the gypsies had made camp.

She shivered and pulled back into the shadows. There were no night sounds now, no creatures of the night passing close by, no feral cats chasing them off. Even the soughing of the wind in the trees had died down. It was uncanny.

And irrational! She had her pistol. She had Dexter. All she needed was to steady her nerve.

Taking a deep breath, she signaled Dexter to follow her and they entered the deserted camp together. There was very little to see, only the blackened embers of the gypsies' fire and the debris of their last meal. Chicken bones, she thought. They would have stolen the chickens from local farmers. That wouldn't make them too popular with the locals. Is that why they'd moved on? Fear of retribution?

She tentatively touched one of the rocks that encircled the fire pit. There was no heat in it, no warmth from the embers. No gypsies and no Nell.

Dexter wasn't interested in the chicken bones. He was rooting about in the tall grasses at the side of the camp. Why had he brought her here if not to find Nell? She gave a shaken laugh. He'd led her on a wild-goose chase. She should have had more sense than to trust Dexter's instinct. He was only a dog.

Without much hope of success, she cleared her mind

of everything and focused her thoughts on Nell. *Where are you, Nell, where are you?*

Where are you, bitch? Where are you?

Eve jerked back as the venomous words filled her mind. White-hot anger. Teeth grinding. Hands clenched into fists. Angelo.

You won't escape me. I know you're here somewhere. Fucking bitch! Fucking vagrant! Come here, my little bitch, and I'll show you what I do with little tinker girls who get in my way.... I see you. Now I've got you!

Eve's throat was as dry as parchment. He was coming for her. He thought she was Nell. She could feel it, sense it. She'd known she might come face to face with Angelo, and she'd thought she was prepared. What a fool she'd been. Sheer terror held her in a paralyzing grip. She couldn't get her feet to move.

"Dexter," she croaked out.

Her dog was sniffing the air. At the sound of her voice, he bounded over to her. As though sensing her panic, he peered into the shadows and he growled low in his throat. The dog's presence, or perhaps it was his fearlessness, was enough to steady Eve's nerves. She moved into the shade of a gnarled lilac tree and leveled her pistol. From the research she'd done for her stories, and subsequent target practice, she knew that she was a fair shot. But she'd never aimed her pistol at a living thing. Angelo was the first, and it did not trouble her conscience one bit. She'd taken his measure tonight and knew that he was a coldhearted killer.

She had one shot. She had to make it count. If only her hand would stop shaking.

"Stay, Dexter," she softly commanded. She didn't want to shoot her dog.

"Eve, where are you?" Ash's voice.

After the first start of surprise, her sense of relief made her legs buckle. "Over here!"

Her concentration was gone and she could no longer sense Angelo's presence. All the same, she wasn't taking any chances. She kept the pistol leveled and pointing into the dense shrubbery.

Rough hands grasped her shoulders and gave her a shake. "What in blazes do you think you're doing?"

Dexter began to dance around Ash's legs, begging to join the game. Eve lowered her pistol. "He's out there somewhere. We have to stop him."

Men came out of the trees and stopped at the edge of the clearing. She recognized Ash's coachman and one or two of Lady Sayers's groundsmen. Some had lanterns, others were armed with pistols or muskets. They stayed well back, as if they were aware a quarrel was imminent.

"Who is out there?"

"Angelo! He is after Nell."

"And who the devil is Nell?"

Impatience threaded her voice. "The girl who escaped from Bedlam. Why are you talking when we should be out there looking for Nell? He's out there. Don't you understand? And he may be after her."

To the groundsmen, Ash said, "Fan out and see what you can find. Be careful. He may be armed."

He turned his hard stare on Eve. "As for you, Miss Dearing, you are going back to the house. No. Don't argue. Wait for me in the library. I want to know exactly what is going on."

She cried impatiently, "What about Nell? You won't let them send her back to Bedlam?"

A nerve twitched in his cheek. "I'd hoped you knew me better than that."

He called Hawkins over. "Have her wait in the library

until I get back," he said. His eyes held hers for one im-placable, uncomfortable moment, then he went after the men.

Her aunt was waiting for her at the foot of the stairs. "Thank the Lord you're all right," Miss Claverley declared. "Now, would you mind telling me what's going on?"

Eve looked into those kind, worried eyes, and the emotions she had locked tight inside her while she searched for Nell spilled over. "I want to keep Nell safe, but she won't let me. She's afraid of people, afraid, I suppose, that we'll send her back to Bedlam. I blame myself for putting her in danger. There's a rabbit hutch close to the house, beside the herb garden. We leave food for her there, Anna and I. I think that the man who attacked Lydia was waiting for Nell tonight as she came for the food and he tried to kill her."

When she stopped to draw breath, her aunt patted her shoulder. "She's safe, Eve. If anything had happened to her, you would know it. And Lord Denison? Where is he?"

"He's out looking for her."

The worry frown on Miss Claverley's brow faded and she smiled. "If she can be found, he'll find her and keep her safe. Ah, here comes Mr. Hawkins. Good night, Eve. I'll see you in the morning."

As Hawkins ushered Eve into the library, Miss Claverley turned and began to mount the stairs. Her ex-pression was thoughtful. Eve, she was sure, did not real-ize how much she had revealed by her impulsive outburst. There was only one way she could have known that the man who attacked Lydia had also tried to kill Nell tonight. She had read his thoughts.

It frightened Miss Claverley. It was a terrible burden to bear, this seeing into the mind of another. Only someone who was exceptionally gifted had that power. Eve's powers were largely untested, but she couldn't advise her niece. Her own gift was a pale reflection of Eve's. There was a purpose to this, and only Eve could bring it to completion.

Eve was Antonia's daughter. Miss Claverley tried to find comfort in that thought.

The burden of Nell was a different matter. There were practical things she could do to help. Whatever she could do to help Eve, she would.

His silence told her everything.

She put down the glass of brandy Hawkins had insisted she drink and got to her feet. "You didn't find Angelo or Nell?"

Ash shook his head. "No to both questions. An army could be hiding out in those woods and we wouldn't find them. It's too dark. And there's no point in getting out the dogs. They wouldn't know which scent to follow. It's a favorite camping ground for gypsies and tinkers."

He walked to the sideboard, poured himself a generous measure of brandy, and took a long swallow, then another.

"Sit down, Eve."

He was trying to intimidate her, and she deeply resented it. She had made up her mind to make a clean breast of things, to tell him of her charisma, but that was before he'd entered the library like a sleek black panther poised to attack. She could well imagine the mauling she'd get if she told him the truth.

She sat, not because she was intimidated but to give herself time to come up with a logical and coherent explanation for her conduct, now that she'd had second thoughts about telling him the truth.

When he came to tower over her, she involuntarily shrank into her chair. His voice was soft, but there was never any doubt of the seething anger behind his words.

"Now let me see if I've got this straight. A week ago, Lydia was attacked right outside your bedroom window. Since then, we've had groundsmen patrolling the area just in case her assailant returns to try again. Earlier this evening, you and I had a discussion about Angelo and we both agreed he is a dangerous character. Am I right so far?"

She nodded.

"Then what in blazes," he roared, "were you doing wandering the grounds by yourself in the middle of the night?"

Because he seemed genuinely concerned for her safety, she kept her resentment in check. "When Dexter scratched at the door to get out, I saw no reason not to go out with him."

He folded his long length into the armchair on the other side of the fireplace and lifted a brow. "Armed with a pistol?"

"I didn't expect trouble, but I'm not a fool." She gave a careless shrug. "So I took my pistol with me. My aunt will support my story."

"Story," he repeated. "Yes, it does have the feel of a story, doesn't it? A fairy tale, in fact! Let's forget for the moment that you and your accomplice, Dexter, stole out of the house by the library door when you might have taken one of the doors where a porter was on duty. Tell me about Nell. I believe you said that she was the woman who escaped from Bedlam. Odd that you never mentioned her before."

Her chin lifted. "I met her the night she escaped from that house of torture. It was late and, believe it or not, Dexter was scratching to get out. However, he didn't go to the back door. He went down another flight of stairs to the laundry room. Nell was there, in a sorry state, filling herself with stale bread. She was freezing cold, hungry, and terrified out of her wits. I gave her my coat and boots. She told me her name. I went to the pantry to get something else for her to eat, and when I returned, she was gone."

His voice had lost its hard edge. "You helped a woman who had escaped from Bedlam? Weren't you afraid she might attack you?"

"Attack me?" She shook her head. "Oh, Ash, she was trembling so hard that she could hardly stand up straight. And she isn't a woman. She's a young girl. I would have done as much for a stray dog. My one regret is that she ran away before I could get her away from this place. I don't blame her. She doesn't trust anyone, except perhaps Dexter."

Dexter, who had been looking a shade glum since Ash arrived, lifted his head from his huge paws and thumped his tail on the floor.

No one paid him any attention.

Ash shook his head. "If she was incarcerated in Bedlam, there must be a reason for it. What did she tell you?"

"I could hardly get her to say a word. She only told me her name after I told her that she was not going back there and that I'd find a safe place where no one could harm her. I was thinking of sending her to Henley."

He was leaning forward in his chair, a hand pressed

to his brow. "You were going to send her to your home in Henley? A runaway from Bedlam?"

"Not alone, of course. My aunt, I'm sure, would have been happy to go with her." She added forlornly, "I hadn't made up my mind what I was going to do with her."

He shook his head. "Let's leave Nell for the moment, shall we? Tell me what you saw when you went out with Dexter, step by step."

He frowned when she hesitated, and that hastened her into speech. "To tell you the truth, I didn't see much when we went outside, but Dexter picked up the scent of something—I don't know what—and he sort of took off. Naturally, I followed."

"Naturally," he responded dryly.

She ignored his sarcasm. "He led me to the gypsy camp. That's why I thought Nell must be there. I'd hoped the gypsies had come back and had taken her in. And I knew Dexter was fond of Nell. If he'd picked up her scent, he would try to find her."

"But you didn't see the girl?"

She saw the trap before she stepped into it. "She was wearing my coat. I caught a glimpse of it."

He pressed his lips together as though he was trying to keep a straight face.

"What?" she asked.

"Dexter was fond of Nell?"

"Of course he liked her. Isn't that obvious? She broke into this house. She was an intruder. But Dexter didn't growl or bark an alarm. He nestled against her to keep her warm. Do you want to hear about Angelo or don't you?"

"Please," he said meekly.

She drew in a breath. Casting her mind back, she said

slowly, "I don't know when I became aware that he was there. I leveled my pistol and . . . and . . . I heard his steps; he was coming straight at me. 'I've got you now, little bitch,' he said, or words to that effect. It wasn't the words that frightened me. It was his rage. He was raving like someone demented." She saw the look on Ash's face and quickly amended, "That's what I sensed, anyway."

"You 'sensed.'"

Her chin lifted. "I'm a Claverley. We sense things."

He let the explanation go unchallenged. "Go on."

"If he'd come any closer, I would have pulled the trigger. But you shouted my name and I"—she gave a shaken laugh—"I sort of collapsed with relief."

"What made you think he was Angelo?"

"Who else could it have been?"

He let out a long, thoughtful sigh. "Keble told me not to say anything to anyone, but I'm coming to see that that was a mistake." He turned his head and captured her gaze in his. "Do you remember the heckler at the symposium?"

"Of course I do. What about him?"

"His name was Robert Thompson, and the night Lydia was attacked, he was bludgeoned to death in one of the arbors in Vauxhall."

"The heckler? Bludgeoned to death?" Her mind was numb with shock.

Her shocked stare prompted him to add, "After the constable interviewed everyone at the Manor, I went with him to Vauxhall to see if I could identify the body." He shifted restlessly. "Keble asked me not to say anything. It's his investigation and he told me, more or less, to keep out of it. We've talked since then, and he believes that Thompson's presence at Vauxhall was a coincidence."

Her mind was reeling with questions. "Who is he? What does he do? Why was he at the symposium?"

"That's what doesn't add up. Seems he was the proprietor of a prosperous inn on Gloucester Road. I've asked myself that same question. What would the proprietor of an inn have in common with Gothic fiction? I have someone looking into it—Jason Ford—but you can see why I was rough with you when I found you wandering outside on your own."

Her mind was racing off in a different direction. Had Angelo killed Robert Thompson? If so, why hadn't she felt the shock of it inside her own mind? Vauxhall was some way from the Manor. It seemed that Angelo had to be very close to her before she could read his mind.

On the other hand, maybe Angelo hadn't murdered Thompson.

"Ash," she said, her voice quavering, "how many villains are we looking for, one or two?"

He lifted his shoulders and let them drop. "I don't know what to make of it, but until I do, I don't want you to take chances. Do you hear me, Eve?"

She nodded. "Don't take chances."

After an interval of silence, he said, "What did Dexter do when this man came toward you?"

She had to think about that. "He growled, but he didn't bare his fangs. I think he growled because he sensed that I was afraid."

"Did he bark?"

"No."

"Or try to attack the man who came at you?"

She shook her head.

"What does that suggest to you?"

She answered slowly, "That Dexter must know him, be

familiar with him." Her voice quickened. "Maybe Angelo is one of the groundsmen or one of the gardeners."

"That's what I think, too, but he wasn't Angelo, just a groundsman who mistook you for a trespasser. I think he panicked when he realized his mistake and that's why he ran away."

He was so wrong, but she didn't know how to convince him. People who heard voices in their heads were candidates for—She couldn't complete the thought.

When he got up, so did she. She wasn't going to sit there like a naughty child and allow him to lecture her. She knew what she knew.

His voice gentled. "Listen to me, Eve. Isn't it possible that everything has become distorted in your mind—the attack on Lydia, Angelo, the girl who escaped from Bedlam? It sounds to me that you've been listening to Miss Claverley. I think she has fired up your imagination till you can't tell what is real from what is fantasy."

She'd heard those words or words very like them from her father. He hadn't wanted her to turn out to be like her mother. And because she loved him, she had tried to be what he wanted, just an ordinary girl.

It hadn't worked. Nothing she did could win her father's love, not then, not now. He still regarded her as a freak.

Well, an ordinary girl would be no match for Angelo.

She looked up at him with hurt and resentment burning in her eyes. It was hard to distinguish between Ash and her father, and in that moment she saw them as one. "Don't patronize me and don't belittle my aunt. I'd rather trust her intuition than your cold logic. She's a Claverley, and Claverleys are extremely sensitive to what people are thinking and feeling."

He was quick to pick up where she'd left off. "What about you, Eve? You're a Claverley, aren't you?"

And she was quick to correct her mistake. "Up to a point, but I also take after my father. That doesn't mean I think my Claverley relations are charlatans. They trust what they feel, and I trust them."

She stood her ground when he dropped his hands on her shoulders. The look he gave her was searching. "Will you listen to yourself? You're an intelligent woman. You can't believe all that rot. No sane person could. We're talking about real life here, Eve, not the fantastic realm of Gothic fiction."

She was glad now that she'd had the sense not to confess everything to him. His skepticism—no, his insulting dismissal fed her resentment. "I don't care what you think," she said. This, of course, was the opposite of what she was feeling, but she had her pride. "I told you what happened tonight. My aunt had nothing to do with it. Nell was out there, or at least Angelo thought she was out there. He mistook me for Nell. He was enraged. If you hadn't come along, I would have shot him."

When he made a small sound of impatience, she gave him a shove and stepped out of his grasp. "I'd hoped you would help me find her. I hate to think of her out there, fending for herself. She could fall into the hands of the wrong person—Angelo or someone who would return her to Bedlam. I promised her that would never happen, and I mean to keep my promise."

His hands fastened on her arms. "You are not going to run around the grounds at night looking for that girl. Not only would you be putting yourself at risk but her, as well." His voice gentled. "Leave it to me, Eve. I'll find Nell, if she can be found. And I promise she won't ever go back to Bedlam. You know how I feel about asylums. I wouldn't allow Harry to go to one. I won't do less for your runaway."

A knot of remorse constricted her throat. She shouldn't be surprised. She wanted to tell him that she wished she hadn't been so hasty to judge him when they'd first met. He was a far better man than she had ever imagined. She didn't tell him because she knew he would give her a flippant reply.

"I won't forget this," she managed to say past the lump in her throat.

He gave her the smile that always melted her heart. The hands digging into her arms released their pressure and slipped around her waist. She became lost in the look in his eyes—appealing, soothing, and if anyone needed to be soothed, it was she. Her encounter with Angelo had left her shaken. There was so much she hadn't shared with Ash, so much she'd learned when she was inside Angelo's head. Could she tell him? Dare she trust him?

His head descended. Hers lifted. Against her lips, he whispered, "This is real, Eve, what we can touch and taste. No crystal ball was needed. I knew it would come to this."

This time, when she shoved him, she sent him back on his heels. Panting, glaring, she got out, "If you'd had a crystal ball, you would have known that what you want you won't get from me. Why don't you try your tricks on Sophie Villiers? Her Gothic bed with its crimson drapes and profusion of gold frogging and tassels is your proper element, if you ask me."

She walked to the door. "Dexter, come."

Dexter was curled up on the hearth, either sleeping or feigning to be deaf. Eve gave her dog one baleful look and marched out of the room. On the other side of the door, she sucked in a disbelieving breath. She had just made a colossal blunder! Would he notice? What would he make of it? Why couldn't she curb her unruly tongue when she was with Ash Denison?

Ash combed his fingers through his hair. How dare she bring Sophie Villiers's name into what, to him, had been a perfect moment of harmony between them? And all because he'd made a little joke. Had the woman no sense of humor?

He heaved a sigh. The one good thing to come out of this was that Eve had not been stalked by Angelo. He believed his own words—a groundsman had spotted her and mistaken her for a trespasser. That Dexter had done nothing more than growl confirmed his opinion.

If Ash believed she'd had a close call with Angelo, he'd be panicking right now.

Nell. He'd promised to find her and take care of her. A runaway from Bedlam? He was beginning to feel like a character in one of Eve's novels, but whether she would cast him as the hero or the villain was still to be settled.

He looked at Dexter. "So now I'm stuck with you, am I?"

Dexter thumped his tail, shook himself off, and padded to the French door.

"If I didn't know better, I'd think you were reading my mind."

Dexter whined.

"Fine," said Ash. "Let's see if Hawkins and the groundsmen have found anything interesting."

Muttering under his breath, he unlocked the French door and followed Dexter out.

Chapter Fifteen

He found Hawkins as he'd left him, in charge of a small troop of groundsmen beating the bushes close to the house.

Taking Hawkins aside, he said, "What's the servants' gossip on this runaway from Bedlam? Have you heard anything, Hawkins?"

Hawkins shook his head. "Not much. They says that she has gone off with the gypsies, but I think that's only to put the keepers off the scent. The maids say that they've seen Miss Dearing and Mrs. Contini leaving food in an old rabbit hutch beside the herb garden."

Ash was incredulous. "They what?"

"That's what one of the maids told me, but they thinks it's for a tinker girl."

Ash breathed out through his nose. "Who is the girl? Who are her people and why was she sent to Bedlam?"

"Nobody knows, not even the keepers. Not that I'm friends with them, but they comes in for a drink some-times at the Black Prince when I'm there, and I hears them talking among themselves. She came straight from living on the streets to Bedlam. That's what I heard. No one has ever visited her. She can hardly talk, but they know one thing: She hates to be locked up."

"Seems to me," said Ash, "you know a great deal—more, I'm sure, than they'd tell me if I went knocking on Bedlam's front door."

Hawkins grinned. "I keeps my ears open."

Ash clapped him on the shoulder. "So what's happening out here?"

"Bugger all if you wants the unvarnished truth. The men are beginning to grumble. They haven't found a thing out of place, not even a dropped handkerchief. I think we should call them off and let them go home to their beds."

Ash agreed. "Tell them there will be beer with their breakfast tomorrow and I'm paying the shot. That ought to cheer them up."

Hawkins grinned again and went off to do Ash's bidding. Ash looked around for Dexter. There was no sign of him. He didn't want to call the dog's name in case he roused the whole house, so he gave a low whistle. A dog barked off in the distance. Not long after, Dexter appeared, tongue lolling, tail wagging. He circled around Ash, then took off again.

Ash recognized the way Dexter was heading, so he commandeered a lantern from one of the groundsmen and struck out along the path to the deserted gypsies' camp. He wasn't alarmed. They had made a thorough search of the area and found nothing. All the same, he had his pistol with him, but that came largely from his training as a soldier. He was always prepared for trouble.

Eve's conduct, on the other hand, was inexplicable. She'd wandered off with a pistol in her hand, in the middle of the night, because her dog wouldn't come when she called. Dexter was well able to look after himself. Any normal woman would have turned back, frightened off by the thought of what had happened to Lydia.

He was annoyed at the sudden stab of admiration that made his lips twitch. It wasn't rational. Eve Dearing had been a thorn in his side from the moment he'd met her, except for a few notable exceptions. The notable exceptions made up for a lot. Too bad that most of them occurred in his dreams.

"You'd better watch your step, old man," he told himself with a chuckle.

He automatically turned up the collar of his coat when a gust of wind funneled through the trees, making the leaves dance and scatter. A fine drizzle began to fall. He debated about returning to the house, but he was too restless to find sleep. He couldn't stop thinking about Eve, couldn't stop wondering what went on inside her head. He always had the feeling that she was holding back, letting him get only so close and no closer.

He wanted to tear that veil she hid behind and know her as possessively and as intimately as he knew her in his dreams—willing, giving, wanting him as much as he wanted her.

He reined in his thoughts as the fantasy began to play itself out in his mind. Mere wishful thinking on his part! He was well aware that he could have her if he made up his mind to it, but that wasn't what he wanted. He wasn't a seducer of women. In fact, he was more often the hunted than the hunter.

Sophie Villiers was a case in point. The only reason she wanted him was because he wasn't interested. A little thing like that wouldn't stand in Sophie's way—just the reverse. Like a lioness on the hunt, she singled out her prey and chased it down till it gave up in sheer exhaustion. All he was to Sophie was another conquest to add to the notches on her bedpost.

That had never bothered him before . . . before what?

Before Eve Dearing came streaking into his life. No doubt about it, her impact had set him back on his heels. And what was her impression of him? That his proper element was in Sophie's grotesquely vulgar bed with its crimson drapes and gold tassels.

He would have been insulted if he hadn't felt like laughing. Eve was jealous of Sophie Villiers? She might as well be jealous of . . . well . . . his favorite dinner. He could not live on a steady diet of steak and kidney pudding any more than he could live on a steady diet of Sophie Villiers. They both gave him indigestion.

He was smiling as he quickened his steps to keep up with Dexter, but that did not last. He was wondering how Eve had come to know about Sophie's bed. *Crimson drapes and a profusion of gold frogging and tassels.* It was a small point, but it nagged at him. Who would be so uncouth as to mention such a thing to Eve? No gentleman of his acquaintance, and Sophie didn't have women friends.

The problem was still turning in his mind when he reached the gypsies' camp. With lantern held high, he made a cursory inspection of the area, not expecting to find anything new, because they'd gone over it thoroughly when he'd come out to look for Eve. As far as he could tell, the gypsies had left in an orderly manner. There was a sandy trail giving locals access for cattle and vehicles, but time and the weather had obliterated most of their tracks. There was no sign of the girl called Nell.

As for the man Eve had encountered, he'd had enough time to make for home, possibly as shaken by his encounter with Eve as she was by her encounter with him.

It bothered him that Eve had evaded the night porters when she left the house and had armed herself with a pistol as though she was prepared for trouble. Did she expect to see Angelo and Nell out here? And why would Angelo want to harm a runaway from Bedlam? What was Eve not telling him?

The rain was steadily becoming heavier, and there was nothing more to be gleaned here. He hadn't set out with the idea of checking out Eve's story. It was Dexter who had led the way.

"Dexter!" he commanded.

Dexter answered with a low-pitched whine, but he did not appear. The sound seemed to come from a dense thicket of underbrush at the edge of the camp. Ash repeated his command with the same result, only Dexter seemed to have moved deeper into the underbrush or had come out on the other side.

Muttering a stream of curses, Ash went to investigate. The thicket was protected by a barrier of rampant briar bushes, their sharp thorns a menace to man and beast. He skirted the bushes until they thinned out. Though he still couldn't see Dexter, he could hear him rummaging around. Dexter seemed to have found something that was far more interesting than a ramble in the rain.

He hoped to hell it wasn't a badger's set.

"Dexter!" he roared.

An answering bark led Ash to a low stone wall on the other side of the thicket. A closer look revealed that it was the remains of the foundation of what might have been a workman's cottage.

"Dexter!" he roared again.

This time the bark came from the bowels of the ruined hovel. Ash felt his way along the wall and stopped when he came to a gap that he suspected was the entrance to the cellar. He could hear Dexter moving around, making a series of snuffling sounds. It didn't sound to him as though anyone was hiding in the cellar, or Dexter would have been barking in excitement or running in circles.

He positioned himself cautiously, close to the gap, and held the lantern up. Dexter was standing at the foot of a set of broken stone steps, looking up at Ash, his eyes shining in the light of the lantern. No one else was there.

Ash let out a breath. "It's raining," he told Dexter sternly. "My lantern is burning low, all I want is my bed, and you want to play games?"

Dexter thumped his tail.

Ash was curious to see what Dexter had found, if anything, so he lowered himself into the cellar one careful step at a time. The cellar was no bigger than a cell, with hardly enough room for a man to stand up. Ash knew at once that someone had been here recently. There were no cobwebs. In fact, the place looked remarkably tidy. In one corner, the driest corner, was a makeshift bed of hay and dried grass.

Just a place to bed down for the night, he thought, a temporary shelter from the elements, but it was hardly snug. Though the walls were made of stone, the floor was earthen, and water dripped in a steady stream from the floor above. It wasn't safe. The crossbeams were sagging either from age or the weight of the roof.

Dexter was taking stock, as well. He was sniffing the makeshift bed, going from one end of the cellar to the other. Finally, he flopped down beside Ash and rested his head on his paws, the picture of abject misery.

Ash went down on his haunches and scratched Dexter's ears. "Who did you hope to find?" he asked. "Was it Nell?"

Dexter's ears pricked, but that was all.

Was this where Nell hid out? Ash shook his head. The cellar didn't have the look of a place that was well used. The girl could be anywhere. There were scores of abandoned buildings like this in these rural areas.

He felt a pang of pity for the girl. She would be moving from place to place to evade capture. No one should have to live like that. He supposed it was better than Bedlam. He thought of his rooms at the Manor and the soft bed that awaited him....

Crimson drapes and a profusion of gold frogging and tassels.

The thought that had been turning in his mind suddenly came into focus, and behind that thought a spate of others: Eve, claiming that the girl was running from Angelo; Eve, braving the elements to take Dexter out—armed with a pistol? Eve, in his dreams, dreams that were so vivid they felt real to him.

How could she describe Sophie's bed so accurately? How could she know that Nell was running from Angelo? Angelo and Lydia. Angelo and Nell. Why was Eve always first on the scene?

He didn't believe what his brain was telling him. What man who prided himself on his intelligence would? But his brain was becoming corrupted by events.

He stayed as he was for a full minute, his head buzzing with a series of questions he could not answer. One way or another, he had to know the truth. But how...

At last, he heaved a sigh. He knew exactly what he had to do.

Nell didn't know where to hide. She had been running in circles all night, first from the bad man, then from the groundsmen who were searching for all the secret places she had made her own. The pain in her ankle was slowing her down, but she couldn't stop or they would find her, and bind her, and send her back to Bedlam.

All she wanted was to get as far from the searchers as she possibly could. But she couldn't go far. This was the only world she knew. Towns were dangerous places. Cruel people lived in them. The ladies up at the big house were kind to her. They left things for her—a sandwich, a piece of pie, an egg. But sometimes she was too scared to take them, because there were people about.

She paused and turned her face up to sniff the air. She could always catch the scent of anyone who was near her. That's when she would hide. The scent she liked best was the scent of Dexter. Animal scents didn't frighten her.

Her eyes widened in fear when she heard a sound on her right. Panic took over. Her feet had never moved faster; her heart had never pumped so hard. She could feel it burning a hole in her throat. Tears were streaming down her cheeks. The only thing that kept her moving was her fear of Bedlam, or what the bad man would do to her if he caught her.

It was raining again, but she hardly noticed. Trees, hedges, and shrubs flew past her in frenzied confusion. Even the pain in her ankle was forgotten, till she stumbled over a tree root and fell headlong, scraping her hands and knees on a patch of gravel. When she pulled herself up, she ached all over.

Ahead of her was a wooden fence. On hands and knees, sucking air into her lungs, she groped her way toward it. She didn't have the strength to climb over it, but she managed to squeeze between the lowest bars. The scent she was picking up was an animal scent. Horses? Donkeys? Goats? Her mind was numb, just like her body, but one thing she knew: animals were her friends.

Shivering, soaked to the skin, she crawled to the darkest corner of that enclosure and came upon a shelter, open on one side, that gave some protection from the driving rain. She gave a heartfelt sob when she felt the straw on the earthen floor. Maybe the good Lord hadn't forgotten her after all.

The animals were restless. They stamped their feet and snorted, letting her know that they didn't want to share their home with her. She was too tired to be frightened of them, too tired to care.

She sat on a cushion of dry straw, hugging her knees to her as she strained to see into the darkness. Long minutes passed before she relaxed and closed her eyes. She wakened when she felt warm breath on her cheek and almost panicked until she realized that the animals were curious about her. The next time she wakened, they had formed a little circle around her, sharing their warmth as though she were one of them.

She had found sanctuary with Anna's donkeys.

Chapter Sixteen

After changing into her nightclothes, she took a chair by the empty grate, ears straining for sounds of Ash. It seemed that every other minute she was looking at the clock, wondering what was keeping him.

He wouldn't have noticed her slip. His mind couldn't conceive of anything that could not be explained reasonably and logically, so if he pressed her to tell him who had told her about Lady Sophie's bed, she would reply that it came to her through servants' gossip.

That ought to give him something to think about.

Sighing, she stared into space and began absently to pick at her dressing robe. A confusion of thoughts buzzed inside her head, and she tried to put them in order. When she'd set off from Henley, she hadn't known Angelo existed. Her primary purpose in coming to London was to attend the symposium, then take in the Season so that she could accurately describe the ways of high society for her next book. At the back of her mind, however, she'd been thinking of her mother, hoping to discover the whereabouts of the quarry where Antonia fell to her death.

She'd been sure she was on the right track. Memories that had slipped from her mind had come brilliantly into focus. She dreamed constantly about that last night and the vision Antonia had put into her thoughts, that premonition about the future. It was all coming together, she'd thought then.

Suddenly, out of nowhere, Angelo appeared on center stage, and her focus had shifted to him. Her Claverley charisma, suppressed for so many years, had quickened to life. She'd been stupefied the first time her mind had locked on his, and electrified tonight.

Electrified, galvanized, and convinced that Antonia had seen this day coming. She had caught up to the future that Antonia had foretold.

And she was scared to death.

She wasn't a defenseless female! She had her charisma to guide her. Use it!

Angelo. She closed her eyes and used her considerable will to recall her impressions of their two encounters. She might not know his name or be able to recognize his face, but she'd taken his measure. He was like a two-year-old child. He couldn't control his temper, and when he was in a temper, he smashed things, *and* people. He was without remorse and thought the sun revolved around him. She remembered his choking rage and the fear behind it, fear of exposure. He wasn't mad. He knew right from wrong.

All those faces she'd seen. Were they his victims? She'd thought so at the time. How could she be so sure?

Where are you, Angelo? Who are you?

There was nothing but a memory of his remorseless rage.

Is that how it worked? Was it his rage that opened the door to his mind? Did she have to be near him? And why had his thoughts come to her? What was their connection? *They were connected.* The thought turned in her mind. The more she thought of it, the more convinced she became that she and Angelo were tied in some way.

His stories were set in stately homes and gardens. Was that how she knew him? Had she met him when she was visiting the gardens with her mother? It was so long ago, and her memories were very sketchy.

She was crossing the floor to the dresser where she kept Angelo's stories, when the doorknob rattled. "Eve?" Ash's voice.

"The door is open," she said.

Ash entered her room. His dark hair was wind tousled and damp from the rain. His boots were muddy. Though he seemed relaxed and was smiling, she never doubted for a moment that some strong emotion seethed just below the surface.

"You've been out in the rain," she said for something to say.

"With Dexter." He shut the door. "I'm afraid he's covered in burrs. He's with my man. Reaper will clean him up before he sends him back to you."

"You took my dog for a walk in the rain at this time of night?"

"Actually, he took me. He led me to what I think is Nell's lair, but there was no Nell. Now don't look like that. I don't think anything bad has happened to her. There were no signs of a struggle or anything like that. It's my opinion that she's safe and snug somewhere else, but that's only my opinion. What do you think?"

She was sure of it. If Angelo had caught up with Nell, his murderous thoughts would have reached out to her.

"Her lair? Where was this?"

"At the edge of the gypsy camp. But why ask me?" She stood her ground as he closed the distance between them. "Look into your crystal ball, Eve, and you tell me where your runaway is."

There was a long silence as she studied the harsh lines of his face. This was not the face of her dream Ash, that one special man in whom she could confide her deepest secrets.

"What?" His tone was derisive. "Nothing to say for yourself? No protestations of innocence?"

Her chin lifted a fraction. "Am I guilty of something?"

His voice rose a notch. "Damn right, you are! How could you know that Angelo was consumed with anger tonight? How was it that you were first on the scene when that devil attacked Lydia? How could you have known he was after Nell? And how could you possibly know about Sophie's Gothic bed?"

In contrast to his heated tone, hers was like ice. "Servants' gossip, in answer to your last question. As for your others, I've told you before. I'm a Claverley. We Claverleys sense things." She injected her voice with equal amounts of amusement and ridicule. "Do you really believe that I look into my crystal ball every time I want to know what someone is thinking or to foretell the future? Then why haven't we found Nell or Angelo?" She gave a credible laugh. "I can't believe what I'm hearing. You've never made any secret of the fact that you think reading tea leaves and crystal-gazing are nothing but flummery."

A look of doubt crossed his face, and he combed his fingers through his hair. "Put it down to fatigue. It's been a god-awful night." Her spine began to relax, then straightened at his next words. "But all this can be settled one way or another if you show me your back."

"What?"

"Show me your back. That's all the proof I need." He grinned when her jaw dropped. "I'll help you disrobe, and I promise to close my eyes until you tell me it's all right to look."

It took a moment for enlightenment to dawn, then, shaking her head, she backed away from him. His smile vanished as he followed her.

"Eve? Tell me it's not true. Tell me I imagined the birthmark on your shoulder. Tell me I was dreaming."

She stopped retreating when she bumped into the bedpost. "It's not possible." She spoke more to herself than to him. If he knew about the birthmark, he must have shared her dream or read her mind.

"What's not possible?"

She held out her hand, palm up, and pushed it hard against his chest. "Keep away from me, Ash Denison."

It was the wrong thing to say. In the unequal struggle that followed, she was no match for him. He turned her around and dragged both night robe and nightgown down in one impatient yank, then he went perfectly still.

His fingers touched her gently, hesitantly. "Your birthmark. The Claverley ruby." In the next instant, he turned her back to face him. "You've been putting thoughts in my head," he roared, "making me want you, tormenting me until I was mad to have you."

She wriggled and pushed to no avail. In truth, she was as shocked as he. He shouldn't have known about the birthmark. It was her dream, damn it! And her dreams were too personal, too intimate, and far too carnal to admit that they were hers. She felt guilty, mortified, but, above all, she felt trapped.

There must be a way out.

"You're hurting me," she said.

His fingers instantly relaxed.

"Thank you." She spoke as coolly as she could manage, although she felt at a distinct disadvantage when she was in her nightclothes and he was still fully dressed.

"I'm waiting for an explanation." His voice was gentle and at odds with the storm in his eyes. "You've been meddling with my mind, putting thoughts in my head."

Her brows lifted. "And how did I do that?"

"By distorting my dreams, not once but night after night. I should have realized what was happening. The dreams were so vivid, and you were so receptive, so passionate. But right before I had the chance to complete the act, you backed off and I woke up sweating like a horse. That's what you meant to happen, isn't it?"

She felt the color rise in her cheeks. Just thinking about her dreams was making her go hot all over.

His eagle eyes narrowed on her face. "So you do know what I'm talking about."

"I can't be held responsible for your dreams!"

"That's no answer. You were there, weren't you?"

She gave a supercilious smile. "I think you must be confusing me with Sophie Villiers or one of your many—"

The rest of her words were lost when he tumbled her on the bed. His face was only inches from hers. "I have never yet dreamed about Sophie Villiers, nor ever will. What is more, she doesn't have a birthmark on her shoulder."

"As you should know!" she interjected crossly.

He smiled grimly. "As I should know. It was you, Eve. You invaded my mind. Well, I want to know how you did it. I want to know *why* you did it."

She struggled to a sitting position, clasped her hands, and gave a helpless shrug. "It wasn't deliberate," she said. "I didn't know you were having the same dreams as I. I thought they were *my* dreams, but if you know about my birthmark, you must have been inside my mind."

He sat back, a look of disbelief on his face. "So it's true! You really were inside my head, meddling with my mind?"

She perked up. "Maybe my aunt told you about my birthmark?"

"You're not going to get out of it by blaming your aunt!"

Her eyes fell before his stare. "I don't know how it works. For all I know our dreams were different."

"Not if I saw and kissed your birthmark." He sounded angry. "Shall we compare notes?"

She glared at him.

"Are we dreaming now, Eve?"

"No," she said at once.

"How do you know?"

"Because now I feel awkward and embarrassed. I don't feel awkward in my dreams."

"Our dreams," he corrected. He paused. "How did you feel?"

She jiggled her shoulders. "If you were there, I shouldn't have to tell you."

"I'll tell you how you seemed to me." He captured one of her hands, opened her fingers one by one, and studied her palm. "You were the loveliest, most desirable creature that I had ever met. I couldn't resist you."

She had to say something in her own defense. "It was a dream. I can't be held responsible for what I said or did in my dreams." He was brushing kisses along her palm, and she was having trouble breathing. "As I remember," she said between breaths, "you encouraged me."

"Do you know what I think, Eve? I think the Eve and Ash in our dreams are more truly us. The people here in this room . . . well, we're only shades of what we could be, what we want to be."

The thought arrested her. Did she have the nerve to be that woman?

"Let's pretend this is a dream," he said.

"What?"

She squealed when he rolled with her on the bed and moaned when his smiling lips touched hers. He kissed her eyelids, her brows, her cheeks, the hollow of her throat, whisper-soft kisses that soon had her purring like a kitten.

"What comes next?" he asked.

"You know what comes next. It was your dream, too."

She tried to stop her inner trembling. He was beginning to look like the Ash in her dreams, the one person in whom she could confide all her secrets and deepest fears. Could she, dare she make that leap of faith?

"Ash," she began, but another kiss sent her thoughts scattering.

He relieved her of some of his weight and stretched out beside her. "We're on a grassy bank," he told her, "and the sun is shining. Can you feel the sun, Eve?"

She remembered only too well. Her face lifted to feel the sun's rays. A warm breeze heated her skin. She could smell the fragrance of new-cut grass.

Her brows knit. "It's only a dream, not real life."

Ash felt the change in her. A moment before, she had

been yielding. Now she was trying to regain lost ground. He wasn't going to let that happen. She'd done more than torment him in his dreams. She'd invaded just about every waking moment, as well. He couldn't look at another woman without comparing her to Eve, and Eve always came out ahead. The things he'd once admired in women had lost their luster. He wanted this difficult, intensely private, eccentric lady with the sharp tongue, whose gentlest touch could bring him to his knees.

She was also the only woman he knew who could make him quake with fear. She was a law unto herself and took the most foolhardy risks. Someone had to put her in leading strings, and, whether she liked it or not, he had appointed himself to the position.

Those lovely, expressive eyes were looking up at him with absolute trust. "Are you reading my mind?" he asked.

"No," she whispered. "I can't read minds. It's my sixth sense I want to talk about. You see, Ash—"

He silenced her by brushing his thumb over her lips. "We'll get to that later. For the moment, let's go back to our dream. You asked me to teach you about pleasure. Do you remember?"

She swallowed and nodded.

"Lesson one: Forget your troubles. They'll still be there tomorrow. Lesson two: Pleasure comes in giving, not in taking. Understood?"

"Ash—" She gasped as he rubbed himself erotically against her. "That wasn't in our dream."

"It would have been if it had been my dream." He did it again. "Don't you like it?" he crooned.

She nodded, then shook her head.

"I'll take that as a yes." He kissed her again.

Her hands spread against his ribs to push him away. Instead, she clutched at his shirt, dragging him closer. The dream they'd shared was only a pale imitation of what she was feeling, what she was experiencing. *Pleasure* was too hackneyed a word. Her heart was full to bursting.

Still kissing her, he opened her robe, then the bodice of her nightgown, and filled his hands with soft, womanly flesh. Her little cries of arousal raced from her lips to every pulse point in his body. His heart was thundering, his breathing was irregular, his body was on fire. He was ready to take her.

Appalled at the lack of finesse on which he prided himself, he rolled from her and flung one arm across his eyes. He gave a shaken laugh. "It's never been like this for me before," he said.

She raised herself from the pillows and lowered her face to his. "That makes two of us," she said. "It's never been like this for me, either." Then she kissed him.

It was the dream that made her bold. He wasn't the only one who had suffered the torments of unsated desire. Night after night she'd wakened, not knowing what she wanted except that it had to be Ash. Tonight she would be his and he would be hers. She refused to think beyond that point. Ash was right. Her troubles would still be there tomorrow. She'd deal with them then.

Ash forced his hands to be gentle as he cupped her shoulders. She was making love to the man in her dreams. What she didn't seem to realize was that he wasn't as docile or chivalrous or harmless as that man. In her dreams, she had tamed him into something she could manage. If he gave in to his baser instincts and took her the way he wanted, she would never look at him with such trusting eyes again. Holding himself rigidly in check, he answered the demand in her kiss with a restraint that surprised even himself.

Eve pulled back and looked down at him. A frown puckered her brow. "What is it, Ash?" she asked anxiously. "Are you unwell? You do look a bit pale. Am I too wild for you, too wanton? Is that it?" She gave a wry little smile. "Is it me? Or is it you?"

Ash was speechless. She thought that he lacked passion? That he had ice in his veins? That he was no match for her in bed? The devil with that!

She gave a cry of fright when he suddenly pounced on her. Between long, wet kisses, he got out, "You want passion? I'll show you passion, but don't say you haven't been warned. I'm not that paragon of chivalry you dreamed up. I'm a flesh-and-blood man, and I'm done with treating you like a priceless piece of china."

"Idiot!" she managed when he allowed her to breathe. "Isn't that what I've been telling you?"

They were smiling when their lips met, but as the kiss lingered, their smiles slipped away. His arms clamped around her, dragging her as close as they could get. She twined her arms around his neck and combed her fingers through his hair. It wasn't enough for them.

In quick impatient movements, he stripped her of her night things, then, swiftly rising, he started on his shirt. She went on her knees and helped him disrobe. There was no false modesty on her part. He'd seen her naked in her dreams, or were they his dreams? It hadn't worried her then and it didn't worry her now. She was caught up in the thrill of the moment, driven by dizzying needs she only half understood.

When he was down to bare skin, she sat back on her heels. He'd been naked in her dreams, but it was different then, foggy, unfocused. Now she saw him clearly. He was, she allowed, a fine figure of a man, but it had never occurred to her that he would have the powerful physique of an athlete. Her gaze traveled from his broad shoulders to his groin, and she stopped breathing altogether.

"Eve?"

Her eyes jerked up to meet his. He saw the uncertainty there and felt a knot of tension gather across his shoulders. He'd never wanted to please a woman as much as he wanted to please Eve. He didn't want to frighten her. The last thing he wanted was to frighten her. But he was a man, and she must see that his strength far outstripped hers. Could she trust him enough to put herself into his care?

"What are you thinking?" he asked softly.

"I think," she said, "that my dreams have led me astray. They didn't do justice to you, Ash."

He let out a telling sigh. Smiling, he snagged her wrist and spread her fingers over his chest. "Everything I am, everything I hold, is yours to command."

She raised her brows. "I'll remind you of those touching words the next time you scold me for not obeying your orders."

With a great whoop of laughter, he used his weight to carry her down on the mattress. Their playful bout of wrestling did not last long. He was hungry to know all of her, from the tips of her fingers down to her toes. She was carried away by the sheer magnitude of his desire, the wild and wanton demands of his lips and hands. Half-understood needs that had kept her awake long into the night were becoming unbearable. She was reaching for something but didn't know what it was.

He'd always felt that her cool exterior concealed a deep reservoir of passion. Now, as she gave him back kiss for kiss, touch for touch, he was dazed by her response and wanted more. Locked together, they rolled on the bed. Heedless with wanting, she arched into him. He tried to tell her to wait, that he didn't want to hurt her. She was too steeped in passion to care. Her fingers dug into his shoulders as her hips moved in unknowing appeal.

Breath heavy, he spread her legs and entered her. She went perfectly still. So did he.

"Ash?" she quavered.

He shut his eyes and gritted his teeth. One slow, careful thrust broke through the fragile barrier. She gave a shocked cry and sucked in a shuddering breath. He tried to soothe her fears with words, but he hardly knew what to say. He told her that he was as much a novice as she. He'd never been a woman's first lover.

"Except with you," he ended lamely.

A smile bloomed on her face, and she lifted her head to plant a kiss on his lips. "Don't look so stricken. I know there's a price for pleasure, and this time I'm willing to pay it."

He wanted to tell her that what they'd shared went beyond pleasure. He wanted to be intimate with her in the fullest sense of that word. How could he expect her to believe him? He had a reputation to live down.

Her nose wrinkled. "Is that all there is?"

He kissed the pout from her mouth. "No," he said. "Now we start over."

She was too impatient to start over. Her hands kneaded his shoulders, his back, his flanks. The little cries she made at the back of her throat made the blood pound inside his head. When she began to move her hips frantically, he could no longer resist what she wanted, what they both wanted. In the flickering candlelight, he watched as her eyes glazed over. His powerful arms locked around her, forcing her to match his rhythm, and together they went hurtling into the void.

He must have dozed, for when he wakened he saw the glimmer of a new dawn through the window. The candles were sputtering in their holders. If he didn't get back to his own bed, the servants would catch them in flagrante delicto. That wouldn't be a first for him, but he was determined that not a breath of scandal would touch Eve.

She mumbled incoherently when he slipped out of bed, but other than that, she did not waken. It took him only a moment to get dressed, then he stood, irresolute, staring down at the sleeping girl. She'd fallen asleep right after the loving, when he was in the middle of telling her that he would do right by her.

He drew the eiderdown up to cover her bare shoulders, brushed a kiss to her lips, then straightened. He didn't like the doubts in his mind or the feeling that had settled in the pit of his stomach. What did a man like him—a drone, a pleasure-seeker, a celebrated skirt-chaser—have to offer this vibrant, intelligent, lovely young woman?

He was cranky when he entered his own chamber, and even more cranky when he discovered Dexter sprawled on the middle of his bed. He tried ordering him off, but Dexter's response was to open one eye and show him his fangs. Undaunted, Ash shoved him to the edge of the mattress and climbed in beside him.

Still fully dressed, arms folded, with his back propped up by pillows, Ash contemplated the events of that night. He hadn't entered her room with the intention of seducing her. All he'd wanted was to see if she had the birthmark or if he'd only dreamed it. So, she had the birthmark. What did that prove?

"There must be a rational explanation," he told Dexter.

Dexter snorted and nestled closer.

But there was no rational explanation. A door was opening in his mind, a door that he was reluctant to go through. Eve Dearing was a Claverley. What else could she do besides play with his dreams?

He was still mulling over that thought when he drifted into sleep.

Chapter Seventeen

It was long after breakfast before Eve came downstairs. She felt a little awkward when she pushed into
the breakfast room, but there was no Ash. There was
only one person at the table and that was Miss Claverley,
and a footman to wait on them.

"Ah, Eve." Miss Claverley dabbed at her lips with her
napkin. "There's fresh tea in the teapot and I've saved
you a slice or two of toast. You haven't forgotten, I hope,
that we're going shopping with Liza this morning?
Everyone has gone upstairs to get ready, except Lydia
and Anna. She's feeling a little under the weather—
Lydia, I mean—and Anna is staying behind to keep her
company."

Eve sank down on the chair next to her aunt's and
thanked the footman for pouring her tea. Her smile was
a little thin. "It never ceases to amaze me," she said,
"how you can answer all my questions before I say a
word."

Miss Claverley beamed at Eve. "It's because I'm a Claverley, of course."

Miss Claverley set down her cup. "That reminds me," she said. "Lord Denison asked me to give you a message before he rode into town. What was it? Now, let me see. He has business with his steward in Richmond but he should be back in time for dinner." Miss Claverley frowned. "He said that you are not to go off on your own, no matter what the provocation. And he is right, you know. We were all warned not to go off alone after Lydia was attacked."

Eve knew that her aunt's words were meant for the footman. They dared not speak openly of Nell.

"Thank you, Roger," said Miss Claverley, nodding at the footman. "You may go."

As soon as the footman closed the door, Miss Claverley turned to Eve. Keeping her voice low, she said, "Anna found Nell this morning, and it all ended well."

"Where was she?"

"With the donkeys, in their little shelter."

Eve smiled so hard, she thought her face would crack. "I'm so glad. Is she all right? What about her ankle? What did she say about last night?"

"You'll have to ask Anna. All I had to do was give you the message. I feel privileged. I don't think Anna said anything to any of the others. The fewer people who know about Nell, the better, I suppose."

Eve let out a heartfelt sigh. "If there had been any trouble, I know Anna would have wakened me."

She reached for a slice of toast and a heaping spoon of marmalade. She felt as though a great weight had been lifted from her shoulders and she laughed. Nell had three champions now to look out for her—four, counting Ash. And where was that knave, anyway?

She'd come downstairs feeling hopeful, fearful, and a little bit awkward, wondering what she would say when they came face to face. Something wondrous had happened last night. Did he feel it, too?

Her aunt was looking at her with a speculative gleam in her eye.

"What is it?" asked Eve.

"You laughed," replied Miss Claverley, "and I haven't heard that lighthearted sound from you in a long time. Oh, in company you can put on a good show, but I know my Eve. What is it, dear? What's been troubling you these last weeks? Is it something to do with Antonia? I know you were hoping to find the quarry where she died. Can't you tell me, Eve?"

Eve had a perfect evasion ready. She could have mentioned Nell's name, but her aunt's words gave her pause, and her thoughts took a new direction.

She took a sip of tea, set down her cup, and came to a sudden decision. "Aunt Millicent," she said, "I've been having the same dream over and over and I don't know what to make of it."

"A nightmare?"

"No." Eve shook her head as she groped for words to explain her dream. "It frightens me, but it's not a nightmare."

Miss Claverley put down her cup and gave Eve her undivided attention. Those never-far-from-laughter eyes had become intensely Claverley eyes, arresting, measuring, knowing.

"Describe your dream, Eve," she said quietly.

Eve began with the setting—the ballroom, the dancers, the glass doors to the terrace, the gardens—and ended with her feeling of dread. There were no interruptions from her aunt, though sometimes Eve paused to search for words. When she had nothing more to say, she looked at her aunt with a question in her eyes.

Miss Claverley took a moment before she spoke. "What do you think the dream means?"

Eve sighed. "I think it was my mother's last message to me before she died." She shook her head. "No, I *know* that it was her last message to me. I think she was looking into the future and she wanted to warn me of danger. It's more than that." She thought for a moment before going on. "I can't avoid what's going to happen no matter how hard I try." She gave a feeble smile. "You can imagine that the first thing I do when I enter a house is sneak a look at the ballroom. I haven't yet found the ballroom of my dreams."

"What about the picture gallery here at the Manor?" Miss Claverley asked with a smile.

"It's up three flights of stairs and there are no glass doors giving onto the terrace."

Miss Claverley chuckled. There was another silence as she took a moment to reflect before she spoke. Finally she said, "I can't tell you what your dream means, Eve, except that you're right to take the danger seriously. But let me tell you what all those elements in your dream say to me. Nothing will be exactly the same when your dream catches up with you and you come to live through it. Everything is a landmark, a signpost, if you like, to get your attention and show you the way."

Eve screwed up her face. "That's it? That's all you can tell me?"

Miss Claverley edged forward in her chair. "It's a great deal, if you think about it. You'll know the moment your dream has become real if you stay alert to all the signs. Antonia would want to protect her daughter. She has given you a map. Follow it."

Eve debated about telling her aunt about Angelo, but the footman came in with a fresh pot of tea, and after he withdrew, Eve saw the change in her aunt. Her eyes had lost their Claverley intensity and mirrored nothing but anxiety.

She clasped Eve's hand. "You will be careful, Eve?"

Eve couldn't bring herself to add to her aunt's worries. "I'll be careful," she promised.

Before getting dressed for the shopping expedition, Eve detoured to Lydia's room. Lydia was dressed for the outing but had obviously changed her mind at the last minute. She was languishing in a chair like a Gothic heroine and the fire was lit.

Anna was keeping her company and came forward to usher Eve into the room. "We'll talk later," she murmured for Eve's ears only. "Wait for me when you leave."

"What did you say?" Lydia called out.

Anna replied, "I said that you had a restless night and weren't feeling you could cope with shopping and afternoon calls and so on."

Lydia gave an apologetic smile. "I don't know what has come over me. I think I must be coming down with something. I can't seem to stop shivering."

"What you need," said Anna, "is a change of scenery." To Eve, she went on, "I'm taking Lydia home with me. There's nothing like good Cornish air and sea breezes to put roses in one's cheeks."

Eve did not comment on Anna's pristine complexion that appeared untouched by the good Cornish air and sea breezes. She was more concerned about Lydia.

Though her wound was healing, she seemed more fragile as the days passed. Eve glanced at Anna. She didn't fit the picture of a motherly type, but her care of Lydia was unstinting, to say the least, and her concern for Nell was sterling.

"I think that's a wonderful idea," Eve said. "When will you go?"

"Oh, nothing has been decided yet. I must do what's best for my donkeys, you see. They can't walk all the way to Cornwall, so transportation has to be arranged for them, too."

Lucky donkeys, Eve thought. *Nothing but the best for them.* She imagined them in a gilded carriage, looking out the windows, waving like royalty. She hoped she and Anna had settled what to do about Nell before Anna went home.

Lydia interrupted her train of thought. "What do you think, Eve? Anna has found a boy to look after her donkeys."

"Really? When was this?"

"This morning," Anna said. "He was in the pasture with them, and they seemed to like him and he them. I hope he'll look after my donkeys, but nothing is settled."

There followed a long, considering silence.

"A boy?" ventured Eve at length.

"His name is Neil," answered Anna emphatically. She gave Eve a straight look. "I hope it works out. He's a wanderer, you know, a vagrant, and they don't like to be tied down. He may come to Cornwall with us, if I can get him to leave here."

Lydia said softly, "Cornwall is so far away."

When tears welled in Lydia's eyes, Anna shook her head. "Don't start worrying about Bertha," she said.

"She'll manage quite well on her own. And it's only for a holiday or until you regain your strength. If you go home to Warwick, you'll only be a burden to her."

To Eve, she added, "My donkeys are just what Lydia needs to take her mind off things. You can't think of your own troubles when you're taking care of these poor abused creatures. And once they learn to trust you, they are very affectionate. You'll love it there, Lydia."

Lydia gave a tearful sniff and nodded.

This new Lydia did not fit with the dasher Eve remembered from the symposium right up to the attack. The thought that she would do anything to have the old Lydia back was startling.

Lydia became quite tearful as Eve made to leave, saying how kind everyone had been to her and how little she'd done to deserve such friends. By the time Eve got out of the room, she was feeling horribly chastened.

She did not have to wait long for Anna. "Well?" was all she said.

Anna did not smile. "I found our runaway and did what I could for her. I'd brought apples for the donkeys, so I gave her those, then showed her a place in the loft where she could hide."

"What did she tell you?"

"Nothing. She was too frightened to say anything. I told her I would go back to the Manor and get food and blankets. When I returned, she was gone."

"Gone?" Eve shook her head. "But my aunt said it ended well."

"And so it did. She'll be back. Meantime, I've left the food and blankets in the loft for her. Trust me, Eve. I know what I'm doing. We have to be patient."

"I know, I know." Eve's anxious eyes searched Anna's face. "I can't help thinking of what happened to Lydia."

Anna reached for Eve's hand and squeezed it. "We can't force Nell to do what we think is best for her. She's like a wild thing. We have to trust her instincts."

Eve was still thinking of Nell as she descended the stairs to join the others on the shopping expedition. Liza caught up to her, looking as pretty as a picture in a blue velvet pelisse with a matching bonnet. Eve would have been satisfied if she could get Nell to comb and brush her hair.

Liza said, "I hear Lydia is not coming with us."

"No, she has decided that the outing would be too long and too wearing. She thinks she may be coming down with something."

Liza gave a short laugh. "And I suppose Dr. Braine will be dancing attendance on her? When Lydia crooks her little finger, he drops everything to rush to her side."

"What?"

Eve was so taken aback by this outburst that she halted on the stairs. Liza went on, stopped, then turned back to look at Eve. Hot color ran under the younger girl's skin.

"I beg your pardon," said Liza. "That was a childish thing to say. I know Lydia is not herself. Anyone can see what she has suffered. But I do think that Archie—that is, Dr. Braine—could remember his manners. I was not in Lydia's room to flirt with him. I thought I could help. Now I'm banished whenever he comes calling, just as though I were a child."

This little speech had Eve firmly suppressing a smile.

She descended the stairs to Liza's level and linked their arms. As they went on down, she said, "What do you care what Dr. Braine thinks? I know that Lydia enjoys your company. If you want to avoid the doctor, change the time of your visits."

"I suppose you're right."

Nothing more was said until they reached the bottom of the stairs.

"Do you know what vexes me?" said Liza. She didn't wait for an answer. "I admire him tremendously, as a doctor, I mean, and he seems to think I'm a flibberti-gibbet. Do you think it's because I've spent the last few years in Paris? Is it wrong to enjoy parties and balls and dressing up? The trouble with Dr. Braine is that he's a sobersides."

"He is a serious young man," Eve allowed, "but that's to be expected in someone in his profession."

Liza blew air through her nose. "Oh, he can be quite charming when he wants to be, but only if you are his patient. Now, if I were to break a leg—" She left the sentence hanging. Coming to herself, she smiled at Eve. "Will you listen to me? Anyone would think that I was sweet on old sobersides. Nothing could be further from the truth. I have plenty of friends who enjoy my company. I can't expect everyone to like me."

"No, indeed," Eve managed.

One of those young friends was waiting for Liza at the front door.

"You remember Jason Ford?" said Liza.

Eve acknowledged his bow. She remembered he was a former Special Branch agent who had set up on his own. She didn't think he was working today. From the comments that were exchanged, it was evident that Liza had invited him to be their escort.

Lady Sayers and Miss Claverley were waiting for them in the carriage, and who should be on the box but Ash's coachman! Eve noted also that the footman who held the door for them was none other than Reaper, Ash's valet. He shut the door after she, Liza, and Mr. Ford had stepped into the carriage.

It seemed that Ash was taking no chances with his little flock of pigeons. She was glad that Reaper was there to guard Lydia and Anna, Hawkins was driving the coach, and Mr. Ford was in the carriage. For her part, she'd left Dexter with the bootboy, with instructions to Andy to patrol the upstairs corridors—just in case.

But who was looking out for Nell?

There was nothing like a shopping expedition to raise a lady's spirits, Lady Sayers declared, and after a few hours of sampling the exclusive shops in Bond Street, everyone agreed with her. They returned home footsore, purses lighter and big smiles on their faces. Not unlike, Eve thought, the night they'd returned home from Vauxhall.

The stray thought took the glow from Eve's smile, and when they retired to their various chambers to gloat over their purchases, she didn't even bother to unpack the red satin pumps that had made her mouth water when she'd caught sight of them in the shop window. She was thinking of Lydia and the man who had attacked her.

Angelo.

Ash had asked her to read Angelo's stories with the hope that something untoward would strike a wrong note, so for the rest of the afternoon she went through them line by line. Nothing occurred to her. She wasn't done yet. She came at the stories again, this time filtering them through her aunt's interpretation of her dream. It made no difference. She could not find one single signpost that connected them to her dream, except the gardens themselves. It wasn't much, but it was all she had to go on, and a plan had formed in her mind, a plan she was eager to share with Ash. Then there was Nell. Her situation preyed on her mind and she wanted to hear what he had to say about that, too.

It wasn't until after dinner, however, that Ash returned to the Manor and her chance came to speak to him alone. She met him at the back door.

"Ash," she said, and that was all she managed to say.

He clamped his arms around her, swept her off her feet and swung her into a clump of ivy in the darkest corner of the courtyard. His weight pinned her to the wall. She made a small, incoherent sound that he swallowed with an all-consuming kiss. She tasted the brandy on his tongue, she smelled the clean scent of his soap, felt the heat of his body as he rubbed himself erotically against her, and she collapsed against him.

She wasn't given time to think. He opened the bodice of her gown. Warm hands molded to her breasts, and she felt her nipples hardening as he rubbed his thumb over each sensitive crest. Her head was swimming, her legs were buckling, she was mewling like a kitten. But when he began to raise her skirts, sanity returned in a rush.

She gave him a hard shove, but all that achieved was that he raised his head and looked down at her.

"Ash Denison," she panted. "What has got into you?"

"Don't you like it?" His smile was almost a leer. "Better get used to it, my love, for I've no desire to act like one of your tame heroes. What did you call them—accessories?"

She pushed at his shoulders and managed to get some breathing room. He was laughing. She was panting. "This isn't the time or place to play the fool!" she shrilled. "I have something *important* I want to say to you!"

"You're right. Let's make love and we'll talk later."

When he fondled her breasts again, she threw back her head and stifled a whimper. If this didn't stop, someone would catch them in flagrante delicto, just like the dairymaid and the stable hand in the story he'd told her. And wouldn't that be good for a laugh?

She fought her way clear of his arms and sucked air into her lungs. "Will you behave yourself?" she finally got out. "I want to tell you about Nell."

That sobered him. In an instant, he changed from a teasing, laughing cavalier into an alert, narrow-eyed predator. "What about Nell?"

"Anna found her with the donkeys. She's safe for the present, but how long will that last?"

She was having trouble buttoning her bodice. When he brushed her fingers aside and did it for her, she wondered, fleetingly, how many bodices he'd buttoned and unbuttoned in his time.

"Let anyone lay a hand on Nell," he said, "and they'll have to answer to me for it. I have friends in high places who owe me favors."

"What does that mean?"

"It means that I stopped by the offices of the *Herald* on my way back here and asked Brand to use his influence to have me appointed to the board of governors of St. Mary's of Bethlehem."

She was awed. "Can he do that?"

"Brand is well known in government circles."

A bubble of happiness started in her chest, spread out, and gurgled from her throat. "You are one of the most generous-hearted men I know," she whispered.

When it looked as though he was going to kiss her again, she ducked under his arm and quickly entered the house. He was right behind her. She slowed her steps in the long corridor that led past the kitchens. Servants were hard at work, cleaning up after dinner.

"There's something else," she said. "I want to show my father Angelo's stories. He may find something in them that I'm missing. He was, after all, sought after as a landscape gardener before he retired. And Brighton isn't so far away."

"I've been thinking along the same lines. I could post down there and be back in time for dinner tomorrow."

"Oh, no, this is my idea. And my father may be reserved with a stranger."

Ash nodded. "Fine. Tomorrow we'll go together." He cocked his head to the side. "Now can we get back to the conversation we were having?"

"We were having a conversation?" She gave him a sideways glance. "Is that what you call it?"

"Damn right I do! The language of love doesn't need any words. I'm fluent in it, but you could do with a little practice." His voice dropped to a whisper. "Why don't I bathe and change out of my riding clothes, then meet you in your room in, say, half an hour?"

At the foot of the servants' staircase, she turned to face him. "It's out of the question," she said.

"Eve—"

"It's my turn to sit with Lydia tonight. And even if it were not, you've moving too fast for me, Ash Denison.

Besides, I need a clear head when I meet with my father and stepmother tomorrow."

"Fine. I'll do my best to be an accessory."

He watched her mount the stairs with a crooked half smile on his lips. She wanted an accessory? He'd be a loaded pistol.

Chapter Eighteen

She hadn't expected to travel to Brighton in Ash's curricle. Brighton was almost a five-hour drive away, and the horses would need to be changed frequently. There was also the problem of the vagaries of the English weather. The sun was shining at breakfast, but who knew how long the fine weather would hold? A closed carriage would at least give them some protection from the elements.

It turned out that there was method in Ash's madness. There was room for only two people in the curricle, and he told her there was much he wished to say to her in private. This gave her a fit of the shivers. She hoped he wasn't going to ask her to marry him. So, they'd made love. He did this sort of thing all the time. He hadn't mentioned the word *love* and neither had she. Did he feel obligated to offer her marriage because she wasn't one of his dashers? That wasn't a good enough reason to marry.

Besides, she had her own reasons for hesitating. She

would only marry someone with whom she could be truly herself, without evasions. Ash was an intelligent man. He must have worked out that she was every inch a Claverley. The question was, could he accept it?

"Let's wait till you meet my father and Martha before we talk," she said.

Much to her surprise, no one objected to Ash's arrangements, not even her aunt. Eve had thought someone would raise the point that an unmarried lady did not travel with a gentleman unchaperoned. From the sly comments and winks, however, it was gradually borne in on her that everyone suspected they were going to see her father to ask his permission for them to marry.

She was thin-lipped when Ash flicked the reins and his team of bays jolted into motion. "What about your groom?" she said. "Isn't Hawkins coming with us?"

"My dear girl, what need have I for a groom? I'm with the intrepid Mrs. Barrymore, and she can outshoot, out-fence, and outgroom any man alive. Isn't that so?"

She remained silent, though she was tempted to laugh.

He was vastly amused. "Tell you what. If we get into trouble, you can act as my groom."

Eve couldn't hold on to her misgivings, not when the sun was shining and the breeze buffeting her cheeks was warm and fragrant with the scent of apple blossoms.

"Did you bring the newspaper cuttings?" he asked.

She patted her reticule. "Right here."

The Brighton Road was the most famous and fashonable stretch of the King's Highway in England, and Ash kept Eve entertained by pointing out various places of interest—where battles of old or duels were fought, where the famous of a bygone era lived or were buried, and where the Prince Regent was wont to lay his royal head before the new road to Brighton cut the duration of the journey from fourteen hours to its present enviable position.

"Without the Prince Regent and the Pavilion," he said at one point, "this would still be a country road passable only by oxen pulling carts."

The last stop on their journey was at the Crown in Cuckfield, where they dined on sandwiches and cake while the horses were changed. Twenty minutes later they were on the road again, and, from this point on, Eve became more and more withdrawn. Ash watched her for some time, then finally captured her hand and squeezed it.

"What's wrong, Eve? Why the sighs?"

She looked guilty. "Was I sighing?"

"Not audibly, but I have an inner ear that is sensitive to your change of moods."

She tugged her hand free. "You're beginning to sound like a Claverley." When his only response was a chuckle, she went on, "I was wondering whether I should have let my father know that we were coming. Martha doesn't like surprises."

"We're not here to see your stepmother but to see your father."

"Martha never lets him out of her sight."

"You worry too much," he said. "I'm the darling of society—your words, not mine. I'll charm Martha out of her sullens."

"Oh, you have nothing to fear. Martha stands in awe of people with titles."

Because he was attuned to her moods, he made an effort to draw her out. She answered his questions but sparsely. He learned that the house in Brighton had never been her home but was acquired by her father after his marriage to his second wife.

"That's when I went to live with my aunt," she said, "when they moved to Brighton."

"You didn't get along with the new Mrs. Dearing?"

She gave a grim little smile. "There were faults on both sides. It began the day she told me to call her 'Mama.' I suppose she meant well, but I couldn't do it. It felt as though I would be betraying my own mother. After that, things went from bad to worse."

"And your father?"

"He was never there. He traveled a great deal in his work, so Martha and I were left to our own devices. It was a great relief to us all when I went to live with my aunt." She pointed to a gap in the trees. "Look, we're almost there."

Ash decided this was not the time to awaken sleeping ghosts, and he obligingly looked where she pointed.

The house was on the eastern edge of Brighton, a red brick Queen Anne dwelling set in an extensive acreage of trees and shrubs. Formal flower beds marched with military precision across the sweep of lawn that led to the front door.

"Martha," said Eve, "is partial to the gardens of Versailles." She gestured to the flower beds. "This is her idea of Versailles in miniature. Papa, on the other hand, prefers the English style."

Ash looked at the flower beds and suppressed a shudder. "Poor Versailles," he murmured.

He drew up outside a stable that was meticulous in every detail, even to the groom who took charge of his team. In his friendly way, Ash tried to banter with the groom, but all he got in return was a look of faint surprise.

The front door was opened by a maid with a funereal expression that was reflected in her mode of dress. For a moment, Ash wondered if there had been a death in the family. The mistress, they were told, was indisposed, but the master was in his study.

The same military precision that was to be seen in the flower beds and stable was also present inside the house. Ash noted the formal groupings of tables and chairs, the uniformity of the rooms, the symmetry of the furniture and ornaments. There wasn't a thing out of place. He was tempted to drop his hat and gloves on a chair, except that he wanted to make a good impression.

"No need to announce me," Eve told the maid briskly. "My father knows who I am," and on that note of authority, she pushed into the room.

The study had a French door giving onto a sheltered courtyard with a fine view of a wilderness of trees, with no flower beds in sight. Set out on the courtyard were wicker chairs and small tables, and this was where Dearing ushered them after the greetings were over. It was the one place, Dearing said with a laugh, that he was allowed to smoke his pipe without bringing his wife's wrath down on his head.

He was, by Ash's reckoning, in his late fifties, but he looked older. He walked with a cane on account of his gout, and there was a decided awkwardness in his gait. If there was a resemblance between Eve and her father, he couldn't see it.

Eve and her father spoke in a general way for some time, catching up on each other's news, then Ash answered the question in Dearing's eyes and explained what had brought them to Brighton.

"I'm trying to locate the person who wrote these stories," he said. Eve fumbled in her reticule and gave Ash the cuttings. "His name is Angelo," Ash went on, "and we believe that these stories incited someone to commit murder."

Eve interjected, "The woman who was attacked is a friend of mine, Papa, a fellow writer, and he tried to kill her."

Dearing's eyes were cloudy with confusion, but he took the cuttings Ash offered him. "What is it you want me to do?"

"Read the stories, sir," said Ash. "They all take place in gardens. Perhaps there is something in them that will strike a chord with you."

Dearing nodded, but he set the cuttings aside and reached for his pipe. It was unlit, but he put it to his mouth and drew on it without appearing to realize that he was sucking on air.

Eve flashed Ash a look of desperation. To her father, she said, "I wondered if Mama had ever visited these gardens. They're all close to London. Perhaps she took me with her."

Dearing seemed to be absorbed in his own thoughts.

A note of urgency crept into Eve's voice. "Papa," she said, "whatever happened to Mama's notebooks? If she had visited these gardens, she would have made notes on them."

He frowned faintly. "You asked me that before." To Ash he said, "There was so much confusion when Antonia died. I asked the landlord at the inn to send on her boxes, but they never arrived. It seemed he asked the Messengers to deliver them. I had to chase them down eventually. Everything was there except for Antonia's notes. No one knows what happened to them."

"You mean the porters lost them?" said Ash, puzzled.

"No, no. The Messengers. You remember them, don't you, Eve? Thomas Messenger and his wife and children. They were staying at the same inn as you and Antonia. We'd had a falling out, so I was surprised he even agreed to take charge of Antonia's boxes."

He shook his head. "What a waste. He was a talented landscape gardener and would have gone far, but he drank too much. I did my best for him, but he wasn't dependable. In the end, the only friend he wanted was in a bottle. Even his wife and children came to mean nothing to him. Sad, isn't it?"

This long explanation seemed to tire him out and his eyelids drooped.

"Do you remember them, Eve?" Ash asked.

"Vaguely."

"Where are they now, Mr. Dearing?"

"Who?"

"The Messengers."

"Oh, we lost touch with the family a long time ago." He darted a glance through the French door. "Does Martha know you're here, Eve? You know she doesn't like to be kept out of things."

"Father," said Eve desperately, "read the cuttings, then I'll go and see Martha."

"Oh, I will. I promise." He puffed quite happily on his empty pipe. "The worst thing I ever did was retire," he said. "Martha isn't like Antonia. She's not interested in landscape gardening, so she never accompanied me on any of my commissions. It was a lonely life for her. If we'd had children, things might have been different." He seemed to drift off again, then slowly came back. "I never meant to give up my business entirely, but Martha wasn't well, and by the time I was ready to take up where I'd left off, other, younger men had passed me by and I was no longer in demand. Oh, I still get the occasional offer, but I can't seem to muster the interest to take anything on."

He stared vacantly into space, then gave a sudden start. "Eve," he said, "you know what she is like when she is taken unawares."

Ash's eyes narrowed on the other man's face. He was beginning to understand why Dearing had difficulty in holding on to one thought for any length of time.

"Eve," Dearing repeated. "Did you hear me? Tell her we have company. She'll want time to make everything nice and tidy."

Eve would have argued the point, but Ash silenced her. He got up and said in his easy way, "I think that's an excellent idea." He escorted Eve to the door. In a soft undertone, he went on, "It's better if you do as your father says. He seems to be distracted with the two of us asking questions. Leave him to me. I know what needs to be said."

She seemed to be reluctant to go, so he gave her a little push and shut the door on her.

Dearing, meanwhile, was on his feet. "My pipe has gone out," he said. "I'll just go and light it."

"Sit down, Mr. Dearing!"

The note of command in Ash's voice had Dearing stuttering a protest, but he did as he was told.

Ash took his own seat and pinned his companion with a hard stare. "How long," he said softly, "have you been addicted to opium?"

Dearing's jaw dropped. "Opium? No such thing! I

take the odd drop of laudanum to relieve my headaches, that's all."

"How often do you smoke your pipe?"

When the older man bit his lip, Ash nodded. "Your tobacco is laced with laudanum, isn't it? That's an old trick. You may be able to fool your wife and daughter, but I'm not nearly so gullible."

"What is it to you, anyway?"

Ash believed in live and let live. He had never wished to convert anyone to his way of thinking or living, but in this case he was prepared to make an exception. This man was Eve's father. His well-being was important to her, and what touched Eve touched him.

"Only this," said Ash finally. "I have no wish to hear my father-in-law described in the terms you used to describe Thomas Messenger. What was it you said? *In the end, the only friend he wanted was in a bottle. Even his wife and children came to mean nothing to him.* Is that how you want to be remembered, Mr. Dearing?"

"What father-in-law?" demanded Dearing testily.

"Why, Mr. Dearing, didn't you guess? My primary purpose in coming to see you was to ask your permission to marry your daughter."

The older man was still gaping when Ash got up. He picked up the newspaper cuttings and slapped them into Dearing's hand. "Read the stories," he said, "and tell me what you make of them."

He sauntered into the house and went in search of Eve.

Martha wasn't as indisposed as the maid had given out. This was only a small deception to put off callers without giving offense while the mistress of the house busied herself with what was really important. In this case, it was tabulating and inspecting every piece of linen in the upstairs linen room, and that's where Eve eventually found her stepmother.

When Eve entered, Martha looked up and clicked her tongue. "You may go, Dora," she told the young maid who was helping her. "I'm sure Mrs. Timmons could do with an extra pair of hands to polish the silver."

"Yes, mum," said Dora, and with eyes downcast, she hurried away.

The names Mrs. Timmons and Dora meant nothing to Eve. Domestic staff came and went in Martha's house with clocklike regularity. Martha was a demanding mistress, and few could meet her standards.

"You look well, Martha," she said.

Martha's thin lips flattened. "How kind of you to say so."

She was younger than her husband by a good fifteen years, a handsome woman with lustrous dark hair that was shot delicately with silver. But that was only a first impression. A closer look revealed a mouth that rarely smiled and eyes that were hard and cold.

She went back to counting her linens. "Your father is becoming very forgetful, as I told you in my letter. That was two months ago. But I suppose a celebrated writer has more important things to do with her time than visit her ailing father."

Eve could not understand why she could never summon the mettle to stand up to her stepmother. She was a grown woman. She had a full and rewarding life. More than that, she knew that she was not wanted here, unless it was to indulge Martha's need for a whipping boy. But Martha had only to pin her with a disdainful stare and she felt like a child again.

As a child, she had never felt safe when she was left alone with her stepmother. It wasn't that she was afraid of physical abuse. Martha would never stoop to that level. But something inside Eve seemed to wither. A slap would have been preferable.

"I've brought a visitor," she said, striving for normalcy. "Viscount Denison." Martha's only response was to raise her eyebrows, so Eve improvised. "He has a spread in Richmond and is thinking of employing a landscape gardener. He wants to ask Papa's advice."

The reference to Ash, an aristocrat, and his desire to seek her father's advice did not soften Martha as Eve hoped it would. Tight-lipped, Martha spoke to the linen napkins as she examined each one.

"Well, you brought him for no reason. Your father isn't well enough to talk about anything. Surely you saw that?" She looked at Eve contemptuously. "I thought I made it plain in my letter. Your father is sinking into senility, and I'm the one who is left to wait on him hand and foot."

Eve's face whitened and she stammered, "No. I didn't know. Your letter was very vague. But that can't be right. He's not an old man. What does the doctor say?"

"Doctor!" Martha smoothed out the napkins and set them on a shelf, then she turned to stare at Eve with her cold, hard eyes. "That windbag? Do you think I want my neighbors to know our misfortunes? And they would know if I called in Dr. Porter. He is nothing but a gossip-monger."

Eve looked blindly at her stepmother. "I can't believe Papa is senile," she said. She thought for a moment. "He was talking quite rationally a moment ago."

"What would you know about it? You're only here on one of your rare visits. I have to live with him."

Awash with guilt, Eve asked, "Isn't there another doctor you could call in? Someone more circumspect?"

"You're a fine one to talk about circumspect!" Martha stood with her knuckles braced on her hips. "Who do you think you are, arriving at my front door in a curricle with no maid or chaperon to accompany you? Oh, yes, my maid told me. What do you think people will say?"

"Nothing!" retorted Eve, conveniently forgetting that she had thought as much herself before setting out. "Viscount Denison is a respectable gentleman. For heaven's sake, Martha, we've been driving on the open road for most of the day! Only someone with a salacious mind would read anything into it."

Martha's cheeks turned an angry red. "A respectable gentleman, is it? Well, let me tell you, miss, I've heard of your goings-on in London, and Lord Denison is anything but respectable! He's a fortune hunter, with no money of his own, and the only thing you'll get from him is a slip on the shoulder!"

"Your mind isn't salacious." Eve's voice was dangerously calm. "It's depraved."

Heedless now, Martha looked as though she would spring at Eve. "And what about your mind, Eve Dearing? Don't you think I know that you're just like your mother? Antonia, with her airs and graces! Oh, yes, your father told me all about her. Her mind was unnatural, seeing into the future, making bargains with the devil! Whose fault is it that I'm childless? It's yours, you little witch! You cast a spell on me, didn't you, because your father preferred me to Antonia. And if that wasn't enough, you would read my mind before I knew my own thoughts and carry tales to your father. So don't talk to me about my mind."

Eve could have accepted Martha's harangue if it had been only against her, but Martha knew she could hurt Eve more by attacking Antonia. As a child, she had put her hands over her ears and run from the room. Now that she was older and stronger, she stood her ground and gave back thrust for thrust.

"You're right," she said. "I did read your thoughts, but I didn't cast a spell on you. You didn't want children, and you were going to make sure that you never had any. I didn't carry tales. If my father found you out, that wasn't my doing. I knew my father would punish me if he knew I had read your thoughts. I tried not to, but you made it so easy. You were always angry, you see, and I didn't know how to shut you out. But I do now.

"As for my mother—" Her voice broke and she cleared her throat. "Antonia used her gift to help people. I'm not so—" She stopped suddenly, bit her lip, and shook her head. "This isn't helping anyone. Can't we put the past behind us, for Papa's sake, and at least be civil to each other?" She put out a hand in a gesture of appeal.

"No!" Martha looked past her and cried in a pleading voice, "You see what she is? She's a witch!" Then more viciously to Eve, "It's a pity they stopped burning witches or both you and your mother would have come by your merits."

Eve didn't answer. She had whirled to face the entrance to the linen room. Ash was propped against the door, arms folded across his chest, looking as sardonic as she had ever seen him.

"In the first place," he said, "let me relieve your minds, ladies. Mr. Dearing isn't senile or anywhere near it. He has been dosing himself with laudanum to relieve his headaches. If I were you, Mrs. Dearing, I'd confiscate his pipe and tobacco. On the other hand, what has the poor man to look forward to in this happy home?"

Martha's face lost all its color. She opened her mouth, but it was only to suck air through her teeth.

"Where was I?" said Ash. "Oh, yes. In the second place, you were wrong about the slip on the shoulder. My intentions toward Eve are entirely honorable. Ask her father. I have just asked him for her hand in marriage."

Both ladies stood there staring.

Satisfied with the effect of his words, he held out his arm to Eve. When she placed her stiff fingers on it, he smiled into her eyes. "You have a lot to answer for, my girl," he said for her ears only, "but let's keep it until we're in more-civilized surroundings."

His eyes fastened on Martha. "I bid you good day, ma'am," and he led Eve from the room.

At the bottom of the stairs, they met Mr. Dearing. He looked angry, but his expression cleared when he saw them. He went to Eve and gave her a hug.

Holding her at arm's length, he said, "Well, well, Evie, you've made me very happy. It was more than time you were married. I know Lord Denison will take good care of you. Your Claverley cousins will give you up for lost now, and that's no bad thing. They're a peculiar lot."

Eve had felt crushed after the scene with Martha, but now she felt totally exposed. She'd wanted Ash to learn the truth about her, but not like this.

Dearing was no less effusive with Ash. The scene in the study seemed to have been forgotten.

When he could get a word in edgewise, Ash said, "About those newspaper cuttings I gave you, Mr. Dearing. I'd still like you to read them and tell me what you think. You can write to me at Grillon's Hotel. Here is my card."

"You're not staying for dinner?" Dearing put the card in his waistcoat pocket.

"Regretfully, no. I have a...uh...an appointment with the Prince Regent's secretary."

"What about tomorrow?"

Ash chanced a quick look at Eve but couldn't tell what she was thinking. "We'll be making an early start for town. Unfortunately, I have an engagement in London that I can't break, either."

Dearing nodded. "Martha will be disappointed. Martha." His brow furrowed. "Yes, there are a few things I wish to say to my wife."

They parted with Mr. Dearing expressing the wish that they have a long and happy life together and that they should visit again when it was more convenient, then he turned and began to mount the stairs.

Chapter Nineteen

They had expected to stay the night at her father's house. They were to learn that finding lodgings in Brighton when the Prince Regent was in town was as hard as finding a needle in the proverbial haystack.

This was the gist of what Ash was told by the landlords of the various hotels he applied to for accommodation for the night. Eve was all for making for London, even if it meant they'd be driving in the dark for the last hour or two. Ash wouldn't hear of it. He didn't trust the weather; he wouldn't risk his horses; he wanted his dinner; and he wanted a heart-to-heart conversation with Eve that was long overdue. That was the most important thing. He wanted to have that heart-to-heart talk with Eve.

Since they'd left her father's house, she'd become more and more withdrawn. He'd expected a fight on his hands over the prospect of their marriage, but she hadn't referred to it, not even obliquely, nor had she mentioned the ugly scene with Martha. She sat in a tight little ball in his curricle, like a whipped dog, and he didn't know how to draw her out.

The quarrel with her stepmother seemed to have crushed her spirit. Had he entered the fray, things would only have degenerated to Martha's level. What he'd been tempted to do was put a gag in her mouth, and he supposed that's what he had done when he'd told her that he was going to marry Eve. Not only had he silenced Martha, but he'd also silenced Eve.

They ended up in the posting house in Cuckfield where they'd changed horses on the last leg of their journey to her father's house. The landlady's brows twitched when he asked for rooms for himself and his sister, a subterfuge he was forced to employ when Eve had no maid or chaperon to safeguard her reputation—his fault, as she reminded him crossly while they mounted the stairs.

The rooms they were shown were unacceptable, in Ash's view—a cramped bedchamber for Eve and a room across the hall that was no bigger than a box for him, where a trundle bed had been set up.

"My dog's kennel is bigger than this," he protested.

The landlady shrugged. "Take it or leave it. This is all I have left."

Eve rallied a little when their baggage was brought up, a commodious leather case for him and a small hand grip for her.

She stared at the case as the boy heaved it into the boxlike room. "What on earth did you bring with you?" she asked incredulously.

"Oh, whatever my valet packed for an overnight stay. And you?"

"The same." She picked up her small grip and walked into her chamber.

There was a spark of amusement in her eyes, and that pleased Ash immensely.

The spark of amusement faded when she closed her chamber door. The scene with Martha had done more than crush her spirit. She felt naked, stripped of every defense, like a spy in an enemy's camp whose identity had become known. It wouldn't have mattered nearly so much to her if Ash hadn't been present, but he'd heard enough of Martha's vile words to put the worst possible interpretation on her Claverley heritage.

As for herself, it had taken her years to throw off Martha's contempt and be comfortable in her own skin. Now she felt like a child again.

The boy came in and lit the fire. Without being aware of what she was doing, she sank into a chair and watched the flames lick round the kindling. *She's a witch! It's a pity they stopped burning witches!* Her stepmother's words drummed inside her head. Martha wasn't the only one who had called her a witch. So had Dulcie, her best friend, but that was years ago, when Antonia was alive. That's when she'd begun to reject the Claverley charisma. But no matter how hard she'd tried, it would flare to life when she least expected it.

Her thoughts shifted to Ash. On the long drive to Cuckfield, she'd waited for him to make some reference to the blatant lie about their forthcoming marriage. She'd hoped...It didn't matter what she'd hoped, because if his only reason for offering to marry her was to do the honorable thing, she wanted none of it.

She didn't know what she wanted. She didn't know what to do. He was in the mood to bombard her with questions, and she didn't know how to respond.

It all came down to wanting his good opinion. Why

in blazes did it matter so much to her? Why couldn't she be herself?

The chambermaid arrived with a jug of hot water, and Eve got up. Maybe when she'd freshened up and changed her gown, she'd find her balance again.

As soon as the maid left, she began to strip out of her clothes.

There were no private parlors in the inn, so they were forced to dine in the public dining room, a small, crowded chamber with barely enough candles to show them who was sitting at the next table. This suited Ash. His being alone with Eve so far from home, in a public hotel, could easily start tongues wagging if they were recognized.

He insisted that she take a glass of wine and kept up a monologue of trivialities while they waited for their dinner to be served. Eve sat in silence with no pretense of listening to a word he said. Finally, he lost patience with her.

"I told you to drink your wine," he said.

She gave him a smoldering look, but she raised her glass and took a long swallow. "Satisfied?" she demanded.

"No. You're not going to put me off by hiding behind a wall of silence."

"I don't want to talk."

"It's too late for that. Too much has been said. Too much has happened. I have a right to know what's going on."

Her chin came up. "What right?"

"Have you forgotten so soon? We're engaged to be married."

"I don't remember agreeing to any such thing."

He almost sighed with relief. She was beginning to come to life again. Crossing swords with him was the next best thing to a tonic. Good. He came at her again.

"You agreed when you didn't contradict your father when he wished us happy and a long and prosperous future. Why didn't you, Eve?"

She adjusted her table napkin. Without looking up, she said, "He was happy for once. I didn't want to disappoint him. And how could I put him right without a long, involved explanation? He wouldn't have understood."

"Too late now. We're stuck with each other."

Her shoulders lifted as she inhaled deeply. He braced for a blistering setdown, but she merely let out a shivery breath and raised her glass to her lips.

The amusement in his eyes softened. He'd won the first round; now it was time to go gently with her, if she'd let him. "Eve," he said softly, "I'm not your enemy, and I'm not a fool. I can accept one or two incidents that I can't explain. I can even accept what happened in our dreams, but after that incident with Martha, I'm at a complete loss. I don't know what to think or what to believe. Help me to understand."

"Are you sure you're ready for this?"

In fact, he wasn't sure. He was a rational man, a skeptic by nature, and the workings of a woman's mind had frequently baffled him. But this was different. Eve was his woman. It didn't matter what he believed but what she believed.

He reached across the table and grasped her hand, bringing her eyes up to his. He was shocked at how fragile they seemed. "Eve," he murmured, "I'm not going to judge you."

When fire flashed in her eyes, he quickly released her hand and sat back in his chair. Obviously, he'd said the wrong thing.

Her voice was low-pitched but fierce for all that. "You mean as you judged my aunt? Reading palms and crystal-gazing—that's always good for a laugh, isn't it? Don't you think I've seen how you roll your eyes whenever I mention my Claverley intuition? Don't tell me you won't judge me!"

"I never roll my eyes!"

"Not literally. But you're not willing to accept me as I am. Don't you think I know it? You reason away anything you don't understand. Oh, you might as well get it over with. I won't lie to you or try to evade the truth. I'm beyond that now."

He took a sip of wine, then another. He didn't want to upset her any more than she already was, but this chance might never come again. When Eve had herself in hand, those formidable barriers that kept him at a distance would be firmly entrenched again.

She looked at him over the rim of her glass. "Well?"

That was all the encouragement he needed. "Martha said you read her thoughts. Can you see into people's minds and read their thoughts, Eve?"

"No. Not exactly. I can't pick on someone and decide I want to read their thoughts. Occasionally, though, someone's thoughts push into my mind and I can't stop it from happening, not once they're in. I can't eavesdrop on strangers, or even those who are close to me." She shook her head. "I thought I'd got over it." More fiercely, "I did my best to get over it. It's only recently that it's started up again."

Suspend judgment, he told himself. *Keep an open mind. Just listen.*

She met his eyes. "'The Claverley charisma,' my Claverley relations call it. It means *gift*."

He nodded. "Yes, I'm familiar with the Greek."

"Of course, you would be, an Oxford scholar. It can be a curse as well as a gift."

In as soothing a tone as he could manage, he said, "Explain it to me so that I can understand. When did it start? How and when did it start up again?"

His soothing words had the opposite effect to what he intended. "You don't have to coddle me. You won't need to worm anything out of me. I told you, I'm beyond lying and evading the truth."

"Fine!" He answered her in the same irritable tone as she had used with him. "But my question still stands. When did you first get the gift and when and how did it start up again?"

Their first course arrived, beef broth with barley, and she delayed replying until after she had taken a mouthful. "You have to understand," she said, "that as Claverleys go, I was not exactly at the top of the class. We all have the gift in varying degrees. My mother, Antonia, was the most gifted of us all, but even she couldn't read people's minds at will. We don't choose our subjects, they choose us—oh, not deliberately but unawares."

She took another mouthful of soup. "I had progressed a little beyond my aunt's level when the most catastrophic event of my life happened."

After a silence, he said, "Your mother died."

She nodded and absently stirred her soup. Without looking up, she said, "When I was twelve. And when the year's mourning period was over, my father married Martha. She came to live in our house—my mother's house, I thought. My father was away a good deal of the time." She looked up. "You heard Martha. You saw what she is like. Because of the Claverley charisma, I was made to feel like a witch—worse, a freak of nature. There was no way we could live together. So I went to live with my aunt.

"But before that, I learned that people were afraid of my gift and I had to keep it a secret. I played too many tricks on my friends—you know what I mean, showing them how clever I was."

"Doing what?"

Her lips thinned. "What do you think? Reading tea leaves and palms! No crystal-gazing, you'll be disappointed to hear. Antonia was the only Claverley who could see into the future, and she didn't use a crystal ball." She shook her head. "It wasn't long before I had no friends. They thought I was weird." Looking up, she went on, "But it was my father who had the greatest influence on me. He felt uncomfortable with a wife and daughter who had visions, and he made us feel uncomfortable. That's when I made up my mind to disown the Claverley gift and become an ordinary girl."

"And you turned it off, just like that?" He sounded dubious.

She gave a short laugh. "There wasn't much to turn off. As I said, I hadn't progressed very far. When I stopped reading tea leaves and palms, all I was left with was my intuition."

"No voices?"

Her brow wrinkled. "I wouldn't call them voices. Occasionally, I could sense someone's thoughts, and I had the most vivid dreams."

"Yes. We both know about that, don't we?" When she glared, his smile died and he moved on to something else. "You said you were supposed to keep your gift a secret. Miss Claverley doesn't keep her gift a secret."

"Only because people think she has mastered a few parlor tricks. They don't take her any more seriously than they would a gypsy telling fortunes."

He didn't want to dwell on the subject of Miss Claverley or fortune-telling. "Eat your soup, Eve. It's getting cold."

Ash topped up their glasses, then gently led the conversation back to where they had left off. He was more careful now, because this was what he really wanted to hear.

"So," he said, "you stopped using your Claverley talents when you were twelve years old, but recently they have started up again?" He left his question hanging, because he didn't want her to see him as a policeman pumping her for answers. He wanted her to know that he had her best interests at heart.

She raised her chin in what looked to him like a gesture of defiance. "The night Lydia was attacked," she said, "someone's thoughts burst into my mind. He was absolutely livid. He was going to kill her. That was how I managed to save her. I knew he was down there before I opened my window.

"The second time I heard the voice, I knew it belonged to the man who had attacked Lydia. Once again, he was livid. He wanted to kill the girl who he thought could identify him. He doesn't know her name is Nell or that she is a runaway from Bedlam. He thinks she is a tinker."

She touched Ash's hand briefly. "I blame myself for putting Nell in danger. She comes out at night to collect the food I've left out for her. I think the night Lydia was stabbed, Nell was coming to the cellar door. The second time, she was on her way to the herb garden. That's what brings her to the Manor—food. It never occurred to me that that villain would return after he tried to kill Lydia. And Nell saw him both times. He knows that."

"*Can* she identify him? Did she see his face?"

"No. She said it was too dark, but he doesn't know this. That's why he wants to kill her." She looked steadily into his eyes. "She's not a good witness. She could never give evidence in a court of law. They would send her back to Bedlam, and she would rather die than go back there."

"She'll never go back to Bedlam," he said, "not if I have to tear it down brick by brick."

His stern avowal brought a fleeting smile to her lips. "I worry about her," she went on. "She can't stay here, not as long as that devil is free to come and go as he pleases. But short of capturing her and abducting her, I don't know what to do."

"I'll increase the number of groundsmen on night patrol and put them on shifts. Angelo won't get past them. And I'll tell them not to go chasing after tinkers or gypsies."

"I wish I had shot him when I had the chance! I won't make that mistake again."

Her fierce words made him smile, but he was disturbed all the same. "Any other episodes, Eve?" he asked easily. "Were there other voices?"

She picked up her glass and studied the ruby-red wine. Her voice was clipped. "Two more," she said. "One you know about. I didn't hear Lady Sophie's voice, but the pictures that came into my mind were very entertaining."

He winced and quickly moved on. "And the other?"

"Martha's voice, after you told her that my father was lacing his tobacco with laudanum." She took a sip of wine before continuing. "It's not true and she knows it."

"What?"

"Oh, I'm not saying that he doesn't take the occasional dose of laudanum for a headache, but that's as far as it goes. It's Martha who has been lacing his tobacco, and now that he knows—and who else could it be?—there will be the devil to pay."

He was appalled. "Why would she do such a thing?"

"Not to harm him. She doesn't want him to accept any commissions, because she doesn't want to be left alone. She has no friends to keep her company, only my father. The laudanum dulls his senses and makes him dependent on her."

"That woman is..." He couldn't find words strong enough to describe Martha.

"Yes. Isn't she?" She looked at him with a question in her eyes. "How did you know that my father was taking opium? It never occurred to me."

A brooding look came into his eyes. Finally, he sighed. "You once asked me about my mother," he said. "Angelo was right. She was a fragile flower in a wasteland. She had only one use to my father, and that was to breed sons. Unfortunately, she didn't have the stamina. After the last child was stillborn, she retreated into opium. It was the only way she could cope."

Stricken, she said, "I'm sorry. I didn't know."

His voice was flat. "Why should you? No one was supposed to know. My father was a proud man. He pretended that my mother suffered from nerves as a result of losing so many infants. In a sense he was right. She slipped into melancholy, then turned to opium."

He brought his glass to his lips and took a long swallow.

"I...How old were you when she died?" she asked softly.

"Fourteen. She died in my arms. I can't remember where my father was. I came home from school for the holidays. Like Harry, she was left to the care of a nurse. My grandmother would have nursed her, but there had been a falling out with my father and she was forbidden to enter our house."

He dipped his head so that she was forced to look into his eyes. "It happened a long time ago. I don't often think of those bad times now."

She saw how it must have been in that desolate wasteland that was Ash's home. He was the buttress that supported both his mother and brother. Who else could they turn to? That was too big a burden for a young boy's shoulders, yet not once had he cursed his misfortunes or complained about the hardships he'd willingly embraced. He met life's vagaries with a smile and a shrug. He wasn't shallow, as she'd once thought. He was as solid as a rock.

"That's why," he said, "I got so fired up when I read Angelo's story. He seemed to know my family well."

The waiter removed their soup plates and soon after, their dinner arrived, steak pie, boiled potatoes and Brussels sprouts. There was no menu to choose from. This was a small inn and all the diners were served the same meal. Ash brought a hearty appetite to his, Eve picked at hers.

"Why Angelo? That's what I don't understand. Why is it his voice you hear?"

"I don't really know but I think, and I'm only guessing, that we're connected in some way. He sets his stories in gardens. Maybe that's the connection."

"But you didn't recognize the settings in his stories?"

"No. But when you've visited as many stately gardens as I have, they all begin to look alike."

He thought for a moment. "No other voices, Eve?"

She shook her head. "Don't you think I've racked my brains trying to think of how I could possibly know a murderer and how he could pass his thoughts onto me?" She set down her knife and fork. "I've been in the Old Bailey as a spectator at a murder trial and no stray thoughts penetrated my mind."

"What does Miss Claverley say about these voices you hear?"

"Only one voice. I haven't told my aunt because I don't want her to worry about me." She exhaled a long breath. "To be perfectly honest, I'm confused. The Angelo who pushed his way into my mind is afraid of exposure. He is heartless, Ash, a cold-blooded killer who will do anything to conceal his identity. The stories in the *Herald*? They're about him, and he wants to silence whoever wrote them before more stories are published. He knows he'll end up on the scaffold if he's found out, and he'll kill anyone in his way to prevent that from happening."

Ash leaned back in his chair as he considered her words. Finally, he said, "I can see why you're confused. Why would Angelo publish the stories if he were afraid of exposure?"

"That's what has me puzzled."

He leaned toward her. "Did he kill Harry?" His voice was harsh.

Hers was gentle. "I think so. And not only Harry. I saw more than three victims."

"What was his motive?"

She was beginning to feel harried. "I don't know. Revenge, I think, for making him feel small."

"You *think*? That doesn't help." His brows snapped

together and he stared absently at a small spot on the tablecloth.

"Maybe," she said, testing him, "it's all a figment of my imagination. Maybe my visions are only dreams and I've read too much into them. Maybe my voice comes from my own thoughts."

He was still thinking of his brother and missed the intense look in her eyes. Suddenly she pushed back her chair and got up.

"We're done here, aren't we?" Her voice was clipped. "I've told you everything I know and I'm quite worn out. If you don't mind, I'd like to go to bed."

He was startled by the change in her. One moment she seemed relaxed and the next she seemed as brittle as crystal.

"Stay and finish your dinner," he said. "There's a lot more I have to say to you."

"Say it tomorrow. I'm not hungry, and I've had all I can take for one day."

She turned and left him before he could think of one thing to say to keep her with him.

Chapter Twenty

She couldn't be still. In that small room she felt like a caged animal, pacing back and forth, with no means of escape. Though the embers in the grate were still glowing, she felt shivery and, after rising from her bed, had donned her robe to stave off the chill. Knowing that she could not sleep, she'd lit the candle on the mantelpiece with some idea of reading the book she'd brought with her, but she could not settle to read. Her thoughts were chaotic, except that they involved Ash Denison and the conversation they'd had over dinner.

She was calling herself all kinds of a fool for letting down her guard and sharing her deepest and darkest secret with the world's most confirmed skeptic. But it seemed as though he was already half convinced. So she'd taken a chance on him. She should have known better. His silence had proved how wrong she was.

Maybe it's all a figment of my imagination. Maybe my visions are only dreams and I've read too much into them. Maybe my voice comes from my own thoughts.

That was the moment for him to make some grand gesture to demonstrate his faith in her. All she'd got was silence.

She threw herself into a chair and after a moment got up again. Her throat hurt. Her head ached. She knew why she was in such a state. She'd wanted him to be the same kind of buttress for her as he'd been for his mother and brother. That was the kind of love she wanted and was willing to give. If she couldn't have that kind of love, she didn't want anything.

She was debating whether she should give in to a bout of weeping when someone knocked sharply on her door. "Open the door, Eve. I know you're awake. There's a light coming from under your door."

Ash's voice.

"Go away! I was just going to bed."

"If you don't open the door, I'll kick it in."

"What," she said, mocking him, "and take the shine off your immaculate boots? What would your valet—"

She fell back with a cry when the door burst open and Ash swept into the room. He was wearing a dark cloak and brought the fresh scent of the rain and the wind with him. His black hair was windblown; rain-drops beaded his lashes, but it was his eyes that trapped hers in their fierce stare.

"I've been out walking," he said, "trying to figure out why you and I always come to a stalemate. Do you know what conclusion I've reached?"

Something in that hard stare warned her to be cautious. "N-no."

"We talk too much."

With that, he seized her by the shoulders, jerked her forward, and crushed her mouth beneath his. She was too stunned to struggle, then too overwhelmed by the instant leap of all her senses to do more than cling to him for support. When she did struggle, finally, it was only to free her arms so that she could twine them around his neck.

He kept her locked in that embrace as he maneuvered her to the bed. Raising his lips an inch from hers, he said harshly, "I don't want to talk about your relations or my relations. I don't even want to talk about us. Understood?"

"Be quiet," she muttered, and going on tiptoe, she fastened her lips to his.

She wanted him. The thought didn't surprise him. He'd known it for a long time, but he'd never expected her to surrender with such instant abandon. Or was it he who was surrendering? He didn't care. Eve, pliant, passionate, wanting him as much as he wanted her, made his head spin. He was dazed by her response.

The ache inside her didn't give her a chance to debate or argue or have second thoughts. She was made for this, made for him. There was no turning back. Her heart was racing, her body was melting, her skin was on fire. Every nerve, all her senses recognized this one man and welcomed him without reserve. Ash, only Ash.

When they broke apart, they were both breathing hard, both out of breath, out of words, and out of patience.

"Eve?" he murmured.

He didn't have to ask twice. She began to undo her robe. He threw off his jacket and began to undo the buttons of his waistcoat. Laughing now, they disrobed in a tangle of limbs and shed clothes. When they were down to bare skin, they sprawled on the bed.

She was wild to have him, and he was wild to give her whatever she wanted. She reared over him and showered him with open-mouthed kisses on his face, his throat, his shoulders. His body fascinated her, the way his muscles clenched when she brushed them with her fingertips, the lean waist, the powerful thighs, the jut of his sex. Her fascination carried her too far. On a pent-up groan, he toppled her to the mattress and surged over her.

"It works both ways," he muttered, and took the same liberties with her as she'd taken with him.

Stroking, nibbling, kissing, he exploited every sensitive spot on her body. Helpless with wanting, she dragged him over her and arched against him, showing him what she wanted.

He tried to prolong the moment. He wanted to capture the image of her as she was now and impress it forever on his mind: the candlelight gilding her skin; cheeks flushed with desire; her dark hair spread in wild abandon across the pillow; her eyes dazed with all the sensations he and only he had ever aroused.

His heart suddenly clenched, and he gathered a fistful of her hair and rubbed it against his cheek. The scent that was uniquely Eve's filled his nostrils, his lungs, his head. He was dizzy with wanting her. He couldn't tell her what he was feeling or what she had come to mean to him, because he couldn't explain it to himself. All he knew was that he had never wanted like this or ached like this. She was his mate, and he would do whatever was necessary to convince her of that truth.

She sensed that he was on the point of speaking, and she couldn't allow it. She wanted nothing to shatter the bubble of happiness that beat frantically in her heart. She didn't want to be sensible or think of consequences. There was no past and no future. All they had, all she wanted, was the present moment. She was going to make it last her a lifetime.

Her whimpered plea tore at the remnants of his control. "Wait!" he murmured, but she wouldn't listen. With her hands on his shoulders, she urged him to cover her. Gritting his teeth, he parted her thighs. When he drove into her, her back arched from the mattress, then she wrapped her arms and legs around him and locked his body to hers.

She was past wanting gentleness, and he didn't give it to her. Her little cries of arousal made him rougher than he meant to be, but she didn't mind. Deliberately, wantonly, she set the pace. At the end, there was only sensation and the sweet, shattering release.

They lay there for long minutes, trying to catch their breath. His face was buried in the crook of her shoulder. She was so boneless that she didn't have the strength to push him away, though his weight was crushing. Sensing her distress, he slipped from her body and lay stretched out beside her, propped on one elbow so that he could see her face.

She lifted her lashes slowly and smiled into his eyes. The look in her eyes told him everything he wanted to know.

"How do you feel?"

"Mmm," she breathed out. "If this is a dream, I don't want to waken."

It had happened so fast, she thought, without time to consider whether she was doing the right thing. Now that reality was beginning to intrude, she felt a ripple of unease, a small ripple that she instantly quashed. He knew what she was and he accepted it, or he would not have made love to her.

Would he? She had to know.

She said carefully, "This surpasses all my dreams about you."

He laughed and dropped a kiss on her brow. "When we are married, we won't need dreams. We'll be in each other's arms every night."

She smiled and let an interval of silence go by. "You know, my father never wanted to hear about my mother's dreams. He could never accept that she was different, gifted—you know what I mean. It made him very uncomfortable."

He kissed her throat. "I can see why it would. Men don't have the same sensibilities as females. They don't rely on intuition, only on their animal instincts and what their brains tell them."

"My mother did not lack intelligence!"

He realized, belatedly, that this was no idle conversation, the sweet nothings lovers exchange when sated with love. This was a trap to ensnare him. "That's not what I said and that's not what I mean. I'm well aware that your mother was gifted."

His words mollified her, but only slightly. "Do you believe in my gift, Ash—I mean that I heard Angelo's voice and have dreams and visions?"

He said helplessly, "What is it you want me to say, Eve? That I have no doubts? That wouldn't be true. All this is new to me. Of course I find it hard to accept. I'd like to explain it away, but I can't."

When she pulled herself to a sitting position, so did he. "Eve," he said quietly, "what difference does it make? You take it seriously, so I'm prepared to take it seriously, too. All I care about is us. Don't you know that I'm willing to take you on any terms?"

She felt a pain in her chest and used the heel of her hand to massage it away. Her voice was so low, it was almost inaudible. "I'm sure my father said much the same thing to my mother when he married her. It didn't work out that way. When you can't tell the person who is closest to you what you are truly thinking and feeling, something precious is lost."

He clasped her shoulders. "I am not your father. I'm willing to be convinced. More than that, I'm willing to act as though I *am* convinced."

"That's not my point," she said. "You say that now, but I've experienced firsthand how it works. Do you know why my aunt has never married, and not only my aunt but many of my Claverley cousins? It's because they've been disappointed in love. No man or woman wants to marry a freak." Her voice trembled and turned bitter. "We learn the hard way to keep our secret locked tightly away. My mother took a chance on my father and, oh, how she paid for it."

She looked at him and shook her head. "I can't marry you, Ash. For both our sakes."

He kissed her then, with a violence that left her shaken. When he pulled back, that same violence was in his eyes. "You think it's that easy? Don't you know anything? We have only to be in the same room and the atmosphere becomes charged. I have only to touch you and you begin to tremble. Hell and damnation, I begin to tremble, too. Even when we're apart, you're with me. I can't get you out of my mind. Isn't that how you feel about me?"

She wanted to say no, but she couldn't get the lie past her lips.

He nodded. "I think you're beginning to see reason. Here's another reason, if you still need to be convinced."

He pushed her back against the pillows and his hands began a slow sweep, from her shoulders, lingering at her breast, trailing to her waist and to the heat between her thighs. He smiled when she gasped and her fingers dug into his shoulders, but he would not be hurried. Slowly, deliberately, he kissed his way up to her lips again.

The brush of his lips had her shifting sinuously beside him. Eyes on his, she said on a thread of sound, "You can't...I can't...Can we?"

He rested his brow on hers. "I wouldn't have thought so, but it seems I can't get enough of you."

Her instant response to his touch went a long way to diffusing his temper, and now that the first rush of passion had burned itself out, he intended to take her slowly, carefully, exploiting his lover's knowledge of what gave her pleasure, bringing her to the peak of fever and leaving her thoroughly sated. He would be unrelenting in his devotions, and she would know that she belonged to him and he to her.

It didn't work out that way. Needs that he had suppressed too long for her sake suddenly overwhelmed him. At the first questing touch of her hands, he became insatiable.

Desire, she learned, fed on desire. One moment she was spent, as boneless as a length of rope, the next she was straining against him, her mouth eager, her touches wanton. While he was gasping for air, she rolled on top of him.

Her hair formed a curtain of silk around him as their mouths met and clung. The fragrance in her hair and on her skin intoxicated him. He couldn't wait. At the first thrust, they both gasped, shocked at how greedy and how impatient they were. Then they began to move.

He wanted to tell her that he had never felt this way before. She wanted to tell him that he made her feel gloriously liberated. The words wouldn't form. Passion stole their breath away. Those little trilling cries she made were driving him frantic. His shuddering gasps of pleasure made her pulse leap. Their movements became wilder, rougher, faster. She gave a little cry as her body convulsed. He groaned her name over and over as he spilled his seed inside her.

On a long sighing breath, she collapsed against him, then rolled to her side.

"I feel..." she began.

"Me, too."

"Good."

They smiled and kissed and nestled closer.

After a while he said softly, "This has gone too far to turn back now. We must marry, Eve. Surely you see that?"

No response.

He pulled back to get a better look at her. At least she had fallen asleep with a smile on her face. He reached for the bed quilt and dragged it over them, then lay there thinking, thinking, thinking. Gradually, his breathing slowed. He closed his eyes.

He wakened when her elbow dug into him as she turned onto her side. He got up and reached for his shirt.

"Don't leave me." She snagged his wrist and held on.

They studied each other, amazed at the feelings that one look could ignite.

"If I come back to bed," he said, "it won't be to sleep."

"I know."

That was all he needed to hear.

They fell into an exhausted sleep long after the candles sputtered and went out.

Chapter Twenty-one

She awoke with the sun streaming in through the dormer window and the sound of horses' hooves and carriage wheels rattling over cobblestones. She turned her head slowly. She was alone. Ash, she vaguely remembered, had gone back to his own bed in the middle of the night, and she was glad that he had. This was all so new to her that she didn't know how to carry it off. She ached with an unfamiliar tenderness in every delicate part of her anatomy.

Rising on her elbows, she surveyed the bed. It surprised her that it was still in one piece. The thought made her wince.

She looked at the clock and gasped. He'd wanted an early start, and she had slept half the morning away. Throwing back the covers, she jumped out of bed and pulled the bell rope to summon the chambermaid.

As she descended the stairs, she tried to bolster her confidence. The maid had given her a note from Ash saying that he'd gone for a walk but would return soon and join her in the dining room. The short respite would give her time to practice some witty observations on the inn and its guests, if only she could unglue her tongue from the roof of her mouth.

When she entered the dining room, she came to a sudden halt. Ash was there, casually reading a newspaper. When he caught sight of her, he laid the paper aside and got up. She knew that she was blushing, and that annoyed her.

He held her chair for her as she sat down. "Sleep well?" he asked.

"Yes, thank you. And you?"

"The same."

To ease the awkward moment, she began to butter a slice of toast.

She was reaching for the coffeepot when Ash's hand closed around hers, preventing her from completing the movement. Her eyes flew to his. He seemed immensely pleased with himself.

He said, teasing her, "I always knew that you were a volcano waiting to erupt, and how right I was."

She countered crossly, "And I always knew that you were an earthquake waiting to happen."

He chuckled and released her hand. "True. I still can't get over the shock of it. I never knew my own nature until I met you. Was it the same for you, Eve, with me?"

Now was the time for that witty rejoinder to floor him. "Pass the marmalade," she mumbled.

He grinned and passed the marmalade. "I don't know why everything has to be so difficult with you, but here's how things stand with me. I detest creeping around strange inns and houses in the middle of the night just so that we can be together, and I detest even more having to lie to people when there's not the least necessity for it. There is a simple solution to our problem, and I'm giving you fair warning. When the time is right, I expect you to do the honorable thing by me."

No words of love, she noted, nothing about building a life together. Were all men this dense? Was bed all they ever thought about?

She struggled to appear as urbane as he. "I'll let you know when the time is right."

"You coward," was all he said, then, much to her annoyance, he went on to make witty observations on the inn and its guests.

They were finishing their breakfast when the door opened and a gentleman in a caped traveling coat entered. Eve saw him first and started up. "Papa! What... what are you doing here?"

Ash was as surprised as Eve, but he covered it better. "Mr. Dearing," he said. "We stopped here for breakfast. You'll join us for coffee?"

He gave Eve a meaningful glance. She got the message. Here was another small lie he'd had to tell to protect her reputation.

Dearing beamed at them. "Most people stop at Cuckfield," he said, "and I was hoping to find you here. Yes, thank you. Coffee will be fine. I thought you'd want to know what I can tell you about these cuttings."

As he spoke, he removed the newspaper cuttings from his coat pocket, laid them on the table, and shrugged out of his coat. A passing waiter took the coat from him, and they all sat down at the table. Ash poured a cup of coffee for the older man.

"It *is* important, isn't it?" Dearing looked from Ash to

Eve. "I seem to remember you mentioning a fellow writer who was attacked by some blighter who had to be stopped."

Ash nodded. "That's right." He was studying Eve's father and quickly coming to the conclusion that Dearing did not appear to be suffering the effects of laudanum this morning. His eyes were clear and focused. He fairly radiated health.

Dearing said, "I don't know who Angelo is, but he didn't write these stories. Antonia did—my late wife, you know?"

"What?" demanded Eve. "Mama wrote them?" She was thunderstruck.

"Are you sure, Mr. Dearing?" Ash was staring at the cuttings. "Why would Angelo claim that he was the writer if he wasn't?"

"I have no idea. But I'm quite certain that these are Antonia's stories. We had words about it, you see. All this superstitious nonsense about ghosts stuck in my craw. I'm sorry to be so blunt, Eve, but your mother, as you well know, had an overactive imagination."

Ash felt rather than saw Eve stiffen, and he quickly interposed, "Then how did Angelo get hold of her stories?"

Dearing shrugged. "All I know is that they were in her notebooks, the ones you keep asking me about, Eve. As far as I know, they weren't in Antonia's boxes when I finally got round to unpacking them. I didn't think it was important. Antonia never intended to publish her stories. It was simply a hobby, something she did after she visited various gardens." He gave Eve a wry smile. "It's no wonder you turned out to be a writer, Eve. You got that from your mother."

Eve was smoothing out the cuttings, frowning as she quickly scanned them.

Ash said, "Are you saying you know the gardens in these stories, Mr. Dearing?"

Dearing nodded. "I bid on them at various times, but each time I lost out to the landscape gardener I told you about, Thomas Messenger. He was a brilliant designer, but not very reliable. Did I mention that he drank too much and wasn't always polite to his employers? These things get around, you know, but when Thomas was sober, he was charming, and everyone was willing to give him another chance. These are the gardens he designed."

Ash said, "Messenger designed the park at Richmond? That's my property, Mr. Dearing, and I have no recollection of anyone by that name."

"It wasn't a big job. As I remember, Lord Denison wanted a terraced garden laid out along a stretch of the river."

Ash nodded. "It's still there. Go on, Mr. Dearing."

"At any rate, I wasn't sure at first that they were the same gardens, but when I recognized the characters, it became patently clear."

"The characters?"

"The maid who fell down the shaft of the well, the footman who fell down the stairs, the boy who drowned? These were tragic events, and people still talked about them to any stranger who came into the area. That's when Antonia got to hear of them, when she visited the gardens."

Eve's mind was buzzing with questions. "Where was I, Papa? I ask because I don't remember these characters at all."

"I should hope not!" Dearing spoke with some heat.

"Antonia knew better than to fill your mind with ghostly stories. You were very young, and these were tragic events. I'm glad your mother protected you from learning the distressing details." He sighed. "If I'd had my wish, Antonia would not have written these stories at all, but she did not think to ask my opinion."

Eve knew why. Her mother could never talk to her father about her Claverley insights. If he'd read the stories, he must have come upon them by chance.

"So I was with Mama when she visited these gardens?"

"Oh, yes. You were very young. It was, I think, in the summer of 1805. I was working up north. I can't remember why you and your mother didn't join me, but you and Antonia made a holiday of it, visiting several outstanding gardens in and around London."

"That was the year before Mama died," said Eve. Her voice was curiously flat. "The year before she fell from the top of the quarry."

Dearing dug into his pocket and produced a handkerchief. After blowing his nose, he cleared his throat. "I thought there might be a story about the quarry garden, but, of course, Antonia did not live to write it."

"A quarry garden?" said Eve. "I don't remember a garden."

Her father replied, "Well, it wasn't laid out then. Everything was still in the planning stages." To Ash he said, "Thomas got the commission to design the quarry garden. There were long stretches, you see, when he pulled himself together and did quite well, and this was one of them. However, it did not last long. He went back to the bottle and there was the devil to pay. He insulted the owners, broke windows, that sort of thing." He shook his head. "Nobody could put up with that. So the owners dismissed him and called me in to finish the project."

When the older man paused, Ash said, "That's quite a coincidence." He was thinking that Messenger had been present at four gardens where a tragic accident had taken place, and the wheels in his brain were spinning furiously.

"What it was," said Dearing, "was a debacle. I started work, and Antonia and Eve took lodgings nearby. The next thing I knew, Messenger had brought his wife and children to the site to have them plead with the owner to give him another chance. They were told to get off the land or the dogs would be set on them. It was all so awkward with Messenger and his family putting up at the same inn as Antonia and Eve."

His voice changed again and he said violently, "I wish I'd never accepted that job. It intrigued me, of course, turning a quarry into a thing of beauty, but after Antonia died, I never wanted to go back. I hear it's beautiful, but I don't want to see it. I couldn't bear to see it."

"Where is it?" Ash asked.

Dearing glanced at Eve before looking at Ash. "I never wanted Eve to go back there. She can be morbid when she wants to be. That's something else she gets from her mother."

"It's all right, Papa," Eve said. "I have a good idea where the quarry is. I'm like you. I couldn't bear to go back, either. Things are different now."

After a lengthy silence, Ash said, "Where is Messenger now?"

Dearing took a gulp of coffee before responding. "I know he hasn't worked on any big projects since he lost the quarry, but he could be doing smaller jobs on his own. On the other hand, it wouldn't surprise me to hear that he had died with a bottle in his hand. I just don't know."

"Or," said Ash, "it's quite possible that he kept Antonia's notes and, years later, when Gothic fiction came into vogue, decided to publish them."

Mr. Dearing was startled. The idea had obviously never occurred to him. "But why would he do that?"

"We don't know. That's what we're trying to find out. It would help if we could visit the quarry and the inn where your wife stayed. Perhaps someone there will remember him. Can you remember the name of the inn?"

"The White Hart." The reply was somber and tinged with sadness.

Eve looked at her father and felt surprise mingled with an emotion that brought a sting to her eyes. "I thought you'd forgotten it."

"No. I remember everything. When your mother died, I thought I might as well be dead, too. For all our differences, I loved her with my whole heart. Of course I remember about that night, every little detail."

Eve could not keep the edge of bitterness from her voice. "Yet you married Martha within the year."

"To give you a home!" he exclaimed. "I thought Martha would look after you. She had no children of her own and seemed a sensible, capable sort of woman. Your aunt did not seem the right sort of person to me to have charge of a young, impressionable girl. She was too much of a Claverley." The handkerchief was brought out and he blew his nose again. "What I did, I did for the best."

"Oh, Papa..." Eve shook her head.

The silence that followed did not seem comfortable to Ash, so he diverted the conversation into a less emotional channel. "Mr. Dearing, you were on the point of telling me, I believe, where this quarry garden is situated."

"It's not far from here, close to Penshurst Place."

"The seat of the Sydney family?" said Ash.

Dearing nodded. "Not that Thomas or I ever worked on Penshurst's magnificent formal gardens. They were laid out well before our time. But there is another fine house in the area, Hazleton House. That's where I was the night Antonia died." He added bitterly, "Working on my designs well into the night."

"Penshurst," said Ash. "It's quite a long detour off the Brighton Road. We won't make it back to town before nightfall. Would you like to come with us, sir? My curricle is too small, but we could hire a chaise and go together."

"Thank you," said Dearing, "but I think if ever I go, I'd like to be by myself, alone with Antonia and my memories."

They left the inn together, and as Dearing walked to his chaise, Ash said, "If you hear anything of Messenger, or something occurs to you, you will let me know?"

The older man looked surprised. "This is important, then?"

"It may be," Ash replied. "I can't say yet."

Dearing nodded. "I'll see what I can find out."

Penshurst was a pretty village dominated by the church that also seemed to guard the gates to the splendid seat of the ancient Sydney family. Memories that she had forgotten came back to Eve in a tide. The whole area was steeped in history, and the proposed quarry garden was the least of what had interested her mother.

"We went to Hever Castle," she told Ash as they drove

through the village, "you know, where Anne Boleyn lived before her marriage to the king? My mother was going to write a story about Anne. She was a tragic figure, wasn't she?" She stopped and gave him a sideways glance. "Do you think my father was right? Was my mother morbid? Am I?"

"Was Aeschylus? Or Euripides? Or Sophocles? They wrote tragedies, Eve, and the world is a better place for it."

"I had no idea," she said quizzically, "that you were such a learned gentleman."

His reply was dry. "Not nearly as learned as I ought to be. I don't know why I missed it. It has been staring me in the face all this time, and like a blockhead I never thought to question it."

"Question what?"

"Why Angelo chose that name when he published your mother's stories. A schoolboy with a smattering of Greek would have put it together."

She threw up her hands. "Put what together? Will you speak in plain English?"

"His name. Angelo. It's from the Greek *angelos*. It means *messenger*."

She wrinkled her brow. "I thought it mean *angel*."

"It does. Same word. Angel or messenger. That's what an angel is, a messenger."

"Oh." She was thinking of golden harps and heavenly choirs.

"Yes, 'oh.' He was using his own name."

"Thomas Messenger." She smoothed a frown from her brow and let out a long sigh.

"What is it?"

"Somehow," she shook her head, "the pieces aren't fitting together the way they should. I haven't changed my mind. I still say that the man who attacked Lydia is afraid of exposure." She looked up at him. "How does Messenger fit into it? Did he have the stories published, or is he the man who attacked Lydia?"

He took his eyes from the road and flashed her an easy grin. "Don't twist yourself into knots trying to figure things out. These things have a way of clicking into place when our brains are rested. Ah, here we are."

He pulled up in front of a half-timbered building with the sign of a white hart swinging in the breeze.

"Poor beast," Ash remarked. "He looks as though he has caught the scent of the hunters." He looked around. "Where am I supposed to water my horses?"

"There's bound to be a lane in the back leading into the yard."

Ash flicked the reins and drove his team to the end of the road, turned the corner, and was soon driving into the inn's courtyard.

The ostler who came to take the reins from Ash looked as sleepy as the village of Penshurst. No one was in a rush. The yard wasn't bustling. People strolled, they didn't hurry.

Ash and Eve wandered into the lobby and, seeing no one, pushed through a door that Eve remembered gave onto the dining room.

"It hasn't changed a bit since I was last here," said Eve.

Small leaded windowpanes let in very little light. Dark oak beams supported the low ceiling. The sooty stone fireplace was set in an inglenook. No more than four tables draped in white cloths could fit into the cramped room.

"We're the only customers." Ash spoke in hushed tones. "Where is everybody? The landlord? The waiters?"

"I think you're supposed to ring the bell at the lobby counter for service."

Ash cursed under his breath.

"What did you expect?" Eve was amused. "This isn't Grillon's."

"Wait here. This will only take a moment."

Eve wandered over to a table by the window and sat down. This was where she and her mother used to sit when they stayed at the White Hart. How long were they here before the accident? A week? She couldn't remember. Her eyes strayed to a table in the corner. That's where the Messengers sat after they arrived.

Her heart began to thunder against her ribs. Her throat went dry. She tried to tear her eyes away, but they were held as if against her will. The shadows took shape and she saw them as clearly as she'd seen them that last night.

The table was set for four, but only three people were there. Mrs. Messenger was almost invisible, a timid woman who dressed to melt into her surroundings. The son, a tall gangly youth, was as sullen as ever, and the man was darkly handsome, with lines of dissipation etched deeply into his face. Thomas Messenger. She thought they'd left, but they were still here.

There was a brandy bottle in the middle of the table. He reached for it, tipped it up, and filled his glass.

Hatred like she'd never known engulfed her—not hatred of her, but hatred of her father. She braced herself as Thomas Messenger's thoughts spilled into her mind.

Dearing! It's all his fault. Just because he kowtows to the gentry, he gets all the credit while I'm pushed to the side. I'm the one with the talent. He's a second-rate hack. This was my job.

He stole it from me. He's jealous of me and always will be. Well, I'll show him! I'll show them all!

The anger flared to a white-hot conflagration. *Tonight, I'll do it tonight. Then there will be no more Dearing and I'll be right here to get my job back.*

The violence of his drunken laughter recoiled inside her head, and she closed her eyes as she tried to shut out the sound.

She jumped when she felt a hand on her shoulder. "Mama?"

"Eve, are you all right?"

For a moment, she stared at Ash blankly, then her breathing gradually slowed and she came to herself. "He—" She had to swallow to get rid of the huskiness in her throat. "He was here, Ash. Thomas Messenger was here that night with his wife and son."

He frowned down at her. "Is this a memory, Eve, or one of your visions?"

That frown brought her out of her daze. "I remember it clearly now that I'm here." And that was the truth. "He blamed my father for all his misfortunes. He was—"

"Yes?"

"I think he wanted to kill him. He was drunk and raving."

She didn't want to argue the point or elaborate on what she had told him. She wanted to go to the quarry. She wanted to make sense of her dream. She had to know what happened the night her mother went out. Her sense of urgency was overpowering.

She got up. "I want to go to the quarry," she said.

"Fine. I've ordered sandwiches and tea. We can go after we eat."

"I want to go *now*."

"At least give me time to ask directions."

"I need no directions. I've made the journey in my dreams a thousand times. Don't look so worried, Ash. It's not far."

"That's not what I'm thinking."

She was almost at the door. Turning to face him, she said coldly, "And I'm not mad, either."

When he came up to her, he draped an arm around her shoulders. "You're not reading my thoughts, Eve, and I must say that's a great relief. What I was thinking, you foolish girl, is that it's high time you learned to trust me."

"I trust you," she said quickly, and she pushed through the door.

The path to the quarry was downhill and protected on either side by a screen of overhanging bushes and thick shrubbery. Then suddenly they came out of the shadows and entered a terraced grotto that was drenched in sunshine.

"This is not how I remember it," said Eve. "It was drenched by the light of a full moon, and I thought it was bigger."

"It's beautiful," Ash murmured. "It doesn't look like a quarry, does it? More like a sunken garden."

On every side, terraces carved into the rock supported a plethora of plants, some flowering, some just coming into flower: bluebells, primroses, lilies, climbing vines, and honeysuckle. On the floor of the quarry, nettles, gorse, broom, and other wild specimens had forced their way in to soften the bare quarry floor. The air was fragrant with the scent of blossoms. The sound of a waterfall was a touch that was almost too perfect, too theatrical.

Ash was enchanted. "This would make the perfect setting for *A Midsummer Night's Dream*," he said.

Eve's eyes were scanning the terraces. "Or a Greek tragedy," she responded. "If I were Iphigenia, I wouldn't linger here."

He was mentally kicking himself for having forgotten that the garden could never be a thing of beauty to Eve.

"I'm sorry," he said. "I wasn't thinking."

She gave him a quick smile. "You don't have to coddle me, Ash. I wonder who designed it."

"I can answer that. I asked the landlady when I ordered our sandwiches and tea. She couldn't remember his name, but he was an Italian fellow who completed the job and turned tail and made for home because he couldn't stand our English winters."

Eve laughed. "I don't blame him. Did you mention my family to the landlady?"

"I did, but she wasn't much help. The inn has changed hands since you were here, and the new people have never heard the name Dearing or Messenger. The same goes for the owners of Hazleton House. The old boy who owned it was the last of his line, and when he died it was bought by strangers."

After a moment, Eve said quietly, "I saw the way you looked when my father mentioned the boy who had drowned. It still hurts you to think of him, doesn't it?"

"Hurt isn't the word for what I feel. Harry would have been about your age if he had lived. I have to know the truth about how he died. You visited the gardens with your mother, didn't you? Did anyone mention Harry to you?"

"No. But they wouldn't, would they? I was only ten or eleven at the time." She leaned toward him. "Antonia wasn't mean-spirited, Ash. She wouldn't have written a story that could hurt the innocent. There was a purpose to what she did. Messenger . . ." Her voice faded and she shook her head. "Too many coincidences," she said softly.

"Yes. I know what you mean. Messenger works on four gardens, and four victims meet with a tragic accident."

"Do you think he is mocking us? Why would he publish my mother's stories and draw attention to himself? It doesn't make sense."

"Not yet it doesn't. When we find Messenger, we'll force him to tell us the truth. We'll make the connections, Eve, I promise you. He won't get away with what he has done."

She put a hand on his arm. "Now who is getting ahead of himself?"

He smiled. "You're right. The thing is, I never believed that Harry would go swimming by himself. Someone had to be there to help him. His death has always weighed heavily on my conscience. I promised to be there to take him out, but instead," he clenched his hand, "I went off to the races with my friends. I never gave a thought to Harry."

Her eyes searched his face. In a voice that was almost soundless, she said, "I know what you're feeling. That's why I'm here. I feel guilty for my mother's death, too, and I don't know why. Perhaps the quarry will tell me."

They fell silent then and moved slowly, aimlessly, into the depths of the grotto. Ash stopped now and again to admire a particularly fine display of wildflowers. Eve scanned the terraces as though she was looking for something.

"What are you looking for, Eve?" Ash asked at length.

"Mmm? Oh, there should be steps carved into the

bare rock going up to the top of the quarry. I never climbed them, I wasn't allowed, but my father used to come and go that way when he visited us."

"Steps, leading up to the top of a quarry?" He sounded doubtful.

She shrugged. "They were old and not very stable. It was a shortcut from the house to the village."

They found them a little way farther on.

"There's a handrail," he said. "Would you like to go up to the top?"

She shuddered and shook her head. "No. But you go up if you like. This is where I found my mother. If you don't mind, I just want a little time alone with my thoughts."

He didn't climb the steps, but he did give her some space and privacy. He understood only too well. When his brother drowned, and even to this day, he didn't want company when he became lost in his memories.

There was a stone bench strategically placed beside a waterfall. Ash sat down and gazed around him with interest. He thought that it was incredible that this beautiful, man-made garden had been created from anything so barren as a stone quarry.

His gaze moved to Eve. She had wandered farther into the quarry and was standing with her head bowed as though in prayer, her hands clenched tightly in front of her. Five minutes went by. One minute more, he promised himself, then he would bring her attention back to the present.

He was moving toward her when she gave a little cry. He quickened his pace when he saw that she was shaking. "What is it, Eve?" He reached for her and gathered her in his arms. "What is it, Eve?" he repeated, his alarm making his voice rough.

She blinked up at him with unseeing eyes. Finally, recognition dawned and she let out a long, pent-up breath. "I know now why I always feel guilty when I remember the night I found my mother. Take me home, Ash. I want to go home."

Chapter Twenty-two

When she said that she wanted to go home, she didn't mean to the White Hart, she meant back to town. Ash decided not to take her to the Manor but to his rooms in Grillon's. At the Manor, she would be surrounded by females, fussing over her and asking questions. He could see that Eve was in no condition for company. She wasn't ill. All she needed was time to come to herself.

He'd done everything possible to make her comfortable on the long drive from the White Hart: hot bricks for her feet, a warm blanket to cover her. She'd slept most of the way, her head resting trustingly against his shoulder. All the same, when he lifted her out of his curricle in Grillon's courtyard, she was deathly pale, and he could feel her start to shiver beneath the folds of the blanket.

"Where are we?" she asked, her eyes blinking as she came awake.

"Grillon's. When you've eaten and are rested, I'll take you back to the Manor."

Her nod was all the permission he needed.

"I can walk," she protested.

He said something soothing and made for the entrance that gave onto the back stairs. Ostlers and stable boys smothered their grins as he passed by. *And why shouldn't they?* he asked himself sourly, struck hard by the irony of the situation. They were used to seeing a steady stream of women coming to his rooms by the back stairs. Why should this one be different?

But she was different, and the next time Miss Eve Dearing came to his rooms, she would come through the hotel's front door, and every groom, stable boy, and ostler would touch his forelock out of respect for my lady Denison.

He was bound and determined to make it so.

The suggestive grins were easily dealt with. A killing look from eyes, as hard as flint, had men hastening to tasks they had either momentarily forgotten or newly invented.

When he entered his rooms, he carried her to the parlor and set her down in a chair next to the fireplace. They were the only two people here, since both Reaper and Hawkins were still at the Manor. He might have rung for a footman or a chambermaid, but he didn't want anyone to see Eve. He didn't want her to be embarrassed, he didn't want her reputation to be tarnished, and, above all, he didn't want anyone to take care of her but himself.

The first thing he did was light the fire. It wasn't dark yet, but dusk was settling over the city, so he lit several candles around the room. He poured two glasses of brandy and brought one to her.

"Drink it," he said, "then I'll order soup and sandwiches from the kitchen. You've hardly eaten a thing all day." He held the glass to her lips.

She obediently took a sip of brandy and choked on it. Pushing his hand away, she got out between sputters, "I'd rather have a cup of tea."

He grinned. "You're beginning to sound more like yourself."

Her smile was valiant though feeble, but at least she was smiling.

"Wait here," he said, "and I'll see about something to eat." He added delicately, "The little room is at the end of the hall if you, uh, want to freshen yourself."

"Thank you," she replied, without a trace of embarrassment.

He wondered whether that was a good or bad sign.

It took him several minutes to find a footman and arrange for their meal, and when he returned to the parlor, Eve was on her feet, looking at everything though at nothing in particular. She'd removed her bonnet and pelisse, and her simple long-sleeved twilled gown, so appropriate for Eve, wiped the smile from his face. He was thinking of so many others he'd entertained in this very room, and the gowns they'd worn had left nothing to his imagination. That she should be the one to capture his heart no longer amazed him. He hadn't known what intimacy was until he'd met Eve. He was everyone's friend but confided in no one. Until Eve. They'd only known each other a short time, but he felt as though he'd known her all his life.

When she looked up with a quizzical smile, he felt that a weight had been lifted from his shoulders. The waif was gone and she looked more like herself.

"You do yourself proud, don't you?" she quipped.

"What?"

She held up her glass of brandy. "The crystal is Waterford. The porcelain is Sèvres. The candlesticks are silver. Or does the hotel supply its guests with only the best?"

"I like the finer things in life," he said, crossing to her, "and the finest and best is standing right before me."

She looked at him uncertainly, and no wonder, he thought. The compliment sounded like the blandishment of a practiced womanizer. In a different voice, he went on, "My father was the one with the expensive tastes. When he died, I inherited all his possessions."

He wanted to tell her that when they were married, she could change things around at his house in Richmond to suit herself. He didn't care whether he drank out of crystal glasses or wooden mugs, just as long as Eve presided at his table. He held his peace because her mood was fragile, too fragile to take advantage of her in a weak moment.

He indicated the fireplace. "Come and sit down close to the fire. Your color is coming back to your cheeks and you've stopped trembling. That's something. You had me worried there for a while. Eve, what happened back at the quarry? I'd like to know, if you feel up to telling me."

She took her chair again, her gaze focusing on the fire as flames licked around the coals. He pulled a chair close to hers and waited for her to begin.

When long minutes had passed, he said gently, "You said that you know now why you feel guilty when you remember that night."

She leaned her head on the back of the chair. "I always wondered," she said, "why my mother went out that night. Well, now I know." She turned her head slightly to look at him. "I told her that Mr. Messenger was planning to kill my father."

He didn't interrupt when she paused, because he didn't want to break her train of thought.

"It all came back to me when we were in the White Hart's dining room. I was twelve years old and he didn't know I could read his mind. Mr. Messenger, I mean. He was sitting with his family at the table in the corner, and I could hear him ranting and raving inside my head. He wasn't supposed to be there. It should never have happened."

She looked a question at him, and when he did not respond to that look, she went on, "I should have told her straightaway. I knew she hadn't absorbed his thoughts. It doesn't work that way. I think I told you that we can't choose who we are receptive to? Antonia's charisma was exceptional, but even she couldn't read anyone's thoughts at will. We Claverleys have a saying: 'Claverleys don't choose their subjects. Their subjects choose them.'"

She paused, then went on, "If I'd told her about Messenger, though, she could have gone to warn my father when it was still light, but I held my tongue because my father had persuaded me that people who heard voices inside their heads were crazy. He was ashamed of my Claverley charisma and made me ashamed, too." She shook her head, a sad little movement that spoke volumes. "I would have done anything to win my father's approval.

"So," she heaved a sigh, "I didn't tell my mother until I went to bed. I couldn't sleep, and she heard me tossing and turning. When she came in to see what was the matter, I poured out the whole story." She gave a faint smile. "And she told me that there was nothing to worry about because Mr. Messenger was sleeping off the effects of a night of drinking. His snores, she said, had the whole inn in an uproar."

She lifted her shoulders in a tiny shrug. "Naturally, I slept, and the next thing I remember is waking in the middle of the night with an awful feeling of doom hanging over me. My mother's dog was there, and Sheba led me to the quarry. Messenger must have pushed her over the edge when she tried to stop him—"

He couldn't help interrupting at this point. "You saw him?"

"At the quarry today, I knew she had been pushed to her death, but I didn't see the face of the man who did it. It had to be Messenger. He had murder in his heart when he thought of my father."

He didn't know what to say. She was talking about things he couldn't get his mind around, no matter how hard he tried. He felt on surer ground when he stayed with the facts.

"You said your mother's dog led you to your mother. Did he go with her when she went out?"

She nodded. "I think so. Sheba was wet when she came in to get me, and it had been raining that night. But Sheba was lame because of arthritis in one hip. She wouldn't have managed to climb those quarry stairs. Had she been with my mother, she would have attacked anyone who tried to harm her."

He tried to sound as neutral as he could manage. "Are you telling me this from memory, Eve, or is this what you've gathered from your visions?"

She looked at him as though he'd said a bad word. "Most of it comes from memory, a memory I locked away in the deepest dungeon of my mind until I stood on the spot where my mother died. There's something else I remember—my mother's voice telling me that it was an accident. But it wasn't. I know she was pushed to her death, so why would she lie to me?"

He smoothed his fingers over his brow. "All that comes to me," he said, "is that she wanted to protect you."

"Protect me from what?"

He shrugged. "Messenger? I don't know. Maybe she thought you'd panic if she said someone had pushed her. Maybe he was still hanging around, waiting to see what would happen next. And maybe..."

"What?"

"Maybe it *was* an accident."

For the first time, her confidence seemed to waver. "Ash," she said, "it wasn't an accident. She was pushed. I know it."

"Fine. Let's go on to something else." Fearing that he'd been too abrupt, he gentled his voice. "What happened to Messenger? Did you see him again? Speak to him?"

"No. I never saw him or any of his family again. Maybe my father would know." Her voice faded as a thought occurred to her. "There was a daughter, too, a sickly girl. I didn't see much of her." She was remembering the fourth place at the Messengers' table.

She looked into space and sighed. He leaned toward her, arms braced on his knees. "You have nothing to feel guilty about," he said. "You did the right thing, didn't you? You told your mother about Messenger."

She rubbed her eyes with the heel of her hands and nodded. "I suppose so." She dropped her hands. "But at the time, I was confused. My father had me believing that there was no such thing as the Claverley charisma, that it was a form of hysteria. I doubted myself and the voice I'd heard. What if I'd sent my mother out that night on the strength of something I'd only imagined? How could I bear it? That's what I've tried to forget all these years."

She looked down at her tightly clasped hands and gradually relaxed her fingers. Bitterness crept into her voice. "From that night on, I became more determined than ever to suppress the Claverley part of my nature. I wasn't always successful, but nothing earth-shattering troubled my mind, until the night of the symposium. That's when it began. I dream, I have visions, I hear voices, and this time there's no denying them."

She gave him a fierce look. "I don't want to deny them. It's who I am, and I won't change myself, not for anybody."

Her words made the fine hairs on the back of his neck rise. "Eve," he shook his head, "we don't know that it's Messenger. It's possible it's someone else. Do you know what he looks like? People change as they get older, and that's especially true for drunkards."

"It doesn't matter what he looks like. I can find him by listening to his thoughts. I'm not sure how it works, but—"

"Damn it, Eve!" He brought his open hand down on the arm of her chair, making her jump. "Will you listen to yourself? This isn't make-believe. This is dangerous. You can be hurt. There's a right way of going about this, and it doesn't involve visions and voices in your head."

When he saw her stiffen, he tried to check his frustration. He hated feeling so helpless, but the stark truth was, he felt more afraid now than he had in all his years as a soldier. At least he'd known who the enemy was.

He lowered the temperature in his voice. "As I see it, we track Messenger down and bring him in for questioning. Once we find him, we can delve into his background, see if we can find hard evidence to tie him to those earlier murders or to Lydia's attack or the heckler's murder."

She spoke in a low, flat monotone. "You don't believe me, do you? You don't believe in my visions or that I can hear his voice."

He dragged his fingers through his hair. "It's not that. I'm thinking of what will happen in a court of law. What kind of witness would you make? You can hardly tell the judge that you know that Messenger is a murderer because you heard his voice inside your head. Surely you can see that? As I said, we need hard evidence to convict him."

He was distracted by a discreet knock on the door. Their meal had arrived. The footman was well trained and didn't lift a brow when Ash insisted on taking the tray himself.

After letting himself out, the footman flipped the coin Ash had given him as a gratuity and held it up to the light.

A passing chambermaid observed him. "That was quick, Ernie. You just this minute entered his lordship's rooms."

Ernie grinned. "There's a lady with him, a lady whose identity he doesn't want anyone to know. I didn't even get a glimpse of her."

The maid looked baffled. "Maybe she's a decent girl," she ventured.

"Don't be daft! You know his lordship only takes up with dashers," and pocketing the silver crown, he sauntered off.

Eve watched as Ash arranged plates of soup and sandwiches on a card table he'd set up close to the fire.

"You still look chilled to the bone," he said. "The fire will soon take care of that."

He pulled up two straight-backed chairs, and she seated herself on the one he held for her.

"Fish soup and salmon sandwiches," he said with a smile. "According to my old nanny, fish is good for the brain."

Though she had little appetite, she picked up her soup spoon and made the effort to eat. He was trying to put her at ease, but she was bracing herself for more questions. Instead, he talked mainly about his place in Richmond and didn't seem to expect a response beyond the occasional nod, leaving her free to dwell on her own thoughts.

Her mind drifted back to the quarry garden. Antonia could see into the future. She could sense all its possibilities and pitfalls, but she hadn't foreseen her own death. Her gift was to help others, not herself, and in those last moments, as her life slipped away, she'd thought only of her daughter.

Things that she hadn't understood before were beginning to take shape in her mind. Now that she knew the stories Angelo had published were her mother's stories, she was seeing them with different eyes. The gardens were the gardens she'd dreamed about, only now she knew where they were and who owned them.

There were no tragic accidents. Messenger, or Angelo, had murdered his victims without remorse, and the ghosts who haunted those gardens did not want peace only for themselves. They wanted Messenger to be stopped.

Who would be his next victim? Nell? Lydia?

Impressions formed in her mind. She was aware of a ballroom, music, the French doors giving onto the terrace. She tried to bring the ballroom into focus, but all she could see were girls in white dresses and their partners whirling around the floor.

Her pulse began to race; her breathing was quick and shallow. Her heart felt as though a hand had closed around it and was squeezing it tight. That was where it would all end. That was what her mother wanted her to see. As soon as she stepped into the ballroom, she would know him. Messenger. Angelo. The man who had thrown her mother from the top of the quarry.

"Eve!"

She jerked when Ash's voice invaded her thoughts.

"Eve! You're falling out of your chair. I thought for a moment you had fainted."

She opened her eyes wide and looked up at him. Worry lines creased his brow. He looked so clean and wholesome and as different from Angelo as day from night.

"What is it?" he asked softly.

"Dreams," she said brokenly.

He drew her to her feet, turned her palm to his lips, and kissed it passionately. "You're tired, that's all. These last two days have been exhausting for both of us. There's nothing wrong with you that a good night's rest won't cure."

The gentle touch of his hands and the worry in his eyes brought the incipient tears spilling over. She cried against his shoulder, great heaving sobs that shook her whole body. She cried for her mother and father, she cried for Ash's brother, for a young maid and an old footman whom she had never met. But most of all she cried for herself. She could not see a happy ending for her and Ash.

Her fate lay where her charisma led her. Angelo was her fate, or Messenger as she now knew he was. With her last conscious thoughts, her mother had tried to prepare her for what was to come. The nightmare would end with her.

Ash's hands were running up and down her spine, trying to soothe her, but she couldn't stop shivering. Suddenly sweeping her into his arms, he carried her to the sofa, reached for her glass of brandy, and held it to her lips, forcing her to drink from it.

When he set it aside, he said, "Don't move from this spot. I'm only going to get a blanket to wrap you in."

He was back in a moment with a quilt and a pillow for her head. Her sobs had faded to an occasional hiccup and she managed a husky "Thank you."

Stretched out on the sofa, she watched as he cleared the card table and set everything in its place. He added more coal to the fire and stirred the embers to give off more heat.

He sank down on his heels at the side of the sofa and brushed back tendrils of hair that had fallen across her brow and cheeks. "What happened?" he asked. His voice was ragged. "What brought that haunted look to your face? Can you tell me about it?"

She gave him an answer she knew he would accept. "Reliving the night my mother died has been too much for me."

What could she tell him? That she and Angelo were fated to embark on the final act of the play he'd set in motion when he'd murdered all those people? This was knowledge too deep for Ash to accept. Even she had trouble understanding it. But she accepted it. She never doubted that that's how it would end.

He nodded sympathetically and kissed her brow. "Get some sleep. I'm going to read for a little while in front of the fire."

"I don't mind if you go to bed."

"My bedchamber is like an icehouse. I'm quite happy to sleep in my favorite chair."

She continued to watch him as her eyelids grew heavy and the warmth from the fire penetrated every pore. When he moved or adjusted his position, her eyes flew open, then gradually closed again. Finally, she slept.

Chapter Twenty-three

They arrived at the Manor in the middle of a domestic crisis. Lady Sayers and her guests had assembled in the music room and Anna Contini was holding the floor. Her stentorian accents blasted their ears, even before they opened the door and walked in.

"Intolerable," she declared. "They should cancel the May Fair, or at least delay it to give me time to make other arrangements."

Lady Sayers put out a hand in a pleading gesture. "But, Anna, dear, they can't cancel the May Fair. It's been the custom for centuries to hold it in the first week of May."

She caught sight of Ash and Eve and quickly rose to greet them. Her look of relief was almost comical. "Lord Denison," she exclaimed, "perhaps you can make Anna see reason. The village common and the Manor grounds have always been taken over for the fair. It's not only a tradition. It was written into the charter granting these lands to the lord and the people of Kennington by royal decree."

Ash nodded, though he was none the wiser. "What seems to be the problem?"

"My donkeys," declared Anna, "and my sheep."

"Sheep?" said Ash, his brows lifting. No one enlightened him.

Lady Sayers said, "They must be moved to make room for the fair, but Anna won't hear of it. My own groom has threatened to hand in his notice if I stable the donkeys with my horses, and what he would do with the sheep, I have no idea."

"My donkeys and sheep must be kept together," Anna interjected.

The story came out in dribs and drabs. Donkeys and sheep, according to Anna, had a calming effect on each other, and donkeys were better than dogs at guarding sheep. It wasn't as though she'd bought a whole flock. She'd started with six sheep, but three had newly dropped their lambs, so now her little flock amounted to nine. Twelve counting the donkeys.

"They know one another," she went on. "They're like a family, and one of my donkeys," she added, clinching the argument, "is about to foal. It would be the worst kind of cruelty to move her now."

Eve used the hiatus in the conversation to take the chair next to her aunt. Liza was silent, she noted, an unusual state of affairs for her. Eve looked at Ash and swallowed a smile. He looked as though he would rather be anywhere but here.

Ash shifted from foot to foot. All eyes were on him as though he were King Solomon. He cleared his throat. "If we don't move your little flock," he said to Anna, "the villagers will do it for us, and the law is on their side.

Bailiffs may come, and they won't be gentle. I'm sure we can find some kindly farmer to take them in for a day or two, at least until the fair is over."

"That's just it," said Lady Sayers. "Dr. Braine has offered to take them, but Anna won't hear of it."

Anna's tone was frosty. "His place is two miles from here. I wouldn't see my little flock more than once a day. And they don't know Dr. Braine. Though I'm sure he's very kind, it's not the same. My donkeys don't trust people, and with good reason."

Lady Sayers put a hand to her brow, Liza sighed, and Miss Claverley stared hard at the Persian rug.

Ash said, "Even if we get permission for you to leave them where they are, they would be terrified out of their wits when the fair gets under way. There will be crowds of people milling around, hawkers shouting out their wares, musicians, dancers. And," he added with heavy emphasis, "a good deal of drinking. There are always a few rowdies at these events who are spoiling for mischief."

Anna was silent as she thought this over. Finally, she said, "I suppose I have no choice. I'll go and tell Dr. Braine that I've decided to accept his offer."

When she left the room, a long silence ensued. No one seemed to know whether to laugh or gnash their teeth. Finally, Lady Sayers said, "Thank you, Lord Denison. That was well done. Anna is very sensitive, but her love of animals is too extreme. Sometimes I think she likes them better than people." She added hastily, "But I truly admire her."

Miss Claverley picked up her embroidery. "Anna," she said, "is sensitive to any creature that has been hurt, whether it's a person or an animal. I believe she loves

Lydia and the boy who looks after her sheep as much as she loves her donkeys."

She was startled when everyone laughed.

"No. I mean it," she protested.

"Well, she doesn't like dogs," said Eve. "She told me to keep Dexter away from her."

"Yes, dear, but if Dexter were hurt or had an accident, she would be devoted to him. So..." she beamed at the company, "what I say is that we should show our appreciation by moving her donkeys and flock for her. I think she would trust us to take proper care of them, don't you?"

Lady Sayers made a halfhearted protest. There was too much to see to. Liza's ball was coming up. The decorators hadn't arrived to paint the walls and she wanted to be there to see that they'd chosen the right colors. The masons hadn't finished pointing the bricks on the west wing, and she wanted their ugly scaffolding gone before the ball. None of this swayed the others. They had made up their minds to help Anna, and her ladyship gave in when she saw that she was in the minority.

Things worked out for Anna better than expected. Not only had Dr. Braine offered to shelter her little flock but, on hearing of Anna's reservations, his mother invited both Anna and Lydia to stay over at Hill House until the fair was over. Then Anna could visit with her donkeys as often as she liked and still keep an eye on her friend.

The following morning, when they assembled in the courtyard, Anna cast a measuring eye over her volunteers. They were making a hen party of the event, except for Neil. Ash had excused himself on a flimsy pretext, which, Anna told Eve privately, relieved her mind. Neil was afraid of men.

"Too many people," Anna observed, and immediately cut her novice shepherds to the most able bodied of the company.

Lady Sayers, Miss Claverley, and Lydia went ahead in the comfort of Lady Sayers's coach, while the others put on stout walking shoes and scraped together a collection of makeshift shepherd's staffs.

Anna's boy—as they were coming to call Nell—was a little apart from the others, a cap pulled low on his brow. He didn't speak to anyone, and only Anna spoke to him. It seemed to Eve that everyone was in on their secret and took their cue from Anna.

It was hot, but not too hot for the long walk or herding the sheep, and Anna kept them entertained with a running commentary on the three donkeys she had rescued—Faith, Fanny, and Fiona. Eve was deeply impressed by the bond Anna had established with her little troop. They were affectionate creatures and brayed softly whenever she scratched their ears. There were no goads to prod them. Anna wouldn't have allowed it. Where she and her boy led, her little flock followed. Poor Dexter had to be left behind. He was too hale and hearty, too much of a dog, to be included in Anna's little infirmary of lost souls.

Eve knew that there were clouds on the horizon that the naked eye could not see. She knew he was out there somewhere, waiting his chance, but she had the advantage of him. She could read his mind. This nerve-racking state of affairs would not go on for much longer, for she had devised a scheme to lure him into the open. It was too late to turn back, and when he came for her, she would be ready.

She pushed the thought to the back of her mind. The danger wasn't imminent, and it was a glorious morning. She intended to enjoy every minute of it.

She plodded on and deliberately opened her mind to the sounds and sensations around her. No surprises here. She received nothing but vague impressions, just what any normal person would pick up with a modicum of intuition. Liza was grumpy because she'd thought she was going to have the doctor all to herself, until Lydia was invited to stay on at Hill House. Anna's laughter betrayed her happiness. She hadn't known she had friends beyond her little band of animals.

Eve's eyes came to rest on Anna's boy, and her lips quirked in a secret smile. Neil made her very, very happy. Her little runaway was becoming domesticated, up to a point. Eve could not remember a time when she felt so much in harmony with a group of people.

She breathed deeply. The shadows could wait. She was just an ordinary girl enjoying an outing with her dearest friends. This happy respite would end soon enough.

The interlude of harmony came to an abrupt end the night before the opening of the fair, when Ash barged into her room moments after she'd come upstairs to go to bed. He was waving a copy of the *Herald,* and he was white with anger.

"I couldn't believe it when I read it," he said. "You've written a story about the quarry garden. You've written about your mother's suspicious death. And your name is at the top of the page as the author of this piece." He slapped the newspaper on the dresser and came toward her. "What I don't understand is how you managed to persuade Brand Hamilton to publish it!"

She kept her chin up and her knees locked. "No persuasion was needed. His editor jumped at the chance of publishing a short story by the celebrated Mrs. Barrymore. Now, if Angelo had submitted a story, I'm sure your friend would have let you know."

"You've set yourself up as bait," he roared.

She almost cowered under the force of his anger, but, of course, she'd been expecting a heated reaction from him when he read the paper, just not as heated as this. "It's the logical thing to do," she said.

Her appeal to logic did not sway him. He stood there glaring at her. She began to pace.

Turning suddenly, she said, appealing to him, "Forget about my charisma. I still say that Messenger is deathly afraid that someone is out to expose him. That's why he attacked Lydia. Now he's not so sure—No! Hear me out!"

When he closed his mouth and folded his arms across his chest, she gave a little nod of approval and picked up where she had left off. "Imagine his feelings when he reads that story about my mother's death. He knows that Mrs. Barrymore and Eve Dearing are the same person, or if he doesn't, he can easily find out. He'll think I'm going to expose him. And who better than I? I know those gardens. I know what happened at the quarry. Oh, yes, he'll come for me. All I've done is give him a little push—"

He drowned out her words. "He could just as easily turn his attention to your father. He knows those gardens, too. He knows Messenger, and you don't."

"My father is not a writer! He couldn't have written those stories."

"Ha! People change all the time. All I'm saying is that we can't know what Messenger will do." He stopped, drew in an angry breath, and let it out slowly. "What am I saying? You're a Claverley. You know everything!"

The jibe hurt. "That's not true. But I do know that this man has to be stopped, and this is the way to do it."

"It didn't occur to you to consult me first?"

"Of course it occurred to me. But I knew you could stop publication if I couldn't persuade you to agree with me."

"You've really thought this through, haven't you?"

She'd hurt him, she realized, really hurt him. Chastened, she said softly, "Try to understand. I'm tired of looking at every man I see, trying to determine whether or not he could be Messenger. Is he the right age? The right height? Would he still have dark hair or would it be shot with silver? My mind is never at rest. There isn't a stable hand or a footman here who hasn't come under my scrutiny. And that's not all. I put my acquaintances and friends to the same test—Leigh Fleming, Philip Henderson, Hawkins, Reaper—"

She stopped when he began to shake his head. "What?" she asked.

"Hawkins can barely write his own name, and the others are too young."

"Well, of course, I didn't really consider them, but you see what I mean? If this goes on much longer, I really will be crazy." She took a step toward him and looked appealingly into his eyes. "Tell me the truth, Ash. If you were in my shoes, wouldn't you do everything in your power to draw this devil out?" She put her fingers over his lips to stop his quick retort. "Think of Harry. How far would you be prepared to go to catch his murderer?"

He shook his head, but his rigid posture gradually relaxed and he gave a wan smile. "Point taken. But I insist that you follow my orders to the letter. Hawkins will be your shadow if I'm not here, and you'll carry that pocket pistol you set such store by on your person at all times."

"It will become my best friend."

"See that it does. Where is Dexter?"

At the sound of his name, Dexter poked his head up from the other side of the bed and slowly ambled over to Ash. When he scratched Dexter's ears, the dog purred like a kitten.

"Make sure he is with you whenever you leave the house," Ash said.

He walked to the windows and shut and bolted them. "And make sure you lock your door behind me."

"You're . . . you're leaving me?"

One brow lifted. "What did you expect?"

"I thought you would stay the night."

A smile tugged at the corners of his mouth as he crossed to her. "You've got the wrong idea about me, Eve Dearing," he said. "I'm saving myself for marriage. *Our* marriage, as you know very well. Just say the magic words and I'm all yours."

Her mouth worked but no words came.

He gave her a moment, then dropped a careless kiss on her brow. "You'll figure it out if you think about it," and he strolled to the door and left her.

After he left Eve, Ash joined Hawkins and they made the rounds of the ground floor together, checking windows and doors, making sure that everything was as it should be. The house was too big to see to everything by themselves, so Ash made a note to have the servants see to it first thing in the morning. "And I want that scaffolding down," he said. "It's the easiest point of entry for an intruder trying to break in."

The last thing Ash did was to assemble the night porters and impress on them the need for vigilance, using the pretext that there were many strangers in the area for the fair, some of whom would be from the criminal classes with their eyes on any grand house that was not well protected.

"They'll rob us blind if they think they can get away with it."

He wasn't sure how seriously they took his warning and wished that he had a troop of soldiers under his command. Dereliction of duty had serious consequences in the army. He thought of offering them a bonus and decided against it. He didn't want to stir up speculation or suspicion in case it got back to Messenger.

It was a good hour after he left Eve before he got to his bed, but he was too keyed up to sleep. He kept thinking about Eve's story in the *Herald*, and the muscles in his stomach tied themselves in knots. To put a woman at risk for whatever reason went against his principles. And Eve wasn't any woman. If something went wrong, if anything happened to her, he would never forgive himself.

One part of him wanted to give her a good shaking, but another part—the logical part—told him that her way was the one sure way of drawing the villain out, whoever he might be. What gnawed at him was that she'd set things in motion without consulting him.

Think of Harry. How far would you be prepared to go to catch his murderer?

He would do anything, give anything, except put Eve at risk.

He was seized by the wild notion of abducting her and carrying her off to his grandfather's castle in Scotland, but that wouldn't do for long. When they came back to London, he'd always be looking over his shoulder, wondering if Messenger was right behind them. Who could live with that?

Eve couldn't have set her scheme in motion at a worse time. The fair would be noisy and crowded with people. Messenger would never have a better chance of getting to Eve than by melting into the crowd.

If only Ash had something solid to go on, but his mind was numb from going over all the details they'd discovered. There were too many bits and pieces to slot into their proper places. He needed to clear his mind, forget his preconceived notions, and start over.

It started for him at the symposium. He was determined to discover who had written those stories. His thoughts moved to Angelo, Lydia, Messenger, Eve and her fellow writers, the heckler. Other names came to him.

A theory was taking shape—imprecise, foggy, a startling change of direction that acted like a magnet on the pieces that had puzzled him for so long. He needed time to think about it, time to prove it, but—damn it all!—time was what Eve had taken away from him.

Time. What the devil was he doing in this lonely bed when who knew how much time was left to them? Eve had practically invited him to share her bed. Masculine pride was a sorry reward for what he had given up.

He got out of bed, dressed himself, and padded along the corridor to Eve's room. She wasn't asleep, either. She opened the door as soon as he knocked and called her name.

"I'm miserable without you" was all he got out before she dragged him into her room.

Their loving was different, slow, pleasurable, and almost entirely physical. In the aftermath, he wanted to talk. Eve wanted to sleep.

He kissed her brow. "What is it, Eve?" he asked. "What's wrong?"

Her head moved restlessly on the pillow. "Don't talk. Just hold me, Ash. That's all I want, to feel your arms around me."

He would have persisted in drawing her out if he hadn't wanted to avoid upsetting her before the fair. She had enough to contend with without having to placate a quarrelsome lover.

Sighing, he gathered her in his arms. Gradually, their breathing evened and they slept.

Chapter Twenty-four

The locals called their fair "the greatest fair in England," and Eve could see why. She had never seen such hordes of people milling about on the common or so many vendors selling their wares from booths and stalls. There were goldsmiths, milliners, drapers, clothiers, sellers of toys, books, medicines, and, on every corner, the marquees of cookshops and taverns with tables and benches strategically placed outside for the comfort of their customers.

Lady Sayers looked around her with satisfaction. "Not the sort of event ladies of quality should frequent," she remarked gaily. "That's what my late husband used to say. Do you know, I wasn't interested in attending the fair until he said those words? After that, you couldn't keep me away."

Everyone laughed, except Ash. In his view, the late Lord Sayers knew a thing or two. There was a darker side to the fair. Prostitutes, pickpockets, and pimps were there in force. The puppet shows were blatantly bawdy, as were the strolling actors and mimers who performed their pieces whenever two or more people gathered to watch. On the far side of the common, roped off from the tents and booths, a ring had been set up, and the roar from the spectators as the pugilists battled it out drowned the din of musicians and the hawkers who shouted their wares. Happily, no ladies were allowed to go beyond those ropes or his little crew would be demanding entrance.

As an afterthought, her ladyship added, "The crowds will thin out when it begins to get dark. That's the time I like best. The rowdies at the fight will wander off to some tavern to celebrate, or drown their sorrows, as the case may be, and the place will be left to the locals."

It was early evening, with the gold-shot sun dipping toward the horizon, and the party from the Manor included several acquaintances and friends from the symposium. This was Ash's doing, thought Eve. He had her hedged about by stalwart men-at-arms dressed up as gentlemen of fashion.

Her gaze touched on each gentleman in turn. Philip Henderson had turned up with that charming, intelligent Miss Rose, and Amanda was ignoring her as though she were one of the painted ladies who made eyes at every gentleman who strolled by. Dr. Braine was there, much to her surprise, looking more like a schoolmaster than a doctor as he lectured Liza on, Eve suspected, her latest gaffe. Leigh Fleming was firmly sandwiched between her aunt and Lady Sayers, which would suit him fine. If there was a brawl, they would protect him. Poor Leigh, he was a bookworm, not a fighter. She doubted if he even knew how to load a gun. There were others she did not know, and others she could not see, but she was sure Hawkins would be hovering nearby. Reaper, Ash had told her, was keeping an eye on Hill House.

Angelo—she couldn't think of him as Messenger—would never get near her. That was the trouble. Her plan depended on her appearing to be an easy target. If he sensed a trap, he wouldn't show himself.

But if she could read his thoughts, she'd have him!

Oh, Lord, she wasn't that brave. What if she got into his mind and never got out of it? A few seconds was all she could stand. Her perception went beyond the words that only she could hear. She could read his character, and what she read made her feel that she'd bathed in a cesspool.

Ash's voice jerked her from her thoughts. "In the meantime," he said, "keep your eyes peeled for pickpockets. Don't let anyone get too close to you." He dropped his voice, and for Eve's ears only went on, "And while you're at it, stop staring at those painted ladies or you may find yourself embroiled in a nasty war of words, and you wouldn't want to hear their words."

She made the effort to appear as though she hadn't a care in the world, knowing that if he guessed how frightened she was, he would whisk her back to the house and bar the doors.

"I know how to win a war of words," she said, and she patted her bulging reticule.

"Your pocket pistol?"

"Need you ask?"

He would have laughed if Liza had not gasped and dashed to one of the booths with the other ladies hot on her heels. He relaxed when he saw that they were only ogling the bonnets that were cunningly displayed on a long table, a lure to draw unsuspecting shoppers into the marquee where the more expensive stock was laid out.

These ladies, he thought acidly, had the instincts of puppies. Every new toy had to be investigated. And the thing that got his goat was that they didn't buy a thing. They wanted to see the wares in all the booths before they made up their minds.

Philip Henderson joined Ash and said conversationally, "I read Miss Dearing's piece in the *Herald*. I hope you both know what you are doing."

"It was Eve's idea. Had I known beforehand what she was up to, I would have stopped publication. It never occurred to me that she was setting herself up as a target."

Philip looked skeptical, but he did not press the point. Miss Rose had returned to the fold, and he gave his attention to her.

Ash's eyes scanned the crush. He wasn't the only one keeping an eye on things. Constable Keble was standing under the awning of one of the cookshops, signaling to two burly fellows who nodded and began to trail a flashy gentleman in a green coat.

He didn't know why he didn't feel confident. Everything that could be done to protect Eve was in place, and not only Eve but Lydia, as well. Not that he expected trouble in that quarter, but it paid to be cautious. Reaper was at Hill House, keeping an eye on things, and Anna was there, too.

But if his theory was right, Lydia was the last person who was in need of protection. All the same, he reminded himself, it was only a theory.

Dusk had taken a firm grip on the May Fair, but the encroaching shadows were held in check by a profusion of hanging lanterns at every booth and stall. Business wasn't as brisk as it had been earlier in the day and, as Lady Sayers had predicted, the crowds had thinned, but there were still plenty of people waiting to take in the dancing once the fiddlers in the bandstand struck up a tune.

"Don't look round," said Liza, "but I think Anna's boy is watching us."

"What?" Eve's head came up.

"I caught sight of him in the trees just now on your left, but she—I mean, he is as nervous as a deer. Something has frightened him off and he's not there now."

Eve glanced surreptitiously in the direction Liza had indicated. She could see what had frightened Nell. One of Keble's mounted officers had emerged from the trees and had stationed himself in front of a dense hedge of hawthorns.

She turned back to Liza with a sigh. They were sitting at a trestle table outside one of the more respectable cookshops, with a good view of the bandstand, refreshing themselves with punch and macaroons. Some of their party were close by or slightly apart, conversing with acquaintances who had stopped to pass the time of day. Others had wandered off.

Her eye was caught by Ash, who was at the other end of her table, conversing with Jason Ford. Ash had used Mr. Ford before, and Eve wondered if Ford had been hired to keep an eye on her. On the other hand, Liza might have invited him along to make the doctor jealous. Poor Liza. She'd get no joy there. Dr. Braine was one of those who had wandered away.

To the question in Ash's eyes, she replied by shaking her head. Nothing was troubling her, no voices or visions. If Messenger was here, she could not sense him.

Liza took up where she'd left off. "What's to become of a boy like that when Anna goes home to Cornwall? He can't speak, or he doesn't want to. He prefers animals to people. You can't get him to sleep in a bed or stay indoors. He prefers the barn to the house." She put down her tankard with a soft thud. "We'll all be going home to our own comfortable lives in another week or two. What's to become of Nell then?" She shook her head. "I meant to say Neil, of course."

Eve had watched the emotions play on the younger girl's face, and she felt a tide of affection well up inside her. Liza was so much more than showed on the surface. She was a debutante. Her ball was only a week away. Decorators were hard at work, sprucing up the picture gallery for the great event. She should be giddy with excitement. But here she was, worrying about Nell. Liza was far from perfect, but in the things that really mattered, she was pure gold.

She squeezed Liza's hand. "Neil has a champion now. Look at the time and care Anna gives to her donkeys. What do you think she is going to do with them when she leaves here?" She nodded. "Yes, she'll move heaven and earth to take them with her. Do you think she'd leave her boy behind?"

Liza did not look convinced. "I hope so, because he can't stay here. It's too dangerous. You know what I mean. If only he would stay hidden, but he comes out after dark—oh, not showing himself openly, but like tonight, watching from the shadows."

Nell was a sad case, thought Eve. She had nowhere to go, no family to take her in. She was like a wild creature that was only half tamed, not a predator but a predator's prey.

If others worked out who Neil was, she knew what

would happen. They'd discover that he was really the girl who had escaped from Bedlam and send for the keepers.

Not if Ash had anything to do with it. He'd promised he would demolish Bedlam brick by brick before he'd let Nell go back there. And if he were appointed to the board of governors, Nell's case, she was sure, would be thoroughly investigated, and not only Nell's. It was in Ash's nature to protect the weak and defenseless.

"Where is Dexter, by the way?" Liza asked.

"He's at the Manor with Andy. Lady Sayers said that no dogs were allowed at the fair, and I can see why. Dexter would have a great time chasing off those mimers and actors."

"Poor Andy. He's missing the fair."

"No. He was here earlier, and he knows I'll reward him well for his trouble."

Liza laughed. Eve smiled, but her thoughts had taken a dark turn. She felt distinctly uneasy, knowing that Nell had been drawn to the fair just when they'd set a trap for a murderer, a man who had good reason to fear Nell, too.

In spite of Ash's warning not to stare, she began to scrutinize every male in her vicinity. No blinding revelation came to her, but she sensed something, just as she had at the symposium. Blocking out the sounds of the fair, she listened with her inner ear.

She was so out of practice that at first she hardly knew what was happening. All she received were insubstantial impressions, something moving at the edges of her mind. She centered on those impressions. Feelings—they were scarcely thoughts—like wisps of ribbon touched her briefly: amusement, derision, superiority.

He knew that she was well guarded, but that only made the game all the more interesting.

She was reading his thoughts.

She clutched her reticule to her bosom in a death grip. The shape and weight of her pistol should have reassured her, but her knees were knocking, quite literally, and she pressed them together to stop her legs from trembling. She deliberately thought of Antonia and how she had found her on the quarry floor, and that steadied her as nothing else could.

The fiddlers struck up for a country dance, and the crowd fell back as a troupe of May dancers stepped lightly through the path they'd made and mounted the steps to the bandstand. More lanterns were lit, and Eve and Liza joined Ash at the edge of the spectators to watch the performance. Others in their party gradually filtered back.

Miss Claverley's eyes kept straying to Eve. *She senses my unease and is concerned about me,* thought Eve. There was no point in worrying her aunt. She would only get in the way if she took it into her head to help, so Eve nodded and smiled, then gave her attention to the dancers.

Behind her bright smile, however, her mind was still occupied with Angelo, and some time passed before the dancers got her undivided attention. The girls in their white dresses, twirling around the floor of the bandstand with their handsome partners, were just like the debutantes at a ball. Just like the dancers in her dream.

It *was* her dream, yet it was different. There were no glass doors giving onto the terrace. *Where were the glass doors? Where was the terrace?*

Her doubts subsided as quickly as they had arisen. It was just like her aunt had told her. Her dream was not an exact replica of what she would find. It was a map, and she should look for signposts. As she watched the May dancers, she knew, without a shadow of a doubt, that she had arrived at the first signpost.

Her breathing slowed and she inhaled a long, calming breath. She could have sworn that she smelled her mother's fragrance, carnation with a hint of clove. Another wisp of ribbon touched her, not briefly but winding itself around her, protecting her in a haze of love.

Antonia.

Then the ribbon floated away.

She turned her head and smiled into her aunt's troubled eyes. *All is well,* her smile said. *I know what I'm doing. Antonia is with me.*

The worry lines on Miss Claverley's brow gradually relaxed. She gave a little nod, but she did not smile.

Eve turned back to watch the dancers. She had come to the first signpost, and from this moment on, all her senses would be alert to her danger. It wouldn't be long now before she came to the second signpost.

They were still watching the May dancers when a man on horseback rode up. "Is Lord Denison here?" he cried out. "I was told Lord Denison was here."

Ash stepped forward. "I'm Lord Denison."

The rider quickly dismounted. "I have an express for you, my lord."

Frowning, Ash tore open the letter the rider had given him and took it to a lantern to read. "It's from your father," he told Eve, quickly scanning it.

"What does it say?"

"It says that Messenger died years ago." He handed Eve the express.

After reading it, Eve was nonplussed. "But this can't be true. We know he is alive."

"We got the wrong Messenger, that's all."

"I don't believe it! My father has made a mistake!"

He brushed her protest aside. "Work it out for yourself. We were looking for the wrong Messenger." To the express rider, Ash said, "Lend me your horse and you'll be twenty pounds the richer when I bring him back."

There was no haggling. Twenty pounds was as much as the express rider could earn in a year.

When Ash was mounted, he called out, "Jason, a word with you?"

Jason Ford detached himself from a group of young men and came quickly to Ash's side. "What is it?" he asked, squinting up at Ash.

Leaning low over the saddle, Ash said in an undertone, "Don't let Miss Dearing out of your sight. I'm not expecting trouble, but it pays to be cautious."

"Where are you going?" Jason asked.

"I'll tell you about it when I get back. Just stay close to Miss Dearing."

Eve watched him ride off with a sinking heart.

"You're Angelo, aren't you?" said Ash. "It was you who arranged for those stories to be published in the *Herald*."

Lydia Rivers stared at him with huge, fear-bright eyes. "How did you find out?" she asked hoarsely.

"You write Gothic fiction. You even claimed to be Angelo for a short time. But it was an express letter from George Dearing that I received not fifteen minutes ago that confirmed my suspicions. Your name is Lydia, the same name as Thomas Messenger's daughter."

He'd learned a lot more than that. Messenger, Dearing wrote, had been hanged for the murder of his wife and son in the city of York eight years before. There had been a ferocious quarrel, witnesses said, and Messenger, enraged with drink, had set his house on fire when his wife and son were asleep in their beds.

Dearing had been working in Bristol at the time and had missed the report of the crime, which had appeared in the London papers. But Martha had seen it and, for better or worse, had kept the information from him so that he would not be distressed. She wouldn't have told him except that he was planning to travel to London to look up a few former colleagues to see what he could find out.

Great, tearing sobs shook Lydia's shoulders and tears spilled down her cheeks. Her eyes darted to the door as though willing someone to enter and put a stop to his questions, but Mrs. Braine, the doctor's widowed mother, was discreetly seeing to refreshments for them, and Anna was in the barn taking care of her pregnant donkey. Had Anna been present, he doubted he'd have much success in getting a confession out of Lydia. All the same, he hadn't expected her to crumble so quickly. If he hadn't known who she was and what she'd done, he might have felt sorry for her. Sighing, he handed her his handkerchief.

Between sobs, she got out, "It's been such a burden not knowing what to say or do. I'm not sorry that you found me out. Yes, I'm Lydia Messenger."

It wasn't much of a confession, but it was a beginning. When her shoulders stopped heaving and the sobs subsided, he went on, "Antonia's notes were never sent on from the White Hart, were they? You kept them?"

She spoke in a voice he could hardly hear. "Yes, I kept them. I didn't think anyone would miss them. I started reading them and I didn't want to part with them. As I grew older, I read Mrs. Dearing's stories over and over. I thought they were wonderful. It was because of those stories that I became a writer. They inspired me, you might say."

"What I can't understand," he said, "is why you published Antonia's stories in the first place. Surely not for the money. What did you hope to gain?"

There was another bout of weeping before she answered him. "It was Robert's idea to publish them in the *Herald*. He thought it would spark everyone's interest in my books—you know, create awareness. Then, when I revealed that I was Angelo, the public would be wild to buy my novels."

"Robert." He stared at her hard. "Robert Thompson? The heckler?"

She nodded. "He wasn't really heckling us. He was only trying to cause a stir so that the public would want to know who Angelo was."

"And what is your connection to Robert Thompson?"

She looked up at him, then quickly looked away. "He was my lover," she said brokenly.

Ash was mildly surprised, not that Lydia had had a lover but that she'd taken up with someone like Thompson, the landlord of a small inn.

When she stopped weeping into his handkerchief, he said gently, "And what if the *Herald* hadn't published Antonia's stories? What if the editor turned them down? What would you have done then?"

"Nothing. It wouldn't have mattered. I suppose

Robert would have come up with another idea to get my name known. He was like that. He was so proud of me."

He looked at her in stunned disbelief. "Didn't you realize that Eve might have recognized you or her mother's stories? She could have revealed the truth. Then where would you have been?"

She shook her head. "I knew she wouldn't recognize me. There have been other symposiums and she didn't know who I was then. As for her claiming that the stories were Antonia's, Robert said that that would only stir up more speculation, and that was all to the good. Eve couldn't prove that her mother wrote the stories, because they were in my possession."

When he swore under his breath, she went on hastily, "I didn't *want* to be unkind to her, but if people thought we were rivals or that Eve was jealous of me, they would think that she claimed the stories were her mother's out of spite."

"Who chose the name Angelo?"

"Robert did. It means *Messenger*. I didn't want anyone to know my real name, but Robert said that no one would remember my father's crime after so many years."

His questions were getting him nowhere, so he decided to be more direct. "Mrs. Rivers," he said. "Lydia. Did you murder Robert Thompson?"

She gasped, and all the color drained from her face. "No! I loved Robert! I didn't know someone had murdered him until I read about it in the newspaper. Can you imagine how I felt? I was waiting for him to write to me or come to me, and all the time he was cold in his grave. I had no one to talk to, no one who could find anything out for me. He was a married man with children, and I had no claim to know anything."

He watched her bent head as her shoulders began to

heave again. Now he understood why she had gone into a decline. It wasn't the stab wound that had brought her so low or the fact that her sister hadn't come for her. There was no sister, and he doubted that there was anyone waiting for her in Warwick. It was grief for the man she loved.

"If you didn't kill Thompson," he said, "then who did?"

Another theory was beginning to form, but this time he wanted to make quite sure of his facts.

She blew her nose and dabbed at her eyes. "I don't know. The newspapers said that he was waylaid by footpads." She looked up at him. "He had no enemies as far as I knew, or none that he told me about."

He nodded and gentled his tone. "I think you know, though, who stabbed you."

She shook her head vigorously. "It was dark. I didn't see his face."

"But you said it was Angelo."

"It was what everyone expected me to say, so I took the easy way out."

He said, suddenly abrupt, "There was no note for you in your glove. You were meeting Thompson, weren't you? So what happened, Lydia? Tell me."

She exhaled a long sigh and stared at the hot coals in the grate. "I was so happy that night. I met Robert at Vauxhall and we arranged to meet later, after everyone at the Manor had gone to bed. That's all we had, stolen hours here and there. Robert would never have left his wife and children, and I wouldn't have asked him to." She stirred and looked up at him. "We were supposed to meet close to the gates of the grounds. I waited a long time, but Robert didn't appear. I was making my way back to the house when I was attacked."

If she was an actress, she was very convincing. But there was something that only she could answer. "Tell me about your brother," he said abruptly.

"M-my brother?" She seemed confused by the turn in the conversation.

"Your brother, Albert Messenger. He died in the fire with your mother, and your father hanged for their murder."

She winced and looked at him with the eyes of a pet dog that had just been kicked by its master. "My father always protested his innocence."

"Where were you when your house burned down?"

Now she was appalled. "You can't think I had anything to do with it!"

"I don't. I'm just curious."

"I'd left home by then. My father's drinking, the constant quarreling—I couldn't wait to get away. So I took a position as companion to Mrs. Northcote in Bath." She added bitterly, "But when it came out that I was a murderer's daughter, I was let go. After that, I changed my name. And that's when I became a writer."

"What about your brother? Was he in school? Where was he when your father was working away from home?"

She looked puzzled. "He was at school during term time, but in the holidays he would join my father wherever he was working. My mother..." She sighed. "My mother couldn't manage Bertie. My father was the only person he would listen to. Why do you ask?"

He was trying to place Albert Messenger at the scene of the crimes. It was possible, but he'd only been a boy then. Possible, but not something he wanted to believe.

He let a heartbeat of silence go by, then asked gently, "Was it Bertie who murdered those people in Mrs.

Dearing's stories? Was it, perhaps, your father? Or was it you, Lydia?"

Her jaw trembled. Shaking her head, she said, "Those were only stories. They weren't true."

"Weren't they? Tell me about the fire. Who identified the bodies of your mother and your brother?"

"My father. But they couldn't be identified, not conclusively. They were burned beyond recognition. Lord Denison, were those stories true?"

"I believe so."

"But they were accidents, tragic accidents. I would never have allowed them to be published if I'd thought they were murders."

Hands loosely clasped, Ash leaned forward in his chair. The last thing he wanted was to frighten her into silence, but they were at a critical point. He didn't have a choice. He had to push her.

"Here's how I see it, Lydia. When you published those stories, the person who murdered three innocent people got the shock of his life. He'd thought he'd got away with murder, but someone was reviving an interest in his old crimes. He'd want to silence that person before it was too late. You practically invited him to the symposium when you advertised the time and place. So he goes to the symposium and what does he find? Lydia Rivers, one of the Gothic writers, is hinting that she is Angelo. That's why he tried to kill you. Are you with me so far?"

She nodded mutely.

"Robert Thompson wasn't as lucky as you. I think our murderer discovered that Mr. Thompson arranged the sale of the stories to the *Herald,* so he had to die, too. I think you know or you have guessed who that person is. You never go out alone. You're practically in hiding. Who is he, Lydia? Who is he?"

She let out a low cry and seemed to collapse into herself. "It's Bertie. He didn't die in the fire. The man who died was his friend. Bertie said that he lost his memory when a beam fell on him. He didn't know he was Albert Messenger until recently. I wanted to believe him. He is my brother, but he frightens me. He has always frightened me."

"He must have taken another name?"

Her voice broke. "Jason Ford. I didn't know he was alive until the night of the symposium."

Disbelief exploded in Ash's brain. "My God," he muttered, "what have I done?"

Chapter Twenty-five

For the longest time, Eve sat in a daze, absently sipping at her jug of punch as the thoughts teemed inside her mind. She was hardly aware of who came and went in the cookshop. All she could think about was her father's letter and how it made nonsense of what she had sensed with her celebrated Claverley charisma.

Thomas Messenger had hanged for the murder of his wife and son eight years before. There was only one Messenger left—Lydia. But if Messenger was dead, that meant that those half-formed impressions she'd sensed from Angelo tonight were either a figment of her imagination or they came from Lydia.

Everything inside her rejected that conclusion. She couldn't bring Lydia Messenger's face to mind, but she did remember that she was just a slip of a girl, perhaps a year or two older than her brother. Thin, shrinking, fearful—that was what she remembered when she thought of Lydia. In fact, much like the Lydia of today.

Her memory could be at fault. After all, she'd only

met the Messengers at the White Hart, and they'd kept pretty much to themselves. She thought of them now and tried to bring Lydia's image into focus. Could she have pushed Antonia from the top of the quarry? Could she have murdered those so-called accident victims in Antonia's stories? Was it Lydia's thoughts she'd read when Nell was attacked? And what about the attack on Lydia? It didn't make sense.

She was missing something. The first chance she got, she was going to read those stories again. The first time she'd read them, she hadn't realized they were her mother's stories. After that, she'd read them believing that Thomas Messenger was the murderer, but if Messenger was dead, what was she left with?

She was startled when someone said her name. Jason Ford had got up and was smiling down at her.

"We've been sitting here too long," he said. "Shall we go for a walk to stretch our legs? I'm beginning to get pins and needles in my toes."

She'd forgotten that Jason had been asked to keep an eye on her. She was still thinking about Antonia's stories and was impatient to go through them one careful line at a time.

On impulse, she said, "I want to go back to the Manor."

"The Manor? That's a long walk. Why do you want to go there?"

She said the first thing that came to her. "To change my coat. The one I'm wearing isn't warm enough now that the sun has gone down."

He hesitated, then lifted his shoulders in a helpless shrug, as if to say, *Women!* "I should tell Lady Sayers where we are going. Hawkins, I know, won't let us out of his sight, so I suppose there's no harm in it. Don't move from this spot. This won't take long."

He was right about Hawkins. She'd seen him from time to time, floating around, always within earshot, but her other protectors had relaxed their vigilance since Ford had taken over. They must know that he was good at his job. As a former soldier and Special Branch agent, he was undoubtedly the best to be had.

The minutes ticked by. She was wondering what had happened to Ford when a sudden burst of energy exploded behind her eyes, blinding her momentarily. When the light faded and she could see again, she could feel that the fine hairs on her neck were raised like a cat's fur.

Angelo. He was here somewhere, and no one and nothing could convince her to change her mind.

Ford was gone so long that she was becoming alarmed. She didn't complain when he returned, however, firstly because she was still shaken from her most recent brush with Angelo and secondly because she felt beholden to him. He should have been flirting with all the pretty girls, not acting nursemaid to her.

"Shall we go?" He seemed a little out of breath.

When she got up, she looked beyond him to the bandstand. The May dancers had left and their places had been taken by girls from the village. Girls in white dresses were whirling around the floor in tempo to the music.

It wasn't a figment of her imagination. This was a signpost. It was time to move on.

Nell flattened herself against a tree as the bad man and the kind lady crossed a short stretch of turf to the path that led to the big house. Her eyes strained through the gloom to keep them in sight. They were leaving the fair, leaving the bright lights behind. It was the sound of the music that had lured her to the fair. It made her feel happy, but that was before she saw the man with the limp. Now she was terror-struck. Where was the man called Hawkins? Why wasn't he following the kind lady?

Eve. That was her name.

The girl dressed as a boy mouthed the word, but no sound came. Eve and all the other kind ladies were her family now, and Dexter, and Fanny and Fiona and Faith. Anna said that families were not always made up of parents and children but of kindred souls who stuck together through thick and thin.

Fear gripped her heart. Her family didn't know that the bad man had taken Eve away. If she went back to the fair, she would lose sight of them. She looked around wildly. No Hawkins, and no Lord Denison. Anna said that they were friends. They would help her, but they were not here.

She had never seen the bad man's face until tonight, but she knew his gait. He wore a boot with a raised heel. She'd heard him when she'd hidden in the tall grasses and he'd run away after he'd stabbed Lydia. She'd heard how he dragged his left leg when he tried to give chase.

She whimpered and looked at the two figures on the path who were melting into the shadows. The bad man had tried to kill Lydia, then her. Was he going to do the same to Eve?

She took a shuddering breath and went after them.

It started with the same vague impressions that she had picked up earlier, something moving at the edge of her mind, and she blocked out the sound of Jason's voice to listen with her inner ear.

Amusement. Derision. Superiority.

She opened her mind, hoping to absorb more, then quailed at the sudden surge of a voice that was jubilant with the prospect of a kill.

She thinks I don't know about the pistol in her reticule. A blind man could see it. That's a good girl, Evie. Keep walking. Keep listening to my inane banter. Only a little while longer and I'll slit your throat.

She didn't stumble, she didn't falter, but only because she was numb with fear. By sheer force of will, she kept her panic at bay, and she had good reason to panic. The charming, handsome man at her side was going to kill her.

Angelo was Jason Ford. She recognized the bitter aftertaste he left in her mind. She would puzzle it out later, if there was a later for her.

Thoughts chased through her mind at the speed of lightning. There was no Hawkins nearby to save her. That blast of energy she'd felt must have come when Ford disabled him. Oh, God, she hoped he wasn't dead. Why hadn't she read him better? Was it because she was too taken up with her own thoughts? Too preoccupied? Just as she was now?

She opened her mind a crack and was overwhelmed by the tide of hatred that pushed inside.

You should have kept your nose out of my business. You shouldn't have stirred up a hornets' nest by publishing those stories. No one gets the better of Albert Messenger and gets away with it. Fucking bitch! How did you come to know so much?

Her mind went blank, then burst with enlightenment. Albert Messenger was Jason Ford! He hadn't died in that fire. And if she didn't get away from him, she'd become his next victim.

One part of her brain was telling her feet to keep moving. Another part was trying to think of a plan of escape. She couldn't get to her pistol because he knew about it. She couldn't outrun him, though it might come down to that yet. She had to do something. *Think, Eve, think!*

He had a slight limp. Maybe she *could* outrun him.

"You're very quiet, Miss Dearing."

At the sound of his voice, she suddenly stopped and clutched a hand to her heart. Stupid, stupid, stupid to give herself away like that!

His eyes narrowed on her face.

She managed a wan smile. "I have a stitch in my side. Could we rest for a moment?"

The suspicion in his voice faded. "Of course."

He turned his head, looking back the way they had come. She could read him clearly now. He was making sure that there were no witnesses so that he could finish her here. If she didn't act now, it would be too late.

"Can you see Mr. Henderson?" she asked, improvising madly. "He said he would catch up to me at the house."

She could tell that he didn't like that.

He took his time to scan the shrubbery and trees bordering the path. "It's too dark to see much beyond the lights at the fair—"

Before he had stopped speaking, she swung her reticule in a great arc, aiming for his head. He was too quick for her. He ducked, and the force of the blow caught him on the shoulder. Down he went, but as he fell back, he grabbed for her skirts and pulled her down with him.

He was above her, and, dark or no, she could see the

silver gleam of a blade as he brought it down. To avoid the thrust, she twisted sideways and rolled frantically. The knife sliced her arm from elbow to wrist, and he raised it again.

Just when she thought her last moments had come, a feral cat—something—catapulted from the bushes, fastened itself around Jason's arm, and bit down on his wrist. His howl of pain as he dropped the knife sent shivers down Eve's spine. She didn't have to read his mind. She could tell that he'd been bitten to the bone. She scrambled to her feet.

Her right arm—the arm he'd sliced—was aching as though a hot coal was embedded in it. Blood was dripping from her fingers. She was in no condition to get her pistol out of her reticule, and she didn't know whether she could shoot with her left hand.

She let out a shaken breath as the wild cat loomed in front of her.

"Eve..." The voice was low, the word not quite perfect, as though a baby was testing its speech. It was Neil who came to her side. Anna's boy. Nell. "Eve...come."

Eve looked past Nell. Ford was searching the ground for his knife. She felt the exact moment his hand closed around it. His savage anger filled her mind with dread. He had a gun in his right pocket, but he would use it only as a last resort.

"Run!" she cried, and she and Nell dashed for the cover of the trees.

If it had not been for Nell, she would have been running in circles. The trees were so dense that she quickly lost her bearings. As they stood in the shelter of a bushy evergreen, Eve sorted all that she knew into slots that would help her decide what to do next.

The house was close by, but all the doors and windows would be locked to keep out the riffraff. By the time one of the night porters answered the knocker, Jason would have caught them, and he would be expecting them to make for the house. But Dexter was there with Andy. If only she could get Andy to let them in… or she could fire her gun to attract attention. That wouldn't do. The porters would come running, but Jason might get to her before they opened the door.

In a sea of indecision, she began to examine the only other alternative—to return to the fair—when, through a gap in the trees, she saw the moon in all its majesty appear from behind a cloud. Its pale, silvery shafts of light glazed the roof of the Manor and the tops of the trees nearby.

Her breath caught. It was just like the night she went out to look for her mother. The moon had come out from behind a cloud to guide her steps. Some would call it a coincidence. She saw it as a sign.

"We're going to the Manor," she whispered to Nell.

Ash left Reaper at Hill House with instructions to shoot to kill if Jason Ford showed his face, then he rode back to the fair at breakneck speed. The moon was up, but the hedgerows, shrubbery, and trees that flashed by him hardly registered. His mind was tortured with thoughts of Eve and how he'd practically invited Jason Ford to kill her. His one hope was Hawkins. That crusty old comrade-at-arms was no fool. He'd never take his eyes off Eve.

His sense of dread took a gargantuan leap when he rode up to the marquee where he'd left Eve. There was no sign of Eve or Ford, but Hawkins was there, hemmed about by a crush of people whom Constable Keble was holding at bay. Dr. Braine was there, too, trying to get Hawkins to cooperate while he examined a gash on his head, and Hawkins was doing his best to get away from those ministering hands. When he saw Ash, he tottered to his feet.

Ash dismounted, handed the reins to Leigh Fleming, who appeared to be numb with shock, and elbowed his way to his groom.

"I never took my eyes off her," Hawkins cried out. "I was in that spinney over there." He gestured to a clump of shrubbery. "Someone struck me from behind. I saw something silver flash, then my head exploded."

The constable added, "We think he was clubbed by the butt of gun. He's lucky that's all that happened to him."

"Yes," said Ash. "A knife can be messy. A gun is too noisy. He's not going to draw attention to himself if he can help it." He looked at Keble. "Miss Dearing?"

"We're making a search, but we haven't found her yet."

"But somebody must have seen something."

"She was with Mr. Ford," Keble said, "but we can't find him, either."

Fear gripped Ash's throat and blood began to beat furiously at his temples. For a moment he felt dizzy and he swayed on his feet, but a blast of anger, savage in its intensity, cleared his brain. He had counted Jason Ford among his friends. He had recommended him as a trusty investigator to other friends. And Jason Ford had counted on his exemplary war record to gain him entry to Ash's world. Ford knew him so well, knew he would go out of his way to assist a former comrade-in-arms, especially one who had been wounded in battle.

He, Ash Denison, had always considered himself a

shrewd judge of character, and all the time he'd been a pawn in the other man's game. All Ford had wanted was to discover Angelo's identity and silence him before his own crimes came to light.

In Ash's opinion, Lydia's silence would not have saved her for long. As for Eve...

If that bastard had harmed one hair of Eve's head, he'd crush him into oblivion!

To the constable, he said, "This is no time for long explanations. Tell your men that Jason Ford has abducted Miss Dearing. He is armed and dangerous."

"What?" Keble looked closely at Ash's face, finally nodded and said, "I'll see to it."

"And there's a Greek folly around here somewhere and—"

"They're local men." Keble patted Ash's arm. "They know where to look. Don't you worry. We'll find her."

"Do you need a description of Ford?"

"Oh, no. I remember him well. He used to work for Special Branch."

After the constable went off, Ash stood, lost in thought, mangling his leather gloves as though he wanted to strangle them. He didn't know where to begin to look for Eve. Why didn't she use her Claverley charisma to tell him? She'd done it once when she'd pulled him into her dream. She could do it again.

Why would she? he asked himself savagely. He had always acted the part of a doubting Thomas. Where was his skepticism now?

The thought that she might be lying dead in some godforsaken place was one he refused to accept. She would survive. She had more than her wits to help her. She had the charisma.

On that thought, he shouldered his way through the

crush of people. "Miss Claverley?" he called out. "Miss Claverley?"

He found her eventually with Lady Sayers, sitting on the steps of the bandstand. She looked up at his approach, and the worry lines on her brow became less pronounced.

Before he could ask a question, she said, "I can't tell you much, but I do know that she is all right."

Lady Sayers looked dazed. "They say that someone knocked Hawkins out and now Eve is missing. What's going on?"

"That's what we're trying to find out." He looked another question at Miss Claverley.

She shook her head. "That's all I can tell you. The rest is up to you."

She was looking up at him with such trusting eyes that he felt like a fraud. He didn't know where to begin to look for Eve.

Liza elbowed her way through the crush and put her hand on Ash's arm. "I saw her," she said. "She was with Jason. I think they were going to the Manor."

Chapter Twenty-six

They moved with the caution of little voles who had caught the scent of a fox. Nell was truly a creature of the night. Her hearing was acute, and whenever she heard a twig snap, she steered them into cover. But Eve wasn't without her own way of detecting their hunter. She was picking up clues as though he were drawing a map inside her head.

At one point, she clutched Nell's arm. "He can see us!"

Her words were no louder than a soft sigh. They both listened. Then they heard him. He was moving ahead of them, trying to cut them off from the house. Caution became a luxury they could no longer afford. With Nell leading the way, they ran like deer, jumping over obstacles, tearing through patches of briars, ducking under branches, unheeding of the scratches and splinters that tore at their exposed skin.

When they burst out of the underbrush bordering the Manor's great sweep of lawns, Nell was all for making a dash for it to the front door. Eve held her back.

The lamps outside had been lit, and unless the porters opened the doors at once, they would become easy targets.

They were both breathing hard, but Eve was ready to collapse. She didn't have Nell's stamina. The little runaway from Bedlam had regained her strength. She was always on the move, roaming what had become her private domain at all hours of the night.

Nell brushed her fingers against Eve's cheek to get her attention. "Come," she mouthed.

Eve frowned and closed her good hand around Nell's wrist, signaling her to wait. Now that they had stopped their panicked dash, the arm that was bleeding was making itself felt. She did her best to ignore it and held her head up, waiting, focusing, anticipating his next move.

"Not that way," she whispered against Nell's ear. "He's waiting for us. We go this way."

There was no argument from Nell. She seemed to trust Eve's instincts implicitly. But Eve had more to go on than instinct. She had locked her mind on Ford's and was reading him like an open book.

It was one thing to avoid their hunter, but Eve had no idea how they would get into the house. All the windows and doors were locked, unless the porters had overlooked the door to the coal cellar, and she couldn't see that happening, not with Ash now in charge of things. Their only hope was to break one of the basement windows and enter that way.

Once again, Nell surprised her. She led Eve to the window that gave onto the laundry, the place where she and Nell had first met. The window was locked, but Nell gave the sneck a sharp tap with the heel of her hand and the window swung open. It was the first time Eve had heard the girl laugh—a sweet, low, melodic sound with a hint of mischief. Oddly enough, Nell's laugh brought a lump to Eve's throat. Nell went first and Eve climbed in after her.

It was warm in the laundry, and the coals from the boiler gave them some light. Now that they'd found a refuge, Eve was beginning to give in to fatigue and pain. She was trembling all over, and her muscles felt as though Anna's donkeys had stomped all over her. But it was her arm that gave her the most trouble. She clamped it to her side, not only to stanch the bleeding but as though she could put out the fire that burned there.

Nell was looking at her with a question in her eyes. Eve said, "We'll go and get Dexter. I want you to stay with him until I come and get you. I'm not leaving you, Nell. I'm going to look for one of the night porters, or maybe some of the servants have come back from the fair and they'll help me. But you are not to come downstairs. I want you to stay in the attics until it's safe to come out." She breathed deeply. "And if anything happens to me, find Lord Denison and stay close to him."

When she put her hand on Nell's arm, she could feel the girl's tremors. "Look." She fumbled with her reticule and produced her pistol. "Take it," she said, but Nell shied away and shook her head violently. Eve tried again. "It's all that stands between us and that monster, and I don't know if I can hit a mark with my left hand."

"Dexter," said Nell simply.

Eve closed her eyes. She was too tired to argue the point. "Dexter," she said. "Fine. We'll go together. Give me a moment first." She discarded her reticule and held the pistol in her left hand.

Since they had entered the laundry, she had been too

wrapped up in her own troubles to try to read Ford, but now she focused her thoughts and opened her mind to him.

And she was blinded by a torrent of frightening images. He was inside the house. The porters trusted him, and he'd sent them outside on a pretext. He knew where they were hiding and he was on the stairs coming to get them.

A moment before, she'd been as limp as a rag doll. Now she started to her feet, every nerve and bone in her body tensed for action. She gave Nell a push. "Get Dexter. He's with Andy in the attics. I'll be right behind you, but don't look back." Nell's face was white with fear. There wasn't time to reassure the girl. "Take the old staircase." Eve stopped. Nell didn't know the house beyond the basement. "I'll show you. Go to the top floor. If you can't find Andy's room, call Dexter's name. He'll let you know where he is."

Nell struggled to say the words. "You . . . come, too."

Eve stared into her anxious eyes. "Oh, I will. But you're more nimble than I am."

They heard a sound and froze. He was trying to be stealthy, but a board had creaked on the servants' stairs. That sound spurred Eve on. She gave Nell another push, and together they crept past the warren of kitchens, closets, and box rooms to the staircase on the west wing of the house.

"Keep going," she urged.

She knew the exact moment he opened the door and entered the servants' hall. So did Nell. The girl said nothing, but she quickened her pace. He heard them and came barreling through that long, long corridor, knocking over small tables and other obstacles in his path. His gammy leg didn't seem to be slowing him down.

Fear bordering on panic had Eve and Nell scrambling up the stairs. Eve's feet had never moved faster. Muscles she hadn't known existed began to cramp in her legs. The pistol she clutched in her left hand got heavier by the second. She could hardly draw breath. If Nell hadn't been there, she would have stopped and taken her chances against Ford. She had the gun, primed and ready, and she knew how to use it. But something else was at work in her. This lovely child–woman had never had a chance in life. If it was the last thing she did, Eve would give Nell that chance. He wasn't going to snuff out her life as he'd done with so many other innocents.

She stopped Nell before she started on the last flight of stairs. A half-formed plan was taking shape inside her head. Gasping for breath, she got out, "This way," and she opened the nearest door and pushed Nell into the main part of the house. Pointing, she said, "Take the main staircase and find Dexter. No, listen to me, Nell. It's best if we split up. I have my gun. You'll have Dexter. Andy will be there. Tell him to get the porters! Use sign language, anything, but get Andy to bring the porters to me. Dexter will be with you. He won't let anyone take you away."

They heard him on the stairs. He was close, very close, and there was no time to lose. "Go!" Eve's voice was rough with strain.

With an agonized cry, Nell went haring up the stairs. Eve closed the staircase door with a snap. She wanted Ford to hear it. Slowly, carefully, she backed away. She knew exactly what she was doing. The picture gallery was only a few steps away, and it had been turned into a ballroom for Liza's ball. It wasn't the ballroom of her dream, but it was close enough to make little difference, if only she could trust her aunt's advice. She was following the map Antonia had given her.

She didn't feel brave or confident. Her whole body was trembling. She was committing herself to a leap of faith. If she was wrong . . . but that didn't bear thinking about. At least she had saved Nell.

There was a lamp lit in the corridor, but it gave very little light. She was aware, but only barely, of an antiseptic smell. The thought faded almost as soon as it occurred to her. Her eyes were fixed on the door he would come through. She wasn't trying to read him now. All her thoughts were focused on her dream.

She positioned herself beside the door to the picture gallery and kept her pistol hidden in the folds of her skirts. Whatever happened to her, she wasn't going to allow this murderous devil to escape.

The staircase door opened slowly, stealthily. She allowed him one glimpse of her, then she slipped into the picture gallery. There were no lamps lit, but light from the corridor filtered in and the moonlight dappled the floorboards. She knew now what she had smelled in the corridors. There was fresh paint on the walls.

For her purposes, the door had to remain open, but she didn't want to be locked in with him. She fumbled for the key, but her fingers were numb and wet with blood, and she couldn't remove it.

She backed away from the door. A curious sense of detachment had fallen over her. The key didn't matter. Here, it would end.

She turned and took in the long gallery at a glance— the furniture under Holland covers in the middle of the room, long windows at one end open to let the fumes of the paint escape, the bare floorboards.

Her eyes were drawn to the long windows. Not

French doors leading onto the terrace, but long windows overlooking the lush gardens and the orchards beyond. She'd come to the final signpost.

She heard a step and turned to face him. She wasn't panicked. It helped that the furniture in the middle of the room was between them. She wasn't brave so much as resolved. She was her mother's daughter and Antonia had prepared her for this desperate, ultimate moment.

He closed the door and locked it, then slowly advanced toward her. He was dragging his left foot. "You should have locked the door, Evie," he said. "Not that it would have made a difference. I would have broken it down to get to you." He glanced at the open window. "You're not thinking of climbing down the scaffolding? My dear girl, you're not a heroine in one of your books."

She was silent, taking impressions. The pistol was in his pocket, the knife was up his sleeve. His wrist, where Nell had bitten it, was a score he was going to settle. He was right-handed and now his right hand was useless.

As he edged closer, she kept pace with him, keeping the stacked furniture between them. He didn't know her pistol was hidden in the folds of her skirts. He thought she was defenseless and easily dealt with.

"I suppose," he went on, "the little bitch from Bedlam is hiding in the closet. Oh, yes, I know who she is. It's an open secret at the Manor that you ladies are harboring a fugitive. I won't hurt her. I'll simply send her back to Bedlam."

He cocked his head to the side. "Don't you remember me, Evie?"

On his lips, the familiar form of her name was an insult. Two could play at that game. She forced a laugh. "I wouldn't show my face in Bedlam if I were you, *Bertie*. You'll be mistaken for an inmate."

That wiped the smile off his face. "So you do know who I am! I know I didn't give myself away. Did you recognize me?"

She chose her words with care. She didn't think he'd take kindly to knowing that she could read his mind, and she wanted to pick his brains clean so that she would know why he had killed all those years ago. She wanted to know what had happened to her mother.

"Not at first," she said. "Well, you're quite the gentleman now, aren't you? But after I published my story about the quarry, I knew you would come after me."

"I wouldn't have if you hadn't signed your name. Do you know, until that point, I believed that Lydia was the author of those stories? Your trouble, Evie, is that you couldn't leave well enough alone. It made things very awkward for me."

She adopted the same conversational tone as his. "Actually, I thought your father would come after me, until I learned that he died a long time ago." She angled her head to the side. "When I think of it, though, you're the image of your mother. I should have recognized you." And that was sheer fabrication. She could hardly remember the family.

"My mother—" He had to drag air into his lungs. "My mother was a sniveling bitch."

"Oh? What harm did she ever do you?"

His memory passed into her mind, and she could have wept with the pain of it. She no longer cared about caution. Her voice quivered with grief and anger. "Your father was drunk that night, wasn't he? At the White Hart? He was drunk, and you decided to take his place and kill my father. Your mother tried to stop you, and when she couldn't, she told Antonia. My mother went out after you, and you pushed my mother from the top of the quarry."

He had stopped moving and was staring at her as though he'd seen a ghost. "How can you possibly know all this?"

She groped for a reasonable explanation and found none.

"Lydia!" he said, snarling the word. "Lydia told you! She and my mother always had their suspicions, but that was all—suspicions. You mustn't believe all the gossip you hear." He paused. "But in this case, I'll let you into a little secret. *Mea culpa*. I did it."

She could see it as though the memory belonged to her. "My mother told me it was an accident, but I knew it wasn't true. You were up there, afraid to come down, and she was afraid that I would climb those stairs and try to find you. She tried to protect me."

"I wish you had climbed those stairs," he said viciously. "Then I would have thrown you off the top of the quarry, too."

Grief made her heedless. "Poor Bertie," she spoke as though she were addressing a little boy. "You were always the little runt whom everyone turned on, weren't you?" She paused and flinched as pictures of his memories formed in her mind, but she went on relentlessly, "The maid who told you to use the back door? The footman who caught you stealing? And Harry, the boy who laughed when you fell off your horse? But you showed them, didn't you, Bertie? No one gets on the wrong side of Bertie Messenger and goes unpunished."

He gave her another obscenely boyish grin. "My, my. Lydia does have a busy tongue, doesn't she? I'll soon put a stop to that. Not that it matters. Those were accidents. The coroner said so."

She couldn't hide her revulsion. "That will change when it gets out that little Bertie Messenger didn't die in that fire, that he assumed a new name and a new life." She stopped and inhaled sharply. "Jason Ford. That was the name of the boy who died in the fire."

Her words obviously jolted him. "How could you possibly know that? I never told anyone."

She said slowly, "You took the identity of the boy you murdered, the boy your father identified as his own son. What did that boy ever do to harm you?"

The suspicion in his eyes was replaced by amusement. "Nothing. I was tired of my old life, tired of being the son of a broken-down drunk. Jason had money and no family or friends who would miss him. I couldn't let an opportunity like that pass me by. Now, could I?"

"You let your father hang for murder?"

He gave a theatrical sigh. "It was supposed to look like an accident. There was nothing I could do to save my father."

"No. I don't suppose there was. There's only one person you love, and that's the reflection you see in a mirror."

His only response was a laugh.

She was running out of things to say, running out of ways to delay him. How long would it take for Andy to fetch the porters? Where was Ash? Where, oh, where was Ash, and why had she never told him that she loved him?

It looked as though his patience was coming to an end. Trying not to sound desperate, she said, "You made a fatal blunder when you attended the symposium. Lydia recognized you."

"I wanted her to recognize me. I thought that she had published those stories and I had to know how much she knew. Yes, I'd changed my name, but so had she. We didn't want to be recognized as Thomas Messenger's children."

"Poor Lydia. Is she going to be your next victim?"

He laughed. "No, Evie. You'll be my next victim."

She brought up her pistol and aimed it straight at his heart. It was in her left hand, and she was praying that at this distance she would not miss. "Your luck has run out, Bertie. I think the phrase is, 'Prepare to meet thy Maker.' No doubt the devil will be happy to see you again."

He shook his head. "You'll never pull that trigger. Not in cold blood. Why, that would make you no better than I am."

He spoke the truth. Tears of frustration stung her eyes, and she lowered her pistol a fraction. She wouldn't put a bullet through his heart. She'd put a bullet in his good leg, supposing she could keep her pistol steady.

They were both startled when something heavy smashed against the door. The snarling and baying sounded as though a lion with a thorn in its paw was trying to attack them.

"Dexter!" Eve cried out.

Her eyes jerked back to Ford just as he leaped for her. She pulled the trigger, but the shot went wild.

"Eve!" Ash's voice. "Hold on! Do you hear? Hold on!"

She couldn't answer. She and Ford were locked together on the floor, and she was desperately trying to keep the point of his knife away from her throat. One thrust would have finished her off, but he didn't seem to have the strength to complete the movement. Then it came to her. Nell had bitten his wrist to the bone. He was handicapped by his injury, forced to rely on the use of his left hand.

The din coming from the door made her heart sing. Dexter's furious snarls were almost drowned out by the shattering sound of the door as it began to give way under Ash's maddened onslaught. She had to hang on. She groped for her pistol and smashed it into the hand that was holding the knife. Ford let out a howl of pain and dropped the knife. She took full advantage and rolled, taking the knife with her.

"Bitch, fucking bitch!" Ford bit out. He sprang up and kicked her in the ribs.

He would have come at her again, and she was in no condition to stop him. She was doubled up with pain, but the door suddenly gave way and Ash and Dexter came in together. Behind them, she caught a glimpse of Nell.

Ford straightened and faced Dexter's ferocious charge. She was inside his mind. He had a pistol. As Dexter tore down the length of the gallery to bring him down, Ford debated. If he shot the dog, he would have nothing to defend himself against Denison or any of the porters.

He made his decision in a split second. Turning, he ran for the open window and jumped. All the air rushed out of Eve's lungs. She could read his horror as he hurtled toward the ground. He hadn't known that the scaffolding had been removed earlier that day.

She pulled herself to her knees, then to her feet, and stumbled to the window. Far below, on the terrace of one of the downstairs rooms, Bertie Messenger lay unmoving, spread-eagled on his face.

The nightmare was over.

Then she was in Ash's arms, with Dexter licking the blood from her hand. There was no emotion left in her, no tears and no anger. "He didn't know about the scaffolding," she said.

Ash's arms tightened around her. After a moment, he pulled her away from the window. His hands shook as he smoothed her hair back from her face. He was having trouble breathing, and not only because of his maddened sprint up three flights of stairs and his frenzied charge against the locked door. He thought he had lost her. His mind could hardly grasp that it was Ford who had fallen to his death and not Eve.

"He didn't know that the scaffolding had been removed," she repeated hoarsely. "He thought he would climb down and get away."

His voice betrayed the violence that was still pumping hard and fast through his blood. "He could never have run far enough to get away from me. Don't talk now. I'm going to get you to bed and have the doctor look at your arm."

She was beginning to sound drowsy. "It can't be that bad. It hardly slowed me down. Only I couldn't use it to hold up my pistol." She had something important to tell him, and she groped in her mind before it came to her. "Do you want to know what happened to Harry?"

"Hush. Tell me later."

He stooped down, hoisted her in his arms, and began to walk to the door. The gallery was beginning to fill up with porters. To one, he said, "Get the doctor. He's at the fair. And if you can't find Dr. Braine, any doctor will do. And see if you can find Constable Keble." To another, he said, "Get everyone out of here and lock the door. There's a body outside on the terrace below this gallery. I want it guarded until the constable gets here. Don't let anyone touch anything."

When they were in the corridor, she whispered, "Where is Nell?"

He replied soothingly, "She was right behind me when I entered the gallery. I'm sure she slipped away when she saw that you were all right."

"Is Dexter here?"

He looked around. "No."

She smiled to herself. "He'll be with Nell."

He saw Andy in the corridor, looking lost and afraid. Ash tried to gentle his voice. The boy was no more than twelve or thirteen. "I want you to help me take care of Miss Dearing. There should be a medicine box in the kitchen. Bring it to her room. Oh, and good job, Andy. You did well."

Andy smiled and ran for the door to the servants' staircase.

As Ash laid Eve on the bed, she said weakly, "I'm sure there are more victims we know nothing about. I had the impression of him once as a two-year-old child in a man's body. So much strength in the hands of a two-year-old in the throes of a temper tantrum. A man like that would kill you as soon as look at you."

"Not anymore," he said, "thanks to one brave, intrepid girl."

She smiled at that, then whimpered when he began to dry her arm with a towel. "That hurts!"

"Not half as much as it hurts me," he replied.

She gave a valiant chuckle as though he had made a joke, but he wasn't joking. None of this would have happened if he had trusted Eve's intuition. He hadn't been lured away from Eve's side. He'd been completely caught up in his own grasp of events and had overridden her protests. And waiting his chance in the wings was his worst nightmare, the monster who snuffed out lives as indifferently as other men snuffed out candles.

He'd handed her over to Jason Ford without a second thought. No thanks to him that she had survived. She'd even explained why Dexter did not bark when Ford had stalked her when she was out looking for Nell. Dexter was used to Ford's scent. He was at the house often enough. As long as Ford did not threaten Eve, he was safe from her dog.

Ash was with her when the doctor arrived. Dr. Braine tiptoed around, casting sideways glances at Ash as though half afraid that he was in the presence of a sleeping lion. He tiptoed out with the assurance that, though Miss Dearing would always carry a thin scar, no real harm was done and a small dose of laudanum would be sufficient to dull the pain.

Ash closed the door behind the doctor and took his chair again. His eyes were unwavering on Eve's face. "Now tell me about Harry," he said. "That is, if you are up to it."

"Oh, I'm up to it. I'm not an invalid. I feel I can breathe again, as though the terrible pressure that was suffocating me has finally been lifted."

He took her hand and waited for her to begin.

She spoke simply and without drama or emotion. "Albert Messenger was afraid of horses. Harry wasn't. A mounted groom took Harry up in front of him and trotted around the pasture. Harry enjoyed every minute of it. Then it was Albert's turn. Well, he wasn't going to let a cripple like Harry show him up. But no sooner had he mounted the horse than he fell off. Everyone laughed, but it was Harry's laughter that incensed him."

She paused to gather her thoughts before going on.

"The impressions I got from Messenger were fleeting, but it was the memory of Harry that I locked on to. I saw him in an invalid chair in the garden, reading a book. He was enjoying the story."

Ash's voice was thick. "Harry was like that. He took pleasure in simple things."

"I can tell."

"Go on. Tell me what happened next."

She gave a tiny sigh. "Albert came along and offered to wheel Harry down to the river. There were no servants about. Albert had chosen his moment with care. You know the rest."

"Did . . . did he suffer?"

"Not for long. He wasn't frightened at first. He thought it was a game gone wrong."

They sat quietly for a long time, not saying anything, then she stirred and pulled herself up. "As I said before, he had the control of a two-year-old child. His other victims . . ." She shook her head. "They made him feel small and he tossed them away like broken toys."

He got up and walked to the window and stared out, obviously lost in thought. After a while she said his name, bringing his attention back to her.

"You can trust what I say, Ash. I didn't imagine any of it. I *was* inside Messenger's mind."

He gave a humorless smile. "The Claverley charisma? Believe me, I'm a convert. I only wish I'd learned to trust it before we got to this pass."

She wasn't sure how to take him. She'd finally got what she wanted—Ash convinced that her charisma was real—but it didn't make her feel the way she'd thought she'd feel.

There was a tap at the door and Miss Claverley entered. "I've brought the dose of laudanum the doctor prescribed," she said.

She bustled about and Ash withdrew, saying that he would tidy himself and return later.

Eve tried to stay awake, but after taking the laudanum, she fell into an exhausted sleep.

Chapter Twenty-seven

The following morning, Ash and Eve had a short conference before they met with Constable Keble. They both agreed to pare the events of the night before to the essentials. Anything else would have caused a great deal of pain to innocent people—Lydia for one and Robert Thompson's widow for another. Nell, of course, had to be protected at all costs. Besides, the truth would sound so far-fetched that they doubted whether the constable would believe them.

They met in a little parlor just off the music room, and though the door was closed to give them privacy, Eve couldn't help feeling that the walls had ears. The house was quiet, too quiet for her comfort.

When Ash gave her a nod, she composed herself and embarked on the story she had rehearsed. Jason Ford, she said, stumbled out of the shrubbery and told her that someone had waylaid him, hit him on the head, and proceeded to rob him. She wanted to summon the constable, but Ford wouldn't hear of it. In retrospect, she thought that the same person who had attacked Hawkins had also attacked Mr. Ford. He complained of a headache, but other than that, he seemed fine to her, and when she mentioned that her coat wasn't warm enough, he offered to escort her back to the Manor so that she could find a warmer one. And that was when everything went terribly wrong.

He became disoriented, and when she tried to help him, he turned on her. Panicked, she ran away. It all ended in the picture gallery, when Mr. Ford threw himself out the window after slicing her arm with a knife.

The constable nodded a lot, occasionally smiled, and asked a few questions to clarify glaring omissions in her recitation. Her replies were vague.

"Some men never get over the war," Ash threw in at this point. "It preys on their minds. I think that's what happened to Ford."

There was a long silence, then Keble looked up at Eve, his mouth quirking with wry humor. "No wonder you're a writer," he said. "That was quite a story. Oh, don't mistake me. I'll write it down word for word in my official report. But to satisfy my curiosity, I'd like to hear the bits you've left out."

Ash smiled sheepishly. "Just between us two?"

The constable nodded. "Word of honor."

Eve got up. "I'll let Lord Denison fill in the blanks. Dr. Braine should be here at any moment to dress my arm. He's a busy man. I shouldn't keep him waiting."

No one tried to stop her. Both men seemed to realize that she had no wish to relive her desperate encounter with Jason Ford. She felt drained, but it wasn't only because of her lucky escape from a black-hearted killer. She couldn't help thinking about all his other victims. How had he gone undetected for so long?

When she entered the music room, three pairs of eyes regarded her anxiously, so she tried to put on a cheerful face. Amanda was there, and she came forward and gave Eve a hug.

"I stayed the night," she said. "I wanted to be near you just in case I could do any little thing to help, but Ash had everything in hand."

Eve swallowed and kept her smile fixed while she nodded to her aunt and Lady Sayers. Amanda led her to a chair and pushed her into it.

"Sherry," said Lady Sayers, thrusting a glass into Eve's hand. "Drink up, ladies, drink up. There's plenty more where that came from."

Eve observed that everyone was nursing a glass of sherry. "Are we celebrating something?"

"It's a tonic, dear," replied her aunt. "After the harrowing events of last night, we all felt the need of something stronger than tea. It will do you good, do us all good."

The reference to what had happened the night before made Eve shiver. Her friends didn't know the half of it. Ash had told them more than she had told the constable, but they didn't know about the murders Ford had committed as a boy.

She looked up as Lady Sayers tucked a shawl around her knees. "That will warm you," her ladyship said softly.

Amanda took the chair next to Eve's. "Are you worried about Nell? You needn't be, you know. Dexter is with her. And Liza has ridden over to Hill House to make sure that she got home safely last night."

Her ladyship made a scoffing sound. "It's not Nell I'm worried about. It's Dr. Braine. Liza can be very persistent when she wants to be. I wonder if that's why the good doctor hasn't arrived yet to dress Eve's arm?"

Everyone laughed, and Eve looked at their dear faces and felt her throat tighten. She had a circle of friends who meant the world to her. She hadn't particularly liked them when she first met them, but life had an odd way of turning a person in an unexpected direction. Now she didn't want to be parted from them.

Miss Claverley held her glass of sherry up to the light. "I think," she said, "Liza is going to surprise us all."

The words were hardly out of her mouth when footsteps came pounding along the corridor and Liza herself burst into the room. Her cheeks were flushed, her hair was askew, and a strong smell of the stables hung on her disheveled clothes.

"The most wonderful thing has happened," she cried out. She sniffed and tears ran down her cheeks.

Alarmed, Lady Sayers cried, "What is it, dear? What's the matter?"

"It's Fanny. She had her baby, and I was there when it happened. I had to help Anna and Archie. It's a boy, and we're calling him Freddie."

"Slow down, child." Lady Sayers had started to her feet. "You're not telling me that Dr. Braine allowed you to assist at a birthing?"

"Oh, Aunt, it was a foal's birthing."

"Even so—"

"And Archie was wonderful. I wish you could have seen him. I was frightened because I'd never done anything like this before—"

"I should hope not!" Lady Sayers interjected.

"And Fanny is really too old to have a baby. She was having difficulty, so ... so I ran and fetched Archie and at the end I helped him. It was a miracle that the foal was saved. But that was Archie's doing. And I wrapped little Freddie in a blanket while Archie saw to his mother."

She beamed at everyone through her tears. "If you had only seen him! I know you all think that he's a dry stick, but he isn't like that at all. He's gentle and warmhearted and the kindest man I know." She drew in a long breath. "I'm giving you fair warning. I've made up my mind that I'm going to marry him."

Amanda let out a sigh.

"What?" demanded Liza, pinning the older girl with a hostile stare.

Amanda jumped. "Nothing. Nothing at all."

"Don't tell me 'nothing'! I want to know what you are thinking."

Amanda said carefully, "Dr. Braine won't like it if you start hounding him. Let him come to you, Liza, or you may frighten him away."

She spoke like a wise big sister to a little sister, and the little sister was true to form. Hands on hips, Liza choked out, "You're the last person to give anyone advice. A blind man can see that you're in love with Mr. Henderson and he with you, but all he gets from you is a cold stare. What's the point of hiding your feelings? Are you happier for it? Wouldn't you rather know where you stand? At least you would have a reason for being so miserable."

"Liza!" declared her ladyship in an awful voice. "You have said quite enough!"

Liza bit down on her lip. "I'm sorry, Amanda. That was uncalled for. It's just—" Her face crumpled and, picking up her skirts, she ran from the room.

Amanda's face was white when she turned to the others. "She's talking nonsense, of course," she said. "Everyone knows that Philip is going to marry Miss Rose."

"Oh, I think you're wrong about that." Miss Claverley

picked up a newspaper. "It's right here on page three. *The engagement is announced between Miss Ardith Mary Rose and Mr. Stephen Willis Lockerby.* Ardith. It's an unusual name, that's why I remembered it."

Amanda stared, then she, too, burst into tears and ran from the room.

Eve felt as though all the wind had been knocked out of her sails. A moment ago she'd marveled at how close they had all become. Now they were behaving like naughty children. She wanted to stamp her foot.

Miss Claverley caught her eye. "It's all going to work out for the best," her aunt said, and she picked up her glass and complacently sipped her sherry.

Ash walked with her in the garden after lunch. He seemed subdued, distant, and that revived her worst fears. Pride kept her spine straight and her expression devoid of all the tortured emotions that churned inside her.

"I'll be gone for a few days," he said. "I don't know how many, but I will be back in time for Liza's ball."

He kicked a pebble along the path. Eve kept her expression serene. "Where will you go?"

"To my estate in Richmond." He flashed her a look that Eve could not read (an annoying aberration for a Claverley), then he went on, "I have to put my house in order, settle my tenants' quarrels, that sort of thing."

"Of course." She knew him better now, knew how much his people liked and respected him. He wouldn't let them down.

"Then I thought I'd visit Colonel Shearer and Lady Trigg to tell them about their servants and how Albert

Messenger deliberately murdered them. I owe them that much."

"How will you explain how you know?"

He smiled. "Don't worry. I won't give your secret away. I'll tell them that all the evidence points to Messenger's guilt, but he died in a fire so he can never answer for his crimes." He glanced at her, then looked away. "I don't want them to be left to wonder, as you and I were left to wonder about Harry and your mother."

She knew he was right. Though she'd wept bitterly for her mother, there was a feeling of completion. She had, in a sense, brought her mother's murderer to justice. It was true that Albert Messenger was only a boy at the time, but he'd murdered others since then.

"I think you know," he said, "that my grandmother is visiting her goddaughter? Henrietta's house is not far from Lady Trigg's. I'll spend the night there and pay homage to the new baby. My grandmother will expect it of me."

"My, you will be busy!" She regretted the pettish words as soon as she'd uttered them. How could she fault a man who always put others before himself?

He let out a long sigh and grasped her hands. "Look, Eve," he said, "you've been under a great strain lately, and I'm giving you a little time to recover your strength. We have a lot to talk about. When I come back, then we'll talk."

She watched him go with a sinking heart.

It wasn't all gloom and doom. The day before Liza's ball, when they had all assembled in the music room after lunch, Lady Sayers burst in.

Face flushed, eyes sparkling, she cried, "My dears,

you'll never guess what has happened. Dr. Braine was here not a moment ago, asking my permission for Liza's hand in marriage. Of course, I had to tell him that she is underage and he must apply to her father. And what do you think?"

Miss Claverley answered, "He's off to France to see Liza's father in person?"

"Clever Miss Claverley!" Her ladyship beamed. "But he won't go until after the ball."

After getting over the initial shock, they all started talking across one another. Liza gave a shriek and bolted through the door. Anna, who was back at the Manor, began to extol the virtues of the young woman who had helped bring dear little Freddie into the world, while Lydia nodded her agreement. Amanda made a few incoherent choked sounds, and Eve began to laugh. By the time her ladyship handed round the sherry decanter, they were all bubbling like fizzy champagne.

The next blaze of excitement came from Amanda. She was gone for an hour, and when she returned, she asked if she could have a quiet word with Eve.

Eve took her to the parlor where she and Ash had met with the constable. Amanda flashed a shy little smile. "Eve," she said, "I want you to be the first to know that Philip and I are getting married. I took a leaf out of Liza's book, you see, and told him that I'd been a fool to let him go all those years ago and that he would always have my heart. I married Mark because it was expected. We'd been engaged almost from the cradle. I shall always feel guilty about that. He was a good man. He deserved a woman who could give him her whole heart."

She shed a tear or two about that, then went on, "My eyes were finally opened when Liza took me to task. Philip shouldn't be miserable just because I feel guilty.

He deserves a woman who can give him her whole heart, too, and he has found her in me. I can't wait to tell the others, especially Liza."

They both cried with happiness, but when Eve undressed for bed that night, she began to feel like a dog in the manger. So much happiness was going around, and none of it was sticking to her.

After slipping out of her gown, she paused. She was thinking of Lydia. She debated a moment, pulled on her robe, and padded along the corridor to Lydia's room. When she knocked on the door, all she heard was a muffled sound. Eve took that to be an invitation to enter.

Lydia was standing by the window with one hand parting the gauze drapes. "I can't stop thinking of Robert," she said. "I keep watching, hoping there has been a mistake." Her voice cracked.

Eve quickly crossed to her and gathered the weeping woman in her arms. She didn't know where she found the soothing words. Lydia cried as though her heart would break.

Eve smiled in her sleep. She held a baby in her arms, *her* baby, and her name was Antonia. Dark gray eyes looked deeply into hers, and little Antonia gurgled with delight. She was dressed in a long, lacy Christening robe with little pink bows sewn to the flared skirt. Eve had sewn on those bows herself.

"Where is Papa?" said Eve to her child, and she looked around the vast interior of what turned out to be a church.

She was in the narthex, and down the length of the center aisle she could see the priest at the Christening font, waiting patiently for her to bring her daughter forward. But where was Ash?

Then she saw him, sitting in the front pew, flanked on either side by a small boy. One was fair and one was dark. Eve's brows knit together. Why wasn't she there with them?

As the priest went forward, Ash and the boys stood up. Ash put his hand on the head of the taller boy. "This," he said to the priest, "is my son Harry, and," turning to the smaller boy, "this is Percy."

Percy? Eve was puzzled. Where had that name come from? There were no Percys in her family or Ash's as far as she knew.

"What is the name of the child who is to be baptized?" asked the priest.

"Antonia," said Eve.

No one seemed to hear her. In fact, she might as well have been invisible.

Her heart plummeted when someone she had not noticed before, a young woman on Ash's left side, got up. She, too, had a baby in her arms. Eve looked down at Antonia, but, as is the way of dreams, Antonia was no longer there.

"The baby's name," began the young woman, "is—"

"This is a dream, isn't it?" Eve said in a hollow voice. "I'm dreaming."

No sooner were the words out of her mouth than a whirlwind surged into the church, carrying everything before it, and Eve was left in a swirling mist.

"Get back here, Ash Denison!" she cried out. "I want my babies, do you hear? You bring my babies back to me!"

She awakened with her heart pounding, tears streaming down her cheeks, and the fierce resolve that when

she next saw Ash Denison, she was going to throttle
him.

It was the night of Liza's ball, but in light of recent
events it was decided not to hold it in the picture gallery
but in a marquee on the lawns. This informal setting
was enthusiastically endorsed by one and all, especially
Eve. She could not think of a ballroom now without suffering a fit of the shudders.

She kept glancing at the entrance for Ash. He'd
promised that he'd be here for Liza's big night, and Ash
always kept his promises. She'd found a quiet spot beside a potted palm, with Miss Claverley to keep her company. Lady Sayers, as the hostess, had no time to sit
down.

The dancing had yet to begin, and Eve's gaze moved
idly among the crush. Anna and Lydia were in conversation with Leigh Fleming. Things had worked out well
for both Lydia and Nell. Anna had added them to her
little menagerie of broken-down donkeys, and they were
all due to leave for Cornwall in the morning. If worse
came to worst, thought Eve with dry humor, maybe
Anna would adopt her, too.

Miss Claverley let out a long, happy sigh. "I knew it
would come to this." She gestured to two couples who
were forming one of the sets for the first country dance.
"Didn't I tell them both that they would find their
heart's desire?"

Eve looked where her aunt had indicated. Amanda
was radiant as Philip led her out, while Liza looked so
grown up and demure beside the tall, smiling figure of
Dr. Braine that Eve hardly recognized her—or him, for
that matter.

She hoped Liza didn't become too demure.

Miss Claverley leaned toward Eve. "Now it's your turn, and remember, when you love someone, don't leave it till it's too late to tell them. Ah, here is Ash now."

Before Eve could respond, Miss Claverley was swept off on the arm of Constable Keble. Eve was rooted to her seat, lost in the awful memory of that dream. Suddenly rising, she squared her shoulders and pushed through the crush till she came to Ash. The babble of voices made conversation impossible, so she grasped his wrist and dragged him out of the marquee. Tables and chairs were set out on the lawn, and she led him to a quiet spot, then turned to face him.

He made some amusing remark about masterful women, but she wasn't listening. Without preamble she said, "Tell me you had nothing to do with the dream I had the other night."

He looked stricken. "What dream?"

She thumped him on the shoulder with her open palm. "I can see by your face you know what I'm talking about. The dream where you stole my baby—yes, and my sons, as well. Who was that woman sitting beside you in the pew?"

Before she could thump him again, he captured her in his arms. Between hoots of laughter, he got out, "That was Lady Dorothy Baird. She's been trying to lead me to the altar for years, but I've always managed to escape her clutches. Last night, in that dream, I kept thinking, *Don't panic, it's only a bad dream, and if it isn't, Eve will come to your rescue.* And you did. When I wakened, I felt as though I'd escaped a fate worse than death."

A dizzying happiness spread through her and she laughed, then she slipped her arms around his waist and dropped her head on his chest. "Oh, Ash," she said, "I've been such a fool. I could no more live without you than I could live without the air I breathe." She looked up at him. "All the difficulties I saw in our path seem as nothing compared to what I felt in that dream when I lost you and our children. I love you, Ash Denison, and I want you to know it before I'm struck with lightning or meet with some equally horrid end."

His eyes glinted down at her. "You're not saying that just for the sake of the children, are you?"

Her cheeks dimpled. "They were adorable, weren't they? But who is Percy? Where did that name come from?"

"A fallen comrade. He was too young to die."

She gave him a hug. To honor a fallen comrade was so typically Ash. He hadn't got to be the darling of society through his charm. Charm was easy. What Ash had went bone deep. Now, why did that make her want to cry?

He tipped up her chin. "If we're going to have those adorable children, we have to get married. You realize that, don't you?"

Her brows rose. "Isn't there something you've forgotten?"

He cleared his throat. "You have my heart. What more can I say?"

"You can do better than that."

"I love you, Eve." He scratched his chin. "And I'm not saying that just for the sake of the children. You're a tigress in bed."

She looped her arms around his neck. "I'm saving myself for marriage," she quipped.

He smirked. "I have a special license in my pocket, so we can be married as soon as you like."

"That's what I wanted to hear."

Anna and her little troop stayed on for the wedding, which took place three days later in Kennington Parish Church with only a few close friends and family members in attendance. Lady Valmede was there, Ash having made the journey into the southern counties not only to see Colonel Shearer and Lady Trigg but also to apprise his grandmother of his forthcoming marriage to Eve.

The wedding breakfast was held on the lawns of the Manor and was so informal that no one thought it odd that three donkeys, one little foal, and their mentors, Anna's boy and Dexter, had the run of the place. Dexter's presence was a great concession from Anna.

"Everyone should get married," Ash told Eve. "It gives a man purpose, something to work for, ambitions. That was what was lacking in my life. In fact, you once pointed it out to me."

"And I was wrong," she said emphatically. "I take it back. You have a vocation, Ash, and that is worthier than ambitions."

"A vocation?" He gave a disbelieving snort.

"You're a buttress, the champion of everyone who needs a friend, and if that isn't a vocation, I don't know what is." She was thinking of his mother and brother and all the people whom he'd helped, including Nell. Her gaze came to rest on Anna. "You're the champion of lost souls, that is what you are."

"And I think you need your head examined."

As they drove away in the carriage that was to take them to Richmond, Eve felt so happy, she was surprised she didn't burst from it. They would all be reunited in Cornwall at Anna's farm when they went for a little holiday after the harvest was in. And next year, they'd all get together for the symposium.

She breathed deeply. The whole world smelled fresh to her.

"What are you thinking?" Ash asked.

"Can't you read my mind?" she quipped.

"I'm working on it. So far, all I can read are your dreams."

"It's not supposed to work that way. You're not supposed to read *me*."

"Nevertheless, that's what happened. Aren't you glad that I can? I know I am. My dreams were never so interesting until I met you."

She gave up trying to figure it out. Maybe her Claverley cousins could explain it to her. "Glad?" she said. "That's too tepid a word. I'm humbled. Are you sure there isn't a wizard hiding somewhere in your pedigree?"

"Not that I'm aware, but it wouldn't surprise me if I fathered a wizard or a witch or two during my lifetime."

Her jaw went slack. "If I thought," she said slowly, "that we were going to make babies who would all turn out to be wizards and witches, I'd divorce you tomorrow and enter a nunnery."

"And give up Harry and Percy and Antonia? Not if I have anything to say about it. Besides, I am not so fainthearted as you." He patted her hand. "The idea appeals to me. Just think. With a little practice, I might get inside our daughters' heads and know where they are, who they're with, and what they're doing. What father wouldn't find that appealing? Of course, I would give our boys more leeway. Boys will be boys."

This provoked a scornful laugh. "If one of them were gifted, I mean *really* gifted, he'd turn your thoughts on and off as though you were a tap."

"Piffle. That's sheer prejudice on your part. I'll work at it. I got into your head, didn't I? You Claverleys think you're so special."

She looked into his eyes, saw the laughter mocking her, and collapsed against him in a fit of giggles. "That's the nicest thing anyone has ever said to me," she said.

About the Author

Elizabeth Thornton was born and educated in Scotland and now lives in Canada. Ms. Thornton has been nominated for and received numerous awards and is a seven-time Romance Writers of America RITA finalist. When not writing, her hobbies include reading, watching old movies, traveling to the UK for research, and enjoying her family and grandchildren. For more information, and details of *The Pleasure Trap* contest, visit Elizabeth Thornton on the Web at *www.elizabeth thornton.com*.